Also by St

DEC
SHADOWS
JIGSAW

"*Deceived* brings history to life in a suspenseful, contemporary tale that sends the protagonists on a research trip to a past close to their hearts. Barcelona's debut book brings an excellent author to the fore; the intrigue blends beautifully with the romance." – Heather Graham, New York Times Bestselling Author

"WOW! *Shadows* is a highly polished, gritty, suspense-packed tale that will have readers hanging on the edge of their seats! Brilliantly written, this story with profoundly unique characters will leave readers gasping while refusing to lay the book down. – InD'Tale Magazine

"Terrifyingly possible, *Shadows* is romantic suspense on steroids. It starts with a bang and never slows down. Not for the faint of heart, but definitely for fans of the genre, this book was just amazing." – Long and Short Reviews

Jigsaw is "[a]n emotional roller coaster of a novel that leaves you breathless. Intelligently written, the plot is both edgy and intense." – RT Book Reviews

Jigsaw is "[a] thrilling world of intrigue, terrorism, love, and hate, where her characters come to life in the pages of her book. ...Ms. Barcelona is a master storyteller and readers will be coming back again and again." – InD'Tale Magazine

"Barcelona writes for those of us who want intelligent protagonists and an intriguing mystery." – Cherry Adair, New York Times Bestselling Author

"[A]bsolutely fantastic...Finally an author who understands romance readers aren't delicate flowers who can't handle kickass action along with high levels of terror." – SherrybytheSea, Amazon Review

"Wow! What a ride! ...*Jigsaw* is everything I expect in romantic suspense. It has the perfect balance of sexy romance and edge-of-your-seat suspense." – Long and Short Reviews

Shadows, RONE Awards Winner – "Best Suspense Thriller Novel 2016" – InD'Tale Magazine

A note about the Concierge cover: The painting of the Saint Louis Cathedral that is featured on the cover is by New Orleans artist Fredrick Guess, of Fredrick Guess Studio and M Contemporary Gallery; for more information regarding the cover, which was designed by Kelsey Richardson of Deborah Richardson Editorial & Marketing Services, visit stellabarcelona.com and the blog: Musings...on the cover of Concierge.

CONCIERGE

Stella Barcelona

To my first hero, Salvador J. Barcelona, Sr.
A wonderful father and a fantastic storyteller.

Chapter One

Andi

Two Years Earlier
New Orleans, Louisiana

Oblivion is the answer. An absence of Andi Hutchenson. A void.

It was Andi's third consecutive morning of going to the spot on the levee where, six months earlier, Victor Morrissey had left her for dead after kidnapping and torturing her. A glance over her shoulder, left and right, confirmed there was no one else on the levee. For now, there was no river traffic.

With the first rays of dawn's sunlight, golden-pink brushstrokes appeared atop the dark swirls and eddies of the Mississippi River's murky water. Ignoring the colors of promise, Andi turned her focus on the flow of the powerful currents. She shivered, pulled her legs close to her chest, and rested her chin on her knees.

No more worrying how I'll make it through the day. No fear. No skin-crawling creeps, as though someone's watching. No more anxiety.

I'm so damn sick of feeling sorry for myself.

On this morning, she'd made peace with her plan to end her life where Victor had dumped her, barely alive.

Ironic. I'm scared to go anywhere but here.

Tendrils of fog drifted above the water as the sun crested over the horizon. Lacy mist hovered long enough to remind her of angel's wings. The fog evaporated as daylight seeped into the grayish-white air. Apropos of her life, if angels had ever looked out for her, they'd abandoned her when Victor had used her as a tool for revenge. And they hadn't yet returned. Andi wasn't culpable for her father's misdeeds, yet Victor had permanently scarred her, in more ways than one.

In front of her, an ocean-going container ship glided downriver. To her right, the distant skyline of New Orleans sparkled, the tall buildings shimmering with the pink and orange light of the rising sun. If she'd ever been a serious artist, this would have been a great setting to paint. Angles, color, and light could easily have revealed the city's precariousness, as it perched so close to the mighty river current.

Sure, I can sit here until hell freezes over, but I've made the decision. It's time.

As a tanker disappeared around the bend in the river, Andi stood. A plump, black river rat, disturbed by her movement, zig-zagged towards her. She screamed a high-pitched yell. The rat froze, its yellow-red eyes locked on hers, then turned and scurried away in tall, dark-green levee grass.

"Goddammit to hell, you damn, damn...rat!"

Gulping in air, she glanced around. No river traffic. It was still too early for joggers, walkers, and bikers on this quiet, remote stretch of the levee. Just grass, the river, and, she sure as hell hoped, no more rats.

The rat had inspired rippling pain along the scars that marked the one hundred and three cigarette burns Victor had placed on her back. When he'd left her to die, she'd been naked, hog-tied, barely conscious, and bleeding. Rats had feasted on her that night. Now they often starred in her nightmares.

Face it. Everything scares the living crap out of you. There's no cure for this kind of post-traumatic stress. Except death.

Pumping adrenaline borne of rat-fueled fear strengthened her resolve. Heart pounding, she walked towards the river.

Fifteen yards to go.

Gazing at her destination, she braced for the cold water. The bone-rattling chill that had seeped into her body and soul on the night of her kidnapping had never left.

I'll only be cold for a few minutes more. Then I'll never be cold again. I'll never be *again.*

It was a mild February morning, but cool enough for jeans, a long-sleeve t-shirt, and a turtleneck sweater. The weight of her clothes would help her sink. She'd worn cowboy boots on purpose. Once they filled with water, her fate would be sealed.

At the edge of the levee, a swatch of flat, muddy earth led to the river's edge, which was lined with broken concrete. She picked a safe path over the rough terrain, reached the water's edge, and kept going. Her heart accelerated as water poured over the rim of her boots. She almost turned and slogged her way back to shore, then stopped and swiped at free-flowing tears.

Keep walking. Keep walking.

She paused when icy water lapped at her thighs.

It's really cold. Damn cold. Oh God. God. God. Please. End this. Fast.

With her teeth chattering, she walked until strong currents tugged at her legs. She kept going. Water crept past her hips, waist, and chest.

God...No. Don't panic. This is it. If there's a heaven, Dad's there. I hope. I'll finally get a chance to tell him I forgive him.

Her long hair floated around her. Fighting panic, she tilted her head back and looked at puffs of white clouds in the dawn sky.

"Hey! What the hell! Stop!"

The distant yell barely registered as frigid water crept over her shoulders. Her boots became weights. Her jeans felt like they weighed fifty pounds. Taking one last deep breath of air, she shut her eyes as her chin slipped underwater.

"Hey! Lady!"

The voice was louder. Closer. She turned towards it. A blond man ran towards the river. Before her ears and eyes slipped under the water, she saw the owner of the voice picking his way across the broken concrete.

She tried to say *no.*

Shorthand for *No, I don't want your help, can't you see I'm killing myself?*

Because her mouth was underwater, she lost the air of her last deep breath. Frigid, foul-tasting river water choked her as she sunk. Her final vision was of the blond man running into the water, then skimming the surface as he dove towards her.

Gag. Cough. Splutter. *DAMN. DAMN. DAMN. I can't breathe.*

A moment of startling, this-is-it clarity hit her as the swimmer pulled at her hair and yanked, hard. A strong arm wrapped around her neck, choking her. Reflex had her fighting back, as the swimmer tried to pull her.

No one touched her without permission. Not since Victor Morrissey. *No one.* She landed a punch on the swimmer's chest, another on his face.

No! Goddammit no!

He pulled her hair, hard, while keeping a death grip on her upper arm. "Geez, lady! Stop fighting! I'm trying to save your ass here."

She clawed at his hands.

"Fuck! Don't—" His words were lost as she fought her way out of his hold. She went under, sucking in a deep mouthful of river water. With his arm on her neck, she bit down hard. He jerked his wrist out of her mouth. He knocked her, hard, at her temple. Gasping in pain, she choked as she breathed in a solid mouthful of water.

Dear God, I'm drowning. Really. This is it.

Her limbs froze with sudden fear. The swimmer pulled, tugged, and yanked her to shore. She gagged, choked, and sucked in more and more water until blessed, quiet, blackness overcame her.

Sometime later, the peaceful, devoid-of-thought darkness disappeared. She opened her eyes. Crystal-clear blue eyes were an inch from hers. His mouth covered hers.

The swimmer.

He exhaled as the contents of her gut roiled up. Lifting her hands to his cheek and forehead, she pushed him away. She turned her face to the earth as sour river water spewed from her mouth. She gasped for air, shivered, and more gray water came out as she struggled to her hands and knees.

Thoughts muddled, she glanced at her rescuer. Wide-eyed with worry, he knelt at her side. "Can you breathe?"

On her hands and knees, gasping in precious air, she nodded. She was gagging, but breathing.

"You have a phone?"

She looked at him through the dripping tangle of her hair.

"Do you have a phone?" he repeated, slowly, as though talking to a child.

"Of course." She spat out more water. She drew a deep breath and *dammit*, her teeth started chattering. She wasn't dead. Instead, she was wet and freezing cold. "It's in my car. But I'm not calling anyone."

His blond hair was wet and plastered to his head and neck. A lock of it fell across his forehead. He pushed it away as he studied her. Broad-shouldered and long-legged, he was lanky. His t-shirt clung to him like a second skin, revealing a faint outline of his ribcage. If he was eighteen, he'd just made it. She guessed he was younger. His blue eyes, made innocent and fresh by a fringe of dark-brown lashes, had a depth that went way beyond his years.

"Wait here." He stood, then ran along the shoreline, downriver.

She didn't have strength to do anything but sit there. She drew her legs to her chest, wrapped her arms around her knees, and tried to absorb the feelings that came with still being alive. Disappointed? Yes. Relieved? Maybe. Maybe even more than disappointed. Worried about what to do next? Of course. Her rescuer left the shoreline, approached a spot on the levee about a hundred yards away, and disappeared into an area that was overgrown with tall grass.

No wonder I didn't see him.

He emerged from the overgrowth holding a backpack, a bundle of clothes, and a guitar case. In a minute, he was at her side again. What she'd mistaken for clothes was a faded blue blanket. He held it out to her. It looked like it had been in the dirt for weeks. Mind numb, she didn't at first understand that he was giving it to her.

He shook the blanket at her. "You're shaking. Take it."

Too cold to unlock her arms from around her legs, she submitted to him throwing it around her shoulders.

"Hold it here."

She looked at him blankly, then glanced over his shoulder, at the river. Another ship glided by. Clouds were starting to build. What had looked like the dawn of a pretty day now looked wintry and dull.

With an impatient sigh, he grabbed her hands and wrapped her fingers around the two edges, forcing her to clench it under her trembling chin.

She drew a deep breath. And another. "Thanks. You could have drowned."

Giving her an it-was-nothing shrug, he sat next to her, facing the river, guitar case and backpack at his side. "It was hard as hell to get you out. Sorry I had to hit you, but you were fighting so hard, I almost lost you. *Man.* Cowboy boots in the mighty Mississippi?"

Unsure of his point, she became aware that only one foot still had a boot. The other was nowhere in sight.

He gave a low whistle. "You were going vertical."

"What?"

He narrowed his eyes. "Vertical slashes on two wrists mean business. Horizontal's for amateurs. The saying's *'go vertical, not horizontal.'*"

"Never heard that before." She shrugged deeper into the dirty blanket.

"It's suicide slang."

Sudden, instant nausea came with a few simple, life-altering truths that made her want to permanently burrow under his blanket. One—she'd attempted suicide. Two—she'd have to live with that fact, because her attempt had failed. Three—she was talking about it with her rescuer, and he was someone who knew suicide slang, for God's sake. "I've never heard of that."

"Lady—"

"How old are you?"

Defensiveness flashed in his eyes. "What's it to you?"

"Whoa. Calm down."

"Twenty."

She studied the taut skin on his cheekbones, the bony leanness of his chest that the wet t-shirt accentuated. He looked like he needed some age on him before he filled out. Maybe sixteen. Perhaps fifteen. Young enough to feel like he had to answer her question, even with a lie.

He bent, lifted a sweater out of his backpack, and held it out to her.

"No, but thanks," she said. "You put it on. Aren't you freezing?"

He gave her a small smile. "It's a hell of a lot colder where I'm from."

Which means he's a long way from home. "Where's home?"

"Someplace I'm never going back to."

Understood.

"How old are you, really?"

"Old enough to pull you from the river. I'd say that's all that counts right now."

He half-turned. When his back was to her, he stripped off the t-shirt, then pulled the sweater over his head. It was blue wool, pilling at the armpits, with loose threads at the neck and waistline. He pulled it down over his chest, then turned back to her.

Her gaze rested on the inside of his wrists as he worked his arms through the sleeves. She saw the imprint of her teeth on his left one. Above that, a thin, pinkish-white line rose above smooth skin. A similar scar was on his right wrist.

His knowledge of suicide slang now made sense. From the direction of the scars, he'd gone horizontal. Not vertical. Hence the reason he was here to see another day if he was right about the most effective way to slash one's wrists.

She dragged her eyes back to his. "What's your name?"

"Why?"

"Because you just saved my life. Sure seems like I should know your name since I owe you a thank you."

"Pic."

"P-I-C-K?"

"Yeah, but without the K. Got it?"

A made-up name if ever there was one.

She nodded, noting the absence of a last name and guessing by his wary look that she shouldn't push for it. He was young and sleeping on the levee. Either a runaway or homeless, which made him one of hundreds of young kids who frequented the streets of New Orleans on their way to somewhere else. Or not. Homeless youth had been a pervasive problem in the city. The large homeless population in New Orleans, young and old alike, was called 'the invisibles,' because the individuals themselves weren't really seen.

"I'm Andi." She extended her hand to the young man who definitely was no longer invisible. "With an I."

He had no way of knowing how big a step the handshake was for her. Post-kidnapping, she rarely let others touch her. He took her hand with a firm grasp. His blue eyes turned serious. "You gotta call someone. You need help."

With the words *'you need,'* she cringed. Pulling her hand away, she said, "Understood."

"Really."

"I'm not seeking your advice, Pic."

Because in the last six months I've gotten more advice than I can handle.

Pic frowned, folded his arms, and cocked his head to the side. "You shouldn't be alone now. Suicide's serious."

"Please quit using that word."

The corners of his eyes wrinkled into a puzzled squint. "What word?"

"Suicide."

"Calling it as I see it. If you can't even admit what you just did, then you really need help."

"It's complicated."

"You need a support system, and that starts with talking to someone and telling them what just happened."

"I have the best support system money can buy. My support network—of friends, relatives, doctors, therapists, counselors, and prescription meds—is so wonderful, it led me straight here, to the river."

The steady, concerned look in Pic's blue eyes inspired a lightning bolt of clarity.

What I need is a goddamn backbone.

"You're not going to call anyone," Pic said, frowning, "are you?"

"No," she whispered, loud enough for Pic to hear it, and pulled the blanket closer around her.

No one will ever know. Because they'll never, ever stop pitying me if they know. They'll never treat me like I'm normal. I've had enough pity for one lifetime.

"But someone needs to know—"

She sighed. "Someone does. You do. And I have a feeling that you're enough."

Eyes intent, he gave her a small, thoughtful nod, as though he was considering the task, and decided he was up for it. The pure concern in his blue eyes reached into her soul, making her forget her own misery.

Dear God, he's a homeless teenager, and he's trying to help me.

"You have to promise me you'll have hope," Pic said. "That you'll believe in tomorrow. That you won't try to kill yourself again. Don't end your story. Make it better. Promise?"

The sincerity in his eyes matched the serious tone in his voice. The combined effect of both muted all of the smart-ass quips she could've made. Instead, in words that held almost no meaning to her, but because he seemed so damned sincere, she said, "I promise."

"You mean it?"

"Yes," she whispered. Oddly, the hope she saw in his eyes made seeds of it germinate deep within her.

"Say you believe."

"You're relentless, aren't you?"

"Sure am." He nodded, with a slight smile. "Say you believe."

"In what?"

"Hope for tomorrow," Pic said.

She almost laughed. "Now you're pushing it."

"Come on." He gave her a nod of encouragement. "Say it."

"I believe in hope for tomorrow."

His smile was broad, with warmth that filtered over to her. He continued, "I meant it just about as much the first time I said it. I'll see you tomorrow. Let's say hi in Crescent Park. By the old wharf near the Piety Street footbridge. Around noon. Okay?"

"I have...limitations, Pic, on where I can go. I've never been to Crescent Park, so I'm not sure—"

"I can't let you go unless I know where and when I'll see you tomorrow."

She sighed. "We'll come up with something. But getting to that point means we have to talk a bit, and I'm freezing. You've got to be as well," she said, standing. "Which is pretty stupid of me, because I left my purse over there." She gestured with her chin to where she'd left it. "My keys are in it, and my car—with a perfectly fine heater—is parked beside the levee. Come on, Pic. Let's go."

"I'm not going anywhere with you." He stood, facing her, arms folded. His face had paled. The fear she saw in his wide eyes made sense of his lying about his age, fake name, and sleeping in levee brush. She guessed he was scared someone would find him. Someone who'd send him back to wherever he ran from. From the fear in his eyes, it was a place as scary as the hell in which she lived.

Fine. We'll be afraid together.

"Yes, Pic. You are. Because I'll turn into an icicle if I sit out here any longer. I want to talk to you, but I want to do it over breakfast. This see-you-tomorrow thing is about trust, right?"

He nodded.

"Trust that we'll both show up tomorrow, right?"

"Yeah."

"So, let's start small. I at least owe you a meal and while we're eating, we'll start building that trust. I trust you'll keep my secret about this morning, and you can trust that I won't push you to tell me anything you're not ready to tell. Sound fair?"

Hunching his shoulders, he dug his fists into the front pocket of his baggy jeans. She eyed his tattered sweater, banged-up guitar case, and overstuffed backpack. He was sleeping on the levee, and she'd bet made-to-order, hot meals had been nonexistent in his recent history. "I know a place we'll get warm. We'll get hot, fluffy pancakes. Eggs. Hash browns. Fat, juicy sausage links. Whatever you want. Sound good?"

She knew she'd caught him at the mention of pancakes, and didn't wait for a reply. With Pic's dirty blanket around her shoulders, Andi turned and walked away, confident her new friend would follow.

Chapter Two

Andi

Present Day
Friday, February 12

Head tilted, eyes narrowed, Andi imagined how she'd capture the perception of time's passage that the 18th century Creole townhome inspired. With its balconies, blue-shuttered windows, wrought iron swirls, and red brick façade, the historic property evoked the contradiction of time standing still, yet racing by. Conveying that feeling on canvas would be a challenge. But the larger question was whether she could force herself to stand on the busy street for the hours it would take to do the painting justice.

I can do this. If not today, one day. I'm almost well enough.

Heart pounding a staccato beat, warning her of the fright that came for her before inevitable flight, Andi tried to block the jarring sounds of traffic on Esplanade Avenue. Rationally, she knew that the tree-lined street that bordered the French Quarter and the Faubourg Marigny, with two lanes of traffic separated by a tree-lined neutral ground, shouldn't inspire fear. Lined with mansions, bars, and restaurants, this stretch of Esplanade was as benign as any street in New Orleans.

A normal person wouldn't be afraid. A normal person would be able to paint for the long hours it would take to do the scene justice. But it had been two and a half years since Victor Morrissey had ended her normal life. It was a full two years after her failed suicide attempt, a life-altering move that no one but she and Pic would ever know about. And it was one year and eleven months after she'd moved into her family's Royal Street townhome, which had been sitting empty since the death of her mother's brother.

Pic had become an instant friend. He'd inspired her to become an artist who worked at creating paintings, as opposed to the kind of artist she'd once been—the kind who talked about painting at cocktail parties. Once she'd mustered the courage to move into the French Quarter townhome, it only took three nights alone in the old house for her to realize she might never be able to live alone again. She had also figured out that trying to practice *en plein air* painting, which required her to be outside, was too much of an undertaking for someone with her brand of post-traumatic stress induced agoraphobia.

So, she'd come up with a workaround for both problems: an around-the-clock protective detail by Black Raven Private Security Contractors. The company was affiliated with her best friend's husband, Brandon Morrissey. Brandon was the brother of Victor, the crazed madman who had forever altered her life. The oddness of getting help from and trusting a man who was related to the man who left her needing such help wasn't lost upon her. But Brandon had nothing to do with what his brother did, and he was driven to somehow, someway, make amends for all she'd suffered. Black Raven specialized in customized security details, and God knew she needed a detail that was customized.

It had been one year, ten months, and three and a half weeks since she'd hired Black Raven. Knowing her security team was there enabled her to breathe. Most of the time. Sometimes though, the anxiety won the battle that she fought every hour of every day. And though she knew she needed the agents, the reality of her situation was far less than ideal. She suspected the agents liked her job as little as she liked having them around her.

Focus on the positive: it's a damn good thing I can afford an around-the-clock security detail.

A car horn sounded a sudden, insistent blast. She flinched, then forced in a deep, calming breath as a red SUV edged around a blue truck, while the driver of the truck tried to parallel park.

A Black Raven agent stood on the neutral ground, five feet away on her left, facing the mansion she was studying. Dark-haired, wearing black slacks, a black leather jacket, his sunglasses concealing the direction of his gaze. Although she paid as little attention to the agents as possible, she took comfort in their solid presence. She didn't bother with their names. Agents rotated in and out of her job as quickly as she could click the 'buy now' button at Amazon for a middle of the night purchase.

Agent Two, a broad-shouldered clone of Agent One, stood on her right, four feet away. Her cart, with her easel, canvasses, and pochade box filled with paints, brushes, and palette, rested at his feet. He faced the opposite side of the street, the French Quarter side of Esplanade.

Breathe. Inhale. Exhale. You're not being taken today. You're never being taken again. It's a perfectly ordinary Friday.

She drew a deep breath and tried to block the rumbling of a delivery van and the beeps of a nearby garbage truck. A cluster of tourists stopped in front of the house she was studying. Three women, four men. One woman stripped off her jacket and posed against the wrought iron fence that bordered the property. She arched her back, showing off her chest through her tight t-shirt, while a man wearing black leather from head to toe snapped photos.

Andi retrained her gaze on the mansion as the tourists meandered down the sidewalk. A bird chirped. She tried to concentrate on the sound of nature rather than street noise as she studied the composite colors of the old brick's reddish brown tones. Pigment would be tricky. Indian Red? Terra Rosa? Brown Ochre? Yes. All of those.

While her left hand craved the weight of a paintbrush, sunlight shifted as more clouds raced across the sky. Limbs of an oak tree in the side yard provided an overhead canopy that filtered the afternoon light. Shadows created by tree branches stretched and reached across the façade.

Screeching tires snapped her out of her reverie. A wide trunk of a gnarled old oak tree stood about five yards away, blocking her view. Hair on the back of her neck prickled. She stepped forward to look around the tree as a cold, heavy sense of dread tightened in her stomach. About a block and a half away, a black van containing a driver and passenger, both male, edged forward into the parking lane along the curb.

Ignore them. He's trying to park. Focus on the house.

Andi tried to return her attention to the house across the street, but her gaze drifted down the street. Sunlight caught chrome, drawing her attention to the van and the passenger-side door as it swung open.

See? It's nothing. He's just dropping someone off.

Yet the passenger didn't move away. The van didn't drive away. A girl, further away from Andi and a bit past the van, was on the sidewalk, approaching the van.

The tourists who had been in front of the mansion were now crossing the street, standing in the neutral ground, within a foot of Agent Two as they waited for traffic to clear. One of the women said something, then the whole group laughed. Andi heard Agent Two give a low chuckle.

Gaze riveted away from the tourists, Andi watched the van's passenger lift his arm, moving towards the girl. Two things got in Andi's way of actually seeing what was happening. One, the van was at least a block and a half away. Two, the girl had been approaching the van from the opposite direction of where Andi stood. Now, her smaller figure was partially blocked by the larger man, who seemed to move towards the girl and the van in a fast, simultaneous action.

Whatever happened took only a second or two. Lightning-fast fear seized Andi, as her mind fabricated a complete picture from the fragmented pieces of the story her vision provided.

Pointing, she yelled, “They’re kidnapping her.”

Ignoring the admonishments of the agents to remain where she was, Andi ran across the street as the van pulled away. Agents One and Two fell in step on either side of her. “The van turned on Decatur. Hurry,” she said. “We’ll catch it. Move!”

“Ms. Hutchenson.” Agent One kept pace with her. “Nothing happened.”

“A woman was taken. Hurry! They’re getting away.”

“Nothing happened,” Agent Two said, echoing Agent One’s statement.

“Call the police.” Andi slowed as she reached Decatur Street, where there was no black van in sight. “She didn’t go willingly! They took her.”

The agents gave each other a long glance that carried an easily readable message. *‘Here she goes again.’*

Unfortunately, this wasn’t the first time she thought she’d seen a kidnapping. The recurrent daymare, the term she used for her wide-awake nightmares, was a symptom of her post-traumatic stress. But today was different because she really had seen a van and a girl. No one was going to tell her that had been her imagination.

Besides, she’d been better for a long time. It had been months since this had last happened.

“You saw the black van?” she asked.

“Yes, ma’am,” they said in unison.

“But neither of you saw the blonde they grabbed in broad daylight?"

Silence was their answer.

“What the hell were you looking at, Agents? The woman with the big boobs crossing the street? Or was the guy with the leather pants more to your liking? Because I know what I saw. Both of you were right beside me. Why the hell didn’t you look where I was pointing?”

She saw the answer in their eyes, right beneath their ever-present glances of pity. They hadn’t really been paying attention to her because they were bored to death with babysitting a crazy woman whose wild-ass imagination made her see things that didn’t exist. “I’m calling the cops.”

"We aren't going to call the police on this, and I don't advise you do it, either. Perhaps we should go home now?" Agent One said. "Maybe you've had enough for one—"

Andi glared him into silence, then spun on her heels, and shot a questioning glance in Agent Two's direction. "Do you agree?"

"I didn't see anything suspicious," Agent Two articulated slowly. Carefully.

"And neither of you plan on backing me up when I call the police, do you?"

Agent Two cleared his throat. "Ms. Hutchenson, we didn't see anything. And we're not going to fabricate an incident."

The words, *'to appease you'* were left unsaid. She heard them anyway.

As her adrenaline surge faded, a wave of fright-induced nausea twisted her gut. Next came a fear-filled jolt, where her mind flashed to the time she'd been locked in Victor Morrissey's pitch-black trunk. Naked, terrified, and cold.

Before she had to use all her present-day energy on combating her memories, she glanced at the two agents. Careful to keep her voice firm, and not reveal her inner turmoil to these two patronizing assholes, she said, "You both should've been paying more attention. To me. Because when I pointed, it was so you could witness a criminal act and take action. We could've prevented a kidnapping in broad damn daylight. You're both fired. As a matter of fact, effective the minute I'm safely home, this entire Black Raven job is terminated."

Chapter Three

Gabe

Outside of Atlanta, Georgia
Friday, February 12

"Heads up, Gabe. Just you and me on this call, but that'll change in a few minutes. Ready?"

Detecting urgency in his older brother Zeus's clipped words, Michael Gabriel Hernandez glanced apologetically at his contractor, architect, and designer. They stood on the slab of what would eventually be his living room. With a hand gesture and a nod, he signaled for them to continue as he edged away. "Talk to me."

"High priority client in New Orleans is extremely dissatisfied." Glancing out towards the stand of pines, magnolia, and dogwood that stood to the east, Gabe detected an edge in his brother's tone. "Client's name is Andi Hutchenson. She hired us for a personal security detail. Her own. Job started almost two years ago. In general, the client is difficult. To say that she's dissatisfied is an understatement. A couple of agents pissed her off this afternoon. She fired them and is attempting to terminate our employment. Firing Black Raven is something we cannot let happen. She's too important a client, for reasons that will become apparent in this call. We need you there, ASAP."

"I'm teaching for the next couple of weeks at Last Resort, starting tomorrow." Schedules at Last Resort, Black Raven's advanced training facility in Georgia, were planned months in advance.

"I've rearranged your course schedule."

"Whoa. Without consulting me? Why is this job so important?"

"That's the reason for this heads up. Figured you'd be annoyed with your schedule change, and I don't blame you. Your courses can be taught in the final weeks of the current training session, which gives you two weeks on the Hutchenson job. Time enough for you to change the course of it. Consider your gracious acceptance of this assignment a personal favor to more than one Black Raven partner."

At least Zeus was giving a nod to Gabe's position of respect within the ranks of Black Raven agents. Gabe had his own client base of repeat customers who asked for him by name. Normally, he had his pick of assignments on the high stakes, international jobs that he, and other elite agents, favored.

"Who needs the favor?"

"Sebastian and Brandon. They want to talk to you."

Sebastian Connelly—founding Black Raven partner. Brandon Morrissey—general legal counsel for the company, and good friends of both Zeus and Sebastian.

"You, plus those two on the line for a job assignment?" Definitely not the norm.

"Ragno will be on the call, too. Client's that important. We just finished a troubleshooting call. Brandon is currently on the phone with Hutchenson, trying to persuade her not to fire the company, then he'll call in. Your buddy, Ragno—"

"She's your buddy, too—"

"Not denying that. I respect the hell out of her intuition. That's why I'm agreeing with her. She's diagnosed the job as needing Gabe-ness." Zeus gave a rare laugh. "Hell. I'm saying it like even I'm starting to believe that magic fucking fairy dust swirls around you. Anyway, Ragno's sending you the file. Brandon and Sebastian are calling in. Ready for a call?"

"Give me a few seconds." Gabe made his way through the semi-framed house. As the construction team stopped their conversation, he said to them, "I'll be back in a few minutes. Most important thing in this whole house?"

The builder, architect, and designer glanced at him with questioning eyes.

"You already know it. The kitchen. I love to cook and I'm a gadget junkie. I need lots of space in cabinets. And counter space. Plenty of it. Got it?"

They nodded and returned his smile.

"Zeus, ready when you are." Gabe jogged across the wooded yard and climbed into his truck. As he fired up the engines and cranked up the heat to ward off the wintry chill, his phone vibrated with a text from Ragno, *'Z gave you the heads up?'*

Black Raven's lead data analyst kept a hands-on approach with various high-profile jobs that required her skills while overseeing the Denver-based think tank that handled investigations and cyber intelligence for in-field agents. Ragno's division alone numbered in the hundreds. The in-field agents, in jobs worldwide, numbered in the thousands.

'Yep,' Gabe replied via text. *'Not like you to let Z beat you to the punch. WTF's going on?'*

'Swamped. Plus I'm working on your job file. Hutchenson deserves better than we've delivered. You need to figure out how to help her.'

Gabe reached for his iPad and started the protocol that enabled access to Black Raven's encrypted databases. Slipping his mic into his ear, he touched a button on his watch that activated his audio line.

After a round of hellos, Ragno used her all-business, clipped tone, to deliver essentials. "Job's a domestic twenty-four/seven detail. Client is female. An artist. Lives in the French Quarter. Her physical world encompasses her Royal Street townhome and a radius of four square miles, give or take a few blocks. She was kidnapped, brutalized, and left for dead by an attacker two and a half years ago. Since then, she's suffered severe PTSD issues. Acute anxiety disorder. Hallucinations. Stress-induced agoraphobia. Night terrors. She's fighting it all, though. Well on the road to recovery."

"I'll cut to the chase, Gabe," Brandon said. "My brother's the reason our client is in this state. You're familiar with what happened in New Orleans involving my wife's family and her father's business partners a couple years ago?"

"Yes." Gabe was connected to the powers-that-be in Black Raven enough to know that Victor Morrissey, Brandon's brother, had, among other things, killed two women and kidnapped two others. One of the women he'd kidnapped was Taylor, who had since become Brandon's wife. The other had been Andi Hutchenson. Absorbing the grim concern in Brandon's voice as the lawyer provided details, Gabe typed a text to Ragno-*'K. NOW I get it. Where's the file?'*

'Hold your horses. Building one for your eyes only.'

'U playing me?'

'Always, Angel. Always.'

"I consider Hutchenson my responsibility, as well," Sebastian said. "I was in New Orleans when it all went down."

Gabe's gaze crawled over tall, skinny pines gently swaying in the winter wind, while Sebastian replayed a few of the tense moments for all in Black Raven as the debacle with Brandon's brother had played out. "Like Brandon, I see our work on this job as a way to make things right," Sebastian continued. "On site agents aren't giving her job the respect it deserves. Our work force suffers from hotshot mentality. Agents aren't understanding that when we're doing our job correctly, the days will be damn quiet."

"I'm trying to rectify that problem in my courses at Last Resort." Gabe reached for the dash and turned off the truck's heat.

"Use your expertise," Zeus said. "Do a trouble-shooting assessment, establish team protocol going forward, and make sure the team that's in place functions in a manner that satisfies Hutchenson's objectives."

"Really, all she wants is constant eyes looking out for her," Sebastian said. "Which means security in her home and safe time outside so that she can paint."

"I'm giving full disclosure here," Brandon said, "she's not easy on the agents."

Difficult clients typically weren't a problem for Gabe, so he listened to the warnings, but focused on the density of the pine, birch, maple, and magnolia trees that filled his two-acre property. Beyond the construction frame, he spotted a couple of locations for a tree house and an elevated deck. He'd make it an outdoor gathering spot for the family he'd one day have. A place to be lazy and disconnected. Read books. Play board games. Strum his guitars. Maybe, finally, one day learn how to sing.

"If you look at her as someone with an intense fear of being taken, but hates that she's so afraid," Ragno said, "it explains her behavior. She wants Black Raven there, but she doesn't like the intrusion or her weakness. She's got rules in the file for agents to follow. They're not outlandish. Nothing like the eye-aversion stipulations our more eccentric clients sometimes put into contracts."

"I can handle rules." *Especially since I'll ignore most of them.* Gabe pushed the seat further back, stretched his legs, and clicked on the iPad to refresh the connection. Inter-office emails loaded, but there was no file on the Hutchenson case.

"Yeah," Zeus said. "We all know rules are subject to interpretation with you. Be careful with this one."

"What was the precipitating event for today's firing?" Gabe asked, looking at the front elevation of the house, imagining the wide expanse of windows that would soon be overlooking the gently sloping front yard.

"We're still trying to figure that out. Pursuant to her request, we're transferring the two agents who were outside with her. The two agents who remain on detail have now requested transfers," Ragno said. "As have most of the other agents who've been assigned the job. We've denied the transfer requests, consistent with company policy. Agents need to learn to embrace the suck and not cry to corporate when a job gets difficult."

"Agreed," Gabe said.

"I'm sending Agent Nathan Marks with you," Ragno said, "assuming you approve?"

Gabe knew Marks. Liked him. "Sure."

"He's a prime candidate to be lead agent-in-charge once you deem the job is running properly," Sebastian said.

"Most of all," Brandon interjected, "make the client feel safe and satisfied. Frankly, I'm worried that if she fires us, she'll spiral downward. I can't let that happen. I feel responsible for everything that went wrong with her. There are strong psychological issues here that aren't your responsibility, but I need you to help me figure out if there's any way we, as a company, can make this job work. Her daily painting excursions seem to be the reason she lives. She cannot handle her daily excursions without Black Raven. You'll get a better feel for it all when you read her file, but..."

As Gabe clicked open the file, Brandon's words fell away. For the cover image, Ragno had chosen a painting by Hutchenson entitled, *'Knockin' On Heaven's Door, Jackson Square, New Orleans.'*

It was a spectacular representation of a pedestrian-crowded, city square surrounded by rust-colored, brick buildings. Lush foliage, a study in hues of green, filled the square. Blue sky hadn't given up afternoon brightness. Thin wisps of clouds imbued pink and gold by an unseen sun, bathing the scene with palpable warmth and soft light.

A lone figure playing a guitar, his face pointed heavenward, was the focal point. Gabe knew the song that was the painting's namesake, knew the lyrics as Dylan wrote and sang them, and knew how to play it on the guitar. Painted abstractly, the musician leaned against a wrought iron fence. His red-velvet lined guitar case was open on the ground. Dollar bills and coins littered the interior.

The guitar's body was a brilliant blue, a traditional color that was a dead ringer for the color on Gabe's favorite of his three guitars. The manufacturer called it Chicago Blue. Gabe called it gorgeous. The people in the painting seemed to lean toward the young man, engrossed in the music.

"Gabe? Sound okay?" Brandon asked.

"Yes."

To whatever.

Any concerns that Gabe might have had, fell away as he studied the vivid painting, inexplicably moved in a way he hadn't often experienced. If ever.

"Thank you," Brandon said. "I know this isn't the high-action job you typically handle. In the ranks of our agents, though, you've got celebrity status. Having you in charge for a while will elevate this job in the eyes of our agents to the position of importance this client deserves."

"No problem. Happy to do it." Gabe answered honestly, flattered that Brandon and Sebastian trusted him to make things right for a client they valued so highly. A natural born protector, and an extrovert who enjoyed meeting new people, Gabe loved most of the work he did for Black Raven. The jobs that he handled were as varied as the clients who needed them. He approached each assignment with a firm appreciation of the human perspective that required Black Raven's expertise.

He clicked to the next page, saw more breath-catching paintings by Hutchenson, and then opened a photo of the client. He drew a deep breath and let it out slowly as his gaze rested on a delicate-featured young woman with a serious expression in her forest-green eyes. Sleek, dark hair framed her face. His heartbeat stuttered as he took in her natural beauty.

My job for the next two weeks is to keep this beautiful woman painting those glorious paintings?

With pleasure.

"Thank you for the vote of confidence. This will all work out. I'm on it. Client's my responsibility now."

As they switched off the call, Gabe kept clicking through the file. Ragno, in cyber-step with him, instant messaged him off and on as he read the data. From Ragno's vantage point in Denver, she could remotely see in real time what he was seeing and reading. Ragno knew how long he hovered on each page, how long he took with each horrific report.

The bright wintry day fell away as Gabe absorbed the hell that Andi Hutchenson had endured throughout her ordeal. The facts of the other-worldly fight she still battled, as she fought to combat the mind-fuck that Victor Morrissey's actions had accomplished, showed deep-from-within bravery.

'Now you understand why I thought you'd be perfect for this job, don't you?' Ragno texted.

He opened forensic photos of the crime, which documented images of Andi's back and the burns Morrissey had left there. He cringed.

He typed, *'I think so.'*

'I've monitored this file for Brandon ever since she hired us. She's climbing up from a really deep ravine. From what I can tell from afar, she's almost to solid ground. She needs a line and a tug. She needs your brand of strength, more than anyone I've ever seen. Be her lifeline, Gabe. Set this job straight. You can give her the confidence she needs to win her fight.'

His life experience—as a child whose father was murdered and an agent who regularly combatted violence—had honed his natural empathetic qualities and his tendency to fix problems that others didn't even diagnose. His work as an agent, often as personal private security, meant he regularly had access to things that people normally kept private. His work was often guided by a reflexive desire to help others when they'd been dealt a hand that was loaded with bad luck.

From what he'd learned in the phone conversation, and the details he was reading in the file, Andi Hutchenson had been dealt such a hand. With his gaze resting on a file image of her, he studied the haunted expression in her eyes and damn well planned to figure out what he could do to help her.

If anything.

Because sometimes, the best thing to do, was to let the hand play out, without interference. Sometimes, fixing things meant leaving them alone.

Chapter Four

Andi

Saturday, February 13, 2:45 a.m.

Dear Journal—

It's been two weeks since I've come in this room and poured out my heart on these pages. I told myself I'd stop coming to you. That I didn't need this crutch. I guess I was wrong.

Maybe I saw reality on Esplanade Avenue. But maybe it was another daymare. A cruel trick played by my damaged mind, where reality enters another dimension.

I think I saw them push her into the van. If I could just stop thinking about what they might do to her...But I can't. Burns? Arms and ankles bound? His hand on the back of her head, while her mouth is on his cock, as he puts out cigarettes on her back?

No. That was my living nightmare.

The men in the van will get away with it because I didn't help her. No one will believe me. And why would they? I've cried wolf too often.

Dammit, I don't trust my eyes either.

The days are long when you're crazy, but the nights are longer.

And no matter how much I pretend I'm fine, yesterday reminded me that I'm just one distraction away from totally losing it.

Brandon's right—I shouldn't fire Black Raven. I'm not well enough to go it alone. I'm too scared to walk outside without protection. Too scared to stay inside, alone, all day. Too scared to be alone at night.

On a night like tonight, with my anxiety spiking, I can hear Victor laugh, as he puts out cigarettes on my back.

And though I know he's dead, when I'm alone, I think he's close. On that one night, he infected me with an insanity that I'll never quite shake. At least if the agents are downstairs, I know that someone is breathing, that someone normal is nearby.

I was doing better.

The funny thing is, I'd almost rather what happened today on Esplanade Avenue be a real kidnapping than a hallucination.

Because if it's just a hallucination, then I'm slipping back into crazy world.

Oh dear God, I was doing so much better. I went months without a daymare, though the nightmares never stopped. But if the daymares are returning, I'll really have no peace.

I promised Pic—and myself—I'd never attempt suicide again. And I won't. I WON'T.

Pic's been in Austin, playing music on the streets, for God knows how long. It feels like forever. He'll be back soon. He told me he'd return by Mardi Gras. I'd love to see him. I worry about him when he's not in New Orleans. I worry about him when he's here, too, but it helps to have him closer.

I'll have to cancel my appearance at the gallery on Sunday. There's no way I can show up in public now.

I'd just like to be able to sleep, but I'm scared. Because with sleep, dear journal, you know what comes. At least my daymares are sometimes about someone else.

When my eyes shut and the world turns dark, I'm the star of the show. And I experience total terror, over and over again.

Chapter Five

Concierge

Saturday, February 13, 10 a.m.

"We acquired a pregnant girl yesterday," I say to my client on the phone. "You placed a right of first refusal on our next pregnant acquisition. Exercise it, or not."

"That's one way of saying hello."

"If you want hello, call your mother. If she still talks to you."

"I'm not necessarily in the market," he says.

I wait for it. After a long beat, he utters the name I train all of my clients to use. "Concierge."

The name has meaning for me and for my clients. It means I deliver whatever they want like no one else can. For that service, I demand payment in currency and respect.

Because he says my name with the respect I deserve, I stay on the line. "I'm offering a six-week rental for five million dollars, with a two million dollar damage deposit. She's young. Think fast."

Amidst the hum of medical monitors hooked to the product I'm offering, a harsh intake of breath through the phone line greets my announcement. Some men and women have an insatiable desire to be intimate with pregnant girls. I don't ask questions, as long as they pay what I ask and return the product uninjured.

This client's slow exhale tells me he is now interested.

Of course he is. Even in the sick world I've created, pregnant girls for lease are big news. They're hard to find because they're typically not the type of person one could kidnap easily, not without someone immediately missing them.

I sit on a chair beside the sleeping girl's bed. As I settle into the negotiation, I push the sheet off and let it puddle on the floor as I study her. "You're interested, aren't you?"

"Hispanic or American?"

I almost smile as he nibbles on my bait. "American."

The reality is, most of my stock is Hispanic. Why? Because it's easy to acquire humans from Mexico, apparently a country full of people who'd sell their future, their bodies, their souls, and even their fucking children, to get to the United States. Mexican border towns are replete with people naïve enough to believe my reapers and their promises of a future. A job. Medical care. A safe passage to this country with golden streets.

God bless America, the greatest country in the world. It's a lure the desperate and downtrodden can't resist. And the beauty of it is that no one in the good old U.S. of A. is looking for someone who isn't supposed to be here in the first place.

Americans barely look out for their own. There's an entire class of people who no one gives a damn about. Call them homeless. Street people. Runaways.

Call them low hanging fruit, mine for the picking.

I don't care what anyone calls them because I call them money. While most citizens avert their eyes from people who put out signs that say, *'will work for food,'* those who've slipped through the cracks of a fractured society, my reapers assess their potential for becoming inventory.

The beauty lying on the table in front of me was plucked off the streets of New Orleans, on Esplanade Avenue, on the fringe of the French Quarter. New Orleans is only one city where I gather my prey.

"Black or white?"

"We'll call her Eve." My non-answer is a delay tactic before I give the final tug on the line. My hook isn't just sharp. It has a barb capable of carving a bloody path through flesh, and I plan to set it in deep.

Naming the product makes them more real. A more tangible product spells more money. So, we name the acquisitions who'll remain whole. Not all are so lucky.

Eve from Esplanade Avenue will bring in a glorious sum. Eve's baby on the black market will produce even more. We've created a no-questions-asked adoption agency. We've made plenty of money and I damn well plan to make more. I have an insatiable desire for fuck-you money. The kind that maintains private jets, yachts, and residences wherever the hell I decide to live. The problem is that the business end of the operation is so easy, it's gotten boring.

"And she's white," I say, delivering the clincher.

His sharp, ragged inhale tells me he's hooked. "Tell me more."

"Exquisite skin. Like satin. More lily-white porcelain than peaches and cream. There's something fresh and...innocent about her."

Innocence.

A magical elixir that even I can't resist. The cliché 'opposites attract' is tired and overused for a reason. Innocence is the screaming opposite of what I am. Destroying purity, hope, and optimism provides me sustenance. Like a vampire's desire for blood, my desire to create darkness where there once was light is insatiable.

I shut my eyes, remembering one particular time when I'd encountered joyful innocence, wrapped in an irresistible, sensuous package that had torqued emotions I'd never before experienced, and didn't know I goddamn even possessed. Feeling alive with such desire had been so heady, so arousing, I'd fantasized creative ways to destroy that innocence. I had planned to take my time with her because I like to build fires within people, stoke them, and then watch as I reduce smoldering fires to ash.

But with the one person who will always be my siren song, I'd been cheated of my desire. Dammit-to-hell. I hate when memories of Andi Hutchenson burst into my day. Because she isn't simply a memory. She's now an obsession that makes a mockery of my overriding rule in life—that I get what I want. Whatever I want. Whoever I want. However I want it. I never lose. Never.

Biting back bitterness, I tell myself that my days without Andi are numbered. That thought helps me regain control. Keeping my voice calm as I lift a hand to Eve's gently swelling belly and feel the heartbeat there, I say, "You have two hours to exercise your right of first refusal. Your two hours started ten minutes ago."

Eve's chest rises and falls with anesthesia-assisted sleep. Leather restraints that had bound her ankles and wrists had been removed a few hours earlier. "She's in the middle of her second trimester. We think she's as young as fifteen. Five feet two. Petite. A natural honey blonde. Even her pussy hair is blond. She has blue eyes. She's beautiful."

A pause. "I'm interested."

Of course you are. "Your first refusal option expires at noon, central time."

"I need more details."

Fingering one of the girl's pink nipples, I look for a reaction. "You know all there is to know."

"I paid twenty-five thousand dollars for this option."

"Yes. That's why you have it."

"Evidence of drug use?" Sexual tension is apparent in the hoarse gruffness of his voice. My guess is that he has his hands on his stiff, hard cock. "I don't want a heroin junkie."

"Marijuana. Nothing else detected."

"Tell me...is she firm, or soft?"

"Firm, but soft where you'll want her to be. Long legs. Tight thighs. A nice, high basketball of a swell at her stomach. You'll have to rub her down with lotion to help her fight stretch marks."

The client groans.

God. This is so easy, it's boring.

"How large are her breasts?"

"B. Almost C. Her skin is creamy. I see a faint outline of veins. Beautiful nipples. Pale pink. Large. I'm fondling them now. She's sleeping, but her nipples are hardening."

I lie. Eve is too drugged to have any reaction. I, on the other hand, am getting horny. Knowing I need to give him time to make a decision, I stay silent as I trace a line along Eve's soft skin from breast to thigh. I thread my fingers through her pubic hair, along the crevices and folds of her sex, then dip the tips of two fingers into her moist, warm vagina while I bend my head to her breast. With a liplock on Eve's right breast and my tongue tasting her nipple, I swirl my fingers into her.

My partner enters the room. Fondling Eve earns me a marked frown of disapproval. I can't really disagree with him. I know better than to play with merchandise this valuable because I tend to leave permanent scars on our inventory.

Breaking away from the sweet flesh, I stand, point to my earpiece, indicating that I'm on a live call and to not interrupt me. I lick the taste of Eve off my fingers as I shrug away my partner's stern glance.

Ignoring his silent rebuke, but nonetheless stepping away from the bed, I leave the medical holding room and walk down the wide, carpeted hallway to my office.

I say to the client, "You'll love her."

"The baby?"

"Ultrasound indicates your favorite. A girl."

The client groans louder, then pants. This is either a sign that he's coming, or that the temptation to jerk off has become physically painful. Both possibilities are encouraging. "Send photos," he says.

Hell. "That will cost you fifty thousand dollars. Nonrefundable."

The network we use is encrypted and requires triple-factor identification. My clients are a select few who provide a myriad of passwords, an offshore bank account with an escrow balance of over ten million dollars, and a retinal scan. This client knows the drill and doesn't need instructions.

The impatient click of fingers on a keyboard comes though the phone line. "I'm wiring money now."

As I sit at my desk, I hear the melodious chime on my computer indicating a direct deposit into our out-of-country, offshore account. I smile, and click a few keys. "I'm sending Eve's photos and videos now. They will disappear in fifteen minutes."

"Got them." His voice is now a hoarse groan. "Tell me the terms."

"We're offering a six-week rental for five million dollars, with a two million dollar damage deposit. A total of seven million dollars, pre-delivery. You can screw Eve until your balls fall off, but you need to keep her and her baby healthy, otherwise your payout will be ten million dollars. Minimal sedatives, which we will prescribe. Proper nutrition, including prenatal vitamins. Throughout your rental term, our medical staff will make a weekly visit."

"Consider the deal done. Is there an option to extend the lease?"

"It can be negotiated. Upon receipt of your money, she'll be delivered in twelve hours."

As this client institutes the procedure for transferring some of his considerable money to me, it's now time to mess with him a bit. "Tell me thank you."

He sighs. "Thank you."

"Now mean it, or else this deal is canceled."

"Thank you," he says, "Concierge. I appreciate the opportunity to do business with you."

Ah. There it is. I have an exclusive network of clients, and they all know the cost of doing business with me. Once I hear the correct amount of gratitude and respect in his tone, my foul mood becomes a little less sour. I break the connection, looking forward to my next transaction.

Chapter Six

Gabe

Saturday, February 13, 12:15 p.m.

In response to Gabe's introduction, NOPD Officer Jack Spagnoli said, "What'd you do to deserve this assignment?"

Considering the question not worthy of a response, Gabe stared at Spagnoli, who didn't bother to reach for the business card Gabe offered. Neither did Officer Cal Thompson, who stood two feet away. The two men were partners. Thompson was the lead NOPD officer tasked with overseeing residential concerns for the French Quarter.

"I'm going to be honest. Crazy thrives in this city," Spagnoli continued, his eyes almost as hard and dark as his tone. "Like humidity, it's part of our oxygen. But your client is a paranoid whack job. NOPD's got real work to do. We'd appreciate it if you keep her out of our way."

With his blood simmering, Gabe dropped his business card on the counter Spagnoli leaned against. "My number's on that card. Save it. Because if anyone ever transports you in the trunk of their car for a five hour drive, puts out a hundred or so cigarettes on your back, then beats you to within an inch of your life and leaves you, naked, for dead, in a place where rats decide you're their midnight snack, I'll pay you a thousand bucks if you give me a call and let me know how well you deal with it."

Spagnoli shot him a hard, pissed off look, which Gabe was happy to return.

Great. Now we understand each other.

To his partner, Spagnoli muttered, "I'll meet you outside."

Thompson nodded, then shifted a toothpick from one side of his mouth to the other as he leaned against a display case of historic weapons, one elbow on the glass top. Hazel-brown eyes and a soft expression at his mouth gave him a slightly nicer demeanor than Spagnoli.

"Sorry about that. Spagnoli's pretty blunt." Thompson's phone rang. "Give me a second to take this call."

Gabe nodded. As Thompson held his phone to his ear, a group of people wearing glistening beads walked into the old building housing the Eighth District station and found their way to t-shirt vending machines. To Gabe's right, officers worked at beeping computer monitors. Gabe heard hooves scraping on flagstone. He looked out the open window to see two officers arrive and dismount their horses, as a cruiser drove away on Conti Street, sirens blaring.

He'd arrived in New Orleans at eleven a.m. His first stop had been the client's townhome. She'd departed for Crescent Park with two agents right before he'd arrived. In the security room, Gabe had an exit interview with the two agents the client had fired the day before. After that, Gabe had walked the few blocks along Royal Street to introduce himself to the local cops.

Into the phone, Thompson said, "We'll be there in five." He gave Gabe an exasperated glance after returning his phone to the pocket of his jacket. "Reality is, we've gotta keep up the charade of good times." He pointed outside, as a trumpeter's crescendo filtered in through the open doors. "While keeping everyone safe. The NOPD can't hold the hand of every resident each time they're frightened by a noise."

Thompson shrugged, his expression seeming sincere—and pained—as he shifted the toothpick again, then continued. "The French Quarter qualifies as a high crime area. People like Hutchenson, who own homes here, have plenty of money. She could live anywhere else. If your client wants an environment where she can paint without seeing the seedier side of life, or an occasional disturbance, she should relocate."

"Sounds like a fatalistic approach to law enforcement," Gabe said.

Hard-ass cockiness surfaced in the cop's eyes, coupled with a sneer. "Perhaps," Thompson said, "but realistic. Where are you from?"

"Miami."

"Then you know about violence."

More than you will ever know, dickhead. "Sure do."

"Here's a newsflash. This isn't Disney World. Despite the atmosphere of forgotten cares—" He gave a nod in the direction of the t-shirt machine, where the tourists were laughing as they pulled out shirts. "—this is real. Gangs from surrounding neighborhoods consider the Eighth District their turf. Plus, half the people here are shit-drunk and easy pickings for criminals. I've got one guarantee for people like your client. If you're looking, you'll see something disturbing." His lips pressed into a thin slash of a line for a second. "Last time I fell for one of her calls about someone being kidnapped, I ended up in the middle of an argument between a boyfriend and girlfriend, who told me to butt out, while a shooting occurred three blocks away."

"Our response times aren't optimal, even for serious crimes, and we've had too many calls from Hutchenson to know there's no need to hurry," Thompson continued. "Since two thirty yesterday afternoon, I've had four messages from her. She claims she saw someone being taken from a sidewalk on Esplanade Avenue. In the last year, she's claimed the same sort of thing at least a dozen times." From his marked frown, Gabe guessed that none of the calls his client had made the day before to Thompson had been returned. "Today's the 13th. There are ten days until Tuesday, February 23. Mardi Gras. You ever been here for Mardi Gras?"

"No."

"Crowds start building, in earnest, on the Thursday before. This year we're shutting down more streets. If I were you, I'd persuade Ms. Hutchenson to stay inside from Thursday on. Trust me, you've never seen anything like it."

Gabe swallowed a chuckle. *Does this asshole think I've been working as a security guard at a mall?*

"She'll want you to call us if she hears a noise in the night." He paused. "Don't. If something's really wrong, call me, or Spagnoli, directly. Don't bother us, or dispatch, unless it's a legit emergency. I take it you know what one of those is?"

"Of course."

Thompson did another cheek-to-cheek toothpick shift. "Keep a firm hold on that reality, 'cause you're officially in the French Quarter now, which is an alternate universe, and Hutchenson is in a distant galaxy. Here's my card." Thompson fished his wallet from his pocket. "Spagnoli's numbers are on the back. But please think before calling."

"Message received, loud and clear. I'll be sure my client understands it as well." Gabe walked out of the police station and turned down Royal Street. Spagnoli and Thompson didn't have to worry. They were the last two people he'd ever call.

He touched his watch to switch on his communication system's audio feed. He called Agent Daniel Tyre, one of the two agents that the client hadn't fired the day before. The other was Agent Jacob Stevens.

"Tyre."

"Yes, sir." Tyre's voice crackled through Gabe's ear mic, competing with a team of street dancers who had boom boxes blasting. They wore red and black leather and were performing for a crowd that was packed onto the steps of a white marble building that identified itself as the Louisiana Supreme Court. "I'm looking forward to meeting you, sir."

"Thank you. And I, you. Location remains Crescent Park?" Gabe threaded his way through spectators.

"Yes, sir."

"Update me."

"Stevens and I are within fifteen feet of the client. We're downriver of the old Piety Street wharf. Easel's up. Client's painting. It isn't too crowded here. Weather's great."

"What else?" To avoid people on the sidewalk, Gabe stepped into the middle of Royal Street, which was closed to vehicles.

"Not sure what you mean, sir."

Gabe reminded himself to have patience. Tyre had been with the company one year. Prior to that, he'd been a Marine for two years. Though relatively inexperienced, he'd scored high on the psych and field tests that Black Raven gave applicants.

"Details." Gabe circled a cluster of tourists who had stopped in the middle of the street for a photo. "Details keep the brain alert on jobs without a lot of action, Tyre."

"Um, there's a great view of the city. We're downriver. The river makes a crescent—"

"Stop. I've studied the file. I know Crescent Park's one of her usual spots. I know what the park looks like and the position of it relative to the city and the river. Tell me something about the client that I don't know."

"There isn't more to tell. She's painting. Other than that, nothing's happening. Typical."

A gold-lettered sign, hanging above the sidewalk, caught his eye. The Stapleton Gallery. Paris, New York, and New Orleans. The sign indicated the gallery was hosting an exclusive showing of paintings by New Orleans artist Andi Hutchenson. All proceeds were to benefit Hope House, providing services to the homeless. Sunday evening, from six to nine p.m.

"Tyre, think about it for five minutes. Then we'll talk again."

Gabe opened the heavy, black-lacquered door with inset glass panels. From the rear of the empty gallery, a chime sounded. As the door shut, street noise faded.

Works of several artists hung on the right wall. The left wall was dedicated to Hutchenson's paintings. In person, her work was even more captivating. Vibrant, unusual colors provided a twist on realism. She used shadows and light to paint in a manner that made her paintings seem like...he squinted his eyes...they were changing before his eyes. Puffy clouds, evaporating into air. Buildings, with once-straight walls slightly leaning, their facades seemingly decaying. Birds, hovering expectantly. Musicians, strumming instruments as they sang. People, taking a step as they walked on a street. The flame of a French Quarter gas lantern, flickering.

In person, *'Knockin' On Heaven's Door, Jackson Square, New Orleans,'* was breathtaking. When he'd first opened the client file, he hadn't known the musician's name. Now that he'd studied the file, he knew that the young man was a street kid whom the client had befriended and given a Gibson Les Paul guitar that was Chicago Blue. The file referred to him as Pic. Gabe smiled as he spotted a discreet *'sold'* sign, a small white tag with black print, on the wall next to the painting.

Yeah. That one's off the market. It's mine.

"A feast for the eyes, isn't it?" The deep, quiet voice came from a doorway in the rear of the gallery.

Gabe touched his watch, muting his mic and his connection to Tyre. Hardwood floors creaked under his weight as he turned to the speaker. "Breathtaking."

The man, with sleek dark hair, and darker eyes, crossed the gallery and extended his hand. "Jacques Stapleton."

"Gabe Hernandez." His name meant nothing to the gallery owner. Gabe had bought the painting using an alias, taking advantage of one of his alternate identifications, a perk that came with being a Black Raven agent with elite status.

Stapleton, about five eleven and fit, gave Gabe a firm, no nonsense handshake, and an easy, *'glad to have you'* smile. He was good looking enough that Gabe bet the man had no problem selling things.

"The painting you're admiring is sold. As are eight of the other Hutchensons." He did a sweeping gesture with his arm, encompassing the wall of paintings, while Gabe noted the ones that had *'sold'* stickers next to them. "An impressive pace, considering this is the artist's first show. I didn't acquire the paintings until yesterday. The artist is reluctant to be in the spotlight." Dark eyes held his, his pause underscoring his last statement. "Putting this show together took months of persuasion. She should be here tomorrow evening."

Should be?

"You're more than welcome to attend the opening," Stapleton continued. "If you have any interest at all, I recommend a quick decision. I didn't correctly assess the demand for her work. These are a bargain compared to what her future work will be."

Gabe reached into his wallet, fished out a card for Stapleton, and handed it to him. "I'm part of Ms. Hutchenson's security detail. We'll do a walk-through prior to the event. Is five-thirty okay with you?"

Stapleton nodded, studied the card, then glanced at Gabe. "That will be fine."

A few moments later, Gabe stepped out again onto the noisy sidewalk. He glanced at his watch, then reactivated his mic. "Tyre. Your five minutes are up. What else?"

"Sir, I'm just not sure what else you're looking for. I've told you everything."

"What is she painting?"

"Um, I haven't really noticed."

"Then you're not doing your job correctly. You're being paid to protect her, watch her, keep any threat from touching her, and make sure she feels safe. On this job, the threat is atypical. It comes from things she sees, and if you don't know what she's painting, then you certainly don't know where she's looking."

"Probably more accurate to say the threats come from things she thinks she sees." Tyre's whisper, low and sarcastic, was said in exactly the wrong tone. His sarcasm matched the patronizing, smart-ass tone used by Officers Thompson and Spagnoli. It was the same tone that the fired agents had used in the exit interview when Gabe had talked to them.

No wonder she fired them. I'm already tired of this attitude.

"Your tone is disrespectful. Agents who disrespect clients don't deserve to be with Black Raven. With me, it's grounds for firing. Understood?"

"Yes, sir."

The crowd got thinner as Gabe crossed Saint Phillip Street and entered a stretch of Royal Street that was open to traffic. Cars snaked along at a snail's pace, slowed by horse-drawn carriages. Pedestrians with go-cups weaved through vehicles.

"To assess potential threats, have your eyes on everything and everyone near her. You need to look where she's looking and see what she's seeing. Try again. What is she looking at, and what is she painting?"

"The footbridge leading into the park, sir."

"What color is it?"

"It's rusty. Sort of orange-ish. It's arched. Steps are steep. Indents on the sides look like piano keys. She's about halfway through painting the bridge. Hasn't started on background."

"How focused is she on the painting?"

"Actually," Tyre paused. "Not very."

"Then what is she looking at?"

"Two people. Invisibles."

"Invisibles?"

"Slang for homeless people. These look like teenagers. They're sitting near the bridge, with a dog on a leash. She's picking up a sketchpad. No. Wait. Her phone's ringing. She's reaching into her bag." Tyre chuckled. "She dropped the phone into her bag. Ignoring the call. She did that earlier, too. Twice. Odd, because, come to think of it, she usually doesn't bother with her phone when she's out. Now she's refocusing on her tablet, and starting to sketch the teenagers."

"Okay. Better, now you know what's in her line of sight. I'll monitor your audio as I work from her house. Do a quarterly status report that includes details. Give me minutia. Stay alert."

Gabe slowed as he reached Hutchenson's townhome, eyeing the gray stucco façade of the corner property. The residence sat close to the property line. Two sides of the house were bordered by sidewalks, while the other two had narrow alleys separating it from the neighboring properties. Tall brick walls, the top lined with shards of multicolored glass that glistened in the afternoon sunlight, provided boundaries.

There were four large windows on the front of the home on the Royal Street sidewalk. Eight windows ran the length of the property. Solid navy blue shutters were closed and locked over the first-floor windows.

A wrought iron gate blocked access to the courtyard. The client didn't own a car. The property didn't have off-street parking. Where there could have been parking in the courtyard, there was a large water garden. Black Raven had one vehicle assigned to the security detail. It was parked in a garage, down the street. Given congestion and lack of parking, the French Quarter and surrounding neighborhoods that Hutchenson frequented were more easily accessible on foot than vehicle.

As Gabe paused at the gate, a walking tour filtered around him. The guide let his group peer through the bars of the iron gate, 'oo-ing' and 'ah-ing' over the lushness of the courtyard and the gurgling fountain.

"This property is an excellent representation of a French Quarter townhome, built in 1825 by the architect Francois Bienville," Gabe heard the tour guide tell his group. "This property has been in the same family since it was built, which is a rarity. You'll note the large home in the front and the slave quarter in the back. Now, we no longer refer to the small buildings behind the mansions as slave quarters, but when these homes were built, that's exactly what they were..."

The tour guide's information was accurate. Gabe's file review had included the original floor plan of the three-story townhome, with its interior courtyard and freestanding two-story, one-bedroom building to the rear of the courtyard. The plan referred to the smaller building as 'slave quarters.' The client had renovated the free-standing building, which she called a guesthouse. As of two weeks earlier, the guesthouse was ready for occupancy. Whether anyone was moving into it was an open question to which Hutchenson hadn't provided an answer.

As the tour group crossed the street, Gabe's mind clicked through logistics of the simple security detail. The client was either in her house, or in the near vicinity of her house. She rarely went anywhere she didn't walk, and liked to have her route mapped before she left the house. She didn't deviate, unless the chosen route was too crowded, and then she went to a back-up plan that she and the agents formulated prior to departure.

Her brothers, Philip and Stone Hutchenson, visited. Her friend, Taylor Bartholomew, Taylor's husband, Brandon Morrissey, and their two children, also visited regularly. Other than that, the client didn't socialize, date, or have guests. Evelyn Parker, a housekeeper whose days she shared with her brothers, came in on Tuesdays and Fridays. Esthetician Juliette Bandeau came in on Saturday mornings, providing spa services. Bandeau had been there earlier that day, for two hours. The client shopped online. A lot.

Four agents worked the detail. Two accompanied the client whenever she was mobile. One guarded her house when she was outside. At night, two agents remained on duty, alternating between moving throughout the property and staying in the security room, where cameras provided visuals of the property. Off time was on a rotation basis at a nearby apartment, rented by the client.

The contract specified that the agents could use one of the second-floor guest bedrooms. The file indicated that the agents preferred not to do that. From what Gabe could tell, in general, the agents had treated the client as though she had a deadly contagious disease.

Rounding the corner and returning to the Royal Street entrance, Gabe lifted his hand to knock on a door of raw, unpainted wood, burnished with a glow from age and care. Agent

Nathan Marks opened the door before Gabe's knuckles rapped on wood. "Saw you on the screen."

Marks, barrel-chested and bald-headed, with dark brown eyes, was a former SEAL. He had five years in Black Raven and a family in Alabama. When called in on the job the day before, Marks had been thrilled for the relatively low-risk stint in New Orleans. "I've made minor adjustments to the cameras. Let me show you the setup."

At the inception of the job, Black Raven had installed a new security system, including the cameras that Marks was monitoring. The security room was immediately inside the front door, on the right. There were two large desks, with computers and comfortable-looking office chairs. Eight monitors showed property views in real time: four potential access doors from the sidewalks, two doors to the main house, the wrought iron gate that opened onto the courtyard, a door to the guesthouse, and skylights on the roof.

"Keys?"

At all times two Black Raven agents had keys to the property. Marks handed him a ring with six keys. In Gabe's wallet, he had a pick and a tension wrench that would have made the keys unnecessary, but this wasn't the sort of job where he'd be picking locks.

Leaving Marks in the security room, Gabe started a visual security check. The room was one of two vestibules that flanked the entrance foyer. Floor plans had indicated that the vestibule on the left of the main entrance was once a cloakroom. Now it doubled as a walk-in closet for guest coats, a place for wrapping gifts, and a repository for a daily stream of incoming UPS, Fed-Ex, and U.S. Mail packages.

Further into the house, Gabe's eyes feasted on the client's paintings. They hung everywhere. On the largest unbroken wall in the center hallway, a series of five paintings of a cathedral, each canvas slightly different, hung together. Each was riveting, and together they were spellbinding. The first few rooms that he walked into—a library, a formal living room, and a dining room—looked like antique furniture showrooms.

Breathing in the essence of fresh lavender and roses, strategically placed in heavy crystal vases, he opened doors and checked the locks on windows. Taking in fourteen-foot tall ceilings that gently curved where they met plaster walls, sparkling crystal chandeliers that hung from intricate ceiling medallions, and wide-planked, golden pine floors that gave slightly under his weight, he expected no security lapses and found none.

Despite the constant stream of traffic on congested streets and pedestrians on sidewalks, thick walls and shuttered windows made the place so quiet, his footsteps seemed loud. Afternoon light filtered in through slatted shutters, and discreet, recessed lighting in each room was turned on.

The client didn't like darkness.

I don't blame her.

His mind clicked through manpower management. Marks, who was sitting in the security room, hadn't yet met the client. Stevens and Tyre were in the park with her. "Marks?"

"Yes, sir."

"Go to Crescent Park. Meet the client, acquaint yourself with the outdoor detail. Stevens?"

"Yes, sir."

"Once Marks arrives, go to the apartment. Rest. You'll be on duty tonight until three a.m. with me. Marks and Tyre will be off, once the client is in for the night."

"Yes, sir."

Pausing at the desk in the library, Gabe inhaled the scent of a fire that had recently burned in the large fireplace. The room was well-decorated. Tasteful. Furnishings and fabrics bordered on extravagant. Yet it seemed cozy, with its deep brown leather-upholstered couch, cream-colored chairs, and matching ottomans. He glanced at the day's newspaper, folded on a silver tray, and neat stacks of AH-embossed stationary. Thick-papered invitations were under an amber-colored fleur-de-lis paperweight. He lifted the heavy glass paperweight and leafed through baby shower invitations, wedding announcements, party invites, and fundraiser details. On each, the client had made a note of the date she'd sent in her regretted absence and the gift she'd sent.

Before her kidnapping, the file indicated Andi Hutchenson had been a socialite, living high on the New Orleans elite party circuit and beyond. From what he could tell, the meticulous attention to invitations, and what gift she'd sent, were an indication of how badly she missed that other life.

Pretty damn badly.

A laptop on her desk was closed. The file indicated the client's internet usage was limited to shopping, email, and Facebook. She had plenty of Facebook friends in her newsfeed, but she didn't do her own posts. Before her kidnapping, she'd done Instagram, Tinder, and Twitter. The file indicated she no longer used those accounts.

Tyre's voice crackled in his earpiece. "Sir, quarterly update."

"Go."

"Client's still working on that sketch of the teenagers. She just picked up her phone again. She didn't say anything. Call lasted twenty seconds. She's applying sunblock to her face and hands. SPF 30."

"Perfect." Gabe stifled a chuckle. He'd wanted details, and Tyre was obliging.

"Now she's returning to the sketch. She's left-handed, by the way. The guy she's sketching is leaning back in the grass, on his elbows. They don't seem to notice that she's drawing them. He's looking at the river, listening to the girl and Ms. Hutchenson is drawing him..."

Listening, Gabe walked through a small room off the dining room that housed china, crystal, silver, vases, and other things that would be useful if the client entertained.

Which she didn't.

An oversized kitchen was sparkling clean. Appliances included a wood-burning hearth for breads and pizza. Immediately thinking about the house he was building, Gabe eyed the pizza hearth and wondered if his kitchen could accommodate one like it.

Back to work.

The kitchen flowed into a casual living room. Above the fireplace, hanging above the mantle and managing to look like it belonged, was a seventy-inch television.

Awesome. I like this woman.

In a corner, children's toys were stacked neatly in a toy box. Gabe guessed the area was for Brandon and Taylor's kids, or her brother Phillip's kids, because the file didn't suggest anyone else who visited had children. A small table with kid-sized chairs had coloring books and crayons. Child-art was framed on the wall. Behind the living room, a large, bright mudroom led to a back door that opened onto the sidewalk and another that opened into the courtyard.

From the floorplan, Gabe knew that the second floor had four living suites, each with a large bedroom, a smaller sitting room, a bathroom, and closets. He climbed the stairs, walked into two suites, mentally claiming the one that didn't have a pedicure chair and massage table in the sitting room as his own.

The master bedroom was locked. None of the keys fit.

"Tyre. We don't have a key to her bedroom?"

"No, sir."

"We're supposed to have access to all rooms."

"Yes, sir. But I think somewhere along the way, that changed. We haven't had a key since I've been on the job."

Dropping to one knee, Gabe studied the brass fitting and the pin and tumbler mechanism. The lock was of high quality, but that didn't mean it would be a challenge to pick. He could also hear his older brother's reminder that meddling in other people's business was an unfavorable character trait.

Over the years, Zeus's admonishment of *'you're such a nosy brat'* had turned into a *'mind your own fucking business'* warning. Lately, Zeus's buzzword was boundaries. As in, *'I thought you'd grow out of it, but now that you're in your mid-thirties, I've given up hope. You might be a great agent. Clients love you. But you've got a character flaw. No respect for boundaries. You've gotten away with it so far. Sometimes, it even works to your advantage. But one day, it's going to get you in trouble.'*

"Quarterly update, sir." Tyre's voice crackled through his earpiece again.

Standing, stretching, Gabe decided against breaking into her bedroom. For now. He'd ask the client for the keys that would get him into the entire property, as the contract specified, and he'd give her a chance to comply. Hutchenson didn't cut the agents any slack, and he doubted she respected agents who let her break the rules. Maybe that was part of the problem.

Gabe turned, studied some of her paintings that hung on the landing, and said, "Go."

"She's finished her sketch of those two kids. She's staring at the painting of the footbridge. She's almost done with that part of the painting. Wait. She's looking at her phone. Hold it a second." After a pause, Tyre said, "Yes ma'am." Then, he added, "Sir?"

"Yes."

"She's done for the day. We're heading to the townhouse. Should be there in twenty minutes."

"Has Marks reached you?"

"Arrived before my update. I made the intro. Client glanced at him and nodded. An accomplishment, considering she typically ignores us."

"Alert me if anything happens." Gabe walked into the second-floor exercise room.

"Sir. The Marigny isn't your average American neighborhood, but still, it's a Saturday afternoon. Nothing's going to happen."

As Tyre spoke, Gabe checked the windows and inventoried exercise equipment. Treadmill. Spin bike. A shelf held dumbells, kettle bells, tombstone pads, boxing gloves, and yoga mats. A television sat on another shelf. Baskets were filled with DVDs. Flipping through the discs, he saw DVDs on cardio workouts, spinning, strength-building, and Krav Maga training.

"Tyre," Gabe growled, as he eyed a red punching bag that hung from the ceiling. "Watch it. She's better now, but file indicates she still has PTSD-induced agoraphobia. If you haven't studied agoraphobia, then you're not working hard enough. Respect her, because the fact that she's out there makes her damn brave. Understood?"

"Yes, sir," Tyre answered.

"Marks. Stevens. You understand?"

"Yes, sir."

"Understood, sir."

"Are you aware of my most recent assignment prior to this one?"

"Yes, sir." The three agents answered in unison.

They knew, because it was company-wide knowledge and because Gabe had been in media reports as he walked with President Cameron and other world leaders through Praptan, Chalinda. Through prior Black Raven work, Gabe was an expert on Praptan. Black Raven, and specifically Gabe, had been hired to provide assistance to the Secret Service throughout President Cameron's tour of the once-thriving city that was now a nuclear disaster zone and, where habitable, a rebel stronghold.

"I do not consider this job any less important than my last assignment. Every Black Raven client is as important as the President. Raise the bar, gentlemen. Let admiration and respect be the baseline for this job and Ms. Hutchenson."

Steep stairs led to her third-floor art studio. Gabe knew she didn't like having agents in her studio. The file was clear on that.

He climbed the stairs anyway. The door was locked. When none of the keys he had fit the lock, he chalked it up to another breach by Hutchenson. While he was tempted to pick the lock, the admonishment he'd given his agents came back to him. Admiration. Respect. Restraint won out over his innate urge to barrel through a boundary that shouldn't exist and could potentially be a danger to the client.

He'd explain the need for the rule and give Hutchenson a chance to comply. Being an optimist, he chose not to worry about what would happen if she refused, or whether she was hiding something he shouldn't uncover.

Chapter Seven

Andi

Sanctuary.

As she stepped into her courtyard, the clang of the gate shutting behind her warmed some of Andi's ever-present chill. After checking the lock, Agent Two walked ahead to unlock the door to her mudroom, then held it open for her.

Entering the quiet mudroom gave her the feeling of slipping into a welcoming cocoon. Wide windows overlooking the courtyard captured radiant beams of afternoon sunlight. The warmth of the narrow, utilitarian room almost loosened the knot that had formed in her belly with each phone call she'd received, and mostly ignored, during the day. Her best friend, Taylor Morrissey, and the gallery owner, Jacques Stapleton, had been persistent.

Don't think about that now.

Agent Three, one of two new replacements for the agents she'd fired the day before, dragged her artist's cart inside. She'd been introduced to him when he arrived in Crescent Park, and promptly forgotten his name. She hadn't met the other new replacement. Agent Three, distinguishable from other agents because he was cue-ball bald, stood in pause mode next to her cart. He was stocky, with warm brown eyes. He evidently hadn't gotten the message that her mudroom time was private.

She slipped her satchel off her shoulder and placed it on a bench. "I'm fine in here, alone."

"Would you like help carrying any of this to your studio?"

"No. Thank you." *Now leave me alone. Go.*

He left, to take position in the security room, or somewhere that she— hopefully—wouldn't see him. Lifting the pochade box to the counter, she opened it and unclipped the canvas she'd been working on.

After placing the canvas on an easel, she collected the filbert, drawing, and flat brushes she'd used that day. Dropping each into a turpentine-filled mason jar, she let them soak. The odor of turpentine, strong and pungent, was comforting. She rinsed the brushes, then placed each onto a stack of paper towels. The tasks were so routine, her mind wandered.

Sunday. Tomorrow. The gallery opening. Which I'm not attending.

After a sleepless night, she'd decided against going to the art opening. Before leaving the house, she'd called Jacques Stapleton. Relieved when he didn't answer, she'd left a short message. She'd ignored his return phone calls. She'd also ignored most calls from Taylor, knowing that Stapleton had called Taylor for assistance in persuading her to change her mind.

Don't think about that now. Decision made.

As the water drained off her brushes, she reached for the wooden palette she'd wrapped in newspaper to keep leftover blobs of paint from making a mess. She unwrapped the palette, then looked in the box for the palette knife, which must have slipped from the newspaper wrapping.

"Ms. Hutchenson, I'm—

Heart pounding at the loud and unfamiliar voice, Andi spun around. He was large. Four feet away. Moving into the room.

Startled, she charged at him, with the fingers of her right hand aiming for his left eye, while lifting her right knee to his groin. Too late, she saw the Black Raven logo on the man's short-sleeved polo shirt.

He did a fast, fluid jump to his left. Her knee barely grazed his outer thigh. As she flew forward with momentum that was off-kilter from missing her target, he flexed his right arm and leaned towards her. A slight elbow jab to her right bicep and a gentle, glancing push with his forearm slowed her so that she didn't fall flat on her face.

While she found firm footing, he backed away and lifted his hands above his shoulders.

"Whoa. Easy now. I'm Black Raven. Not here to hurt you."

Gasping for air, she steadied herself.

"You okay?" he asked.

Her heart pounded so fast, she couldn't answer. Eyeing his broad shoulders, his bulging biceps, trim waist, and long legs, her one thought was, *hell.* He had almost a solid foot of height on her and at least seventy-five additional pounds of what looked like pure muscle mass. If he had used any of his considerable force, he would've knocked her on her ass.

Finally, she managed to breathe. "Have you lost your goddamn mind?"

"I knocked, but—"

"There's no damn *'but'* that's acceptable. I don't pay Black Raven to scare the hell out of me. Turn around. Disappear."

Staying a short distance away, in the doorway, his hands fell to his side. “I’m sorry I startled you. Michael Gabriel Hernandez. Everyone calls me Gabe.”

“I don’t care what the hell everyone calls you.” *To me, you’re officially Agent Idiot.* With adrenaline-fueled aggression slipping out of her body with each slowing pulse of her heart, her hands started shaking.

“Ms. Hutchenson, are you okay?”

“Yes. Fine. But you obviously aren’t familiar with my background, so go read my file so you know exactly what you’re dealing with.”

“I have studied your file. I’m really sorry, ma’am. I certainly didn’t intend to scare you,” he added, his tone deadly serious, his light eyes grave with worry as he assessed her. “I knocked. Thought you heard me. File says you hyper-focus, and that’s what I thought I was watching as you cleaned your palette. File also says you tend to ignore agents, so that was another possibility.”

What he said was perfectly plausible, because she did all that. Focusing on tangible tasks was an anxiety-coping mechanism that worked better than the drugs her doctors had prescribed.

She resumed her position at the sink, turning her back to him.

Focus. On the moment. Nothing bad is happening in the mudroom. Agent Idiot will disappear. Take a deep breath. Relax.

“That was a pretty decent move. Looks like you’ve used those DVDs in your exercise room.”

Spinning to face him, she said, “Don’t patronize me—”

“I’m not. If I hadn’t studied Krav Maga, you would’ve hit your mark.”

He gave her a slight smile, looking at her as though he was expecting...what? A conversation?

“Let me reiterate, in case the file doesn’t make it perfectly clear. I really, really don’t like to be startled. If you can’t comprehend that, or the reasons for that, please remove yourself from my job now.”

“Once again, I apologize. I’m the new agent in charge of your job, I certainly understand the reasons why you don’t like to be startled, and I don’t plan on leaving for a while.” Unlike the other agents who knew her history, he looked deep into her eyes with a natural directness. “As I said, everyone calls me Gabe.”

“I heard that the first time. I don’t do nicknames. Or names for that matter, where Black Raven personnel is involved. Agent will do. If you’d like, I’ll call you Agent-In-Charge. Or would you prefer Agent One?”

“Really?” He arched an eyebrow. “You really do assign us numbers? The file mentioned something about that, but I didn’t think—”

“It beats trying to remember names as you guys filter through the revolving door of this job.” She lifted her chin and leveled her eyes on his.

Why he thought there was anything to smile about, she couldn’t fathom, but a smile played at his lips. As much as she usually didn’t dwell on details about the agents, her fear—which was now fading, thank God—made her hyperaware of everything around her. Which, for the moment, meant him.

His black hair was cut short and neat on the sides, a bit longer on top. A few pieces fell in curved spikes onto his forehead. Not quite curls. He had high cheekbones and a square jaw, but his eyes were what held her attention. They were mostly a light green that reminded her of the Pthalo green pigment.

In fact, in the brilliant sunlight of the mudroom, the sparkling color was so close to the oil color that was in her pochade box, she wanted to compare the color to the real thing. On the outside of his irises, the pure green picked up a crystalline-blue, which was perfectly set off with an olive-green rim. Rarely had she seen unadulterated nature put on such a riveting display.

Hell. Focus on the task at hand. Not his damn eyes.

“Frankly, if you’re in charge, the team’s in trouble. Do not startle me. When you come into a room, especially behind me, make some damn noise. That isn’t rocket science, is it?”

“No ma’am, it isn’t. Next time I’ll make a hell of a lot more noise.” Voice dry, eyes twinkling, he added, “I’ll even wear bells on my shoes to avoid scaring you.”

For fear of encouraging him, she bit back her smile. “Great. I fired two agents yesterday, tried to terminate the contract, and corporate responds by sending a joker.”

“I’m just trying to put you at ease.”

“Doesn’t my file say that I don’t interact with the agents?”

His smile drifted away, but the tilt at the corners of his lips told her it would quickly return. “Yes.”

"Good. Then you understand that I pay Black Raven to protect me. Not startle me into defensive moves, joke with me, or engage in extended conversations."

"Understood." The direct look in his eyes seemed honest, but she narrowed her eyes, looking for the overly-effusive look of pity she'd learned to spot. Sooner or later it always appeared. She could suss it out like a grizzly bear could smell strawberry jelly donuts at a campground.

She lifted her chin, squared her shoulders, met his gaze, and braced for it to appear in his stunning eyes. Yes, life had thrown her a curve ball that she still hadn't figured out how to hit, but she was fortunate. A hell of a lot of people carried far worse burdens. Pity was best reserved for others, those who truly were living a life of despair. Once someone looked at her with the off-color filter of pity, they'd never really see her. Which meant she had no use for them.

Nope. No pity.

"Bells on my shoes, noise when entering a room, and no humor. Got it, ma'am. If you don't mind, I'll start over with my official intro. Here goes. I'm the new agent in charge. I've already reconnoitered the property, both inside and out, with the exception of your bedroom and studio, for which I do not have keys." Serious eyes, a frown, and a pause suggested not having keys was a problem for him. "I'll get back to that. Your security equipment's in top form, we've re-calibrated the cameras, and all locks are intact."

"Good to know." Attention on him, she was still waiting for pity to make an appearance and trying to figure out how, and why, 'Everyone-Calls-Me-Gabe' was so different than the other agents Black Raven had sent her way. His broad shoulders matched his oversized height. He wore black slacks, with a pistol holstered at his hip, and a fitted, black polo shirt. He looked...at ease. Content. And happy. In his skin. In the moment. Just damn happy.

Happy? Yes. That's it. That's what makes him different. It's as though he's standing in the one place in the world he wants to be, which is...damn weird.

None of the other Black Raven agents had seemed happy to be assigned to her job. Upon meeting her, they'd all been professional to a fault, but not genuinely pleased with the assignment. The agents typically gave her a wide berth. A little too much body space. As though her brand of crazy was a contagious cough.

"I'd like to have a general discussion with you about the job. But first, what are your plans for the rest of the afternoon and evening?"

"Staying in. Like always." *I'm too scared to be out at night, didn't you read the damn file?*

A nod amped up the niceness in his smile, as though she'd just said something that was perfectly normal for a single twenty-nine-year-old on a Saturday night.

"That makes our logistics easy." His deep, smooth voice was that of a man who liked his job, had confidence in his ability to do it, and planned to do it efficiently and well.

The charming nature of his smile was unexpected and...was seemingly genuine. Oh, who the hell was she kidding? At full beam, Everyone-Calls-Me-Gabe's smile wasn't merely charming or nice. It had eye-pulling magnetism that hit the upper stratosphere of gorgeous; a place with air so thin, mere mortals became lightheaded. With his full smile, the corners of his eyes crinkled where a thick fringe of dark lashes accented the light and warmth that his gaze conveyed.

Such inner joy, easily worn for the world to see, reminded her of...the person she used to be.

Never mind. That Andi doesn't exist any longer.

She gave him a nod that was intended as a dismissal. He may as well learn her body language now, because his engaging nature was...off-putting.

Turning back to the counter, she picked up the palette knife and started scraping paint from the palette and onto a newspaper. He moved closer to the counter, leaned his butt against it, and faced the opposite wall, as though settling in for a chat. "If it's convenient, I'd like to discuss your expectations for the security detail and work out any kinks that might need addressing."

She sighed as she cleaned the palette with baby wipes. Best to get his introductory comments out of the way, then he could fade into the background. "Talk while I work."

"Yesterday's incident suggests there are some things Black Raven can improve upon."

"Fine. I'd say that's an understatement. Do it within the specified parameters of the contract." *Now go away.*

After setting the palette on the counter, she picked up her paintbrushes, examining each to see if another turpentine rinse was warranted. The brushes were clean enough.

Nope—not taking a damn hint. Butt in place against my counter, with his eyes on me.

"I'd like your input on any adjustments to the detail."

She focused on blotting out leftover water with a paper towel and reshaping her brushes as she spoke. "Great idea. Why haven't any of the prior agents asked for my input?"

"I can't answer that. All I can do is ask now. I'd like your opinion as to what went wrong yesterday."

Andi crossed the mudroom and sat on the bench. She pulled off the dusty cowboy boots that were her current favorite for long days of painting and sketching. Instead of staying across the room, he moved to stand just a few feet from where she sat.

He leaned against the doorway, looking down at her. "I'm all ears."

"Yesterday's incident boiled down to one simple problem. My version is I asked the agents who were on the detail with me to investigate something I saw, which they should have also seen, had they been paying attention to me."

Eyes on her, he gave her a nod. "Go on."

"They refused to investigate it. I asked them to call the police and report it, because the cops no longer listen to a damn thing I say. They refused to do that, too."

She pulled off her socks, dropped them next to her boots, and stood, facing him. Angling her chin upwards so that she could meet his gaze, she folded her arms at her waist. For a second, his eyes were on her bare feet and her pastel painted toenails. Juliette, her in-home spa service provider, had painted them the Saturday before with Andi's favorite standby—Loire Valley Lavender. This morning's session with Juliette had been a long massage, and help with the haircut Andi had given herself the night before. With the tension this agent had inspired, she longed for more time on the massage table.

When his gaze returned to hers, his eyes were serious. A slight frown played at his lips. She continued, "So those two agents were fired. Look. I know Black Raven keeps me safe, but what I really need the agents to do, is—"

She paused, thought through the next words she planned to say before they popped out of her mouth, and then thought better of them.

Dear God, what is it about this man that has me spilling my guts?

"I've forgotten your name. Not the nickname. The real one."

"Michael Gabriel Hernandez. I answer to Michael, Gabriel, or Hernandez, but, for the third time now, most people call me

Gabe. One close friend even calls me Angel, but no one else gets away with that, so don't try." His 1,000-watt, positively beatific smile reappeared. It warmed the chill from her in a way no one had been able to do since Victor Morrissey had used her for an ashtray.

"Rest assured," he continued, "I'll answer to Agent, Agent One, Agent-In-Charge. Even a 'hey you' will work. What were you saying?"

Andi stepped toward the doorway and waited for the man who was named after not one, but two, archangels, to move. Chiseled and muscular, he didn't resemble the sweetly innocent, cherubic angels that had been painted by Raphael Sanzio in the Madonna di San Sisto. Nah. If angelic at all, he was a dark angel, one who'd fight evil, inch for inch.

"Ms. Hutchenson," he prompted, "you were saying—"

"All I need to say. Fine." Lifting her right hand with a slight wave of dismissal, she continued through the living room.

He cocked his head and arched an eyebrow as he studied her. "Fine?"

"Meaning I'm through talking. Make any necessary adjustments to the security detail. Discussion over. I've been outside for hours. I'll spend the rest of the evening upstairs."

She walked through the kitchen and entered the hallway, to go upstairs, where she wouldn't have to see him. Agent Hot-Guy's gaze was too penetrating, and that smile? There was just no damn reason for it.

"Ms. Hutchenson?"

Now what?

She turned. He was right behind her. She mentally renamed him Agent Can't-Take-a-Hint. "Yes?"

"I'd like to talk a little more." He walked with her to the base of the stairs. The quiet of the house fell around them as he stopped just short of her, giving her the minimum amount of acceptable body space. As though he carried an invisible tape measure and knew the number of inches required for her comfort level. Climbing onto the second stair gave her enough height that when she turned towards him, she could look directly in his eyes. Hands resting on the banister, he returned her gaze.

"Well?" she said. "Go on."

"You were saying you need the agents to do something. I'd love to know what was on the tip of your tongue, because—if you pardon my bluntness—this job has been lacking guidance from you, except when you fire one of us." He arched an eyebrow. "So, what were you about to say? You need the agents to do what?"

"Keep me safe."

He nodded as he flattened his hands on the banister, running them a few inches up, then down the smooth cypress. "That's a given. You were talking in the context of yesterday's incident, though, and you didn't finish your thought."

She inhaled in exasperation, detecting a light, woodsy and citrusy scent as she studied him. His intense focus on her, his interest in what he could do to make the job run smoother, seemed genuine. Okay, so on top of the compassion that poured from his eyes, he had great listening skills and the attentiveness of a dog with a bone.

"I'd like the Agents to humor me. If I see something that needs investigating, I damn well want the agents to check it out, then explain to me in rational terms what happened, if anything did at all. Without making me feel that..." She drew a deep breath, catching again his aroma. Deciding it was something akin to a pheromone-borne truth serum that she was apparently powerless to overcome, she said, "I'm crazier than I am."

Without a trace of judgment, he nodded. "Understood. To implement an investigative component, we'd ideally have a third man on your outdoor detail. You see, standard protocol for the type of security detail prescribed by your contract requires two agents to be at your side whenever you're outside, especially on a busy street with vehicular traffic. Which is why those agents couldn't leave your side and investigate anything yesterday."

"You are an optimist, aren't you? You think that is why they didn't listen to me?"

"Yes, and yes." He paused for a second. "Logistically speaking, the most effective way of accomplishing what you're requesting is with a five-man detail, because agents need off time so they can be alert in the field. Until now, your detail has had four agents. More manpower means higher fees. Roughly twenty-five percent higher than contracted."

"Fine."

He pushed hair that had fallen over his forehead back, cocked his head, and arched an eyebrow. "Fine?"

"Yes."

"I'd prefer not to have to read between the lines, Ms. Hutchenson. That might've cut it with the other agents, but it also might have been part of the lack of communication that led to job problems." His tone had hardened slightly and his smile had almost disappeared. "Ambiguous responses to my questions will perpetuate the problems that have been pervasive on this job. Communication between you and us needs to be clearer. The sooner the better."

"I communicate just fine." His firm tone and blunt message broadcasted that he wasn't a pushover. *Fine. Neither am I.* "The agents choose not to listen. Yesterday, they looked at me like I was crazy and treated me that way. I'd say that's what damn well led to their firing. Not a lack of communication on my part."

Serious eyes regarded her for a moment. "My question stands. Would you like me to incorporate a fifth agent into the detail?"

His direct question hit her with a reality check. The round-the-clock private security detail cost her a small fortune. Yes—she had the money for it, but she hated throwing her money away as a reaction to what she thought she saw the day before.

Face it. I'm not even sure I saw anything at all. Oh dear God, did I fire those agents over nothing? Because, except for yesterday afternoon, they didn't irritate her, and this new guy sure as hell did.

"No," she said. "Hold off for now."

Eyes serious, hands clasped together on top of the banister, he gave her an understanding nod. "Then I'll see what we can do with the existing manpower. Especially as the Mardi Gras season peaks, flexibility is warranted. Once I'm on the job for a few more days, I'll have a better feel for your expectations."

"Thank you. Tomorrow I'll paint outdoors from ten to four. Assuming the weather's nice." *And assuming I sleep at all tonight.* "I usually meet with the agents at nine thirty to plan the day."

"I'm aware. Before you go upstairs, there's the matter of the keys."

"What about them?"

"Protocol requires that we have access to the entire premises. Including your bedroom and the studio on the third floor. Keys would be the most efficient way of having access."

"On this job," she said, "and on the issue of locking my bedroom and my studio, I define standard protocol."

The play of a slight smile at his lips suggested he was enjoying their conversation. "That's not the way it works, Ms. Hutchenson. The contract sets standard protocol. We're to have access to the entire premises. Every room, every attic, every crawlspace. It's a standard clause in all of our security details, and not one that I can override."

His doggedness was damn irritating, despite his high cheekbones, mesmerizing eyes, broad shoulders, and captivating smile. “About six months ago, when I requested a new team of agents, I took the key to my bedroom and studio out of the sets the agents use.” *Keep your tone unwavering, your voice pitch perfect. Enunciate. Speak up.* “You’re the first agent to call me out on it.”

“Can’t say that’s a fact that earns me a star. It’s a discrepancy that should have been rectified.”

“I leave those doors unlocked when I’m in the house. I simply ask that agents knock before entering.”

“Part of providing security means constant access to the client. And, in your case, the file specifies that there are times when you explicitly request that we lay eyes—”

“Yes,” she interrupted, feeling the heat of embarrassment burn her face.

His steady eyes held her gaze. Still no pity. Thank God. But plenty of compassion, as though he appreciated the enormity of her struggle. “We need access to the premises. Which means I need a key to every lock, on every door. In an emergency, we can’t have anything slowing us down, and due diligence requires me to survey the entire property today.”

“I’ll give them to you. But...” From out of nowhere, she inexplicably felt pathetic and she didn’t want her voice to reflect her inner turmoil. Drawing a deep breath, she prayed that she could keep her voice steady. Through sheer force of willpower, and buoyed by the concern that flooded his eyes, as though he was willing his strength to her, she kept it together. “Those are the rooms I consider the most private and frankly, I can’t stand the fact that I need you guys to be here in the first place. Please. Respect my privacy.”

He gave her an understanding nod. “Don’t worry. We’ll treat those rooms with the respect they deserve. May I follow you up now, for a quick check?”

“Fine.”

Chapter Eight

Gabe

As Gabe trailed a couple of stairs behind Andi, the fresh scent of lavender, and a lingering whisper-like trace of oil paint and turpentine surrounded him. He enjoyed the view of her long, slender legs and tight butt in faded jeans that were splotched with paint.

Odd, but with the plethora of details and all the photographs that were in her client file, his due diligence hadn't prepared him for finding her so...interesting. Complex. Compelling. Adorable.

Oh hell—just plain mesmerizing.

There was no denying she had the physical attributes of his favorite type of woman—long-legged, dark-haired, with a heart-shaped face. Physically, she was exactly the kind of woman he'd made a habit of avoiding, for fear of getting too attached. But there was something more than her looks. In the bright sunlight of the mudroom, throughout their conversation, until now...he'd never before felt whatever the hell he was feeling now.

Almond-shaped, expressive eyes had looked almost velvety-brown at first glance, but with the sun of her mudroom hitting them, he'd seen deep, forest green undertones. The intense color did justice to the roiling emotions underlying each of her glances, each pause before she spoke, each carefully thought-through word and sentence.

His fascination had begun as he'd watched her focus on her cleanup tasks, as her slender hands washed her paintbrushes. Or it could've been when she'd surprised the hell out of him by almost succeeding with her attempt to knee him in the groin. Or possibly, it was as simple as she'd stoked his love of a challenge, and, with her steadfast refusal to say his name, she'd given him a flashing 'game-on!' signal.

It could've just been her delicate feet, with lavender toenails, which were now padding up the stairs, her footfalls silent on the runner. Or perhaps it was the smudge of brownish-orange paint on her left cheek, where her creamy flesh lifted and rounded over the delicate, high arch of her cheekbone.

Or maybe it was that her voice sometimes fell to a whisper. There was something about that whisper that yanked on every fiber of his heart, in a way he'd never felt before. When she said she wanted the agents to not make her feel crazier than she was, her voice had been so quiet, he'd almost missed the words.

As they reached the landing at the top of the townhome's first flight of stairs, the doorbell rang. Andi paused, and turned towards the front of the house. Gabe turned as she did. On the first floor, at the base of the stairwell, Marks stepped out of the security room. "Ms. Hutchenson. Ms. Morrissey is here."

Andi hesitated, then nodded. Gabe moved to the side, allowing Andi to pass him as she retraced her steps on the wide stairwell. "Let her in."

Taylor entered, her heels clacking on the marble floor of the foyer, as Andi reached the bottom of the stairs. Gabe stopped mid-way down and stood to the side.

"Hey, honey." Taylor stepped further into the foyer. Marks shut the solid door and slid the locks into place. "I've tried calling all day. Why are you avoiding me?"

"Don't get too close. I'm a mess. I've been outside for hours." Andi lifted her hands, waving off Taylor's outstretched, ready-for-a-hug, arms. "Even though it's chilly, the sun was bright. I'm sticky with sunblock and probably wet with paint and you, as usual, look perfect."

"Doesn't matter." Taylor stepped forward and wrapped Andi in a friendly hug despite her friend's resistance, then held onto her shoulders, at arm's length.

Marks glanced up the stairs. Gabe gave him an *I've-got-this* nod, and the other man disappeared into the security room.

The file indicated the two women had been best friends since they were toddlers, and Taylor was the only friend from Andi's pre-kidnapping days with whom Andi maintained regular contact. As Taylor gave her friend a lingering, scrutinizing glance, Gabe studied the contrasts between them. Andi—barefoot. No makeup or jewelry. Choppy hair short, with blunt edges that barely touched her shoulders. Faded jeans. A loose, over-sized white, long-sleeve shirt that was half tucked into the waistband of her jeans. Taylor—in pumps. Dark blue slacks. A soft, cream colored sweater. Bright lipstick on a fully made-up face. Long, golden-brown hair pulled into a sleek ponytail.

"The new haircut's fab," Taylor said. "Did Juliette do that?"

"I did most of it. Juliette had to help with the back this morning."

"Seriously? You did it?"

"I couldn't sleep last night. When I got sick of feeling sorry for myself, I watched a few YouTube videos. I had scissors, and you know the rest." Andi pushed a chunk of hair behind her ear, then slipped her hands in her back pockets. "Really? It's okay? Juliette wanted to kill me. But then, after she tweaked it a bit, she thought it would work."

Had he not been in silent mode, standing on the stairs and being as unobtrusive as possible, Gabe would've told her *'don't worry. It's perfect.'*

"Are you kidding? It's fantastic. It's stylish. Better than the Chanel models in the latest ads."

Andi pulled her hand out of her back pocket and gestured to the stairs. "Come on up. The new agent is finishing a security check, since I had a couple of doors locked while I was out."

"Oh. Hi, Gabe," Taylor said, looking up the stairs. "Welcome to New Orleans. Brandon told me you were arriving today."

"Hello, Taylor." Gabe moved to the side of the wide stairwell, allowing them to pass in front of him.

Andi kept her attention on her friend. "You know him?"

"Gabe's the brother of Zeus Hernandez. He and Brandon are good friends. So yes, we've met a few times." Taylor smiled at Gabe. "Brandon thinks the world of you."

"Thank you," he said as they passed in front of him. "Always good to hear something like that."

Pausing at the door to her bedroom, Andi pulled a key from her pocket and unlocked it. She pushed it open, and moved to the side so he could pass. The room had a neatly made king-size bed, white linens with lavender-colored *AH* monograms, and bouquets of fresh lavender in vases on bedside tables. His gaze locked on the embroidered H. As he observed the scrolls and curls of the ornate stitching, he admired how special a plain old H could look when it symbolized generations of family wealth, an enormous inheritance, and more than a little good taste.

Gabe walked to the far window and checked the locks, then moved to the other window. They stood in the doorway as he did his check. The eye aversion and straight face required for personal security jobs came with training, as did his ability to observe every minute move the client made while appearing not to be looking at her.

"I'm sorry, Tay. I just can't go." Andi drew a deep breath.

Ah. So she does use nicknames.

"I know you put a lot of effort into the opening. From personal assurances with Jacques and Sonja that I'd show up, to a social media push. Flowers. A caterer. But I just can't. I'm sorry."

"Judith's done the leg work. She's been happy to act as a party planner for the event." Taylor rested her right hand on her friend's shoulder, while giving Andi a soft, reassuring glance. "I shouldn't have pushed you into it. I let Sonja's enthusiasm carry me away. I was blinded by the Stapleton name."

The Stapleton Gallery. Gabe had just met the owner. Sonja was Sonja Long, the wife of Doctor Walter Long. Both were in Andi's former social circle. The client file had provided a few details, since Sonja, after spotting one of Andi's paintings at Taylor's house, had been the impetus for the opening. The Longs were fervent art aficionados and philanthropists. They'd made New Orleans their primary home five years earlier. Walter had made a fortune in designing and patenting surgical devices. Sonja, his younger wife, had inserted herself into the art and social community by volunteering with art museums, taking classes at the art academy, and chairing large-scale fundraisers.

"Sonja's enthusiasm is warranted..." Taylor was saying, as Gabe stepped into the walk-in closet. He was suddenly surrounded by hanging sweaters and shirts. Plenty of jeans. Shelves held folded exercise clothes, as well as linens and blankets. Cowboy boots, tennis shoes, and other casual shoes were in racks. Rods where dresses would've hung were empty. "Look at how fast Jacques leapt at the chance to represent your work once he saw the photos. Jacques wouldn't take on your work if he didn't believe there was tremendous potential. And he isn't doing you a favor, Andi. I know you two were friends—"

"Don't know if I'd call him a friend." Keeping her tone matter of fact, but lowering her volume slightly, Andi added, "I slept with him. More than once. Which doesn't make him any different than the other people I slept with, and we both know there were quite a few. That doesn't necessarily make him a friend. It isn't a big deal, considering how much I used to sleep around."

In the closet, using a footstool to check the lock on a window, Gabe was unable to stop himself from listening. Pre-kidnapping social media use, provided in the file as background information, had given him a hint that she'd been active. The casualness with which she now acknowledged her past behavior gave him another view at how different her life was now.

"I was only being polite," Taylor said.

"I know. Hell." In a voice that suddenly carried a bit of regret, she continued, "I just can't believe how...available I was before the kidnapping. I know. You tried to tell me sex wasn't a sport. Geez. Why didn't I listen?"

"Don't beat yourself up. You were younger then—"

"I was bored. I was an adult, but acting like a spoiled rotten teenager—"

"We were all spoiled rotten. But look what you're doing now. You're helping people, Andi. The gallery opening will create awareness about a very good cause. Back then, your artistic calling wasn't very strong, so you had way too much time on your hands. You always had too much energy for your own good. I love that you're pouring that energy into your paintings now, but—"

"But it would be better if I had a more well-rounded life, right? How long is it taking this agent to check the closet?"

Too long, because he couldn't help but listen to every word. Gabe stepped out of the closet and glanced in Andi's direction. With her hands tucked into her back pockets again, and a slight frown playing across her lips, her discomfort was palpable as she gave him a passing glance, then refocused all of her attention on her friend. Gabe walked into the sitting room, which had another television that was almost as large as the television on the first floor, and lingered there.

"I was going to say it would be better if I could figure out a way to persuade you that you're doing exactly the right thing, right now, and not to waste any of your energy on worrying. Stop second guessing yourself," Taylor said. "Anyway, I shouldn't have pushed you into it. I'm sorry."

"I should've stood firm from the beginning. After yesterday, I know that I'm not ready for such a big public appearance." Her voice was softer, dropping to that darn heart-torqueing whisper. "I'm not blaming you, Tay. I'm just sorry I can't do it."

"No apology needed. That's all I wanted to tell you when I called. Don't overthink this."

"Dammit Taylor. I was the person who jumped without looking. Maybe too impulsively, and definitely without thinking, but still...did you ever think you'd have to tell me not to overthink something?"

"No." Her tone soft and gentle, Taylor let that word sink in for a second. "But I love this part of you, as well. Look. The opening would be better if you were there, of course, but it will be perfectly fine if you don't go."

Gabe re-entered the bedroom. "Ms. Hutchenson. The file indicates that you do not keep a weapon on the premises. Is that still accurate?"

"Yes." She gave him a serious glance. "Black Raven is my weapon."

He gave her a nod. "Then consider yourself ready for anything." He tried to keep his voice as serious as her eyes, but he couldn't help but give her a small smile. In return, she stared at him with a slight scowl furrowing her forehead, which made him drop the smile and give her a serious nod. "Shall we go upstairs?"

Andi led the way up to the third floor, with Taylor at her side and Gabe trailing behind. Pausing at the door to her studio, Andi's hand shook as she tried to unlock the door.

Hell.

"Andi," Taylor asked, concern in her tone, "are you okay?"

"Fine."

Yet her hand was shaking so much she couldn't get the key into the lock. *Fine*. Her go-to word, when she was anything but fine. Gabe stepped closer, careful to keep an arm's length between Andi and him. He stretched out his hand, palm up. "May I?"

She dropped the key in his hand. "Thank you." Turning to her friend, she said, "I was getting better, Tay. It's been a long time since I saw anything like that. Or thought I saw anything like that. I just wish the goddamn cops would call me back. I've left three messages for Officer Thompson."

Pushing the door open, he let them walk in ahead of him. "Excuse me, Ms. Hutchenson. Couldn't help but overhear. I went to the station and met Thompson and his partner, Spagnoli. They won't be calling you. They have an odd perception of their duty to serve the public. I could tell you after meeting them in person how little I think of them, but that would be counterproductive."

She shot him a grateful glance. "I appreciate the honesty."

He entered the studio and inhaled the lingering aroma of oil paints. Sunlight flowed in from six large skylights. Gleaming wood floors were partially covered with area rugs scattered throughout. But something was off.

On the left, there were four easels, each with a canvas. Floor lamps were placed around the room, near easels or at standing worktables. Canvasses were stacked against the walls. Others hung on the walls. There was a cream-colored couch, with throws and pillows. A coffee table was full of magazines and books on painting techniques. Next to the couch, shelves were crammed with more books. A kitchenette had a coffeemaker, a small refrigerator, and a microwave. A couple of bags of chocolate chip cookies were in a basket.

It looked like an artist's studio, but the dimensions of the room were wrong. The floor plan had indicated the third floor consisted of one large room. The studio was cavernous, but it didn't seem large enough, given the footprint of the house. If there was a crawlspace or attic behind any of the walls, the floor plan hadn't included it. Aside from wiring the skylights for the security system, Black Raven had left the third floor alone. The walls were windowless. Nonetheless, the room certainly looked secure. Impenetrable.

I'll figure it out later.

In the far corner of the large room, the walls were covered with sketches. In stark contrast to the vivid colors that saturated her paintings, the sketches were pure black and white. Or, more accurately, done in shades of grey, with hints of darkness.

The people she'd sketched looked young. Some sketches were close-ups, just head and shoulders. Some were full bodies, with a hint as to background. Their faces seemed so real, their eyes so lifelike. Their gazes burned into his skin, as though they were calling to him. Goosebumps prickled on his arms. He walked closer, unable to resist the pull.

Weird. I can't stop looking.

Taylor crossed the room and stood next to him, as they both stared at the sketches. Voice a low whisper, Taylor said, "Not many people have seen these, Gabe."

"They're phenomenal," he said, with a smile at Taylor and a longer glance at Andi.

Hands in her back pockets, Andi gave him a full smile, the first he'd gotten from her. "Thank you."

A large oak table held dozens of sketchpads, some open, some closed. "May I look?"

Relieved when she nodded, because he couldn't pretend his interest had anything to do with security, he lifted one of the pads, and thumbed through the pages. Some subjects had smiles. Some were sad. Some stared vacantly. Stoned? In some, they played music. In others, they were panhandling. Clothes—old and tattered. Hair—long and disheveled. At the bottom of each sketch, she'd marked the date, time, and place. Names—not full names—were in quotes. "Daisy." "Honey." "Sam." "Lu." "Monica." "Beth." "Liz." "Pic." "Tank."

Dragging his eyes from a tablet where she'd made notes about who she'd sketched, when, and where, he realized it was organized by name. "You keep track of them."

She gave him a one-shouldered shrug. "I like to note dates and times when I do a sketch. I've gotten to recognize a lot of these people."

Gabe closed one sketchpad, and opened another. He expected her to give him a short, dismissive signal indicating he should leave. When she didn't, he kept looking. He flipped the pages, lost in the raw emotion in the subject's eyes, the way they held their chins, the way they held their shoulders. A young girl, playing a flute, seemed to look directly at Gabe with soulful eyes. One girl had a flower in her hair. Another had eyes that looked so sad, they tore at Gabe's heart. One young man held a dog.

A common thread in the sketches was the subject's vulnerability. All had a subtle touch of something being off—whether it was tattered clothing or a look of despair—as though the artist had captured an underlying trace of something being wrong in a young life.

Unable to define the mesmerizing hold the sketches had on him, he could only acknowledge that there was something magical in her talent. The drawings reflected the souls of the subjects, but also revealed that she felt compassion and empathy for the people she sketched. The sketches left Gabe with the inescapable conclusion that there was way more to Andi Hutchenson than what he'd learned so far.

"I can't stop looking at them. I thought your paintings were something, but these..." He shrugged, pausing midway through one of her sketchpads, as he stared at a drawing of 'Pic,' playing a guitar in Jackson Square. "Rarely am I at a loss for words. But I am now."

Her whispered, "Thank you," was accompanied with a full smile that lit her eyes.

In her smile, he found another goal while on her job—to see more of the same smiles.

"Did you know that you've already sold eight of the pieces that are at the gallery?"

Lifting her hand to the base of her throat, her mouth fell open. "Eight? Sold? No."

"That's wonderful news, Gabe!" Taylor said, clapping her hands together as she turned to her friend. "See? You're going to be a sensation."

"They're magnificent. I was blown away when I walked in the gallery, which I did after visiting the cops. And I'm not just saying that because I'm on your payroll." He gave Andi a warm smile, then turned his attention back to the sketches.

"Agent Hernandez, did you notice which ones sold?"

It isn't Gabe, but Agent Hernandez is better than Agent One. Or Agent-In-Charge.

"I can't remember all the titles, but *Knockin on Heaven's Door* is sold."

Joy transformed her features. "Wow. That's the most expensive. Hope House will be thrilled."

"Aside from being the beneficiary of sales for the opening, what is Hope House?"

"A charity providing services to the homeless in the French Quarter and surrounding neighborhoods," Andi said. "They're opening their doors next month. In addition to helping them by donating proceeds, one of my goals is to get the word out about them."

Taylor pulled up Stapleton's website on her phone, and told Andi which pieces were sold. Gabe alternated his glance between them and the sketchpad he was holding as he continued thumbing through the pages. When Taylor was through, he said, "If you change your mind about going, say the word. We can adapt with just a bit of warning."

Focusing on Taylor, Andi's voice dropped to that low, almost-whisper that torqued at his gut. His acute sense of hearing was going to come in damn handy on this job. "My appearance would be better for Hope House. I know it. But there will be too many people. They'll all stare at me with that look people give me now. That look I can't stand."

Gabe wondered if Taylor detected what seemed obvious—underneath Andi's insistence that she couldn't go, her voice conveyed a solid, unmistakable yearning to be there.

Andi walked across the room. She paused at a table, where tubes of oil paints were laid out two inches apart, four inches from the edge, by color and shade. Behind her friend's back, Taylor gave Gabe a long, meaningful glance.

Yep. She gets it.

Taylor turned from Gabe, crossing the room to where Andi was rearranging the tubes. "You can't change the way people look at you, and the people who matter don't define you by what happened. The night will be all about your paintings." Taylor rested a hand lightly on her friend's forearm. "Don't overthink it. Whether you go, or don't go, isn't a big deal."

"Damn. Damn. Damn. This angst is going to kill me." Hands clasped together, she turned to Taylor. Gabe made a point to look at the sketches, while keeping his peripheral vision—and 100 percent of his attention—on the two women.

"With so many people looking at me, I don't want to appear like I'm a freak who can't be out without security. When I agreed to do this, I thought I'd be able to have the security in the background, but after yesterday, I can't."

"We'll dress in sports coats," Gabe said. "No Black Raven logos. I can just look like your very attentive date."

As Andi rolled her eyes at the suggestion, Taylor said, "That's a great idea, Gabe."

"What, Ms. Hutchenson? I'm not your type? How about Agent Marks or Tyre being point man?"

Andi gave him a dismissive shake of her head. "It doesn't matter who acts as point man."

Got it. We're all the same to you. No worries. That's how it should be.

"I know these people," she continued, shuddering. "They're touchy feely. Hugs hello. Kisses on cheeks." Andi shuddered. "I can't do that."

"We'll keep that crap to a minimum. Taylor will stay on one side of you. I'll stand on the other. We'll keep a wall behind the three of us. No one will come at you from a blind side. Your left hand will hold a drink—"

"I don't drink. Not since—"

"That fact was in your file. It'll be club soda. Or something. Your right hand will hold my left one."

"I'll be holding your hand?"

He chuckled at the stark dismay on her face. "You said it didn't matter who acts as point man, so I'll act as your date. Holding my hand has to be more palatable than having to shake hands with everyone there—"

"I'll carry a clutch, and hold that instead—

He nodded. "That'll work, too. I've acted as security at enough meet and greets to know that we can't give people an inch. Once they're shaking hands, they're leaning in for hugs and kisses. With both your hands occupied, close contact will be impossible. Taylor will run interference. Brandon will be on Taylor's left to help her. The guests will move down the receiving line without realizing they didn't get to touch you. I know exactly where we'll stand. It's near the front door so you won't feel overwhelmed by the crowd."

A twinge of annoyance crossed her face. "You have all the answers, don't you?"

He gave her a nod. "Yes, ma'am. Remember that communication thing we were talking about earlier? As long as I know your concerns, I can formulate a plan."

"It's too long. Three hours." She shook her head. "I can't stand the thought of it."

"You'll show up late," Taylor said. "Make an appearance around six forty-five."

"And we leave whenever you're ready," Gabe said. "I'll be on you like glue—"

"I don't like to be crowded. Or touched for that matter," she said, accentuating her words with a glare. "Hell, I could very well get there and have an anxiety attack that forces me to leave."

He chuckled. "I'll be so close a whisper will do the trick. When you've had enough, for whatever reason, tell me. Whether it's fifteen minutes, twenty minutes, or two hours in. I'll get you out of there in a matter of seconds. If you go, things will work out. You'll be glad you went. You just have to believe it."

"Agent Hernandez, do you still believe in fairytales? Because that just sounded a whole lot like 'look, here's a beautiful yellow brick road'." She stared straight into his eyes, with a frown playing at her lips. "And we can find a magical wizard who can make Andi courageous, bright, and smart."

"Andi! Don't be mean," Taylor said, "just because he's sharing the optimist's point of view."

"I'm not offended," Gabe said. "Besides, *Somewhere Over the Rainbow* gets me every time I hear it."

Andi glared at him, but enough of a smile played at her lips that he felt a cautious hopefulness. As she turned to Taylor, though, her smile slipped away. "Don't forget the biggest problem with me making an appearance tomorrow night. I look like hell."

"No," he offered, busting over the speed bump that should've kept him from getting personal. "You don't. Even with that paint on your cheek."

Glancing again at him, Andi lifted her hand to her face. A faint pink blush appeared as her smile disappeared.

Taylor's smile was gentle, her eyes assessing. "Your appearance is in my wheelhouse, honey. Not that you need it, but I'll come over and help. I went shopping earlier. I've already got the outfit. A black Donna Karan wrap—"

"Sounds clingy. Showy. I don't want people looking at me."

"You have no idea how gorgeous you are," Taylor said, "do you?"

"Nice of you to say, Taylor. But I might've been pretty. Before. When I tried. Now I look nothing like I used to."

"You're prettier now," Taylor responded, without hesitation.

True.

Drawing in a deep breath, Andi's gaze encompassed both of them as she gave a slight nod. "How I look is actually the least of my concerns. I'd have to get some sleep tonight. Last night I didn't sleep at all."

"Decide tomorrow. No need to worry about it now." Gabe walked to the doorway, then turned to face them as he leaned against the door jamb. "Because you're worried about what happened yesterday, we could go back to the scene. Maybe a crime cam in the area picked up something." As he spoke, concern over the opening gave way to something lighter. He shrugged. "Wouldn't hurt to ask."

She focused on him, with unabated gratitude shining through her eyes. "Thank you. Let's go now. There's at least two hours of daylight left."

This has the potential to be my favorite job ever. If I can get her to look at me like that, more often, simply for doing my job, I'll be floating on top of the world.

"Let me mobilize the team," he said, as he moved to the doorway. "Give me five minutes."

"Wait. Agent Hernandez. When I tried to knee you in the groin earlier—"

"Andi! You've got to treat him with respect. Gabe's part of the elite force, one of the superstar agents. He was just with the President, for—"

Ignoring her friend, Andi talked over Taylor. "How'd you move so fast to deflect me?"

"You hesitated."

Fire lit her eyes as she folded her arms. "I did not."

"You did. When you turned, you sized me up and drew a breath. That action broadcasted your move. But, to be honest, I achieved black belt Krav Maga status a couple of years ago. Even without hesitating, it's highly unlikely you could get an edge on me."

She shook her head. "I didn't hesitate."

"You can only learn so much from DVDs. Let me teach you how to be better." He couldn't help but smile, though he felt deadly serious about the subject matter. Apparently, he was powerless to stop smiling around her. "As much as I love the idea of a magical wizard at the end of the yellow brick road, I believe that teaching people an effective way to kick ass is more reliable for instilling confidence and peace of mind."

Andi thought about his offer for a second, then nodded. "You're on. We'll start tonight."

Chapter Nine

Gabe

"I was right here, studying that house." Andi pointed across Esplanade Avenue. "Thinking how I'd paint it."

Gabe, Marks, and Tyre flanked her in the wide, tree-filled median. Traffic crawled along the narrow street. Parked cars, pedestrians, and bicyclists added to the congestion. With tall palm trees and sprawling oaks on the lawn, the red brick house was majestic.

She'd washed the smudge of paint off her face, and had pulled a brown-leather bomber jacket over her loose white shirt. A breeze tousled shiny strands of her hair. As it fell back in place, the result was a perfect, edgy frame for her serious eyes and pale pink lips.

"What seemed off first?" he asked.

She frowned and bit her lip. Glanced at him, then gave him a small nod before refocusing on the street. "I saw movement out of the corner of my eye. There."

As she pointed, Gabe looked where she indicated. Her voice, barely above a whisper, was hard to hear with the traffic noise. "About a block and a half away. At the corner of..."

A passing truck, with its engine roaring and radio blaring, drowned her words. As he leaned closer to her, she backed a step away. "Don't crowd me, Agent Hernandez."

"Not trying to, ma'am. There's too much noise. I can't hear you when you whisper."

She drew a deep breath, squared her shoulders, tilted her face up, and met his gaze with a determined look. "Perhaps you could do something with that mic in your ear," she said, loud and clear, so there was no missing the words, "so it's a hearing aid?"

Marks and Tyre turned fast so she wouldn't see them laughing. In his ear, the open audio carried their chuckling. "There's nothing wrong with my hearing. Your voice drops when you—"

"Fine. I damn well know when and why my voice drops, but—" She lifted her chin, and he realized then how pale she was. "—I can't seem to stop it from happening." The flash of fire in her eyes told him she hated it. "Do what you need to do, Agent. Just try not to crowd me. It was there," she said, pointing again. "Right before the corner of Esplanade and Decatur, on the

Marigny side of Esplanade. Where that Yellow VW just pulled away. A van pulled up and I thought I saw them kidnap someone."

Eyeing a walking tour of fifteen or so people meandering along the sidewalk, a horse and buggy loaded with tourists turning onto Esplanade from Royal Street, and the never-ending traffic, he asked, "Was the area this crowded yesterday?"

Andi gave him a slight headshake. "No. Yesterday was Friday. It happened before most of the TGIF'ers hit the Quarter, before most of the weekenders arrived. A few tourists were crossing the street." She frowned. "I think they distracted the agents."

"Back up a minute. What made you notice the van?"

She flinched as a nearby car backfired. Gabe almost reached for her, to reassure her with some kind of contact. Studying her, knowing everything the file had included about her PTSD and her agoraphobia, Gabe knew that standing in the median was terrifying for her. Yet she was doing it.

Damn brave.

"Let's cross the street, to the sidewalk, Ms. Hutchinson," he growled. *And you're never going to paint that house, if this is where you'd have to stand to do it.*

At a break in the traffic, he led her to the French Quarter side of Esplanade. He placed himself between her and the edge of the sidewalk, with Marks and Tyre on either side of them. Her back was to a brick wall. She had a view of the area in question. "Better?"

She nodded.

"Try to tell me why you noticed the van."

"It was the sudden movement. It wasn't that he was driving fast..."

Her words, mixed with traffic noise, trailed when Gabe leaned closer to hear her, his feet a mere eight inches from hers, his head bent down to her, as her voice lowered to a whisper. "What was that last part?"

"It was that he stopped so fast," she said. "Fast enough for the tires to screech." Her arms were tightly wrapped around her waist.

Oh, shit. She's hugging herself.

As she torqued every protective instinct he'd ever had, it took everything in him not to grab her, take her in the shelter of his arms, and hold her tight. Gabe planted his feet and straightened his back as she once again tilted her head up and looked directly at him. She looked irritated—with herself, him, or the situation, he couldn't tell. "I'm really trying to speak up, Agent Hernandez."

"Your whispers don't bother me one bit. You could make up your own sign language and I'd figure out a way to understand it. Okay?"

His comment won him a small smile. "Do you always find a way to joke?"

"That wasn't a joke."

She shook her head and drew a deep breath. "At first, my view was partially blocked by that tree. When the tires screeched, I turned, and saw a black van pull along the sidewalk, heading away from the river. A man got out on the passenger side."

"There were two people in the van?"

She nodded. "A driver plus a front seat passenger."

"Both got out?"

"Only the passenger."

"Two men?"

"They were broad-shouldered. Larger than the average woman."

"Can you describe either one?"

She bit her lower lip. "No. They both wore baseball caps. Driver's was dark. Passenger's was black. He wore a long-sleeved dark brown shirt and dark pants. The passenger grabbed a woman walking on the sidewalk, pushed her into the back seat, and got in there with her."

"Can you remember details about her?"

"She was a lot smaller than him."

"Are you sure the person on the sidewalk was a female?"

Andi was quiet for a second. "She was walking towards the river. Away from me. Yes. I'm sure. She had on a loose, pale pink dress. A black leather jacket. Maybe she had light blond hair. I just saw a flash of it. She had most of her head covered. A purple head wrap. Not Muslim. Trendy. Like Old Navy. Once she was in the van, they took off."

"Did she scream?"

She gave him a slow headshake. "Not that I heard."

"Okay, Ms. Hutchenson. I'll look around and see what I can find out. Marks and Tyre will stay with you. It's getting dark soon. Would you like to stay out here or head home?"

I know not to tell you what to do. But please go home. The strain in your eyes tells me you've had enough of the great outdoors for one day.

Andi glanced down the street, to where the incident may—or may not have—occurred. She didn't need to voice her internal struggle; worry and self-doubt flooded her eyes. If it had happened, someone could very likely be in peril. If it hadn't, her imagination was playing tricks on her, and in her world, her runaway imagination was a scary, scary thing.

"I'll go home," she whispered.

As she left with Marks and Tyre, Gabe walked to the spot where Andi said the van had screeched to a halt.

Well, well.

Tread marks blackened the road. It wasn't a big skid. Just one solid foot of four black marks. Definitely an indication of a sudden stop. It could have been any one of hundreds of cars, vans, or SUVs that had passed in the last few days. Probably, it meant nothing. But—probabilities didn't always pan out.

Turning from the street, scanning the sidewalk, he saw no evidence that anything had happened there.

"Tyre," he said into his audio mic, his eyes returning to the skid marks.

"Sir?"

"When you get back, check to see if there were any missing person reports filed since yesterday that could be relevant. Here and in neighboring jurisdictions."

"Yes, sir."

From what he could tell, only one potential outdoor crime camera would've picked up the area in question. When Gabe walked into Bailey's Lounge, where the camera was perched above the entry, he looked at the video monitor set above the bar and the bartender confirmed that Gabe was SOL. The camera's permanent view was set on the bar's entryway. Not the area in question.

Pug's Po-boys, on the opposite block, didn't have an outdoor crime cam but it had outside tables with a view of the corner. Inhaling the aroma of roasting meat, and scanning the clean restaurant where most of the tables were empty, Gabe introduced himself to a young waitress with blond pig-tails. She wore a t-shirt with a Pug's Po-Boys logo, a short jean skirt, and red tennis shoes. She eyed him up and down in a friendly, but suspicious way, as he asked to speak to any of the wait staff who'd been working at two the day before.

"Well, Gabe," she asked, "are you a cop?"

"No. A private investigator, and I'm not investigating anything having to do with you or anyone who works at Pug's. I'm investigating an occurrence that happened across the street."

"Like a pickpocketing or an armed robbery?"

"Something like that." He decided he was hungry, too. He'd last eaten on the plane, and that had been hours ago.

"Well, things like that happen all the time on Esplanade. Cops take their time, unless someone's shot and bleeding to death on the sidewalk. Took them twenty-three hours to get here when we were burglarized last month. I was around yesterday afternoon. I'm Cat. My brother John was here, too. That's John, slicing the bread behind the counter. My dad, Pugs, was here, too."

Cat, Pugs, and John, hadn't seen anything matching, or coming close to, what Andi had witnessed. The day before had been quiet, and none of the outside tables had been taken at the time in question. As Gabe glanced at a menu, Pugs told him he wouldn't find a better po-boy in town. "I roast the meat myself. Most shops don't these days. We deliver in the Quarter and the Marigny."

"I'll be calling around eight."

Gabe left the restaurant. Walking back to the townhome, using the audio mic, he said, "Tyre."

"Yes, Sir."

"Missing person's reports?"

"Nothing relevant. I'll monitor."

Tell Andi about the tread marks, or no?

With most other clients, it would be an easy question. He didn't believe in hiding information from his clients. But this client had runaway paranoia fueled by post-traumatic stress.

Don't tell her. The tread marks, alone, mean nothing.

At the townhouse, after checking in with Marks in the security room, he climbed the stairs. He stepped along the hardwood risers and not on the carpeted runner, letting his footsteps fall heavy so that he wouldn't startle her. He found Andi in her gym. She was jogging on the treadmill, which faced the open doorway. She pressed the pause button when she saw him, immediately slowing her pace, then stopped.

Holy shit.

Her purple exercise micro top—barely larger than a jog bra—left almost nothing about her breasts to his imagination. Not the perfect swell of them, not that they'd be a bit more than a mouthful for him, not anything but the exact color of her nipples. The micro top didn't even cover her midriff. Her abs weren't a he-man six-pack, but she was definitely toned and ridged. Fitted shorts with a rolled waistband hit low on her hips, below her delicious-looking belly button, and just an inch or two down her thighs. Her legs were muscular. Lean, and perfect.

Lifting a towel from the treadmill's handrail, she glanced his way as she wiped her forehead. "Anything?"

"No one in the area could confirm or deny it. One crime camera could've picked it up at Bailey's Lounge, but it wasn't focused on the area. I talked to the people at Pug's PoBoys, where there's a view of the corner. No one there saw anything."

A stoic nod concealed all emotion. "Even if it means I'm crazy, I hope that it was just my imagination at play. Thank you. I'm really, really grateful that you tried."

It hurt him to his core that she was so appreciative, when all he'd done was exactly what any Black Raven agent should've done for their client. In the face of her appreciation and worry, he made a decision. "I did see tread marks that are consistent with a sudden, short stop."

Her eyes gleamed with fresh interest. "Where I said the van stopped?"

"Yes ma'am. But that isn't conclusive proof of anything. On that busy street, tread marks, without more, simply mean that someone, at some point recently, stopped abruptly."

"But the tread marks could've been made by the van."

He nodded. "Maybe."

"So, a woman really could have been taken." Her voice fell as she spoke. "And no one knows?"

Not what he meant, yet he gave her a slow nod, because the *'maybe'* he'd given her could mean that as well. "Possibly, though if a woman was there, and taken, she could've been an errant wife, or girlfriend, a runaway teenager found by her parents. Several scenarios are possible. If a woman was abducted, someone will report her missing. We're monitoring missing person reports. No female has been reported missing in this state in the last twenty-four hours."

"Do you really have that much faith in the system? In missing person reports?"

"Not sure what you mean."

She gave him a cool look, folded her towel, and replaced it on the handrail. "You're a private security contractor, for God's sake. You're called in when the system has failed." Leveling her eyes on him, she asked, "Am I right?"

"That's one way of putting it."

After carefully lining up the ends of the towel, she glanced at him again, vulnerability showing through her eyes. "Let's try it this way. You read my file enough to be familiar with the facts of my abduction. Correct?"

Oh hell. Wrong move telling her about the tread marks. "Yes, ma'am."

"I've always had a safety net surrounding me. More so now, with Black Raven, but even pre-kidnapping, I had the cushion that comes with having the constant, loving concern of relatives and friends. The cushion that comes with wealth. Gated neighborhoods, with security. Staff that would notice if I was gone."

He moved to the side of the treadmill. Gripping the towel-covered handrail, he leaned against it so that he could better hear her whispered words. He was so close, he could smell her delicious, sweet, lavender-tinged perspiration.

"When I was kidnapped, I was in a secure house, in my bedroom, with an alarm system, in a guarded, gated community. I was taken, and no one who made up the considerable components of my safety net knew about it. For hours, no one knew."

"I know that, Ms. Hutchenson."

"I'd have died on the levee where he dumped me, but for the fact that Victor Morrissey had a message to give, and the fact that I somehow managed to live until Taylor and Brandon found me."

He now understood yet another reason why she was so afraid to be alone, why she tolerated the presence of a security team when she obviously considered the agents an intrusion. She remained afraid of going missing and no one being aware of it until it was too late—a fact that hadn't made it into her file. "I know."

"Did you really pay attention to the sketches when we were in my studio, upstairs?"

"Yes. They're unforgettable."

"They're real people. Most of them, young ones." She was now looking at him, leaning against the opposite handrail, her voice barely audible. "They're runaways—Agent Hernandez, you really have to quit getting so close to me."

"But you're whispering again."

And we're both lucky I have considerable restraint here, because what I really want to do is wrap my arms around you and tell you everything's going to be okay.

She sighed in frustration. "Fine. My therapist says the same goddamn thing. I'll try to speak up, because having you leaning into my space is...disconcerting." She cleared her throat. "Some of the people I sketched don't have a single person looking out for them. Who, exactly, would report one of them missing, if they were abducted? Isn't it conceivable that someone who lives on the streets could be gone for days, and no one would know? Who, exactly, would file a missing person's report for someone no one is looking for?"

"That's a great question."

"Are you patronizing me?" Her voice was loud and clear. And pissed.

"No. I'd never do that."

Studying him for a long moment, she nodded. "Good. Don't." Turning to the treadmill control panel, she pressed a button and upped the speed to a fast walk. "I'm through with our conversation. I'm ready for my workout."

"Fine," he said, realizing her multi-use word was just perfect.

She glanced sideways at him, arched an eyebrow, taking in his polo shirt, slacks, holstered gun, and street shoes. "Don't you need to change?"

"I will." He pressed the incline on her treadmill to a slight upgrade and increased her speed to a fast jog. "Don't fool with the settings. I'll be back in fifteen minutes."

His duffel bag was in the security room, where he'd stashed it when he'd first arrived. Using one of the bathrooms on the first floor, he changed into exercise clothes, then went into her kitchen. Opening the pantry, he saw few food options. He'd have to rectify that. He ate a high-protein power bar that he found on the shelf before returning to the gym.

"Warm up's over," he said. "Feeling okay?"

She nodded as she slowed the treadmill. Her cheeks were pink. Tendrils of her hair were wet with perspiration. "Fine."

"Good. Drink some water, then we can get started."

Turning her back to him, she slowly walked to the shelf where the weights were organized. Her water bottle was stashed on the top shelf.

His gaze slide over his first real visual of the scars on her back and down her legs. The scantiness of her crop top and shorts revealed the majority of the scars. He wondered if that was her intent. Keeping her back to him, she lifted her arms and stretched her fingertips to the ceiling.

Yep. She's testing you.

The file had photographs from police and medical reports. When the wounds had been raw and festering, they'd been worse. But not much. The circular welts were still purplish-red, raised, angry remembrances of that horrific night. Plastic surgery would have made the raised pucker marks better. The file indicated she hadn't had one of the recommended five surgeries.

Lifting the lid off her bottle of water, she made a slow turn to face him. "Answer honestly, Agent Hernandez. Do my scars bother you? I can put on a t-shirt if you'd prefer."

"No. I just wish the circumstances that led to those scars could've been different, wish like hell you never acquired them. So, no, Ms. Hutchenson, the scars don't bother me, only the fact that you have them at all. That bothers the hell out of me."

"Ah." She took a long swig of water, then replaced the lid. "There you go with that fairy tale theme again."

"Excuse me?"

"Wishes don't come true, Agent. Except in fairytales. You've figured out today that when I'm uncomfortable, I whisper. I figured out today that when you're uncomfortable, you either joke or spout fairytale-ish nonsense."

He smiled at her. "Well, with all due respect, ma'am—

"Don't ma'am me when we're working out."

"Okay. Would you prefer Andi?"

She shook her head. "No. Don't use my first name. No need for us to pretend that we're friends. You won't be here that long. Ms. Hutchenson will work."

He nodded. "Got it. Well, with all due respect, Ms. Hutchenson, you're wrong."

"What exactly have I gotten wrong?"

"I haven't been uncomfortable today. My jokes, and what you're calling fairytale nonsense, well, that's just me. And I don't think any of it is nonsense." He gave her a smile.

She gave him a cool nod. "So no t-shirt. What kind of exercise are we doing? I'm trying to become proficient with Krav Maga so I can use my own body strength and movements to subdue an attacker, no matter the size, then get the hell away."

"Perfect. You're preaching to the choir. This evening, I want to assess your strength. Three thirty minute sessions. I'll call out the exercises. Follow my lead. I'll be doing most of the exercises with you. Mat work first. Push-ups, sit-ups, then squats."

They unfurled yoga mats, and got started. When they were through with squats, he asked, "Know a bear crawl?"

She nodded. "They're hard. I just started them."

"They're great for mobility, stability, coordination, and total body strength. Can you do forward and reverse?"

"I've never done reverse."

"Then let's just do forward. Tomorrow we'll work on reverse. By the end of the week, I'll have you doing forward, backward, and lateral."

He led her through a basic workout. There were no rules for Krav Maga fighting. There were also no rules he knew of to teach it to someone in a private studio, when the student didn't want to be touched. In most workouts, casual touches just happened.

Keeping her aversion to physical contact in mind, he avoided contact, figuring that she'd warm up to the idea of him touching her in the exercise room. When they were through with forward bear crawls, he picked up tombstone pads and assessed the speed and power with which she was able to punch.

"Good, but give me more follow-through."

Pausing for a breath, she asked, "Meaning?"

"Don't stop at the point of connection. Whether you're hitting pads or if you're in a situation when you're striking someone, don't pull back once you touch. Power through. Aim for maximum damage. If you're poking out someone's eyes, try touching through to their brains. You want gray matter under your fingernails—"

"Ew."

He chuckled. "Yeah. If you're hitting the ribs, reach through their lungs so you can wrap your fingers around their spine. Inflict as much damage as you can. If you're fighting, there's a reason, right?"

A dark shadow crossed over her eyes. "I should've been able to get away."

"You didn't know how to fight. And there's no shame in that. Most people don't." He lifted the pads, and nodded to her. "But now you do. You're good. Fast. Strong. Smart. As long as you don't hesitate, and power through, you'll be able to fight effectively. Now...go!"

She hit the pads with a force that was beauty to behold. Again. And again. And again.

"Water break," he announced, when she was breathless. "Fantastic job. Great follow-through. My arms are tired." As she took a long swig of water, he added, "You've got good strength. But there's still a bit of hesitation. Remember, victims hesitate. Survivors don't."

"What's the work around?"

"Strength building, practice, and," he said, smiling, "more practice. Keep your mind clicking with your plan, even if you're not moving. Don't cower. Play possum. Trick your opponent."

"Meaning?"

"Even if you're acting like you're not going to fight, keep thinking how you're going to kill. Plan, then implement. Think fast, plan, then implement. Have confidence you will get out of any situation you find yourself in. Exercise drills will give you confidence in your moves. Drop to the mat. Let's start over with sit-ups, then more squats."

After another hour, she was dripping with sweat and he was impressed with how fit she was. Her reflexes, though, became slower as the session progressed.

"Let's call it quits. We'll continue tomorrow."

"No." Prone on her yoga mat, where she'd just completed her hundredth sit-up, she gave him a headshake. "I can do more."

"I know." Standing about a foot away from where she lay, he extended a hand to her, wondering if she'd take it for an assist up. "But I'm starving."

She stood without using his offer of help. "Fine. Thank you, Agent Hernandez. I'll clean up in here."

"I'll help. It's my sweat too." He sprayed the mat he'd been using with antiseptic spray. "I'm ordering dinner from Pugs. Want anything? I could have it delivered here, rather than to the apartment across the street. We could eat downstairs, in your gorgeous kitchen."

She gave him a wide-eyed look of surprise.

He chuckled. "What? Ms. Hutchenson doesn't eat with the hired help?"

The corners of her lips twitched. Her eyes lightened with her almost-smile and the unmistakable gleam that came with wanting to laugh. It lasted long enough for him to know he was getting to her—in a good way. Long enough to reach into his chest and steal his heart like no one ever had before.

As the light disappeared, she pushed a clump of sweaty hair behind her ear. "I don't think I would've said it quite that way."

"Yes, you would have. No worries. I'll order a salad and an extra po-boy for you. Trust me, I've looked in your fridge and freezer, and, aside from apples and peanut butter, nothing looks appetizing. You had one hell of a workout. Carbs and protein should help you sleep."

At the mention of sleep, she shot him a doubtful look, which was quickly replaced with one he'd come to expect from her in their afternoon and evening together. Brow slightly furrowed, she broadcast a cross between cool disinterest and plain annoyance. "Really? Now you're offering advice on sleeping?"

He chuckled. “Consider it part of your training regimen. To build strength and endurance, rest is as important as what we do in the exercise room. I’ll leave your food on your kitchen island. I’ll eat in the security room, so you don’t have to fraternize with the help.”

“Thank you, Agent Hernandez. You may leave now. I’d like to be alone for the rest of the evening.”

Chapter Ten

Pic

Saturday, February 13, 10:30 p.m.
Greyhound Bus, en route to New Orleans

'You're strong. Brave. Smart. Remember that, Lucas.'

Pic's mom used to say crap like that with a heartbreaking smile. Her blue eyes had seen through to his very soul as she wished for a hopeful and positive future for her only child. *'You'll grow to be a good man. You'll live a wonderful life, filled with joy and love.'*

It was a prediction that hadn't come to pass. Half-asleep, and pretty thoroughly miserable, Pic coughed. His mom's voice faded, no matter how hard he tried to hold onto memories of her whisper and the sweetness in her eyes. She had been equal parts naïve, self-destructive, and solidly lacking common-sense, but that was the side he worked hard on forgetting about her.

Pic became aware of the older lady sitting beside him on the crowded, noisy bus as she stirred. He was riding from Austin, Texas, to New Orleans, Louisiana, on a direct route that had taken only one stop in Houston. He'd been stupid to think the streets of Austin would offer a better life for a homeless guitar player than New Orleans.

Plus, cheap food tastes better in NOLA than Texas. I'm sick of Tex-Mex refried beans and tacos. And the bigger goddamn reality is my problem isn't where I live. My problem is...me. Because I'm so sick of living on the streets, I wanna die.

He knew Andi wanted him to move into her guesthouse so that he could get on his feet. It was a move he was dying for, but it was one he couldn't make. It came with too much risk that someone—like one of the armed security agents who were always with her—would figure out who the hell he was, what he was running from, and send him back home.

Without lifting his head from the cold window, he checked the large-faced watch Andi had given him.

Almost there.

His cough once again pissed off a man one row ahead of him, who grumbled, "Shut up, asshole. I'm goddamned sleeping."

Pic coughed again, more to piss off the guy than to clear his throat. He squeezed his eyes shut, trying for a few more minutes of sleep, before he'd have to get off the bus and walk for miles to the place on the river he planned to spend the night. The dreams of his mom came with a steep price, because his good memories were like battery acid, opening a fissure in the hard shell he'd built around his heart, a crevasse into which bad memories poured.

Clarence. His mom's dickhead boyfriend. Pic had hated him at first sight. He usually hated all men his mom brought home, 'cause they typically looked at him like he was a pain in the ass. They made it clear they were coming over for one thing, and Pic had nothing to do with it. He hadn't realized until Clarence came along, though, that he should've counted his blessings all the times his mom was the only one the slime balls wanted to fuck.

When he'd been twelve, they'd been new to town. His mom had promised him West Virginia would be different. But after one look at Clarence in their second week there, entering the trailer at two in the morning, and listening to them behind the bedroom door as he lay on the pullout couch, Pic knew two things. One—West Virginia wasn't going to be any different. Two—Clarence was just another in the long stream of losers his mom brought home.

It took him a while longer to realize who, and what, Clarence was. The closest town to their trailer park with more than one stoplight was Mapleton. Clarence Adams Walker was Chief of Police of Mapleton. Clarence had money and a way of inspiring fear and hatred with just a glance. He was known to play favorites as he enforced the law, was married, and had a family.

Pic had learned how to quickly fall asleep. But now, though he tried to fall back asleep, even though he knew he was safe on a bus and far from West Virginia, his meandering thoughts prompted a flashback image of Clarence's beefy hands unzipping his jeans. The memory of Clarence's strong fingers fondling Pic's cock, with hoarse whispers of all the vile shit that would happen if Pic wasn't a good boy, still inspired heart-pounding terror.

Clarence's threats had usually involved the difference between living under a roof with running water and heat, or living in their old, stinking car. And Clarence knew how to drive the point home in Pic's young brain. And then the fun would start. *'Give me your hand. Yeah. Wrap it around me. Like this. Squeeze. Hard. Now your mouth. Relax your jaw, kid. Yeah. That's it. Oh, ye—*

Giving up on sleep, Pic sat up. Clarence-inspired cold sweat dripped down his forehead. Pic hated that he'd ever been so weak, hated that he'd let it go on for so long.

Grow a pair and shake it off. You were twelve, for God's sake. And thirteen. And fourteen. Aw. Fuck.

Wide awake, he fought the urge to puke from the too-real memories. As the disgusting images receded, he was better able to focus on his current, and comparatively lightweight, hell.

Chest aching from his stinking cold that wouldn't go away, his eyes gritty and mouth tasting like he'd eaten mentholated bird shit, Pic wiped his snotty nose on one of the tissues the lady beside him had handed over earlier. Yeah, he felt like crap, but he was happy to be going back to New Orleans, and Andi, his only friend who wasn't homeless and on the run from a shit existence with the guarantee of a shittier future. Plus, on the bright side, he'd managed to sleep—a little.

The bus was packed with Mardi Gras tourists, families, businesspeople, and road-weary travelers on their way to good times. He was aware of the two half-drunk guys a couple of seats back who'd passed out moments after climbing aboard. He was also aware of the girl, probably a runaway, with too much makeup and resignation in her haunted eyes, curled in a ball in her seat in the very back. She was pretending to be asleep, probably afraid to be noticed, but more afraid that no one was even noticing she was there.

Been there, done that.

The grandmotherly-looking lady beside him had boarded alone. She smelled like home-cooking and mothballs and seemed to knit as easily as she could breathe. The air in the bus hung heavy with the smell of desperation, booze, and day's old sweat. The passengers had mostly dozed off after an hour or so. It had been quiet once night fell as they traveled Interstate 10. Now, as the interstate wound its way through suburbs, phones beeped, chirped and serenaded as people yawned, talked and stretched.

The bus took a right fork in the interstate. Pic saw cemeteries. Acres and acres of floodlit tombs, with crosses and winged angels, lined either side of the roadway. It was a fitting sight for the kind of dreams he'd been having.

Though he was now wide awake, he was seized with a sudden longing for his mom. Mostly, she'd called him Luke. Or, if she had something important to say, she'd call him Lucas. She'd never known him as Pic. Sometimes, when she'd been distracted, irritated, or tired, she'd use his full name—Lucas Tanner McShane.

Clarence's brand of evil had vaporized all the white light from Pic's life. When Pic's suicide attempt didn't work, and knowing Clarence was just going to dish out more of the same, Pic planned the exact words he'd tell his mom. Her reaction shocked him. She accused him of lying. She yelled at him to take back the words. Then Clarence arrived. Everything became a blur of swirling darkness as his mom continued her rant, slapping and punching Pic while she told Clarence what Pic had said.

He'd let his mom hit him, disappointment rocking his core with each blow. If Pic started hitting her back, he didn't remember. There was a lapse in his mind, blank space he couldn't fill. Then his mom was lying on the floor, and Pic was trying to wake her. Blood ran over his fingers as he smoothed her hair.

He didn't remember what happened, but Clarence was there to tell him all about it. Clarence stood across the room, leaning against the wall with a sick smile on his face, and a simple statement that sealed Pic's fate. *'You killed her, kid. Now you're mine.'*

Pic had frozen for a few seconds, then he'd sprung forward. Not towards Clarence, but towards the door. He'd run, and he was never going back.

Pic looked between the two seats in front of him. Through the bug-speckled windshield, he saw the city skyline. He hoped Monica was still in town. He'd blown it with her, he knew, but maybe she'd still look at him as a friend. And God, but he was looking forward to seeing Andi. Yeah, he knew not to get too close to Andi. Yeah. Yeah. Yeah. But she was nice. She cared, and he knew he could trust her. But he didn't trust the security that was always around her.

Plus, in some weird way, he understood that jumping in the river to save Andi—a move based on pure gut instinct—had been his first step towards altering his own life. He'd told Andi he'd be back for Mardi Gras.

It was high time to check on her again, 'cause if her yearning for suicide was like his, it was never going away. Pic knew firsthand that sometimes a friend saying *'see ya tomorrow'* was all a person needed to make it one more day. He'd started the *'see ya tomorrow,'* thing with her and it was time to make an appearance. As much for her, as for him.

"Five more minutes," the lady on his left said, her face lit by the glow of light from her cell phone. "You feeling any better now that you slept some?"

The gray-haired lady had boarded the bus when he did in Austin. By the time they'd passed through Houston, she'd given him cough drops, tissues, and advice on how to get rid of his cold. "Think so. Your cough drops helped. Thanks."

"You going to get your Aunt to take you to the LSU Health Center like we talked about?"

Pic nodded yes, 'cause that was the right answer. When she'd asked earlier, he'd made up a story about visiting relatives in New Orleans.

She gave him a doubtful frown, evidently seeing the lie for what it was. "If you don't, you'll end up with pneumonia. That's what our humidity does to that kind of cough. You make sure you go, okay? Like I said, health services are free there. You may as well use them."

"Yes, ma'am." He wasn't going. Free didn't mean no questions, and word on the street, which Pic knew from having spent time on the streets of New Orleans, was that the LSU Health Center asked a lot of questions. Not happening. He'd been sick before—sicker—and he'd lived.

"Here. This scarf's for you." She lifted her hand. In it was the bundle of stuff she'd been knitting ever since they'd departed Austin. "The lighter blue matches your eyes. Yarn's a wool blend. It'll keep your neck warm. Go on." She shook her hand that held the scarf. "Wear it. It's chilly out there."

For the first time in days, Pic felt his mood lighten as he took the soft scarf and wrapped it around his neck. "Thanks. That's really nice of you."

"You're welcome." She smiled at him as she nodded. "Looks good. You're a handsome boy. You take care of yourself, you hear?"

"Yes, ma'am."

As the bus tires thumped along the interstate off-ramp, a fresh bout of coughing built in his chest. Working hard to suppress it, he wondered for the umpteenth time what the hell was wrong with him. The meds he'd gotten in Austin a couple of weeks ago, from a clinic known to ask minimal questions, hadn't done anything to take the edge off the feel-like-shitness that now greeted his every day.

Maybe Andi will know what to do.

He'd be careful not to seem too sick in front of her, because Andi would use his illness to press the point of him moving into her guest house. He couldn't do that. Not now, not ever. She didn't know his reasons for running. She'd never know. No one would. Keeping the truth to himself was the only way he could guarantee that he wouldn't be sent back to Mapleton, West Virginia and Chief of Police Clarence Walker.

Pic shook off the feeling of comfort and safety that sitting on the bus had provided. He'd used up a good chunk of his cash for the eighty-five dollar fare from Austin to New Orleans, but it had been worth it. Living on the streets was one thing, but hitchhiking was another matter entirely, bringing a set of risks he didn't feel like encountering. Especially when he wasn't fit to fight and able to protect himself physically.

He lost the battle for cough suppression as the doors opened and a burst of moist air blew into the climate-controlled bus. He'd felt sick, off and on, since New Year's Eve. He could handle the constant feeling of having a cold, but this was different than any cold he'd ever had before. His head heavy and full of snot. His voice was raspy with a nasal tone. He hadn't been able to sound good while he sang for the last three weeks. Without singing, the money he made from playing the guitar was down to just a few dollars a day. He had enough cash to get by for a few more days, but he liked to have extra. Just in case he had to go a few days without making any at all.

After grabbing his guitar from baggage claim, Pic slung his backpack on one shoulder, the guitar case on the other, and started walking along Loyola Avenue. The place he planned to sleep was about an hour's walk away, if he hustled. He took his brass knuckles out of his pocket and slid them onto the fingers of his left hand. Slipping his fingers into his right front pocket, he made sure his knife was in position. He was ready if trouble came his way.

He walked through the business district, using Loyola, then South Rampart Street. He kept going, crossing Esplanade, then into the narrower, quieter streets of the Marigny neighborhood. He paused on the sidewalk of a street that led to the river to adjust his things.

A black van slowed but continued, without stopping. A red Mercedes went by, close behind it. It stopped in the middle of the street. The blond driver lowered her window. After hiccupping, and turning down the radio, she asked, "Hey, can you tell me how I get back to Esplanade? These twisty one-way streets always screw me up."

Sure it isn't alcohol that's fucking with your sense of direction?

"Go left at the next corner, then go a few blocks up. The busier street's St. Claude. Take a left. Next big street will be Esplanade."

She lifted her hand, waved, and hiccupped again. "Toodles."

With her brake lights rounding the corner, the street became quiet again. Some houses looked occupied, some abandoned. Cars were parked along both sides of the narrow, tree-lined street.

With his guitar case readjusted, backpack straps tightened, he continued. He was almost at the levee, near the old abandoned warehouse where he'd sometimes slept before heading to Austin.

Only eight more blocks. Then I can stretch out, rest, maybe even sleep, and hope like hell I wake up feeling a ton better.

When he passed under the few and far between streetlights, he saw tiny droplets of water swirling, making a fine mist of tiny white dots on the sleeves of his black leather jacket.

The first and only warning of impending doom was footsteps. Soft footfalls, but fast. Heavy. Close.

Too close.

Turning, he reached into his pocket and pulled out his knife. Pressing the smooth button with his thumb to release the blade, he dropped into a fighter stance. He shrugged his shoulders in a practiced move that let gravity take the backpack and guitar from his shoulders.

Everything he owned fell to the ground with a sickening thud. He debated whether to run or stand and fight the two thugs, who were dressed in head to toe black. Ski masks covered their faces. They were almost on him, but still ten paces away and taking their goddamn, sweet ass time as they approached.

One laughed. "Well, pretty boy guitar player's a fighter. Nice knuckles."

Leave his shit and run? No. Fuckitall.

Arms up as a shield, careful to keep the blade visible so maybe they'd reconsider, Pic softened his knees so that he was in a slight crouch in the center of the sidewalk, ready to jump, assessing which one posed the most immediate threat.

"You're messing with the wrong guy," Pic said, using his street-wise, *'don't fuck with me'* tone.

"Nope. You're just what we're looking for." The answer came in a flat, matter-of-fact tone. "Your kind fetches big bucks."

I should've run.

Thug One, closest to him, had something shiny in his left hand. Pic lunged forward as the man broke his leisurely pace and came at him in a run. Pic kicked at the man's extended arm.

The thing that had been in Thug One's hand—whatever the hell it was—flew into the air. Thug One dove for it. "Fuck!"

Thug Two lunged forward, his right hand outstretched. Something black was in his hand.

Holy shit. A stun gun? These assholes mean business.

Energized by a fresh burst of adrenaline, Pic leapt to the side, then squared himself in a new, ready-to-fight position. He landed a full-force, brass-knuckled punch on Thug Two's lip, and ground the knuckles down the guy's jawline, while narrowly avoiding a jolt from the stun gun. He wasn't totally in the clear, though, because Thug Two's left hand connected with Pic's eye, and his beefy right shoulder connected with Pic's gut. Pic lost his balance and flew forward a few steps.

"GoddamnsonofaBITCH!" Thug Two said, more than an arm's length away. His hand was on the jaw where Pic's knuckles had made impact. Bright red blood covered his lip. He spat blood in Pic's direction as he readied himself for another attack. "Your hours on this goddamn earth are numbered, asshole. Starting right this..." He spat more gunk out of his mouth. "Second. You smart enough to figure that out?"

"Take my shit." Pic's heart pounded as he regained his balance. "There's three hundred dollars in my backpack. Guitar's worth two thousand."

Thug Two laughed. "We don't want your shit, dumb fuck."

Thug One was on his knees, reaching under a parked car. His hand was in the gutter, looking for what Pic had kicked out of his hand. "Got it."

Something in Thug One's hand captured streetlight as he got to his feet. "Let's finish this."

Whatever it was in the man's hand, it was too small to be a gun. Black. White. Narrow. A blade? Pic couldn't tell. As Thug Two made another lunge in Pic's direction, and Thug One came closer, Pic jumped to the side, his hip knocking into a car parked at the curb.

The jarring thud set off the car alarm. The thugs froze, giving Pic a split second to see what Thug One was holding.

A syringe!?

The car alarm kept going. The thugs glanced at one another, as though silently debating whether to stay, or go. Pic was so ready for them to advance on him, that it took him a second to realize their indecision was giving him an opportunity to get away.

Holy Fuck! Go!

Chapter Eleven

Gabe

Sunday, February 14, 12:17 a.m.

A loud, piercing scream slammed into the security room with the force of a rogue wave, electrifying the air. The echoing shrillness sliced through Gabe. Pulse ratcheting, he jerked upright in his chair. The fearful pitch was unlike anything he'd ever heard, and he'd heard plenty horrific sounds in his tenure as a Black Raven agent. The stark terror chilled him to the marrow.

"Holy shit." *Move your ass. Now.* As Gabe stood, a quick glance at the cameras and digital read out on the security system confirmed that the perimeter hadn't been breached.

Stevens, with curly brown hair, brown eyes, and a steady look in his eyes, shifted, his chair squeaking under his weight. He glanced at Gabe with tension underlying his businesslike, '*everything's normal*' expression. "Unnerving, right? Night terrors, Sir."

Gabe's mind shifted to agent protocol for handling the client in this situation, which she'd dictated. Yet it was hard to focus. Even though he'd read the reports, and thought he was prepared, he was still shocked by the reality.

"Happens most nights I've been on the job," Stevens said. "Last night included."

Gabe knew the facts and frequency, but the details in the file didn't convey enough. "File reports said loud. I had no idea."

Some high-risk personal security jobs required an agent to be stationed at the door of whichever room the client was located. This job wasn't high risk and, when the client was home, threat factors were low.

He'd completed his most recent perimeter check at eleven forty-two; his last visual check of the client had been at eleven twenty-five. He'd knocked on the partially open studio door before opening it. Paintbrush in hand, standing at an easel, she'd acknowledged his presence with a slight nod.

Confident the house, and his charge, were secure, Gabe's attention had been alternating between the surveillance monitors and his iPad when the first scream started. He'd been reading about *en plein air* painting when her screams startled him out of the world of techniques for painting outdoors and into the world of *how the hell do I deal with this situation.*

The contract stated, *'ascertain client is not in jeopardy through an in-person visual observation, then resume normal sentry position.'* In her contract, she acknowledged that Black Raven wasn't liable for damage she did to herself when the night terrors occurred. Gabe knew how the agents who had preceded him had interpreted the contact—check on her as unobtrusively as possible, ascertain she wasn't in jeopardy from an external threat, and then leave her alone.

As the scream pulsed, ebbing and building to a new crescendo, he said, "I'll go up, then do perimeter."

"Thanks. Appreciate it." Relief flooded Stevens' voice. Stevens had been scheduled to do the next perimeter check, with the visual on Andi.

The night terrors were one reason the agents hated this job, and Gabe now understood why. The job they did required steadfast confidence in their ability to conquer all forms of evil. But this was evil that couldn't be fought.

As he ran up the first flight of stairs, another scream pierced the otherwise tomblike silence of the house. He took the landing in three steps. Her bedroom door was closed, but not locked. Bedside lamps—on. Bedroom—empty. Bed linens—untouched. Sitting room—empty.

He took the stairs, three at a time. The door to her studio was partially ajar, as he'd left it. Opening it and charging through, ignoring her knock-before-entering rule, he stopped in mid-stride. She sat on the couch. Her small, delicate hands were balled into tight fists on either side of her knees. She was screaming as though the gates of hell had opened and the devil and his best friends had their fire-hot hands on her.

Her face was flushed red, her eyes were unfocused but open and darting, and she was trembling, as though she was freezing. She wore a tight black tank top. Long black leggings. One blanket had fallen to the floor. Another had slipped mostly off her lap. A couple of lamps, close to the couch, were on, but the overhead bright lights and artist's lamps were off. She had a pillow next to her on the couch.

She'd settled in for a snooze, for God's sake, and this is the hell that came her way.

He wished she'd snap out of it and rip him a new one for barging into her studio without knocking, but the unfocused look in her eyes, coupled with the high octane intensity of her fresh scream, told him that wasn't about to happen.

Gabe had done research. People with night terrors could appear awake, like Andi did now. She lifted her head, and seemed to focus her attention on the skylight overhead. For the stark fear in her voice, Gabe glanced up, cringing. He half expected to see something horrific attached to the skylight, but knew he'd only see exactly what he saw—the pure inky darkness of the night sky.

He dropped to his knees in front of her. With her mind's eye focused on a distant horror that only she could see, she gave no indication that she sensed his presence.

"Andi?"

His mic remained open to Stevens. In a lull in her screams, Stevens said, "Sir, we're not supposed to wake her. Waking people from night terrors can result in scaring them even more. Wouldn't be a good thing." The lull in her screams was over as a new scream climbed to a crescendo. "Besides, her client contract—"

"Speak up, Stevens." Gabe's mic system was sensitive enough to pick up a whisper, but with Andi screaming, he had to talk louder to be heard. "Hard to hear with her screaming."

"Yes, sir. Contract says we get a visual, then leave her alone. You've gotten a visual, now you're to leave. As per the client's orders."

Gabe was well aware of the terms of the contract and the scope of his job. He also knew that waking people from night terrors was nearly impossible and, if accomplished, could very well make things worse. Her horrific screams, though, had amped up his natural instinct to fix all of God's broken creatures.

He'd been the kid who brought stray animals home, fed orphaned kittens with bottles, and cooked for his older brother and his mom so they'd have something to eat after work. He'd also been the kid who made sure he befriended everyone in the class, even those who were typically left out. As an adult, he'd carried on the habits he'd formed as a child. Doing nothing in the face of such suffering went against every fiber in his being.

Hell. Hell. Hell. How the HELL can I comfort her?

The depth of her fear, when she wasn't consciously being the tough woman he'd been with throughout the day, made him realize that every kindness he'd ever bestowed on anyone, every broken-winged bird he'd ever fixed, was merely training that would come in handy for now.

Identify the source of the suffering. Then fix it.

But the source of her suffering was a memory and the perpetrator of that memory was undeniably dead. Which was a good thing, because right now Gabe would kill Victor Morrissey with his bare hands if given the opportunity.

Gabe sat on the floor in front of her. "Stevens. File indicates episodes last anywhere from ten to twenty-five minutes. What's been the average that you've observed?"

"I'd say fifteen to twenty-five. Last night, twenty-three. Started at eleven thirty-one. She was on the couch in her studio. I checked on her. By eleven fifty-five last night, it was over. When I went up there at one a.m., she was on her feet, painting. Focused. If she noticed I was at the door, she ignored me. Typical."

Stevens's tone was detached. Almost clinical. Most agents stayed in cool professional mode when working, but it wasn't in Gabe's nature to be detached. He typically became friends with his clients, as long as they were likable. His list of good friends was long and they were scattered around the globe, because no one he met for any length of time stayed a stranger for long. They either became friends, or, like NOPD Officers Thompson and Spagnoli, they weren't worth knowing.

Gabe's track record indicated that his personal, friendly style worked. Clients usually requested him by name after one job with him. School was still out on whether his style was going to work here, but he'd made inroads that afternoon and evening.

Not that anything she'd said suggested it to be true. He just got a sense that something had shifted in the course of the day. Her tone had become less clipped. Her eyes more pensive than irritated. Her glances just a tad more...trusting.

Now, eyes on her, listening to the abject horror in her voice, he understood the depth of her fears in a way that reading the file, or spending the day with her, hadn't revealed.

He was inexplicably at a loss as to what to do to make things better, and being at a loss was foreign to him.

As a fresh scream flowed, then ebbed, he drew a deep breath, before gently covering her fisted hands with his own. His hands barely hovered over hers, but he was surprised when she turned hers in the cup of his so their hands were touching, palm to palm. A fresh scream tore through her, and she gripped him. Her fingernails dug into his palms as she held onto him, her body trembling with the scream.

"That's it, Andi," he murmured. "Hold on to me."

With a jolt, he realized he'd been thinking of her as *Andi* for the better part of the day. Not *the client*. Not *Ms. Hutchenson*.

And saying her first name came naturally. "You're safe. Understand?"

She relaxed for a second. Her fingertips flexed against his. She wasn't quite gripping his hands. It was only a touch. A feel. Not much, but he took it as a sign that she knew he—or someone—was there. Someone who wanted to help her, not hurt her. That this woman who so hated casual touches when awake would accept one now, when her subconscious fears had taken over, told him that he was doing the right thing.

He interpreted her fingertips curling against his as a scream for help. Maybe, just maybe, he was figuring out a way to answer.

"That's it. Hold my hands. Hold on. You're safe."

Her hands stretched open, then pressed against his. The tone of her screams changed, to more of a mewl of fear, like someone in a deep, deep sleep, unable to awaken from a nightmare. Her unfocused eyes were now looking straight through him.

Keeping his voice low, he said, "Stevens. I'm staying with her for a while—"

"Sir, I know you're my superior. But with this job, there are lines we don't cross."

"Not interested in that right now."

"She'll fire you if she wakes up and you're right there. Contract says—"

"Fuck the contract. My mic will be open. I'll be listening for you, but I'm muting my audio. I'm going to help her. Not listen to you tell me how not to help her."

Loosening his right hand from hers, he touched his watchband to mute the mic, then covered her hand again. She didn't reject it. "Andi, you're going to be okay. You're fine. You're safe. Nothing bad's going to happen. You're in your home, in your studio. I'm here. Gabe. Agent Hernandez. You're safe with me. Do you understand that? Safe. Sleep easy now."

She turned her wrists, threading her fingers through his. Whimpering. No longer screaming. Her gaze shifted downwards. If she'd been looking at him, he'd have thought she was looking at his chest. But she wasn't focused on him. Her eyes were heavy, the lids half-closing. He drew a deep breath of relief as even her whimpers quieted.

She inhaled deeply. Exhaled. Once. Twice. Then she tightened her fingerlock on his, yawned, rolled her shoulders, and did a slow head rotation.

Oh. Hell. She's waking up.

She gripped his hands tightly, as though he offered a steel-clad lifeline capable of pulling her from a fiery hell. He tried to ease his hands from hers, but she held on tighter. She had strong fingers, and her nails, clipped short, dug into the back of his hands. Even if he could get her to let go of his hands, he was a solid fifteen feet away from the door.

No way I'm getting out of here without her seeing me. And she's going to be pissed as hell. Fuck me to hell and back.

Wide-open, forest-green eyes looked at him. She shifted her head to the side, and yawned again. "Wh-what are you doing here?" Her voice was sweet and gentle. Nothing like the curt tone she'd used throughout the day—when she didn't whisper. "Did—did I fall asleep?"

Relief coursed through him when he realized she wasn't pissed. Rather, she seemed confused.

Thank God.

"Checking on you," he whispered. "You were having a nightmare."

Goddamn understatement of the year.

Heavy eyelids closed in slow motion over her gorgeous, forest-green eyes.

Slipping back to sleep? I can only hope.

He knew that night terrors resulted in a confused fog upon awakening. The person usually had no memory of the terrors, or coming out of them. Chances were, she wouldn't remember this moment.

Hope she doesn't, buddy, because if she remembers that you hovered over her when she was having her night terrors—breaking the explicit terms of the contract—Stevens will be a prophet, and your sorry ass will be fired.

As her eyes remained closed, she took a few deep breaths. He breathed with her, loving the hell out of her lavender scent, the way her choppy hair fell every which way, and the small bit of cleavage that he couldn't help but spot at the top of her tank top.

She half-opened her eyes again, studying him, but seemed to have a hard time keeping them open. Gripping his hands even tighter, she tried to stand, but fell back onto the couch. "I'm so, so tired. And cold. I want to go to my room. Need a blanket there. But I can't even st-stand."

"Let me help you."

Nodding, she shocked the hell out of him when she lifted her arms to him. Frozen in place, he almost choked when her forearms came to rest on his shoulders and she leaned forward.

Eyes shut, with a deep breath, her head fell forward. She seemed to fall into a dead sleep as she rested her forehead on his chest.

Gabe scooped Andi up, his left arm at her shoulder blades, his right under her knees. Her head flopped to his chest as he stood. She weighed one twenty to one twenty five, at most. Too little for her muscular, five seven frame. Easy to carry. Glancing down, he edged his left arm up a bit, making the angle of her neck more comfortable as she rested against his chest.

Not waking up. Thank you, God.

He carried her out of the studio and down the stairs. Pausing at her bedroom door, he managed to open it with his right hand without waking her. At her bed, he bent with her, then used his right hand to gently pull the covers down. Once she was on the bed, he pulled the covers up over her shoulders. Pausing for a second, he watched her breathe in and out. Slow and even. She looked too small to be in the large king-size bed alone.

He hoped that there wouldn't be that many more instances that he'd be standing at the side of her bed, looking down at her. A passing glance—he could handle. This, though, was something different entirely. Staring at her while his arms remembered the weight of her and his chest remembered the feel of her leaning into him, made him ache to hold her. To comfort her even more. And not just comfort her. With her dark hair framing her heart-shaped face, with the memory of her nestled against his chest as he carried her, his body was telling him in a classic way that her bed was made for more than just sleeping.

Move on. Idiot.

The bedside lamps had been on when he entered the room. He left them on for her. Hopeful that her night terrors wouldn't return that night, he turned to leave, despite the compulsion to linger.

"Agent Hernandez." Her soft voice, a bit louder than a whisper, stopped him when he was ten feet from the door.

Oh, damn. Not as asleep as I thought.

He made a slow, hesitant turn back to her, grateful that what had been the beginning of an erection wasn't yet at full force. A telltale bulge in his pants wouldn't be well received. "Yes, ma'am?"

She sat up, the covers dropping to her waist as she leaned against the headboard, and folded her arms. As building irritation in her eyes replaced the grogginess, she seemed to grow larger in stature. "How the hell did I get here?"

Thanking any lucky stars that were shining in his direction for the fact that her night-terror-induced-confusion seemed to prevent her from remembering what had transpired in the last few minutes, he was nonetheless at a loss for a cover story. By the fire building in her eyes, the flare of pink in her cheeks, and the flush crawling up her neck, he knew the cold hard truth of '*I carried you*' wouldn't be well received. Not being a good liar, or even any kind of a liar, Gabe settled for a non-answer. "What do you mean, ma'am?"

"I don't usually awaken in rooms where I didn't fall asleep and I damn well didn't fall asleep here." She kicked aside the covers, stood, and walked over to her closet. She opened the door, but didn't walk in. Instead, she turned to him and, with her voice almost a snarl, said, "Sleep walking isn't a symptom of my night terrors."

"I'm aware, ma'am."

"Well?" Folding her arms against her chest, the steady tap-tap-tap of her left foot produced a soft, ominous thud on the hardwood floor. She glared at him as she waited for an answer. "Well? You're going to stand there and not explain? The question is simple, Agent. How the goddamn hell did I get here?"

"I can't really say, ma'am—"

"Let's get one thing straight, Agent Hernandez. You can stop the overly polite 'ma'am' bullshit right now."

Oh hell. Hell. HELL. "Standard protocol is we're supposed to be polite to clients. It isn't an age thing that's getting to you, is it, because—"

"Seriously? No. I'm not that old. It's—"

"Just saying. We refer to females under eighteen as Miss. Ma'am is for females over eighteen. The other agents say ma'am when they address you. Would you like us all to stop ma'am-ing you?"

"No. The other agents are fine." She shook her head in exasperation, then turned from him and disappeared into the closet. As he reached the doorway, she emerged from the closet, a red sweatshirt over her tank top, carrying a neatly-folded electric blanket. The third floor was drafty, but not that drafty. And last he checked, the temperature outside was a balmy sixty-six. Inside, seventy-two. A cold front was forecasted, but it hadn't arrived yet.

"Stupid try, by the way. Don't use typical male deflection techniques with me to avoid the issue—"

"Wasn't trying to, ma'am."

"Are you even listening? I don't want to hear ma'am again from you. Let that be your last and final one. The other agents can say it twenty times in one sentence, for all I care. I don't want to hear it once more from you. My problem, Agent Hernandez, is with you and the way you say it. Are you understanding that my problem is with you?"

"Um, since you're being personal about it, can you be just a bit more specific in why I'm such a problem for you?"

"Seriously?"

"I believe in knowing all issues up front so I can address them."

She gave him a cool nod. "Sure. For one, you've got to stop being so..." She ran a hand through her hair, standing an arms-length from him as he stood in the doorway of her bedroom, looking up at him. Her arms were around the blanket, clutching it to her chest. "So goddamn present."

"Present? My job is to be present. I asked for specifics, Ms. Hutchenson." Too dumbfounded to be irritated, with just a small amount of frustration simmering in his gut, he realized she'd been whispering. Like it had throughout the day, her whisper got to him. She was being a royal bitch, but she was whispering, and that made her seem vulnerable, no matter how bitchy her words.

Question: What is it right now that has her so goddamn bothered that she's whispering? Answer: Me. That's what she's saying, so listen up, dumbass. Figure it out. Make it work.

He gave her a nod, drew a deep breath, and started over in a tone that was as businesslike and non-threatening as he could make it. "Look. I'm really not trying to be obtuse—"

"Well, perhaps you should look up that word and think about what it means, because you obviously don't know the meaning of it. O-B-T—"

"I know how to spell obtuse. Also, know what it means. For future reference, I only use words when I know their meaning." *Oh dear God, please don't let me start laughing. I know this is serious, but I could stand here and argue with this beautiful woman all night.*

Keeping a straight face, he continued, "You're paying me to be your guard and I'm doing it the only way I know how. If I'm annoying you so badly, it might help if I have a better understanding why."

Still clutching the blanket, but keeping her chin up, she met his gaze with a firm glance. "Look, I appreciate that you went to Esplanade Avenue with me this afternoon. I also appreciate the workout. Even appreciated the dinner that you ordered. But you're...too much. I know I'm paying for security, but I don't want to notice you every time I look up. It starts with the way you say, ma'am. With that look in your eyes." There was no whispering. She spoke loud and clear, in a tone that matched the fire in her eyes. "That smile that you have that never quite seems to disappear. All that sincerity is either way too goddamn fake, or..."

Damn curious to hear her complete thought, he folded his arms and waited in the extended silence that followed her trailing words. In her anger, or whatever the hell he was witnessing, she was goddamn adorably sexy. When it became clear she wasn't going to finish her statement, he suggested, "Perhaps real?"

Eyes flashing with irritation, she lifted one hand and waved it in a dismissive gesture. "You're blocking the doorway. See? A perfect example of being too present."

Biting his tongue, he stifled a laugh. A mere chuckle would be a lethal spark in the gunpowder he'd inadvertently lit. Plus, given the precariousness of the job, and the importance of the client to the powers that be, the situation wasn't funny. "I apologize, Ms. Hutchenson. Thought we were having a conversation."

As he stepped out of the doorway, she glared at him, walked past him, and paused on the first stair that led to the third floor. He met her on the other side of the banister, careful to keep some distance from her. "Here's your conversation, Agent Smart-Ass. Reread the damn contract. The American Sleep Association calls the disorder night terrors." He leaned closer as her voice fell to a whisper. Her cheeks became flushed with the prettiest shade of pink he'd ever seen.

"I call it a living hell. But it's my private hell. You agents aren't invited to the freak show. No one is. The contract provides the protocol, and I'm pretty damn certain—" She lifted her hand and jabbed her index finger into his chest. "—you didn't follow it. When I start screaming, you're supposed to make sure Victor Morrissey hasn't returned from the dead, or some other freak hasn't hijacked my lame excuse for a life, then leave me the hell alone. Understand?"

"Yes, ma'am."

Oh fuck!

As angry spitfire lit her eyes, any amusement he'd felt, and if he was honest, there'd been way too much, evaporated. He'd been so caught up in her raw pain as she'd said, '*freak show,*' he hadn't put any thought into his habitual agent-to-female-client response.

Dropping her hands to her side, hands and fingers fisting into tight balls of frustration, she said, "If you say ma'am one more time, you and Black Raven are fired. Understand?"

Get a grip. If she tried, once again, to fire the entire goddamn company, he'd be disappointing Zeus, Brandon, Sebastian, and Ragno, and creating a steaming, shitload of a mess. Totally unacceptable. Failing at anything—and disappointing others—wasn't his goddamn style.

Shit. Make it right. NOW, numb nuts. But how?

"Agent Hernandez, I asked if you understand you're just one overly polite, overly effusive, annoying as hell, ma'am, away from having this entire Black Raven job terminated. I'd prefer to go it alone than deal with you. Do you understand me?"

"I understand perfectly. You won't hear that again from my lips. Can you offer a suggestion for what I should call you in its place, because I'd like to have something a little more shorthand than Hutchenson."

Head tilted, she studied him with eyes that held so much pain and frustration, his own chest ached. "Make something up. And while you're at it, stop being such a smart ass. This job won't get better, you know. To be one hundred percent honest, there's something about you that grates on my nerves."

Well, that's a breath of fresh air. At least I'm getting to you. Because you're certainly getting under my skin.

He stood in silence as she continued. "The other agents have all managed to blend into the background while they do their jobs. The ones I've fired had issues with doing their job. You, on the other hand," she said, shaking her head, "I don't think blending into the background is your style."

"Not quite sure how to answer that one."

"That wasn't a question. And you're smiling again." She stamped her bare foot on the carpeted stair. "As though I'm joking. Goddammit! I haven't had to fire an agent simply because I didn't like him, but...I have the option to terminate due to personality conflict." Lifting her hand to shoo him away, she climbed a few steps, giving her a couple of inches of a height advantage on him. She lifted her left hand again and gave him a firm push on his right shoulder. "Get the hell out of my personal space."

"But you were whispering again."

"I'm not now," she said, glaring at him as she ran her fingers through her hair only for it to fall back exactly as it had been, curling softly over her cheek. "Am I?"

"No," he said, his tongue almost twisting with the urge to say ma'am. "Yelling's more like it."

She glared at him. "Because you're more than a little obtuse. Your word. Not mine. You're on duty a while longer tonight?"

He nodded. "Yes."

"Read the contract. Top to bottom. Especially the part about night terrors. If you can't follow it, leave before daybreak. You're the brother of a partner. Taylor said you're one of Black Raven's best, recently on duty with the President, for God's sake. I don't know what the hell you did to deserve my job, but surely you have sway if you're that good. I bet they'd let you off the hook. Now that you've gotten a full dose of what my security entails," she continued, giving him a curt nod, "you may leave at your earliest opportunity."

Stunned into silent stillness, he watched her climb the stairs, slowly, her back erect, without a backward glance. Maybe he'd accept her invitation to leave—if she hadn't held onto him as she'd come out of her night terrors. If there hadn't been those moments during the day when she'd thanked him with so much sincerity, she'd torqued every protective instinct in his body. If she hadn't captivated him from the moment he first saw her photo in the file. If he'd been the type to quit anything.

I really should leave. Because this job is destined for failure. I should be gone by morning, as she's suggesting.

In his world, where things always worked out, this seemed impossible. He hadn't one single clue how this job was going to possibly work out. He was here to make the client feel safe and be happier with Black Raven. Given the actual threat level, and the fact that people tended to really like him, the Hutchenson job should be simple. Yet, she almost fired him for being too present? For saying, ma'am?

When lost in her night terrors, she'd held onto him as though she was drowning and he was a lifeline. But when fully awake, she'd delivered a message that she perceived him as a threat. To what? Her peace of mind?

He couldn't reconcile the contradictions she presented. Maybe the best thing was for him to leave the job—if he truly did irritate her that badly.

But as the studio door clicked shut above him, he realized that in midst of her sparks and outright indignant fit over the way he'd said ma'am, there was a glaring omission from her fighting words.

Organs farmed, ready for shipment. Six hundred thousand per body."

"That petty-ass price is a no go. Next time you open that shithole of a mouth, make your brain talk and not your ass."

Gentle chastising doesn't work with the Butcher. That's why we get along so damn well. I deliver what he wants. Opening a sketchpad and picking up a pen, I doodle in his extended silence and shrug off my budding frustration.

The Butcher's more interesting prior orders have run the gamut of our products. From our stock of living people, he's made rentals and outright purchases. He's also ordered dead people. To be more specific, he places an order for organs, we find inventory suitable for killing, and then we farm the organs that meet his specifications. Sometimes he orders bodies intact. Apparently, the Butcher has lots of clients who like to fuck dead women, so he orders age-specific dead females, with bodies preserved, dressed, and beautiful, in high Concierge-style. Who knew necrophiliacs would be so specific?

Those are among my favorite orders to fill. I love to watch as we transform a corpse from a cold-blue dead person to a fuck-worthy dead person. If the client wants, we send them out beauty-pageant ready, waxed, tanned, wearing lingerie, with toes and nails painted. All for a fee, of course. It's damned hard to find a manicurist willing to paint OPI's latest color on a corpse, unless I'm paying top dollar.

Personally, I don't like having sex with dead people. Yes, I've tried it. Screwing a live person until they're dead is different than starting off with a dead one. Dead people can't scream and God knows there's nothing like a good, horror-filled scream to get my juices flowing.

"Rework your opening number," I say, prodding him, "we sell people. Not garbage. Six hundred thousand apiece is unacceptable, even for our dead ones."

He sighs. I brace for whining.

"My offer results in two point four million dollars to you," he says. "Doesn't that figure have value?"

"No. Adding four inadequate amounts equals a total of don't-fucking-bother-me."

I open a tube of seven-inch matches, pull one out, then run the head along the strike pad. An orange flame ignites and crawls along the match as he stews. From the Butcher's end of the phone line, "Summer Wind" plays. Incongruously, and always as annoying as hell, the Butcher favors Sinatra. I hate every goddamn tune Sinatra ever sang.

Letting the small orange ball of fire lick my fingertip, I feel a twinge of burning heat before dropping the match on the silver tray, next to where my lit taper has started dripping a steady stream of hot wax. I dip my index finger in warm wax that has puddled in the tray, then lift my finger to the candle flame, letting the fire melt the wax. I lean back in the desk chair, hoping to hell the Butcher's call will end soon.

Face facts. Business is getting boring. It's still as lucrative as anything, but...boring. Tedious. Ho-hum. Too goddamn easy.

What good is money when everything that can be done with it is boring as a predictable 7:30 a.m. trip to the crapper?

Last night, after we shipped off Eve, I'd been hopeful that a few hours of playtime with another recent acquisition would take the edge off my growing restlessness.

Nope. Restlessness remained. I barely even came. No surprise there. My prerequisites are specific and our acquisition was a poor imitation of who I'm craving. Now, last night's plaything needs medical attention and my partner's pissed off because I created work that slices into profits. A larger problem is that I got virtually zero satisfaction and not enough sleep.

Sinatra's "Summer Wind" ends, and "My Way" starts. The Butcher, steadfastly silent, can go fuck himself. Here's a dose of my way, asshole. For being so goddamn tedious and annoying, I'm mentally figuring in a fifty-thousand dollar pain-in-the-ass tax to this morning's bottom line.

It's time for some goddamn excitement. Don't care if I'm not being rational. I want. I want. And I get what I want. That's my way.

"I can go up to seven hundred thousand per body. Parts harvested," the Butcher says.

"One point one million per," I counter, eyes on the orange-red dancing flame on the candlewick. "There's nowhere else you can make these kinds of purchases. We've got a monopoly and even you, with your pea brain, know it."

"Too high," he said.

"If you were here, I'd take a bullwhip to you. Fifty lashes across your back." He groans. I can't tell if it's a groan of frustration or desire. Truthfully, with the mood I'm in, it doesn't matter. "While you think about your naked self getting bullwhipped, your back bleeding, think for a few minutes about your offer. You want us to harvest the organs. You want said parts shipped separately. It's one hell of a lot of work and we damn well don't work for free. One point one. You in, or out?"

"At that figure," he says, "there's no profit for me, even with you harvesting the organs. A liver and a heart will fetch $400 thousand. Kidneys, perhaps $200 thousand. Eyes—"

"I don't give a shit about your bottom line. I'm well aware of current market prices for body parts." Lifting an index finger and threading it through the flame of the candle, shivering with the burn, I add, "remember the potential value of what I'm selling."

"Meaning?"

"Your lowball offer isn't considering the intrinsic value. Frankly, my products are worth more alive than dead. If you want bargain-basement organs, go somewhere else on the black market. But if you're dealing with me, you need to up the offer."

As he stews in silence, "My Way" gives way to "Mack the Knife."

"At least that one has lyrics I can relate to."

The Butcher chuckles. Nervously. "Eight hundred thousand per."

Now we're talking. "To confirm. No blood tests on our part. No tissue typing. No prerequisites?"

"None."

While it could be interesting to know just who would buy organs from the Butcher without blood type and cross matching, identification of the Butcher's clients is none of my business. Fingers threading through the candle's flame, I consider the offer and the bottom line numbers for some of our inventory that, truth be told, really needs to move. Like last night's plaything, who is now almost damaged beyond repair.

Knowing something that the Butcher doesn't know warms my heart almost as much as the hot wax into which I'm dipping my finger. Mardi Gras in New Orleans offers a way to generate inventory quickly. Always a haven for the homeless, due to its tolerance and temperate climate, during the carnival season the streets become full of people no one will miss when they disappear.

Last night my hunters had a glitch, but that's highly unusual. The typical ease with which acquisitions can be snagged from the crowded streets of the Big Easy during Mardi Gras means there's play in my price. Even with a pain-in-the-ass tax factored into the bottom line.

"Nine hundred seventy-five thousand per. It's a bargain basement price." Flicking warm wax off my fingers, I reach for my laptop and send the Butcher an email with an encrypted data package, then stand and stretch. "And you pay me today for all four. Three point nine million dollars, wired into my account by ten a.m., Central Time."

"You're killing me."

"No. Trust me. This isn't what death by Concierge feels like."

He chuckles and then—*Fuck me*. Yes. The playlist switches to the song I've been dreading. "New York, New York."

"I'll make this quick." Because I have a lot to do on this Sunday, and even more than that, I hate that gravel-pit of a voice singing that lame-ass song. "I have something else that might interest you. I'll give you first refusal. At three p.m., we're opening an auction of two prime male specimens. Minimum bid is one point one million apiece. I expect they'll go, at auction, for at least one point five apiece. Maybe more."

"Not interested. Got what I needed, and that's organ donors. One point one is too high for organ donors. I know most of your assets have become higher end, but I'm adapting to what I can sell fast. There's been a spike in demand for harvested body parts. Surely you know that?"

"Of course. But before you go, check your inbox. I sent a data package with photos and a video. Normally I charge for this sort of thing, but I'm giving you a break. You know the viewing protocol."

"Not going to open."

Before he finishes the sentence, I hear his fingers clacking on his keyboard. "Bullshit. I'll bet your cock's already hard."

"Blow me."

"Probability is sky high that won't happen in this lifetime."

"Give me a minute. Damn decryption programs take forever."

Finally, praise-Jesus finally, the Butcher shut off the music and there is silence in the background. Through the phone line, I hear only heavy breathing as he examines the photos and videos of the high-end merchandise, who no one in their right mind would harvest for pieces and parts.

At least not right away.

"Oh. My word."

"Yeah. Happy Valentine's Day. Special, right?"

He groans in answer.

"I'll sell them now at pre-auction for one point three million dollars apiece. On the other hand, if all you're interested in is organs, we're done for the day."

"How old are they?"

"Seventeen and sixteen." I'm guesstimating their age. Like an animal shelter does with cute dogs, the ones who have a chance of not going to the gas chamber. Yeah—I'm looking for a loving home for them. As long as someone will pay my price, they can love these two anyway they see fit. "Both handsome, healthy and athletic. They'll be ready in one week. I need them for stud for a few more days."

The Butcher moans as he gets an eyeful of the fair-haired boys.

I smile. "Your access to the data package disappears when I hang up. Unless, of course, you buy the goods."

"Give me a few minutes to run some numbers."

Run some numbers? My ass. The Butcher knows his goddamn numbers and profit margins down to the last dime. Give him a few minutes to jerk off over what the two drugged-to-the-gills teenagers are doing to each other in the video, thanks to the threat of imminent death and libido-enhancing drugs.

I know not to hang up. I also know it takes the Butcher about three minutes to jack off once he starts moaning and groaning. I've listened to him do it enough over the last few years. Keeping up the pretense that he needs this time to contact clients, I tell him, "I'll hold for three minutes. When I next hear your voice, it better be saying a resounding yes. Otherwise, you won't be getting first refusal options in the future."

Having three minutes to kill, I glance at a large screen video monitor hanging on the office wall. Turning it on requires a series of passwords. Once the screen comes to life, I click the channels of the camera feeds at the farm, where the chores are never ending. Simply checking on whether our highly paid assistants accomplish their work is a full-time job. Baths. Food. Meds. Vitals need to be checked. On this Sunday morning, my partner is at the farm, overseeing operations.

For the assets in our mating program, sexual performance drugs are administered. Mating works better when both male and female actually want to do the act. Ah. The mating. A big part of the reason impregnation at the farm typically occurs the old-fashioned way is because I love to watch it.

Ownership, after all, has its privileges.

It isn't yet fucking time at the farm. Baths are just starting. A disappointment, but that's okay, because as I click through camera feeds and eye the inventory, I decide to study my personal work in progress.

Six months ago, we acquired her from San Francisco after she made the mistake of propositioning one of my reapers. Once

I studied her for valuation purposes, I realized I had a rare prize. Her lean, angular body, her long, naturally muscular arms and legs, the set of her jaw, and the way her narrow neck met her shoulders reminded me of my one true obsession—Andi Hutchenson.

Mostly, it was the surprising fragileness of her bone structure. The way her back was thin, where I could almost see the outline of her ribs through creamy, translucent skin.

I'd immediately directed her to our clinic in Mexico. This once-homeless prostitute has now been pampered and transformed, Concierge-style. I call her Andi, for reasons made obvious by a few surgeries to make her look like the woman of my dreams. I had her nose fixed, because her wide, flat nose ruined my fantasy. I had her eyelids redone, because hers didn't have as much of a crease as Andi's. Dental implants and breast work completed the package.

She'd arrived at the farm a week ago, and, this morning, I zoom in on her and study her face. My mood lifts. I smile, because she's healed nicely, and the latest round of cosmetic surgery did the trick. She's almost become the woman of my dreams.

I have a busy day planned. Sunday services. Brunch. The gallery opening—a nice end of day event to look forward to. Just knowing that I'll see the real Andi sends a shiver down my spine. So much of a thrill, I suddenly know what I need for my own after party. And the acquisition who is currently pictured on the screen will be my entertainment.

All of which makes the end of this negotiation with the Butcher easy, because his three minutes are up and I now really no longer give a shit about business.

I take the call off mute. "One point three," I say. "Decide now. Going once. Twice. Thr—"

"I'll take them both."

We click off the call, and I immediately make another call to my stylist.

"It's Sunday," she answers, tone clearly indicating annoyance.

I hear air swooshing through the speaker, so I know she's driving the Porsche that she's able to afford because I pay her a fortune. I swear—I know physicians who make less money than this beauty school dropout.

"This is personal," I say, working to keep my temper tamped down.

"Not necessarily a way to entice me to work," my stylist says, between smacks of gum chewing. "I'm on my way to goddamn church, then I'm throwing a princess party at Chuck E. Cheese's for my four-year-old niece. I need to show up with cake and balloons and presents that I haven't even managed to buy yet, because you had me working most of the day and into the night yesterday. Know how important this party is to her?"

At first, I stay silent, because I've got nothing to give this woman. Nothing. Honesty on this subject will not accomplish my goal. I think the world would be a better goddamn place without four-year-olds and whatever it is that might be important to them. But does this woman really want to hear that I've never met a four-year-old I give a rat's ass about? No. And all told, that isn't true, because I've sold a few and I certainly cared about the money they brought in.

"Aw man. Geez, why did I even ask you that question? Of course you don't know how important a princess pizza party might be for a kid, because you have no goddamn soul."

"Lose your whiny-ass attitude and start to think about what I'll pay you for working on a Sunday."

"Yes, I'm thinking about it. But no matter what you offer, I'm not working on a corpse. Not on a Sunday."

"Goddammit, are you listening? I said it's personal, and you know I don't fuck corpses."

She gives an extended harrumph. "Like that's an important distinction, given what you do to the people you do fuck."

I smile, because the truth is this woman amuses me. Few people have the nerve to throw attitude at me, and I find rare moments of joy in the ones who actually do. Which is part of the reason I fell so hard for Andi.

"I'll pay quadruple your hourly fee for you to do the work today." I split my screens, looking at the acquisition who caught my eye a few weeks ago. I open a video montage I've put together of the real Andi, from the eyes that I have on her. "We did the heavy lifting with surgeries, and she's healed. I estimate you'll need eight hours."

"Jesus H. What do you want me to do to her?"

"I want...everything. I'm sending you a file. Some of photos you've taken. Some are other photos. Clothes. Shoes. Underwear. Hair color. Cut. Nail color. Toenail color. Makeup. Make my faux Andi as close to the real thing as you can. If you can fool my eyes, there's bonus money for you."

My eyes linger on the video feed of the real Andi, our first time together. She's naked. There's a moment before I move in the way, where the hidden camera captures her spreading her legs for me, the treasure that lay between them calling me home and glistening in dewy, lust-driven splendor. Holy shit, but that image does it for me every goddamn time. The reckless abandon Andi brought to fucking was so intoxicating, I'll never lose the craving for that high. "Even down to the way you wax her pussy hair. And I want her ready by ten p.m."

Chapter Thirteen

Andi

Opening the door to her bedroom, Andi froze as the aroma of something baking greeted her.

Biscuits?

Had to be. She'd grown up in a household with full-time kitchen staff. Certain culinary memories were ingrained in her senses. Nothing else in the world had the floury-doughy scent of a fresh-baked biscuit. Metal clanged against metal. A lid against a pot? Inhaling deeply, she shut her eyes, while her mouth watered.

Good God, is that bacon?

She'd painted until four in the morning, ignored Agent Smart-Ass each time he checked on her, finally fallen into a dreamless sleep in the studio, and woken up at eight forty-five.

Now, post-shower, she was starving, and a few minutes late for the nine-thirty meeting with the agents. But while the idea of a good, home-cooked breakfast was great, the fact that she smelled food being cooked on a Sunday, when her housekeeper Evelyn wasn't working, meant that one of the agents was hosting a breakfast meeting.

Really?

None of the other agents had ever cooked in her house. She'd bet her left hand that the agent/chef was the one she'd invited to quit the night before. Agent Obtuse. Agent Do-Everything-Different. Agent Can't-Take-a-Hint. Agent I'll-Teach-You-to-Fight. Agent Happy-to-be-Here.

Agent Hernandez, dammit to hell, had decided not to leave. She walked with purpose down the stairs, determined not to start the day with him under her skin—when the truth was, he was already firmly embedded there. Determined that her walls were going to be firmly up—even though her walls inexplicably crumbled every time he looked at her.

He's an agent. Simply an agent.

But he's Agent I'll-Carry You-to-Bed. Agent Unafraid-of-Night-Terrors, when they freak everyone else in the whole goddamn world out.

He's just another agent. One in a long line.

Forget that he carried you to bed. That somehow it didn't freak you out. Most of all, forget that it made you feel like crawling into his muscular arms and staying there for the rest of your life. Forget the way his easy smile lights his eyes. The way his deep, smooth voice makes you feel as though you've been stroked by a velvet glove.

Hell. The man is like...

Careful. Careful. Careful. He might be different than all the other agents, but he's the same, in one important respect. He's getting paid to be here.

Okay. Reality check taken.

He's like...New Orleans humidity on a hot August day. Seeping into every space. Everywhere. The warm, steaminess of the fresh air he carries with him might feel good for a few minutes, a fresh change from the perpetual chill that was wrapped around her soul. After a while, though, he'll be just as annoying as the ever-present, thick-as-pea-soup humidity. A few days of him, or even a week, and she'd damn well welcome the freezing chill that came with being her post-kidnapping, post-traumatic stressed-out self.

Maybe.

Two more steps down, she reached the first floor, where male voices traveled from the kitchen to the hallway. "Can't do a level one job without an AK, or similar firepower. No way. Would be the same as not wearing pants in Times Square."

"Yeah. Like pizza without pepperoni."

"That would be a damn shame. I prefer double pepperoni." Agent Pain-in-the-Ass's voice, the very tone conveying a smile, sounded more authoritative than the others, but no less engaged in the easy, relaxed banter. "Better analogy—Krav Maga sparring without a cup."

His comment produced an *"ouch!"* and a solid round of laughter. That was something else that didn't happen in her house. When the agents typically assembled for the morning meeting, they were near silent until she arrived. Businesslike. No chatter. No laughter. All work. No play.

"Jokes aside," Agent Hernandez said when the laughter died down, "Black Raven wouldn't send agents on a Level One job without adequate equipment. Okay. Cookie dough done. You can tell me tonight what you think of my recipe. Some say they're better than sex. I wouldn't go that far."

Andi paused in the doorway of the kitchen. Agents Two and Three were sitting on stools at the kitchen island, gazing at Agent Hernandez with adoring eyes and smiles, obviously drinking in everything he said. To Andi, cult leaders and Kool Aid came to mind.

Agent Two took a bite out of a biscuit, glanced in her direction, then put it on his plate as he stood. Agent Three followed suit. They looked at her with sheepish expressions, as though they'd been caught doing something illegal.

"Good Morning, ma'am," Agent Three said.

Agent Two gave her a nod as he chewed, then worked to swallow a mouthful. "Morning, ma'am."

Leaning against the counter, next to the stove, Agent Hernandez wore faded jeans that hugged his perfect thighs, a snug Black Raven logoed t-shirt that accentuated his broad shoulders, and tennis shoes. His gun was holstered at his hips. Dark hair, spikey and damp, looked like he'd barely brushed his fingers through it as he'd towel-dried it. He gave her a nod as he placed a skillet on a burner. "Perfect timing, Captain. How do you like your eggs?"

"Alone."

He smiled, as though finding great wit in her words. Not her intent. Arching an eyebrow, he asked, "No biscuit or bacon?"

"No. Meaning I prefer to eat alone, Agent Hernandez. I thought we settled that last night."

He pursed his lips, cocked his head, and studied her for a second, before giving her one of his interminably optimistic '*that'll work*' nods. "No. Last night we were talking about last night. Don't worry. We won't do this at every meal. I figured we'd multi-task this morning. I've gotta be present at the morning meeting, and I'm starving. You need to eat, and my guys don't know how to boil water. Cooking skills aren't part of the Black Raven training program. There's only so much take-out a person can eat, and Tyre and Stevens have eaten take-out since they've been on the job." He did an over-the shoulder gesture with his chin to Agents Two and Three, who still stood at attention. "Tyre's put on five pounds, Stevens has put on ten since they've been in New Orleans. That right, guys?"

"Yes, sir." Said in unison, the agents' voices gave every indication they'd agree with anything Agent Just-Plain-Happy-to-be-Alive said.

Andi glanced at the two agents. If they had gained weight, she couldn't tell. Then again, she'd barely noticed them. As a matter of fact, she didn't know which one was Tyre, or which one was Stevens. All she knew was that the man she now thought of as Agent Two had reddish hair and light brown eyes, and the man she thought of as Agent Three had brown hair and dark brown eyes. If they both had brown hair, she doubted she'd have distinguished them at all. They looked young, lean, fit, and with the neat, serious, professional look she'd come to associate with the Black Raven agents who'd been sent her way. They didn't look like take-out had done them one pound of harm.

Turning her attention to Agent Jokester, she folded her arms, "And their weight gain is my problem, how?"

"If I'm cooking for me, it's just as easy to cook for the team. So why shouldn't I cook for you?"

"You're not answering my question." Glancing at the island, she eyed the unwrapped stick of butter and a bag of shredded cheese. "You do understand that bacon, egg, and biscuit sandwiches won't help weight gain issues, don't you?"

As one of the other agents chuckled, Agent Hernandez reached over to the platter of bacon, lifted it, and offered it to her. "I bought nitrate free bacon. And you forgot the grape jelly. I put that on the side. For dipping."

"And I heard you say you made cookie dough. That won't help, either."

"But they're chocolate chip. Which means the calories don't count, because it's Valentine's Day. Nothing with chocolate has calories on Valentine's Day. Actually, if you don't eat chocolate today, there's an automatic two-pound weight gain."

Andi marveled at how he could keep a straight face while spouting such ridiculousness. If he was waiting for a reaction, she refused to give him one.

He lifted the platter of bacon an inch or so higher. Shaking her head 'no' to his offering, she ignored the grumbling in her stomach as he set the platter down.

Grocery bags lined the far wall. "When did you get all of this?"

"I went to the grocery store on Royal Street when I knocked off duty at six thirty. I put up the cold stuff before I started cooking. Those are the dry goods." He nodded in the direction of the bags, then smiled, conveying a look that said, '*today's going to be great, whatever it brings our way.*'

Oh dear God. Next, he'll break into a chorus of *zippity-damn-doo-dah.*

"I'll organize it later. As you suggested, I reread the contract. Decided I'd be here for a while. Figured it would be a shame not to make use of your fabulous kitchen. Looking forward to pizza night."

Aw. Hell.

The man could cook. And he actually liked to grocery shop? To save herself from falling for this man who irritated the hell out of her, she needed to fire him. *Fast.*

"I'd prefer if you cooked across the street, in the apartment I've rented for the team."

His megawatt smile didn't falter. "I'm not staying there. Or cooking there." Glancing at the two agents, he said, "Finish eating. We have work to do." As the agents sat down, he turned back to the stove, returned the skillet to the burner, and gave her a sideways glance. "The contract says one of the agents can stay in a guest room upstairs.

Oh, hell. Damn, but he's correct.

"For now, that will be me."

"None of the agents have slept here before."

He cracked an egg and put it in the pan, then cracked another. As the eggs sizzled and popped, his eyes slid to where she stood, feet firmly planted in the doorway. "Doesn't mean I can't stay here now. Have you seen the kitchen over there?" Lifting a spatula, he flipped the eggs. "It's a narrow galley. In case you haven't noticed, I'm not a small man."

He didn't need to pause to let that sink in, but he did, giving her a smile that made her want to groan. Of course she'd noticed that he wasn't small. He was huge. Tall. Muscular. Broad shoulders, long legs, big feet. Big hands. He brought new meaning to DaVinci's theory of the golden ratio. Everything visible was in perfect, harmonious proportion, which made her wonder about the parts of his anatomy she couldn't see.

"I can barely fit in it," he continued. "Much less cook. If you'd prefer, I can stay in the guesthouse across the courtyard. Even that kitchen is better than what's in the tiny dump the agents stay in."

"My guesthouse is for someone else, and the place I rented for the agents isn't a dump."

She glanced at Agents Two and Three. Silent, mouths stuffed with food, their eyes bouncing between the senior agent and herself, they looked like a pair of oversized kids who had settled in for a serious discussion between parents—thoroughly enjoying themselves, while having enough wisdom to stay silent.

Agent Hernandez glanced at her, one eyebrow arched. "Who's moving into your guesthouse? File lacks that detail."

Not waiting for a reply, he reached for a plate on the island. He took a large biscuit off a pan, split it with a knife, placed a pat of butter on the top half, spread it, sprinkled a bit of cheese on top of the butter, then laid two pieces of bacon on the bottom half. After placing a knife full of grape jelly to the side of the biscuit, he turned back to the stove, plate in hand.

"Well," he asked, "who's moving in and when?"

"None of your business."

She told herself his efficient moves between the stove and the island weren't mesmerizing. It was a total lie. The short-sleeved t-shirt revealed muscles that rippled as he moved, even when he cooked. The bulge between his bicep and tricep produced a horseshoe of an indent, which got her back to thinking about proportions, angles and curves. He'd make a great model to sketch. Nude. A class she'd taken at the academy had used nude models that posed for timed intervals, while the students sketched. She'd love to have this guy pose for her.

Holding the plate where he'd partially assembled the biscuit sandwich, he flipped the eggs again. After pressing the spatula down, he lifted the eggs onto the biscuit, and pressed the top down. "Clause in the contract says we do security clearances on people who live on the premises."

"If and when someone moves in there," she said, "I'll let you know."

Damn, but she was starving. For food. And, face facts, him.

Humidity, remember? That's all he is. He's only attractive because he's warm and you're freezing. He makes the air feel different. That's it. You've been cold for too long.

He gave the plate with the loaded biscuit a not-too-gentle push. It slid along the island, stopping magically at the edge closest to her.

If I tried the same move, the plate would've crashed to the floor.

"That's yours. You missed the opportunity for a special order. If that isn't to your liking, don't worry. It won't be wasted." He reached for the platter of bacon, grabbed a piece, took a bite and chewed as he studied her. "I'm starving. That's how I eat it. If you don't want it, I'll eat yours and mine."

He turned back to the stove and cracked two more eggs. "Morning meeting officially convened while I cook my eggs. Marks?" Talking to the agent who wasn't present was a reminder that the agents were connected to each other by a comm system. It was easy to forget, as their earpieces were nearly invisible. Agent Hernandez paused, then chuckled. "Well, next time I'll add more cheese. Tyre, if you're through, start cleaning. Make it spotless. I don't clean when I'm cooking for able-bodied people over the age of five or under eighty. Stevens, pull up a map. Tell us your plans for the day, Kemosabe."

He glanced at her with a smile that made her insides melt, while her brain screamed *'fire this guy.'*

Chapter Fourteen

Gabe

He'd never been so happy to see a woman reach for a plate of food.

Using peripheral vision, he watched her carry the plate to the counter space closest to the refrigerator. She lifted the top of the biscuit. Dipping the knife in the grape jelly, she smeared some on the egg. After reassembling the sandwich, she leaned her hip against the counter, took a bite, chewed, then bit into it again.

Hallelujah.

She wore faded jeans and an oversized blue-green sweater. Her feet, slender, smooth, and elegant, were bare.

He'd figured out she didn't wear shoes in the house, except in the workout room. Sometime, he didn't know when, he'd evidently developed a thing for a woman's feet. As he studied the gentle curve of her toes, he realized her feet could do it for him.

Matter of fact, they were doing it for him, because he was going from soft to semi-hard, and...dammit.

Think about something else.

She opened the refrigerator, looked inside, shot him a look that was somewhere between surprise and annoyance, and pulled out a bottle of orange juice. He'd bought a fresh bottle of the brand that had been almost empty. Fresh squeezed, calcium enriched, and pulp-free. He'd also filled the shelves with things he liked to eat and made a few guesses as to what she'd eat. She poured a glass of juice, then ate another bite. He assembled his biscuit, then sat on a stool, facing her. "Plan for the day?"

"Before that, the missing person reports you said you were monitoring. Was anything reported overnight?"

Gabe had already gotten a report from Tyre on that. "No. Not yet. We'll alert you if that changes."

She nodded. "Today, I'll paint in Crescent Park. Near the old wharf and the Piety Street footbridge. Same as yesterday. These agents know the streets I like to take." She glanced at Tyre, who was now standing by the sink, scrubbing a skillet, and Stevens, who had pulled up a map of the area on his iPad. Her gaze fell to Gabe. "We'll leave in a half hour."

"Tyre and Stevens will get you there," Gabe said. "Stevens. Map the routes for me."

Stevens reached for his iPad. “For Crescent Park, we have a main, and two alternates. Ms. Hutchenson lets us know if she’s uncomfortable on any one route.”

“Understood.” Glancing at Andi, he added, “Can you estimate how long you’ll be there?”

With her mouth full, she paused as she chewed. “A few hours, likely.”

“Okay. I’ll go to the park at two, assuming you’re still there. Plans for this evening?” Taking a bite, Gabe waited for direction from her on whether she was going to the gallery opening.

Do it. Come on. Just do it. Beat the goddamn fears that have you by the throat. Take that first step. If you falter, I'll be there to catch you.

Plate now empty, she drank the last of her juice. When she moved towards the sink, Tyre extended his hands. “I’ll take that, ma’am.”

“Thank you.” The slight smile she gave Tyre faded as she glanced at Gabe. Deadly serious forest green eyes held his. Thick dark hair in chunks surrounded her delicate face exactly how he liked it—a tossed, just-got-out-of-bed look. “As of now, I’ll go to the gallery opening. Exactly as we discussed. You guys in sports coats concealing your guns. We arrive late. Quarter to seven, at the earliest. We leave early. I’m thinking I’ll be there an hour. At most. All subject to change, though.”

He finished the last piece of bacon and pushed the now empty platter to Tyre. “Understood, Chief.”

She gave no indication that she noticed his interpretation of her ban on ‘ma’am’ usage from him provided free access to any other title he deemed appropriate. Instead of showing annoyance, she studied him with a slightly puzzled look, without a smile. But there wasn’t a frown, or her slight scowl, either. He took it as a sign of encouragement.

“We’ll adapt to whatever you decide, whenever you decide it,” Gabe said.

A half hour later, Tyre, Marks, and Andi were gone. Stevens was in the security room, and Gabe was supposed to get a few hours of sleep. *Later*. Pressing his watch, he climbed the stairs from the second to the third floor and hit speed dial for Ragno. His ear mic automatically picked up the call. He muted the other agents. His conversation with Ragno was private.

“Hello, Angel.” He heard her fingers racing across her keyboard, as she multi-tasked with agents positioned in jobs worldwide.

“Have a few minutes?”

“Yep. It’s been busy, but I’m in a lull. How’s the Hutchenson job?”

“Interesting.” Studio door was locked. Using the key that Andi had provided the evening before, after their workout, he unlocked the door.

“How so?”

“Would’ve helped me if you gave a clue how gorgeous she is. The pictures in the file were one thing. But damn. In real life? Stunning. I’d have braced myself.”

Ragno laughed. “That’s a surprise, coming from you.”

Stepping into the studio, he glanced around the expansive room, trying to get a feel for where the proportions were wrong. He’d studied the floor plans again during the night. There was no indication of a hidden room. There was also no mention of it in the file. The studio was windowless, save for the skylights.

“Meaning?”

“She’s not your type. Frankly, I didn’t think you’d even notice how pretty she is. She’s not all that curvy. Boobs aren’t more than a full B. No long blond hair.”

“And you think that’s my type?”

“Excuse me? Giselle. Heather. Kaity. Georgie. Stacey. Any of those names ring a bell? Because in the last calendar year, you told me about them. They were all the lingerie model, blond and curvy type, right? And Heather and Georgie are actual models, right? Or was it Kaity and Georgie who wore the wings on the runway? Whatever. Oh, damn. Hold for a minute.”

On hold, Gabe eyed the four walls. There was only one option for which wall had space behind it. He walked across the room, to the wall opposite the doorway and stairwell. Canvasses leaned against every inch of the wall space. One painting was larger than the rest—a six-foot tall, oversized, painting of the Saint Louis Cathedral, the historic center of the French Quarter. It was spectacular, with a side view of the grayish building and its crosses that reached up into a brilliant blue sky. Sliding the painting to the side, he found a small, frameless door.

Bingo.

He’d been clear with Andi that he needed access to the entire premises. He’d given her a chance to provide it, and she’d broken the rules. Sitting back on his heels, he studied the four by two foot wide, frameless door that blended almost seamlessly into the wall. The brass knob-style handle didn’t match the others in her house. Too new, too shiny. Too Home Depot.

Maybe the door led to an old attic, with trunks of old clothes and long forgotten memorabilia. Dusty suitcases. Mousetraps. If so, the narrowness, and the low lintel, would make taking bulky things in and out tricky. Not practical. Didn't matter. He'd see for himself. It was going to be some feat to squeeze his six feet four body through the short and narrow opening, but he'd do it.

He tried the brass knob. Locked.

No surprise.

If Andi knew what he was doing, she'd fire his ass. No one in the company would blame him, however, because it was his job to cover every inch of space. Reaching into his back pocket for his wallet, Gabe opened it and pulled out a card-sized set of titanium tension wrenches and pick rakes. He inserted a wrench in the bottom part of the keyhole, moved it counterclockwise, then clockwise. When he felt the right amount of give, he slid a ridged pick rake into the upper part of the lock, getting a feel for the torque necessary to manipulate the pins.

Pulling the tools out, Gabe stretched his fingers, chose a different rake with more ridges, then started over as Ragno started talking again. "Okay. I'm back. My point is, all the women you've dated look so much alike, they're a blur of forgettable. Or did I imagine that those cookie-cutter women have been your type over the last decade?"

"You mean the type of women I date."

"Is there another type?"

"Sure there is. The kind of woman I'm going to marry doesn't look like the kind of women I've dated for the last decade or so." Inserting the pick rake and tension wrench, he shut his eyes, feeling the subtle movement of the lock's pins.

"God. I love you," Ragno said. "There is never a moment when you don't have me smiling, you know that? What the hell are you talking about?"

"Didn't want to date my marrying type until I was ready."

"For?"

"Marrying." Ah. The lock turned. Done.

"You're ready now?"

"Yep. It's part of my life plan."

"But you're not even dating anyone seriously."

"Always figured I'd find her, once I started looking."

"You've spent most of your time traveling far from the U.S. in recent years. Not exactly a lifestyle suited for settling down."

"I'll teach more, which is what I always wanted to do. I'll take more domestic jobs."

"You have it all planned, don't you? This is funny, Angel. Borderline ridiculous—"

"I'm not joking." He pushed the door open. "I'm building my house now. You know that. I've always known what she'd look like. I just have to find her."

"Okay. I'll bite. What are the features of the type of woman you plan to marry?"

Bending to fit through the small door, he said, "She looks just like Andi Hutchenson."

"Stop joking."

He flipped on the light and entered finished attic space. The narrow room ran the entire length of the third floor. Standing in the middle, he could flatten his palms along both sides. The ceiling sloped. At its highest part, the ceiling was eight feet high. There was no furniture in the room. To one side, the floor had a soft rug, on top of which were full, oversized pillows and a soft blanket, neatly folded.

"I'm not joking. Dark hair. Green eyes. You see, my dad had green eyes and dark hair. I want my children to have a fighting chance to look like him. She'll have a heart-shaped face, 'cause I think that's pretty. A slight turn-up to her nose. Tall, but not too tall. Lean. Muscular. Gorgeous feet. Artistic. Creative. Likes to be at home."

"Are you kidding me?"

"Nope. Look. I'm not saying I'm marrying Andi Hutchenson. Far from it, considering we're off to a somewhat rocky start. But I can't deny that she damn well looks like the type I always thought I'd marry. Actually, she looks better than I imagined."

"Whoa. Back up. A rocky start?"

"Yeah, though we seem to have moved past it. But if you really think I'm kidding about this, go to my latest personality profile interview. The part about personal goals and objectives. It was about a year ago."

Andi's secret room looked like a cozy reading nook. A low table held a lamp and a small pile of books beside a tray filled with black pens. One leather-bound book was separated from the others. Fresh lavender and roses in a crystal vase told him she came in here often.

"Then you're due again. I'll put a tickler in the file for when you're done with this job." He could hear her fingers pecking at her keyboard. "Give me a second. Okay. I have it open."

"See the question about personal life plan?"

"Got it." She fell silent, presumably reading through his answers to the battery of questions that Black Raven's teams of psychiatrists asked, which were designed to make sure agents weren't going to go crazy mid-job. The questions elicited life goals and objectives. Gabe loved to give details of his life plan, because he'd always had one. At the beginning of each year, he tweaked the one, five, and ten-year goals.

As Ragno read, he looked at small linen-covered boxes that were neatly stacked against the wall opposite the door. Opening a box, he saw photographs of Andi, with friends. Looking at the date, he realized it was two years before her kidnapping. The smile on her face—positively captivating and full—looked nothing like the serious look on the face of the woman she now was.

Another box held newspaper clippings. Rifling through, he realized she had saved reports of her kidnapping. The local press had provided endless details of what Victor Morrissey had done to the three daughters of the three prominent New Orleans families. The reporting style of the local press bordered on voyeuristic gossip. He wasn't surprised, just pissed off that the press had made the details of what the *'former debutante,'* prior *'queen of carnival,'* and *'talented student of the New Orleans Art Academy'* had suffered so public. Right down to the goddamn cigarette burns and the message Morrissey had left on her back.

"Gabe, this is amazing." Ragno's voice broke his concentration. "Who gives this much detail? You said when you were thirty-six you were going to marry the girl of your dreams and when you were thirty-four, you were going to start looking for her. By forty, you hope to have your first and second child. Going to have three."

"How old am I now?"

"As of this past December, thirty-four. So, you're now looking for the woman you're going to marry?"

"Of course. Was glad to hit thirty-four, actually. I'm getting tired of blondes. Though quitting cold-turkey means I haven't had sex since my birthday."

"TMI, and by the way, a whole two months? Careful. It might fall off."

He chuckled, then continued his mini-rant. "Been working non-stop and I haven't had time to transition to the different dating realm. Hell, Ragno. Every female I know is blond."

"Poor baby," she said, sarcasm flag flying high.

"Yeah. It's wearing thin. Go back to the file. How did I describe the woman I'm going to marry?"

"Dark hair. Green eyes. Heart shaped face. Tall. Not too tall. Lean. Muscular. Artistic. Creative. Likes to be at home." Ragno drew a deep breath. "Oh holy hell, Gabe. Wait a second. I'm not falling for this. Did you plant this in the file just to jerk my chain?"

He chuckled, then walked to the far stack of boxes, looking for something happier than media reports of her kidnapping. "Now why would I do that? Besides, personnel files are encrypted and off limits, remember?"

"Like that's ever stopped you. Hey," she chuckled, then her voice turned serious. "Wait. This bit about liking to be at home. Yeah—I get it. I know you love to be at home when you're not working, know your favorite dates are long weekends at home. But you do understand that someone who has post-traumatic stress induced agoraphobia is way different than someone who likes to be at home, don't you?"

"Of course, but I'm an optimist." Crouching on the floor, he opened a box and realized she might have been the cutest baby in the world. A few old photos in the farthest box were of her in diapers. She had fat cheeks, wavy dark hair, a light in her eyes, and a smile that made her seem like she was laughing.

"Of course you are, Angel. You live and breathe optimism like no other. Oh, and by the way, there's nothing about gorgeous feet in your personality assessment."

He chuckled as he thought about the pale lavender paint on the nails that graced each of Andi's delicious-looking toes. Gently curved and obviously well cared for, her toes looked ready to nibble. And that thought produced yet another blood-pumping reminder of why abstinence from sex wasn't good for him.

Hell.

"Yeah, I just decided that I have a thing for feet over breakfast." Gabe closed the box, went to the reading nook, sat at the pillow, and opened the black leather-bound journal that was on the table.

Not a reading nook. A writing nook.

If the locked door didn't dissuade him, if the oversized painting that blocked the secret doorway wasn't a strong signal of what he should do, the words '*dear journal*' should've been a red clanging light that brought him to a smoking stop and made him do a screaming U-turn.

"Gotta go. I'll check in later."

"Roger."

While Gabe had never respected a boundary in his life, he almost did this time. But like the eyes of the young people she'd sketched, her handwriting drew his eye, enticing him with a glimpse into her soul from which he was powerless to turn.

The journal in his hand was the most recent in time. The others, piled neatly to the side, were dated earlier. There were ten. All black-bound leather, all about two inches thick. The first page had the dates covered on the interior pages. The earliest one, at the bottom of the stack, was dated one month after the kidnapping.

Sinking to the floor, he settled himself on the carpeted area next to her writing table. Leaning against a wall, legs stretched out in front of him, Gabe heard the ring of the front doorbell. Touching his watch, he opened the channel to the agents. "Marks?"

"Yes, sir. Fed Ex. Amazon packages."

"Still not used to Sunday deliveries. Feels weird. Anything happening downstairs I need to know about?"

"No, sir."

"Tyre?"

"We've arrived at the Piety Street entrance to Crescent Park. Quiet out here today."

"Okay. Unless anything crops up, I'm taking a few hours to rest. Alert me if you head back, though. Give me a heads up call at one-thirty. I'll be there at two, if she's still painting. Stevens will come in when I arrive. Tyre, you'll stay out with me. Marks."

"Yes?"

"Alert me if there's anything I need to know about." He needed sleep, but with her journal in his hand, he was wide-awake.

Chapter Fifteen

Gabe

Cursive writing, in black ink, on thick, unlined paper, delivered her points in an understandable, precise manner. Not too flourished. Barely loopy.

Her first entry was dated in the month after her kidnapping, which made it two and a half years earlier. Her words drew him in, becoming a deep hook in his flesh that yanked him into the nightmare from which she hadn't fully awakened.

Once he started reading, he couldn't stop, because he had a close-up, exclusive seat to a horror show. It only took a few page turns to realize that the dread that had emanated from her while in the midst of her night terrors had been relived, time and time again, in her mind.

Dear Journal (Aug. 4) –

I brush my teeth so much my gums bleed. I gargle five times a day. But it's 31 days post-kidnapping, and the sour taste of him lingers every time I swallow.

Will I ever get the foul and disgusting taste of VM's cock out of my mouth?

The police asked me if I was sexually assaulted. I told them, no. They even asked about the teeth marks they'd found on VM's cock when they recovered his body. I told them they weren't mine. I lied.

Can't tell anyone about this.

Did the devil's version of a blow job really last for an hour, or is the length of time my imagination?

Dad's carrying enough guilt. Dammit. I know I need help. Help, though, can only do so much if I don't tell them everything. And I can't do that, because this is already killing Dad. He's aged a decade in a month.

If I told anyone, it would be leaked to the press. Eventually. Former Mardi Gras Queen sexually assaulted, too! Besides, telling others would make it more real, and the burns on my back are real enough.

So many regrets here, but keeping silent isn't one. What I regret more than anything is that I lacked the courage to bite down harder. When VM's hands were holding the back of my head, with my hands and ankles tied together, my mouth wide open on him as I choked and gagged, I should have bitten down so hard, he became angry enough to kill me.

His endless stream of burning cigarettes punished me. I wish he had killed me that night. Dead would be better than this.

Icy dread raced through Gabe's veins.

Could it be she hadn't yet told anyone that the kidnapping had included a sexual assault?

He read again, and again, her words.

Yeah—he'd never respected a boundary in his life. Didn't mean he was stupid. He should stop reading. Now. Instead, he held onto the journal. With the push of one finger on his watch, he redialed Ragno. "Hey. Need your help with something. I just uncovered a fact about the client that didn't make it into the file that you gave me. And this needs to be kept between us. As in, I'm deadly serious, Ragno. Don't stick this in her file."

"Caution bells are clanging, Angel." Sternness crept into Ragno's tone. "Exactly where did you get this fact?"

"Not relevant."

"Always relevant."

"You don't want to know."

"With you, probably true. Zeus is correct about boundaries, you know. One day—"

"Ragno. Not now. I'm worried."

"Tell me what you've got. Perhaps the client file I built for you was incomplete in some way. I don't usually make that kind of mistake, but there's always a first."

Momentarily relieved that Ragno had more data, he asked, "So you know more about her than what you put in my file?"

"Yes. She's a high priority client and her data is sensitive. Only my hands and eyes have touched the entirety of the data we accumulated on her, then I personally determined what went into the agent files. Give me your question, and I'll double check your material with my file."

"Here's my question, and it's a doozy: Did you know she was sexually assaulted during the kidnapping? Did she ever report that fact?"

Ragno's keyboard was silent. "No. I know without looking. She didn't, and hasn't, reported that. Not to anyone. Medical or police. As a matter of fact, when she was interviewed by police, she told them, no. And remember, I've done a Black Raven-style profile on her."

Meaning Ragno had collected data that even the client didn't realize Black Raven had accessed. Black Raven operated under the assumption that a job well done required both knowledge and power.

"That's exactly what happened." Gabe heard Ragno's fingers pecking at the keyboard. "She was sexually assaulted, and she didn't report it."

"Okay. I'm now in her file. She was hospitalized for a few days afterwards. Contemporaneous medical records indicate there was no sign of sexual trauma."

"I know," Gabe said. "I read that in the file. I don't think medical personnel found the signs, and from what I'm reading, she didn't tell them about it."

"What happened?"

He shut his eyes, trying to fight rage. "Forced oral sex. He burned her back with the cigarettes when she didn't cooperate. It lasted for a long—"

"Don't need more." Ragno went quiet for a second. Totally quiet. No words, no keyboard clacking. Only a few deep breaths, as she absorbed the fact.

"Sorry. That was stupid of me. You okay?"

"Yes. It's just that..." Ragno drew a deep breath as her words trailed, "Over the two years that I've monitored her job for Sebastian and Brandon, I've identified with her in some way, you know?"

Yeah. He could fully understand why, and he felt like an ass for reminding Ragno of her own history. "Sorry."

"No need for that. I'm just saying, I get it. I admire her determination to overcome what happened to her." Her voice faded. "At the same time, I hate that she has that to overcome."

"Yeah. Me too."

"And how, exactly, do you know this fact?"

"Journals." He rolled his neck and shrugged his shoulders, trying to loosen the tension that was building.

"Please tell me you're not reading her personal diaries."

He drew in a deep breath. "I am."

"Oh, Gabe. That's the worst sort of privacy invasion."

"I know. I'm damn sorry I started, but I can't unknow what I now know."

"Stop. Now. If she truly has never told another soul, she certainly doesn't want you to know."

"I can't. Have to know more. I'll call you later." As he ended the call, the stark quiet of the attic room settled around him as he read.

Dear Journal (Sept.20) –

Every second, of every day, I'm afraid. Terrified—of noises, of shadows, of people. Nighttime is the worst. I scream in my sleep and I don't know what to do about it. I don't even know when I'm screaming.

My dad and my brothers are insisting I see a psychiatrist. I don't need a shrink. I need for VM to have never touched me.

I had to give up my own house. I'm too scared to be alone. Dad's house has twenty-three rooms. Over fifteen thousand square feet. I've moved into the housekeeper's quarters. I've taken over the small room next to Evelyn's room, where she does her ironing and watches television. It has a Murphy bed. She tells me she doesn't mind my nightmares.

Evelyn's living area is the furthest I can be from Daddy's bedroom. I'm here, because my brothers tell me my screams are horrific. When I awaken, Evelyn is always nearby. I never remember the screams, but I sometimes remember the dreams. My screams while I'm sleeping are killing our father, so my brothers say.

I'd move out, but I'm too scared. I really need help.

I feel like a scared, frightened child. All of the time. Phillip and Stone just don't get it. I want Dad to be strong again. I want him to be his sweet, funny self. But, I can't forget that what happened to me is partially his fault. Dear God, I'm not blaming Dad, but I hate myself, and him.

The reality is I'm not sure I'll ever forgive my father. And I think he knows it. If Dad wasn't alive, I'd kill myself. I know just how I'd do it, too.

Gabe reread the last two sentences. More foreboding twisted his stomach into a hard knot. He wanted to shut his eyes from her suffering and torment, but there was no way he'd stop. Though he knew he should walk out and leave her secrets to her, behind the locked door of the room she'd tried so hard to keep secret, he kept reading. If she had the courage to live and write it, the least he could do was have the courage to read it.

Dear Journal (Oct. 15)—

I haven't left Dad's house in a month. I can't. Haven't slept more than three hours at a time in weeks. I can't. "Friends" are making it worse. They have no clue. If one more friend calls to check on me, then starts telling me what I need to do, I'll scream. "You need" to get out. "You need" to go for a walk. "You need" to eat more. "You need" to get a good night's sleep.

NO! I need to forget. Any idea how? If not, shut the hell up!

Phillip, being the ever-responsible older brother, has called a psychiatrist who makes house calls. I've lost eighteen pounds since the kidnapping. With the taste of VM in my mouth, it's no wonder I have no appetite. Worse, no attention span for anything other than the gory details of what he did to me, which play over, and over, and over again in my mind.

I'll talk to the psych. I'll tell him what I told the police. The doctors. The nurses. Not one fact more. Aren't the rest of the things he did to me bad enough?

Gabe kicked off his shoes and pulled a pillow between his back and the wall. He then picked up the journal again, placed it on his lap, and kept reading.

Dear Journal (Nov. 1) –

Three visits with the psych, and I like him. But I don't trust him with all of my secrets, because he's a friend of my brothers. If I told the psych that I'm now craving death like I used to crave chocolate, he'd have to hospitalize me. At a minimum, there'd be some type of intervention. My dad wouldn't be able to handle it. And I'm freezing. All the time. Doesn't matter what I wear or whether the temperature is really cold. The chill comes from within, and the chill is almost as bad as the urge to scratch my scars. The ever-present coldness makes me think VM reached into me with those soul-less eyes of his and drained all the warmth from my body.

The doctor has a good idea—something to do, rather than a pill to take. Because pills aren't helping me.

I'll start painting and sketching again. I will. I will. I've been an artist all of my life, though I never took my ability seriously. Life was too much fun to do anything seriously.

The doctor thinks painting will force me to focus on things that I can see, rather than things I'm imagining. Or remembering. I did have a knack for it, in my other life.

I'll start slowly. Sketch. Pencils. Paint. A canvas. A paintbrush. I'll start with the view of oak trees in my father's backyard, from the room next to Evelyn's room, now the only room where I feel like I can breathe.

Painting is a solitary endeavor. While painting, I won't have to interact with anyone. That might be the best part of it, because everyone I talk to now looks at me with eyes clouded by what happened to me. They pity me. They tiptoe around me. Yet, they can't stop looking at me. In this small city that's always been my home, I've become a curiosity, for one very wrong reason.

By one o'clock, he was midway through the journal where the entries were dated mid-December, 2014. She was painting, and she was able to leave the house. She usually went out with either Taylor, or her brothers, Phillip and Stone. Destinations? All with her art in mind. A drive to see something she wanted to paint. A walk on a quiet street, or in a quiet park. A place where she could paint for a couple of hours.

There was one place where she would go alone. She'd go to an area she described as *empty*, where *any wharves where work was getting done seemed far away*, where *the levee grass was tall*, and the *buildings of the city rose on the horizon on her right as she faced the river*. She'd visit the *place on the levee where VM had left her for dead.*

Early in the morning, she'd drive herself to the river. She'd go along Tchoupitoulas Street and drive downriver from the Uptown neighborhood where she lived in her father's mansion, through the French Quarter, past the Marigny neighborhood, and beyond. She'd drive to where Cold Storage Road hit the River Road.

Dear Journal (Dec. 20) –

If I just walk into the river, the current will take me. The Mississippi River has some of the most powerful water currents in the world, and I'm not that great a swimmer.

It will be an easy way to die.

I'll wear cowboy boots and heavy clothes and I'm betting it will happen pretty quickly. The murky water will suck me under. In all likelihood, no one will ever find my body. I'll leave a note in Evelyn's evening prayer drawer. By then, it will be too late, but they'll know that I'm gone. It will give them closure.

My brothers will be okay without me. Dad? I can't do it to him. It would kill him.

Gabe knew her father had died that Christmas. He hesitated before reading more, then drew a deep breath and continued. He'd been ten when his father was murdered. The pain over losing him was something Gabe would never forget, and Andi's words told of heartache and longing that reminded him of his own abject grief. He kept reading, though, because of what she'd written earlier. He wondered whether she'd tried to kill herself, once her father's death removed her one obstacle to suicide.

Gabe's watch vibrated as he turned pages. He glanced on the digital readout. Tyre, with his one thirty call. Activating his mic, he said, "Tyre. Details."

"Relatively quiet afternoon, sir. Except Ms. Hutchenson has now decided she is not going to the opening. Asked me to communicate that to you."

"She offer a reason why?"

"No, sir."

"Any idea why she changed her mind?"

"Seriously?" Said with the tone of, *'as in how the hell would I know,'* Gabe let out a breath of exasperation.

"Was there a precipitating phone conversation?"

"No, sir." Dropping his voice to a whisper, he said, "Absolutely nothing I observed. And trust me, I'm being observant. Do you know how many colors she blends to make rusty orange? Well, I do. And there's a parade on the other side of the French Quarter, so this end of the park is quiet, and..."

He tuned out Tyre. Though it was almost time for him to get his ass out the door and to the park, he kept reading. Six months after her kidnapping, a few days into the start of a new year, he found the answer.

Dear Journal (Jan. 5)—

I tried to kill myself this morning.

Obviously, my plan didn't work.

A boy/young man (he's lying about his age) named Pic (not his real name) saved me. I've never met anyone like him. Homeless? A runaway? He won't say.

He has a haunted look in his blue eyes that makes me pause and forget about my own problems. The ages-old, sorrowful, sad, hard, cynical look in Pic's eyes tells me the horror of what he might have experienced parallels my own. And that says one hell of a lot.

My mom used to tell me, before VM, when I was young and the world was perfect, that all I had to do was look a little past my nose and I'd see others who are less fortunate, others who are walking a path that's much harder to bear than my own.

I'd forgotten that pearl of wisdom, until I looked into Pic's eyes, after I tried to kill myself.

Oh dear God, why is this sweet kid living on the streets? Was there no one around to help him? Here I live, in a mansion, with all the help and comfort money can buy.

Yet I tried to kill myself today.

Pic tells me I need to admit it, and move on. I'm so desperate, I'm taking advice from a homeless runaway. Okay–step one. Admit it and move on. So I keep writing it, because I can't believe I'm even alive to write about it.

I tried to kill myself.

I failed, even at that.

So, what's left for me? Not sure, yet. Today I tried to kill myself. I'm still in shock over it. Today I tried to kill myself.

It's a secret that I'll take with me to my grave.

Only Pic—my new friend, who I have to figure out a way to help—will ever know. I'll never tell anyone else. God, I'm ashamed. Ashamed that I allowed VM to almost win. Ashamed that people will pity me even more if they discover how sick I really became. If anyone (other than Pic) knew I tried to kill myself, I'd shrivel up and die. I couldn't live with the shame.

Today I tried to kill myself.

I have to become stronger. Have to be braver. VM almost won. Almost succeeded in killing me. He sure as hell killed the Andi I was. And no one will ever love the 'me' I've become. Because for true love, they'd need to know everything. And telling the whole truth isn't an option.

One thing is certain—I have had enough pity from my own sad, sorry self to last the rest of this lifetime. Pic, thank you. I didn't tell you this today, because I was worried I'd scare you off, but I swear, one day I will get to the root of why your eyes tell me that you've experienced a hell as bad as my own. I'll figure it out, and I'll fix it. I promise.

Pic, thank you. You have given me a reason to live.

Dread shot through Gabe's core, with the focused precision of a bullet hitting its mark. Gabe shut the journal, placed it where he found it, rearranged the pillows, and stood.

Sick to his gut with a premonition that reading her journals had resulted in an inevitable, cliff-hanging dead end, he tried to remind himself of a truism that guided his life.

Everything always works out.

Unfortunately, his mind produced scenarios where things hadn't worked out. His thoughts raced across a finish line, marked by another of his guiding principles. *Help her. She's pushing a burden uphill that's far too heavy for her to carry alone.* But the details of her burden weren't his business, because he shouldn't know anything that was written in the journals.

She's doing better now. Coping. She's brave. Living with her fears, and doing a damn good job of it. Doesn't want or need my help, except for what she's paying me to do.

And I shouldn't forget it.

Shake it off. This is just a job and she's just a client. Yet he wanted this job to work out for the better and right now, he couldn't fight the unease that snaked through him, telling him of impending personal doom. Because the longer he stayed on the job, the more he'd care about her. And the more he cared about her, the more he was lying to her by knowing things that she didn't want a soul to know. Blatant lying wasn't his style. Not on important things.

Yeah, that's me. Honest. One day, I'll have to tell her I read her journals.

He could only imagine her reaction. Exiting the room, he relocked the door, and moved the painting of the cathedral back into position. As he descended the stairs, the nagging foreboding stayed with him.

Dammit. I should've respected her boundaries. Joke's on me, though. As Zeus had told him a million times, *'There will come a time that you overstep and can't fix the damage you've created.'*

Walking down the stairs, Gabe tried to shake off the uneasy feeling with another life-guiding principle. *Embrace the suck*—a Black Raven mantra.

Jobs tended to mirror real life, and, like life, every job had a certain amount of suck. But this job was going to have suction force like none other. He'd inadvertently created this unique, multi-faceted suck by snooping through the pages of her journal after he'd allowed her to get under his skin.

And there was only one thing he could do about it. Accept it. Embrace it. Own it.

He couldn't un-know what he now knew about her. Couldn't undo what he just did. This job's suck was going to pull like none other. All he could do was open his arms wide and embrace it.

Chapter Sixteen

Andi

Backing away from her easel and canvas, Andi studied the greenery and arched footbridge she'd painted, then let her gaze wander through the park. Though Crescent Park attracted fewer people than the French Quarter, plenty of locals frequented the sliver of green space that ran along the river.

Today, though, only an occasional jogger or biker passed the grassy, off-path spot where she'd set up her easel. There were none of the young homeless who so frequently grabbed her attention.

She stood with her back to the river. A wharf positioned at the water's edge, once used for moving ship's cargo, was now wide-open recreational space. Agents Two and Three stood behind her, in her line of vision if she looked over her shoulder. Silent. As they should be.

A biker approached on her right. He wore neon exercise clothes and a helmet. Going fast. Really an exerciser. He stayed on the bike path and showed no indication of veering from it. Not someone who seemed likely to stop anywhere near her. No threat.

The park was downriver from the city, stretching from the Marigny to the Bywater neighborhood. The parade route was a few miles away, on the upriver side of the Quarter. The noise of the afternoon parades was too far away to be heard where she was, and that was fine with her. Parades drew people like magnets drew steel, and the parades that were rolling today had drawn people out of the surrounding neighborhoods, including the park.

The actual day that was Mardi Gras, Fat Tuesday, was nine days away. The streets of the Quarter and surrounding neighborhoods would grow more crowded with revelers as the day approached.

I've gotten better, but I'm not ready to test my limits with that wild crowd.

She shivered. It would all be too much. By the Thursday before Mardi Gras, in just four days, the streets would be choked with people and Andi would have to be inside for the remainder of the season. Thank God the mayhem abruptly ended on Tuesday night at midnight, when Lent began and the city officially started cleaning itself of the evidence of the weeks-long party.

She focused on the entrance to the park, then the sky. Zipping her jacket to ward off the chilly, humid breeze drifting off the river, she pushed her hair out of her eyes and glanced at her palette. Sure, the cobalt blue and titanium white she'd mixed would work, but, as her gaze bounced from palette to sky, she realized it wasn't optimal. The resulting color wouldn't come close to giving the canvas the shimmering brilliance of the sky she was seeing. The hue wouldn't appropriately set off the greenery of the park, or the rusty orange of the footbridge.

Glancing away from the palette and her canvas, she focused on the footbridge. Movement where the rusty-orange, arched structure met the sky caught her attention. Agent Hernandez was on the downward slope, taking the stairs at an easy, long-legged pace. Efficient. Fast.

He'd said two. Was it that late already?

A quick glance at her father's wristwatch confirmed the time. Telling herself she was using her creative eye, she let her gaze follow the agent as he approached. Wearing all black, his windbreaker was zipped enough to cover the gun that she knew was holstered at his waist. He walked the pathway with an athlete's grace. His physique had the harmonious proportions that were found in fine art depicting men who weren't mortal. Sketching him in just about any position would be a pleasure.

Hell. Be honest. He's smoking hot. Back in the day, I wouldn't have wasted one second thinking about sketching him. Only one thing would've come to mind, and woo-hoo. I'm thinking about it now. One. Delicious. Thing.

He gave her a cool hello nod as he passed, continuing along the path on his way to his agents. She bit her lip and tried to keep her face impassive, while a blush burned her neck. Erogenous zones, areas of her body that had once loved to be touched, were tingling with a feeling that had once been familiar and normal. Now, as nerve endings—between her legs, along the back of her neck, at the peaks of her breasts—awakened, the sizzling feeling was foreign.

Hello, lust. I've missed you. I think. Why is it you've decided to make an appearance, after two and a half years, when I'm looking at a man who annoys the hell out of me? No way. Down, girl. Not gonna happen.

Focus on the task at hand. Focus.

The color she'd mixed on her palette had too much cobalt in it. She glanced up again at this afternoon's sky...clear and brilliant. More of the lighter hue of cerulean than cobalt. Squinting her eyes, she studied the horizon. She'd use a bit of cadmium yellow, and perhaps a bit of Naples yellow, to give the horizon that feeling that the earth was rising into the sky.

Okay. I have my road map. I know what to do.

"Stevens. Head back to the townhouse. Let me know when you're there."

The brown-headed agent walked towards the footbridge, presumably following Agent Hernandez's instructions.

Don't listen to him. Aw. Hell. Impossible not to.

Instead of thinking about painting, she listened to the timbre and tone of his voice as he continued talking to the agent who was present, and the other team members who were elsewhere. It had taken her a while to get used to the communication system Black Raven used. The earpiece was so tiny, it was almost invisible, which gave the agents the appearance of talking into thin air. Normally, when they spoke, she didn't hear them and she usually didn't pay attention if she did.

It wasn't a surprise that his voice came through as loudly as if he was shouting, because, as she'd told him the night before, everything about him annoyed the hell out of her.

"If we're going to be here much longer, I'll..."

Damn. Damn. Damn.

None of the other agents broke her concentration. Or made her need to squeeze her legs together to combat the sudden, strong urge for sexual release.

What the hell is my problem? I don't even like him.

Okay. Breathe. Don't fixate. She picked up a tube of blue and almost squeezed some onto her palette, before realizing she'd inadvertently picked up cobalt blue. She was about to make the mistake she was trying to avoid. Not cobalt. She needed cerulean blue.

"Marks? When Stevens arrives, head to the gallery for recon. It's a simple set up. I've talked to Stapleton, and here's the layout..."

Grinding her teeth in annoyance, the urge for sex was forgotten at his mention of the gallery. She squeezed out too much cerulean blue on the palette.

"...a three-man team at the gallery, with one behind at the house. And heads up, Brandon Morrissey will also be at the open—"

Andi spun on her heels. Five feet behind her, Agent Hernandez continued instructing his men. "Hey! Megaphone Mouth. Keep it down. I'm not going to the opening, so—" She lifted a hand and waved it at him. "—do whatever you need to undo the plans you just made."

Dark sunglasses, aviator style, covered his eyes, so she couldn't see the preternaturally happy, at-peace-with-the-world look that she'd come to expect from him. Not seeing his green eyes made everything about him seem off. Even more off was the absence of a smile. There wasn't even a play of an upward tilt at the left corner, where there was usually a twitch that revealed constant inner mirth. Or whatever the hell it was that usually had him so goddamn happy.

Since she'd seen him last, something had handed him a great big dose of seriousness. The effect on him was...chilling.

He spoke, presumably into his mic for the agents. "Proceed as directed. Over."

"Didn't you hear me?"

He nodded. "Of course I did, Honcho—"

"Dammit, would you stop calling me names—"

Finally, the beginning of a smile played at his lips. "Excuuuse me—"

"Oh my God. You're really going to act like a ten-year-old?"

He chuckled. "That, from the woman who just called me Megaphone Mouth? At least I have a reason for getting creative with names for you, since you've prohibited usage of my usual form of addressing a female client—"

She snapped her fingers, cutting him off. "Focus on your job. I said I'm not going to the gallery opening. No one needs to proceed as you just directed them, which I heard, due to your voice being so godawful loud. I don't think you need your mic system to get the message across to anyone, even if they're on Mars."

He folded his arms. "Fine, Ms. Hutchenson. Heard you loud and clear."

Yet he wasn't doing anything about it. Sure as she was breathing, she knew why he felt inaction was warranted. *Hell.*

"Taking a bathroom break." She dropped her palette knife into her pochade box.

"Tyre, I've got this. Stay with her things."

As Andi walked to the footbridge that arched over the levee and led to the park exit, he fell in step with her, walking at her side.

"You're thinking I'll change my mind. Yet again."

"Actually, I was thinking things would be easier if you called me Gabe. And perhaps saying nicely, '*hey Gabe, pipe down. I'm trying to figure out why this painting is coming out flat—*'"

"My painting is fine. Fooling with color is part of the process, Agent Smart-Ass. Don't dodge the question. You think I'll change my mind again, and you don't want to say that, because you know that's going to royally piss me off. Am I right?"

"I'm confused. Are you asking whether you're right about what I'm really thinking right now? Or are you asking about whether I'm worried about pissing you off?"

"What the hell is the difference?"

He chuckled as he glanced sideways at her, then resumed looking forward as they took the first few steps of the footbridge. "Let's just say I'm damn glad you're not a mind reader. Although you may not believe it, there really is a filter between my mouth and my brain. Oh. And about the opening. Yep. I'm preparing for the slim possibility that you'll decide to go. We need to do preliminary work so we're prepared in case you change your mind about changing your mind."

"I won't. So you can stop worrying about it. Having your agents plan for my appearance there is a wasted effort—"

"Look," he said, pausing on the stairs and folding his arms. She stopped with him. The breeze blew hair in her eyes, which she pushed to the side. "I won't tell you how to paint, Kemosabe, and you don't tell me how to do my job. And if you've got that much of a problem with me, that my voice is going to annoy the living shit out of you every time I speak, then..." He shrugged, with a full-on smile. "I could buy you ear plugs, or you can go ahead and fire me."

She gave him a glare and kept walking. She couldn't imagine telling Taylor and Brandon she'd fired their friend from her job because she didn't like his smile, or the way he spoke, or because he seemed to care too much. "I told you last night, this job wasn't going to get better. Everything about you annoys me. I told you to leave."

"You're not looking at a quitter, Ms. Hutchenson. And this job suits me just fine, as it is. And about it getting better, I'm...an optimist." He walked alongside her as she took the last few steps to the top of the arched bridge.

"I was once, as well." Talking to herself as much as to him, the words escaped before she thought twice about them. "Let me be living proof that sometimes, things don't work out. I used to have your kind of smile, Agent Hernandez. Used to beam it out at the world and pull everyone into the illusion of happiness I created with it. What I didn't understand was how fast that kind of happiness can be shattered. I also didn't understand that some people have nothing to smile about. Didn't realize how fast my world could turn into a nightmare, how pathetic I could become, how I'd never return to normal. And before you tell me to stop feeling sorry for myself—"

As the top span of the bridge gave way to a descending flight of stairs, his large body blocked her from taking the first step down. He lifted his sunglasses and pushed them over his hair. Eye level with her, he gave her a serious, searching gaze. "Just so we're clear—because you really aren't a mind reader. You have no idea what I'm thinking. I wasn't going to say that. You understand me?

"I don't think that you're feeling sorry for yourself. To be perfectly honest–I wouldn't even try to judge you. You lived through a terrible ordeal. You're doing more than coping. I think you're brave. Damn brave. God blessed you with unbelievable talent, and you've found a way to let your creativity shine. I think you're being way too hard on yourself."

Shocked into silence by his words and uncharacteristic seriousness, she looked away from him. She glanced at the spectacular view their vantage on top the bridge provided, but her eyes bounced back to him. Fast. He was better to look at. The cool air and gentle river breeze inexplicably carried a bit of the magic that was in his earnest smile and the light in his eyes.

Holy shit, this guy's good.

"Thank you, Agent Delusional."

As he arched an eyebrow, the gleam of inner laughter returned to his eyes. "Fine. Miss Can't-Take-a-Compliment. And don't you think 'Gabe' would have been an easier name to roll off your tongue just now?"

"Agent Gabe?"

"No." He smiled. "Just Gabe."

A mish-mash of annoyance, warmth, desire, and irritation zinged through her as she held his gaze. Deep inside, she wanted to laugh with sudden relief.

Weird. Now I'm really going crazy.

"I really do have to go to the bathroom."

He chuckled, and gestured for her to walk ahead of him. They moved through the parking lot of the park, then waited for a car to pass before walking across Gallier Street.

"Kevin! I'm not..." As an old truck passed in front of them, the cough and splutter of engine noises drowned out the words. "I told you, Kevin! I'm not..." Andi turned her head in the direction of the female voice. At the end of the parking lot, a girl was pacing in the grass, with a cell phone to her ear. "No! No way! You're a..."

There was more than a bit of distress in her voice. Hard to tell what was going on, from this distance. The girl turned to walk the other way and her voice faded. Long brown hair, in a ponytail. Early twenties. Black and white running clothes. Hot pink running shoes. An athletic belt, with a bottle of water tucked into it, at her waist. This wasn't one of the street people Andi had sketched. She had a photographic memory for the invisibles, and this girl didn't look like anyone she'd ever seen. The girl turned in their direction, as a red four-door sedan passed in front of them.

"I don't know..." the girl said, her voice a little calmer. "Maybe."

Andi glanced at the agent. His eyes were also on the young woman, then he turned to her. "Looks like a jogger. Possibly pausing to call her boyfriend with whom she's had a fight. Upset, but she seems to be getting over it. Doesn't look like she needs any help at the moment."

Nodding in agreement, Andi crossed the street. It was disconcerting to be read so well by a man who hadn't known her before yesterday. Even more disconcerting was how much comfort she found in his matter-of-fact, rational assessment. Tone? Not patronizing one bit. It inspired not only reliance, but confidence.

Careful. Don't read too much into him. He's only doing his job. He'll move on soon and leave you exactly as he found you, without a backward glance.

Squaring her shoulders, she drew in a deep breath and re-erected the walls that seemed to be crumbling every time he glanced at her. He paused with her in the wide doorway of the casual, bright restaurant, scanning the Sunday brunchers as she stepped in. She'd been there enough times to feel somewhat safe, knowing there was an exit door beyond the bathroom, knowing that the people who ran the restaurant liked her and valued a safe atmosphere in their well-kept establishment. Still, she paused at the doorway, standing side-by-side with the agent as she likewise scanned the diners.

"People drinking enough mimosas and Bloody Marys in here to float a boat," he said, reporting his observations in a low voice as he scanned the twenty tables that made up the dining room. "Two men at the four-top, in the far left corner. Possibly military. Maybe FBI or DHS. Brunette at the closest four-top with only two people at it? That purse might be concealing a weapon."

Andi glanced at the brown leather purse sitting on the table next to the woman's place setting. "Looks like a purse to me."

"All purses can carry weapons. She's got hers on the table, though, near her right hand, and she's eating with her fork in her right hand. Grillades and grits. Looks good. Most women put their purses on the back of their chairs, or at their feet. We have to assume hers is on the tabletop for a reason." He paused, looked down at her, and gave her a nod. "People are more focused on their food than us. Shrimp and grits look good. I'll have to come back one day when I'm off. As a matter of fact, no one except for those two military men has even glanced in our direction. You're safe."

"The other agents usually just give a nod. Or some other silent signal for me to proceed inside."

That provoked one of his smiles, but with his sunglasses firmly in place, the smile was like seeing a cake, without icing. "We all have our individual style, Boss." Turning to face the restaurant again, he said, "Is that...okra...sticking out of a Bloody Mary?"

"Hey Andi," the bartender called, walking through the kitchen's swinging door to stand behind the long wooden bar.

Thank you, Jesus, for the interruption. Because I was staring at him. Staring. And getting ready to tell him he shouldn't wear sunglasses, because they cover those gorgeous eyes. And that, my dear, is flirting. What, for the love of God, has gotten into me?

Squaring her shoulders again, she reminded herself of the need to be distant.

The bartender asked, "The usual?"

In winter months, the usual was scalding hot coffee, with steamed milk, and plenty of sugar, in a Styrofoam go-cup, with a lid. "Yes. Thank you, Brooke."

Tall and blond, Brooke was one of the restaurant owner's college-age daughters. Her eyes were immediately drawn to the agent at her side.

Slowly dragging her gaze back to Andi, Brooke asked, "An order of praline bacon today?"

"No, but thanks. I already had my daily allotment of bacon." She glanced at the agent. He'd seemingly ignored Brooke's longing glance, and her offer of bacon. The agents didn't typically eat when on duty, so Andi wasn't surprised that he didn't place an order.

He was walking in step with her to the bathroom. "I use the single bathroom, off the hallway—"

"I'm aware. I'll go in first, and check." Which he did, then gave her an *all's clear* nod as he paused in the doorway of the bathroom. "Clean and tidy. And safe. Nice soaps and hand lotion by the sink. I like this place."

"Not relevant, Agent Hernandez."

"What's not?" Deadpan expression on his face, he looked down at her as he slowly exited the bathroom to stand next to her in the narrow hallway. He smelled of a forest after a rain—fresh, and woodsy. There was something undeniably, deliciously male underlying his scent. Just a few inches from her, she felt heat emanating from her body, reaching hers. Beckoning.

In his arms, I wouldn't be cold. Not even chilly.

She shook her head in an effort to shake these nonsensical thoughts from her mind. "Whether you like this place or what vegetables are in the Bloody Marys. Like I said last night—"

"I'm being too present?" Head cocked, he gave her his million-watt smile, as though he enjoyed anything she said, even if it wasn't complimentary.

She drew a deep breath. "Look. Nothing I've said is intended to make you smile—"

"So now I'm not supposed to smile? Because I said I think you're brave? You're going to make me pay for that moment of honesty?"

"If you're not going to quit, perhaps you should just stay in the security room while you're on my job. Out of my eyesight. Like I said, the other agents are better at putting the 'un' in unobtrusive."

She walked into the bathroom. She closed the heavy door hard enough so that it thudded. Scowling at her reflection in the mirror when she saw a flush of pink at her cheeks, she splashed her face with cool water. When she was through in the bathroom, she stepped out, left Brooke a twenty, and grabbed her coffee.

The agent opened the door to the sidewalk, then stepped through it as he held it open for her. As she passed him in the doorway, he said, "Traffic's picking up. Foot traffic and vehicular. The jogger we noticed earlier is still across the street, about a block down."

Normally, when she first stepped outside of a place where she felt safe, sights and sounds assaulted her. To fight off a breath-stealing anxiety attack, she had to process each observation individually, and focus on the reality that nothing bad was happening. With Agent Hernandez's calm voice ticking through her own observations, she didn't have to struggle to keep her anxiety in check as she gathered her bearings on the sidewalk and let the bright sunlight of the afternoon warm her skin.

"Looks like the jogger is still on the phone," he continued, his tone calm. "No issues there. Traffic's coming. Wait till the white SUV passes. Can't believe you said no to praline bacon, by the way. Sounds like a sweet and salty home run. Heads up. On your left, a guy's turning the corner. Hoodie. Moving fast. Towards us. Six paces away. Five. Four. Andi—back! Behind me."

With his right arm, Agent Hernandez gripped her forearm, and pulled Andi between the building and into the shelter of his body. His broad back became as much of a barrier as the blue stucco wall of the restaurant. At the same time, he lifted his left arm to halt the man's forward progress.

She got a partial glimpse as the agent stepped forward to intercept the man. Sunglasses and green hoodie concealed his face. Worn leather jacket. Backpack over one shoulder. Tall. Not as tall as the agent.

As Agent Hernandez shifted to distribute his weight, Andi caught another glimpse of the man. From her new vantage point, she spotted the top of a black guitar case slung behind his back.

Pic!

Chapter Seventeen

Andi

Before she could say anything, the agent slammed his palm dead center on Pic's chest, stopping him in his tracks. "Close enough. Give the lady some breathing room."

"What the fuck! Hands off, asshole." Pic tried to peel the other man's hand off him, but the agent kept him at bay.

"No! Stop!" Andi grabbed Agent Hernandez's arm. A gnat had more of a chance of pushing an elephant. His hard, thick arm had the strength of a steel piling and he had it poised, ready for a forceful push, if needed.

The agent used his other arm as a barricade. "Stay back."

"I know him." She couldn't blame him for holding Pic away. With sunglasses and hoodie concealing his features, there was no way to identify him. "He's my friend, Pic!"

"Andi, call off your guard dog." Backing up, out of reach, Pic stumbled and almost fell before regaining his footing. He shifted his right shoulder, letting his backpack slip to the sidewalk, then pulled his guitar case off his left shoulder and laid it down. Breathing heavily, he spread his feet, bent his knees slightly, lifted his fists and focused on the agent. "Touch me again and I'll break your face."

Andi cringed at the put-on, cocky tone in Pic's voice. Knowing him as she did, she knew the aggression was an act. Hernandez dropped his arm, stepping to the side to allow Pic access. She wanted to hug her friend, but he and Hernandez were posturing, each waiting for the other to make a move.

"Asswipe jerk." Despite his words, Pic shifted his shoulders, relaxing just a hair's breadth out of his on-guard stance.

"Didn't realize you were a friend. Pic, right?" Extending his right hand, he added, "Name's Gabe Hernandez. I'm leading Ms. Hutchenson's security detail."

The agent's outstretched hand may as well have been carrying a steaming pile of shit, because Pic didn't reach for it and his sneer, along with his stiff-shouldered, fists-clenched posture, broadcasted loud and clear that he didn't accept the Agent's not-quite-an-apology. Which seemed to matter not one lick to Hernandez, who continued talking, in his matter-of-fact, everything's-A-okay tone. "You shouldn't come in so fast, especially with your face concealed."

Agent Hernandez dropped his hand, shifting to face Andi. Touching his ear mic, he said, "Tyre. No problem here. Return to position. You good, Chief?"

When she nodded, he added, "If you'll step back, closer to the restaurant, you and your friend can talk there."

Andi followed the directive, as Pic dragged his backpack and guitar case closer. The agent planted himself between Andi and the street, within an arm's length of either of them. While they stood in his line of vision, the direction of his sunglasses suggested his gaze was focused elsewhere, and shifting, as he surveyed their surroundings.

Drawing a deep breath, Pic focused his attention on Andi. "Was heading to the park to find you, rounded the corner, and realized you were right here. I got so excited, I ran to hug you." Pic's voice, usually smooth and deep, sounded hoarse and nasally. He gave her a sheepish smile. "At least this oversized fucker's doing his job."

Since the 'oversized fucker' stood close enough to hear everything they said, Andi was impressed that the agent maintained his jaw-set, stone face.

"I missed you!" She reached for Pic with outstretched arms.

Pic wrapped his arms around her, squeezed hard, and lifted her off the sidewalk. "Pic. Stop! I'm going to spill my coffee..." Agent Hernandez reached for the cup and took it from her before the lid popped off. "Dammit Pic! You can't leave for that long again. Please tell me you're staying a while."

"Yeah." He paused, coughed, then reburied his head against her neck. "Not going anywhere anytime soon. Missed the hell out of you."

"When did you get back?" She held on tight and buried her face in his loose, shoulder-length hair, as she inhaled the essence of strong, industrial-strength soap and shampoo. She'd been around him long enough to know he took full advantage of homeless shelters and the showers they provided.

"Last night." He turned his head, broke from the hug, coughed again, then quickly recovered with a smile. "Had to make good on my promise to my favorite girl to be back in town for Mardi Gras, right?"

She stepped back to assess him. The hoodie of the sweatshirt he wore under his leather jacket had slipped off his head. Sunglasses concealed his eyes. Turning, he covered his face with his elbow and gave in to another deep, chest-wracking cough.

As Pic coughed, Agent Hernandez returned her coffee to her, then stepped back into guard position. For once, Agent Everywhere was being unobtrusive. He didn't even appear focused on them, yet he was close enough for her to reach out and touch. Near enough to hear every word. Closer than the agents normally stood when she had a conversation that was supposed to be private.

Yet another thing that's different about him.

His slight smile and nod in her direction jolted her.

Great. I was staring.

She dragged her attention to Pic, who had finally stopped coughing, and was watching her and the agent look at one another. "That cough sounds godawful."

"Just a cold," Pic said, shrugging it off. "Sounds worse than I feel."

"You sure? Because if you feel anywhere near as bad as that sounds, you need a doctor. Now."

He cleared his throat and nodded. "I feel fine, Andi. Really."

"And what the hell happened to your eye?" Pic, who seemed taller than she remembered, had about five inches on her height of five seven. From her vantage point, she saw a ring of purple under his right eye and a scrape along his cheekbone. His sunglasses almost hid it, but the lenses were a little too small for his face. He'd probably picked them up at a secondhand store for a few dollars, or fished them out of a surplus bin at a shelter.

"It's nothing. Don't worry about it."

"Take off the sunglasses."

He frowned. No movement.

Sipping the coffee helped her keep her tone calm. "If it's nothing, let me see it."

He pulled off the sunglasses, folded them, and slipped them into his back pocket. "See? Nothing."

"Black, blue, swollen, and your cheek's scraped. Looks like something to me." His blue eyes studied hers as she let her gaze crawl over him, looking for other signs of trouble. With smooth skin, cheeks ruddy from the cool outdoor air, and sandy-blond hair, he looked like an advertisement for outdoor clothing. Not new clothes, though. He wore faded jeans. The green hoodie was zipped midway up his chest, revealing a grey t-shirt underneath it. Tennis shoes and the black leather bomber jacket she'd given him last winter completed his outfit.

"Well?" she prodded, taking another sip of coffee so she didn't appear as worried as she felt. "What happened?"

He gave a shoulder roll and a slight headshake. "It isn't worth talking about."

"You have a black eye. It's worth talking about."

As he stood there, silent, Andi drew a deep breath, then gestured with her chin to the guitar case and backpack. His Gibson Les Paul, ensconced in its hard black case, and a lightweight, battery-powered amp designed for portability, neatly tucked into his backpack, were things he'd let her buy him. She knew that all his other possessions, secondary of importance to him, were wrapped around the guitar and its paraphernalia. "Did someone try to rob you?"

He shrugged. "Don't worry about it. I can protect myself."

"I told you to give up your things if someone tries to rob you. I'll buy you a new guitar, or whatever you need."

He shook his head and gave her a slight, rueful smile. "I don't need you to buy me things. I'm not a charity case. I'm doing okay."

"No. A person who lives and sleeps on the streets, moving from one shelter to another—or worse, sleeping outside—is not doing okay. You're going to be hurt, or killed, or...worse. You can't live on the streets for the rest of your life. And how'd you get away with your things last night? If someone was close enough to punch you in the face, God knows what else they could've—"

"Please don't freak out. I don't want to talk about it, anymore. This sort of shit happens all the time. I got away from the two assholes last night—"

"There were two of—"

"—and I'll get away if it happens again. That's all that counts. A black eye is nothing," Pic said, turning his head with another cough, then giving her a smile. "You cut your hair. I like it."

"Thanks," she said. "But don't think your flattery means you're changing the subject."

As Pic stood there, steadfast in his silence, Agent Hernandez said, "Pic." His voice, low and steady, was authoritative. Commanding, as though he damn well expected Pic to pay attention.

Instant animosity sparked from Pic's eyes. A rapid pulse started beating at his temple as he gave the agent a sideways glance. "Yeah?"

"Tell Ms. Hutchenson what happened last night."

Pic's eyes narrowed. "Just 'cause you're on Andi's payroll doesn't mean I can't tell you to fuck off, asshole."

"Pic!" Andi said. Two restaurant patrons had stepped out in time to hear Pic. They glanced at the three of them, then took a right on the sidewalk, walking fast, away.

A flush of pinkish-red color flooded Pic's cheeks, making his irises look a clear, cobalt blue, and the bruising around his eyes even blacker. "Our conversation's private. Did you change security companies? All your other bodyguards knew to keep their fat mouths shut when you're talking to a friend. Knew your conversations are none of their business. What's with this guy?"

"Been wondering that myself," she muttered, while she stared at the purplish bruising around Pic's eye, and her mind raced one hundred and fifty miles an hour with worry. "Security company's the same. Agent Hernandez is new, but he's right on this. I need to know what happened."

Pic, breathing hard, studied her as he studiously ignored the agent, who stood still, studying Pic. With his sunglasses in place, Andi couldn't read Agent Hernandez's expression, but the smile that had a way of appearing so frequently was nowhere in sight. He growled, "Start talking."

Pic kept his shoulders and his body facing Andi, yet his glance was directed at Agent Hernandez. "Have the steroids you've taken to blow up those muscles made you dumb?"

"Pic! What's wrong with you?"

"His job is to protect you." Eyes flashing with anger, he turned to face the agent. "Not question me about anything. And newsflash, big man. Brains go first when you take steroids, then your cock goes second. By the time you're permanently limp, you're too stupid to care. Can. You. Understand. Me?"

Agent Hernandez's chuckle was deep and throaty, with genuine humor. "Really? I understand you perfectly, you little punk. Trying to pick a fight with me doesn't earn you an A for smarts."

"Goddammit, Agent Hernandez! Both of you—stop it. Pic, tell me what the hell happened."

"Sorry, Andi." Pic paid only lip service to the word. His face was beet red, his hands were curled into fists, and he was glaring at Agent Hernandez. "But this guy's out of line."

Pic broke the staring contest first, with a glance at her, then he did a one-shouldered shrug, looked at his feet, and she suddenly got it. Knew why he wasn't saying any more about the black eye. Knew why he'd worn sunglasses, when he didn't typically wear them. Her young friend knew way too much about her. Knew why she'd tried to kill herself, because she'd told him some of the details. Knew why she needed to have men like

Hernandez protecting her. And that's what Pic was trying to do—protect her by not giving details.

Agent Hernandez slid his glasses off, folded them, and put them in his back pocket. With his gaze intently on the younger man, he turned his shoulders slightly, stepping forward a few inches. The agent was taller than Pic, his shoulders were broader, and Andi had no doubt who'd win in a fight, if it came to that.

"Pic, you're one hundred percent correct that my job is to protect Ms. Hutchenson, and that's exactly what I'm doing. Might be hard, but can you be an adult about this?"

"Fuck off."

"Stop acting like a twelve-year old. Ms. Hutchenson's file doesn't state how old you might be, but—" He paused, studying Pic from head to toe. "I'm guessing you're just short of eighteen. Nineteen, at most. Act whatever-the-hell age you might be and tell her what caused your black eye. Clearly, she's already worried. Not divulging details will worry her more. Is that what you want? To give her more stress?"

"If it was important, I'd come clean. It's not." A breeze lifted a clump of Pic's hair. He swiped it off his forehead and pushed it behind an ear, as some of the flush faded from his cheeks. Glancing at Agent Hernandez, Pic shifted his posture by straightening his back. He was imitating the agent's stance, arms at his side, shoulder's square, as he glared into the larger man's face. "If you've studied her file, you know why I'm not giving her details. So, butt out."

"Wish I could. But I can't. Not if I want to do my job the right way." His voice became softer. More conversational. "Come on. You've got to know that if you don't tell her what happened, she'll worry. And you've got to know that worrying about your safety is about the worst thing that can happen to her."

She'd had enough of the testosterone-driven pissing contest, with both of them being overly protective, in their own way. "Stop talking about me like I'm invisible. The agent is right, Pic. Please tell me."

Agent Hernandez gave her a nod, but kept his attention focused on Pic, who kept his attention on the agent. Without glancing at her, Pic said, "He's the one with the problem."

"You've got a skewed perception of problems. But that's irrelevant." The agent softened his expression, "She's the most important person in my world right now and I'm betting she's pretty damn important in yours. I'm guessing you're trying to protect her as much as I am."

Pic glanced at Andi, drew a deep breath, then gave a chest-wracking cough behind his hand. "Stupid cough," he muttered, shaking his head in frustration as he turned his attention back to the agent. "Stick to your muscles and guns. I know her better than you."

"You started the story by showing up with a black eye. If you didn't want her to know what happened, you should've stayed away until it faded."

"Couldn't," he mumbled. He glanced at Andi, with a frown. "I need to ask you something."

Andi's irritation with them was forgotten as a black van passed in the street. Through the front windshield, she saw two men in front, but as it passed, they were concealed by dark-tinted, side windows. About ten yards past them, there was a brief tap on the brake lights, then it continued down the street. It was similar to the van she'd seen on Friday, on Esplanade. As she tore her gaze from it, she saw the agent and Pic were focused on it, as well. After it turned a corner, Agent Hernandez looked in her direction, and gave her a nod and a shrug that echoed her first thought—*It's nothing. There are millions of vehicles like that.'*

But then other thoughts took hold. *That could've been the van I saw on Friday. Hell. The van I think I saw on Friday, on Esplanade, when I saw them—those two men—take that girl. Or when I think I saw that...Damn. Damn. Damn. Breathe.*

"Pic," Agent Hernandez's low, thoughtful voice grounded her as he stared at Pic. "Did you see a van that looked like that last night?"

Okay, so maybe I'm not crazy, if his thoughts went down that path, too.

Chapter Eighteen

Gabe

Of course, Pic ignored the question. No surprise there.

Not giving me an inch. Protecting her as much as I am. But he's wrong on this one.

Gabe could barely tear his eyes from the kid, who had turned pale when the van passed. Clean shaved, clear skin, and blond hair. Tall. At least six feet. Not enough meat on him. Probably still growing. Broad-shouldered. Even with straggly, shoulder-length hair, first glance revealed all-American good looks. If he had weight on him, he'd look like a star on his high-school football team.

But Pic's eyes revealed a suck ass life that had nothing to do with the American version of happiness. Even when the kid was drawing upon anger and spitting out curse words, or smiling with slight bravado when he glanced at Andi, his eyes had an underlying look of weariness and cynicism that didn't fit with a person so young.

Gabe had seen the ages-old, beaten-down, hopeless look before. Mostly, he'd seen it when Black Raven jobs took him to war zones. Poverty-stricken areas of third-world countries. Terrorist strongholds. Places where intelligent people were afraid to travel or conduct business without Black Raven, or one of Black Raven's competitors, watching their backs. In the United States, Gabe had seen the same look in the eyes of victims of horrific crimes. He'd even seen it in Andi's eyes—when she whispered. When she struggled with her memories.

Seeing that dark, hopeless look in Pic's eyes pissed Gabe off. No matter what had started the rolling avalanche of bad shit that had pushed the kid to the streets, Gabe's firm belief was that the greatest country in the world should've had resources that would have provided better options.

"Before you share the details," Gabe said, glancing at Andi, "what do you say we take this inside, Honcho? You've had enough street corner exposure. Plus, it's chilly out here. We can sit at a table for a few minutes, and if anyone's hungry..."

Andi nodded, taking his not-too-subtle hint. *Let's feed this kid.*

"Yes." Andi's eyes telegraphed her gratitude, and Gabe felt a rush of warmth at what—suddenly—felt like an intimate connection. "Inside's better."

"Okay if I tell Agent Tyre to pack your art supplies?" Gabe asked. "He needs to move in closer."

She nodded. As they walked inside the restaurant, Agent Hernandez gave Tyre instructions, slipping into the barely audible tone that he typically used when on the job. So low that someone standing right next to him would have to strain to hear his words, but the mic picked up what he said, amplified it, and made it audible for all the agents on the job.

There were a few empty tables, so they had their choice. He pointed to a four-top, square table, at the corner of the restaurant furthest from the door.

"So..." Andi glanced at him as she walked in step with him, "Your earlier, much louder, running dialogue as I tried to paint. Was it designed to irritate me?"

"Not at all, Chief." *Yes. You're right. I was trying to get your goat. And I did. And I'm screwed. Totally screwed. Because I can't stop wanting your eyes on me.*

He was unable to resist smiling, which prompted a scowl from her. Which made him smile more. He pulled out a chair for her. Pic settled his backpack and guitar against the wall, then took the chair next to Andi. After they ordered food from the waitress, Gabe sat in a chair that provided a view of the entire restaurant. He turned his chair away from the table so his legs had stretching room. He nodded to Pic, who was drinking a soft drink. "Whenever you're ready."

Andi pushed the breadbasket to Pic. "Bread?"

Pic took out a slice, held it, but didn't do anything with it. "Bus got to town around 11:30. I was walking from the station to the levee. It was too late to get in a shelter. The ones I like here close at nine and they're usually full by six, when dinner's served. So, I was going to the old wharf at the edge of the Bywater. Streets were quiet."

Alone. Vulnerable. An easy target as he schlepped everything he owned on his back.

"I saw a black van pass. Same kind as the one that just went past us, I think."

"You notice the plate?" Gabe asked.

"No." Pic slathered butter on a slice of bread, took a bite and chewed. His skin looked clammy. He cleared his throat after he swallowed, as though the bread got a little stuck going down. "As a matter of fact, I didn't think about the van again until that one went by just now, 'cause this blonde in a red convertible came by right after the van. She asked for directions. She was pretty, but drunk. I hate drunks."

"Makes two of us," Gabe said. "What street were you on?"

"When I saw the van and the red convertible, I was on Dauphine. I turned the corner." Pic put the bread down on his bread plate. "I was distracted. And I was almost where I was going." He shrugged, coughed, then chased the cough with a long sip of soft drink before continuing. "I don't know. I felt like shit, so I wasn't focused. I just didn't hear them. Freaky, 'cause normally I know what's going on around me."

"Could've been your cold." Gabe scanned the restaurant. The late-lunch dining crowd was dwindling. As four people stepped out, he glanced out the door. Tyre, now on the sidewalk, gave a no-problem nod. Gabe returned his attention to Pic and leaned forward. "Your ears stopped up?"

"Everything's stopped up," Pic said. "But that's no excuse. I'm better than that. They were almost on me when I heard them."

The waitress deposited a double-order of praline bacon onto the middle of the table. In front of Pic, she placed a bowl of steaming gumbo and a side order of potato salad. Andi had a salad with blackened shrimp. Gabe typically didn't eat when on duty, and particularly not when he had the Raven's view, meaning his eyes were on the client. But his willpower with food was a finite resource, and it rarely included resisting bacon. Gabe reached for a slice of bacon and took a bite, savoring the salty sweetness. He'd underestimated how good it would taste. "You used your knuckles on them?"

Pic's eyes widened with surprise. "How did you know?"

"Fade marks on your jeans pocket. Smart of you. It's a warning. I figured you'd had to use them, since they got close enough to blacken your eye, yet you managed to get away. Meant you put up a good, effective fight." Gabe reached for another piece of bacon and took a bite. "Come on guys, don't make me eat it all."

Andi reached for a slice. Pic did as well, but he took one bite and put it down, next to his forgotten bread. Looking like he was tasting pond scum, the kid turned even paler than he'd been when he started eating the bread. Beads of perspiration were now visible on his forehead.

That does it. He needs a doctor. Antibiotics. Sooner, rather than later. Because this bacon's more addictive than any drug and he should've gobbled down five slices by now. He's probably running a fever. On his way to passing out.

"I already had the knuckles on. Always wear them when I'm on the move that late."

Gabe nodded. "Even smarter."

"My eye's black, but I promise," he said, giving Gabe a slight nod, "his face looks worse."

But now you've got a problem, kid, 'cause the thug you clocked with those knuckles considers you public enemy number one. The next time he finds you, you're not walking away with something as benign as a black eye. And this town's way too small for someone who's got a vendetta not to find somebody with your pretty-boy looks as you tote your guitar through the streets. You got away last night. My money says you won't be so lucky next time.

Gabe most definitely wasn't going to say what he was thinking in front of Andi, and his heart sank as he studied Pic. *Holy hell. This kid's got no business on the streets. He's too...tender.*

Pic's eyes took on an earnest, worried expression, as though there was a lot more that he wanted to tell, while Gabe seriously hoped he didn't spill it all in front of Andi.

Just give her enough details, kid, then shut the hell up. Work with me here.

"One of them had a stun gun. Not a big deal," Pic hastened to add, with a glance at Andi, and another shrug. "I'd rather face down a stun gun than a real gun, any day. But still—it's not what I'd expect the typical shitbag to carry. When I saw it, I hesitated, and that's why he was able to land a punch. They were big and slow, so I managed to punch the crap outta one of them. The other one got distracted 'cause I kicked something out of his hand. He went down on his hands and knees to get it."

"What was it?" Gabe asked, his gaze glued on Pic. *The shrug's his tell. He's either lying when he shrugs, or omitting direct information. Fine by me, because she's heard enough.*

"A gun?" Andi asked, fear palpable in her voice.

Pic glanced from Andi to Gabe, held Gabe's gaze for a long second, then shrugged. "No idea. I didn't see it. The guy went down after it. I bumped into a car, which made the alarm go off. They froze. I ran." Pic shrugged, took a bite out of his gumbo, then laid the spoon back down and pushed the plate away, as though he'd had enough, when he'd barely eaten any of it. He gave Andi a one-shouldered shrug, and attempted a smile. "And that was it. See? Nothing, really."

"You saw where they went?" Gabe asked.

"Hell, no. I grabbed my shit and got the hell out of there."

"Did you hear a car?" Andi asked. "Or see a van again?"

Pic shrugged, then shook his head. "No, but I wasn't listening for one, either."

"Would you recognize them?" Agent Hernandez asked. "If you saw them again?"

"No," Pic shrugged. "They were wearing ski masks."

"Andi," Gabe said. "Any other questions for Pic?"

Lips pursed in a pensive line that was neither a smile nor a frown, her eyes conveyed a boatload of sudden determination.

She shifted her attention back to Pic. "My guesthouse is ready for you. You'll be safe. No more living on the streets. Out of the shelters." Her voice was calm as she fished a key out of the back pocket of her jeans and placed it on the table. She'd put it on an oversized brass safety pin. "Here. You said you'd be back at Mardi Gras. I've been carrying this, hoping I'd see you, for the last two weeks."

Hell. I should've seen this one coming.

Pic eyed the key, and gave Andi a hard headshake. "We've talked about this."

Andi reached across the table and, with her hand shaking a bit, she pressed the key into Pic's hand. "Six months ago. Keep the key. Come on, Pic. What happened last night should help persuade you it's the right move. You don't have to live on the streets. No one can force you to go home, right? You've got to be eighteen by now."

Gabe watched the kid's eyes darken with a flash of...worry? Fear? He gave her another firm *no* headshake. "Not going to move into your guesthouse, Andi."

But the fact that the key remained in Pic's hand, with his fingers curled around it, told Gabe that Pic was considering the idea. The prospect of Pic moving onto Andi's property raised a host of issues from the security prospective, but those concerns took a backseat to worrying about the kid. Because his refusal of Andi's offer didn't add up.

"Look, if it's too much for you to think of it as moving in, just stay there until you get over your cold. Please?"

As she pleaded, Andi's voice took on that whisper-soft quality that torqued Gabe's heart. As though her heart was so full of emotion, some of it spilled over into the very air that carried her words. *If ever, for a second, she makes a request of me with that voice, I'd move heaven and earth to give her anything she wants. I'd give anything. Do anything.*

"There's a comfortable, warm bed," she continued. "It's yours. You can leave in a few days, if you'd like. Or move in permanently. You understand that, don't you? You can come and go as you please. No questions asked."

Pic drew a deep breath. He looked at the key in his hand, as though studying the dull brass finish. He closed his fist around it for a second, then pushed it across the table, back to her. "I can't."

"Tell me why not," Andi said. "I can help—"

"Maybe one day. Not today."

Something's really wrong here, and it's a hell of a lot more than just the obvious.

Pic's quick glance at Gabe told him that the kid wasn't going to say another word about it with him at the table. Gabe stood, stepped a few feet away, hoping to give them the feeling that their conversation was private. Listening to their every word wouldn't be a problem, as long as Andi's voice didn't sink into a softer whisper. It was three o'clock. The late-lunch crowd had cleared out. He turned his back to the bar, placing Pic and Andi solidly in his peripheral vision, though pretending not to look. In reality, he was staring. The key was now on the table, in front of Andi.

"I was just passing this way to say hi," Pic was saying, "and ask you a question for some friends of mine. This morning I went over to the St. Claude Mission for breakfast and a shower. Hooked up with Tank and Honey. They've been working a corner at Chartres and Conti Streets. They say there's a great crowd and asked me to play the guitar for them for the next few days. Monica's been playing for them for the last few months, but she's a little unpredictable. As usual. She's supposed to be there today."

"Ah," Andi said, leaning forward. "Monica. Interesting."

As the waitress left their table with the plates of food that Andi and Pic had barely eaten, Pic frowned. "Monica's pregnant."

"Oh," Andi's expression was a perfect blend of horror and shock, then she quickly recovered back to neutral. "How far along?"

"Hell, Andi. I don't know."

"Is the baby yours?"

"No!"

"You sure?"

"Course, I'm sure."

Poor kid. His face was flushed bright red. Discomfort rolled off him in waves.

"How do you know?"

Come on, Andi. Give the kid some credit. And by the way, he doesn't want to have this conversation with you. And I don't blame him.

"We didn't even have sex. I—" He paused. "—wasn't ready, I guess. I don't know. Anyway, she told Honey and Tank last week. It was some guy she hung with after I left town. But he's gone now. Didn't give a shit that he got her pregnant, and picked up and left town, and she's alone now—"

Red flag. Not ready? At his age, whatever it is. Interesting. Why?

"If you move into my guesthouse, Monica could stay there too. She can't stay on the streets if she's pregnant, Pic—"

"You'd do that? You'd let her stay there?"

"Yes, but only if you're staying there. And I mean it. You have to be living there. Night after night, and working on school. Monica would be welcome, as long as you're there, too."

Gabe bit back a smile. It was a brilliant move on Andi's part. It also raised a host of issues from the Black Raven perspective, but he'd sort through them when and if the time came.

Some of the red flush faded from the kid's cheeks. He looked wary, but also...hopeful. "I'll figure out what's going on with her today. If she shows. She was supposed to work with them yesterday, but she didn't get there, and that's got them worried, though I think it might just be her. She's kinda unpredictable. On the flip side, from what I gathered at the Mission this morning, people are sort of worried. That's why I needed to talk to you. Told them I would."

"About what?"

"Look Andi, you gotta promise me you won't get all freaked out. I wouldn't be bothering you with this, but soon enough, somebody you've sketched would. They all know you're nice. Know you're always on the streets, watching. As a matter of fact, Tank and Honey wanted to be here with me now, but I told them to go ahead and secure the corner. I figured you should get a rational assessment from me rather than the sort of story someone else would tell you, 'cause it's weird shit."

Andi leaned forward, toying with the key with her left hand, her eyes intent on Pic's face. "Spill, and don't sugarcoat it."

"There's talk of people coming up missing. But most of what I'm hearing are stories that are being retold from what somebody else said. Except Banjo Richie is now looking for Jake. You know Richie, right?"

Andi nodded.

"Richie would have been here with me, but he had a parade gig this morning over on Poydras. So, I told him I'd find you and ask you if you've seen a guy that nobody seems to be able to find. You know Jake? He plays a silver harmonica."

"Young kid. Hangs out with Richie. Spends a lot of time on the old wharf in Crescent Park, sort of in that back corner." She was quiet for a second, evidently searching through the catalog of street people in her mind, thinking through things that made Jake distinctive. "His eyes are a lot like yours. Dark blue. Blondish-brown hair. Has a tattoo of a dove in flight on his neck. Right side."

"Jake says he's eighteen, but everybody thinks he's younger."

"I sketched him a couple of weeks ago, in Crescent Park." She swiped her hair back, behind her ear. Otherwise, she seemed calm. But by the way her fingers were trembling, and her voice was dropping, Gabe guessed the air of calm she was projecting was fake. "He was playing his harmonica near the old wharf with Richie."

Pic nodded. "You seen him since?"

"Give me a second." She shut her eyes, thinking. "I did the sketch of Jake with Richie two weeks ago. I sketched Jake by himself the following Thursday, again at Crescent Park. I'm pretty certain I saw Jake last Sunday."

"Where?"

"Armstrong Park. It was relatively early. Maybe eleven. I was walking there to see if it would be quiet enough for me. It wasn't. So I just walked through and left. But I saw him strolling along the pond, near the statue of Louis Armstrong. Jake was playing his harmonica. Last time I saw him was this past Monday, in Crescent Park. Around four thirty in the evening. I was packing up for the evening. He was heading downriver."

"No one saw Jake after this past Wednesday. He was supposed to meet up with Banjo Richie on Thursday evening, and he didn't. And I wouldn't believe any of it, but Richie isn't the only one talking about this. Others are, as well."

"So Jake has been missing since Wednesday?"

Pic leaned into her. "Don't jump to that conclusion. Get that look out of your eyes."

She swallowed. "What look?"

"That scared look. Like really bad shit is happening. Right now."

Gabe let his gaze linger on her face for a couple of seconds. Pic was right. *That look. Like that subhuman devil who tortured you has come back to life. And you're too afraid to move.*

Forcing herself to breathe evenly, she nodded. "I'm fine, Pic."

Come on, kid. Shut the hell up. She's had enough.

"I shouldn't have said anything." He coughed, then gave her a slight smile. "It's probably nothing. For all anybody knows, Jake decided to go home. His real home, wherever that might be. Maybe Jake didn't want to tell anybody he decided to leave. Going home is viewed as a cop-out, you know? Anyway, it's probably urban legend bullshit. Banjo Richie gets stoned. A lot. He could've seen Jake yesterday and not remembered today. You know nine out of ten people who live on the streets are bat-shit crazy, don't you?" Pic gave Andi a full, teasing smile.

Some of the terror slipped from her eyes. "Everyone's a little bit crazy, Pic. Doesn't mean we shouldn't listen—"

"Yeah, but we need to filter out the noise from the music. Let's just say after a few hours at the Mission this morning, my head's swimming with a whole lotta noise. Time for me to make some music and settle into town the right way." He stood, lifting his guitar case and backpack. "Thanks for lunch. See you tomorrow. Really. In Crescent Park? You'll be there?"

She nodded. "Yes."

"Cool. You'll get to tell me all about your opening tonight—"

She gasped. "How'd you know about that?"

He chuckled. "Like I said, I spent a couple of hours at the Mission this morning. Street people know everything going on in the Quarter, so they know about your opening, they know that it's benefitting Hope House, and they know you're my friend, so I got a great big earful. They watch you as much as you watch them. They're pulling for you to be a huge success, almost as much as me. See you tomorrow, Andi?"

She nodded, clearly speechless that he'd known about the opening.

"You gotta say it, Andi."

"See you tomorrow, Pic."

On his way past Gabe, Pic gave him a lingering glance. The corner of his lips lifted in a smirk. Not quite a 'we're friends' smile, but definitely warmer than the sneer that had accompanied their sidewalk conversation.

"Well," Gabe said, sliding into the chair next to her, drawing Andi's attention from Pic's back as he opened the door to the restaurant. "Does that settle the question of whether you're going tonight?"

She gave a quick nod, as though the gallery opening was the least of her problems. Eyes intently on him, with none of the irritation she usually shot in his direction, none of the on-guard filter that was normally there, she asked, "What did you think of Pic? No jokes. Nothing glib. I want your honest assessment."

Gabe reached for the guesthouse key, then slid it across the table, closer to her, and dropped his hands to his side as he thought through things he should tell her from the security perspective. All the reasons why she shouldn't enmesh herself with people like Pic and his friends, like pregnant Monica. He should tell her the type of security check that Black Raven needed to do before Pic and his friend could move into the guesthouse, which opened onto her rear courtyard. But as he looked into her eyes, he couldn't tell her any of those things. One word overshadowed all the rest, minimizing all the bullshit, lame-ass excuses that would keep him on a steady path past need and desperation.

"Heartbreaking." As her eyes welled with tears, his next statement—so goddamn honest and sincere, he couldn't imagine the kind of man he'd be if he didn't feel it in every molecule of his body—tumbled from his mouth. "I have to help him."

Eyes immediately awash with warmth, gratitude, and determination, her focused gaze carried a sudden connection between the two of them that took his breath away. It was as though she was suddenly seeing him for the first time. "You mean that. You totally get it, don't you? You really do."

As she whispered, swiping at her eyes with her fingers, he muted the audio on his comm system by touching his watch. Her heartache over Pic was palpable. He was privileged she was sharing it. It wasn't anyone else's business. "I've dropped the other agents. These mics pick up every word. Other agents don't need to hear this. But yes," he said, leaning forward, both elbows on the table. Close enough to smell her lavender-scented perfume. "I get it. I'll help you help him."

"Thank you," she smiled through her tears, "Gabe."

"Whoa," he said, as his heartbeat accelerated hearing her voice his name. "What did you just say?"

She chuckled, swiped at her eyes again, and leaned a bit towards him. "You earned it."

"Say it one more time."

"Gabe."

"Amazing to hear it from you." *More amazing, though, is the way your eyes look at me when you say it. Steady. Thoughtful. A little more light in there than normal.*

Should I use your first name? Nah—not even going to ask that question. It's much more fun to make up names for you.

"Your name's beautiful. Michael Gabriel Hernandez."

"Mom had a thing for angels."

"Had?"

"She died a few years ago."

"I'm sorry."

"Thanks. It was hard when we lost her. Still is. And I know you know how that feels. Dad died when I was ten." He cleared his throat. Debated whether to tell her what that meant to him. *What the hell? She used my name. By her rules for dealing with agents, that officially means we're now on a different playing field. Right?* "My dad's death was sudden. It tore us all apart. Mom. Zeus, my brother. Me."

"How did he die?"

He had planned to omit that fact. The serious look in her eyes told him not to soft pedal the truth. "He was murdered."

She drew a deep breath. "That's brutal."

"Yeah. But my family situation makes me think about Pic. You see, my brother was sixteen when dad died. Zeus took on the responsibility of being the man of the house. Worked his ass off so I'd have a normal childhood. That's when I learned how important it is to smile, because Mom used to say my smile was often the only thing that brightened her day. Most importantly, Mom and Zeus were there for me—when I got in trouble at school, got caught smoking, got caught drinking, had my first crush on a girl and was too embarrassed to talk about it, when I made the basketball team. You name it. Whenever, and for whatever. My brother—who pushed me to be better—is still my best friend. I thank Zeus almost every day for all the things he did for me. Which gets me back to Pic."

Her eyes turned serious. "Pic didn't have a Zeus to help him when the bad stuff—whatever it was—happened."

Gabe nodded. "Yeah. That's exactly right. And he's obviously not figuring things out on his own."

"I'm going to be real honest here—he's one of the most important people in my life."

And I sure wish you'd tell me why. Because I know Pic saved your life, and it would be damn helpful if you told me that yourself, rather than me knowing because I overstepped and read your journals.

"But I haven't been able to help him," she continued, skipping right over the 'why' of it. "It kills me to see him on the streets. Temperature's dropping to the forties here tonight. That's cold for New Orleans. He might make it into a shelter, but chances are, he won't. And it isn't just tonight. It's the big picture," she continued. "The older he gets, the more the problems compound. He's painting himself into a corner."

"Any idea why he left home in the first place?"

"No. He's never talked about what happened." She shuddered. "I hate to imagine—"

"Don't." He wanted to take her hand, the one that was shaking now as she held onto the key. Yet he didn't. If ever he was going to touch her in a way that had nothing to do with the job for which he was hired, she was going to have to make the first move.

She nodded. "I try not to. Mostly because all the speculation in the world doesn't give me answers. I don't even know his real name."

"I can find out."

She shook her head. "I promised I wouldn't ask questions."

I didn't make that promise.

As he hesitated, she frowned. "Don't."

"He won't know."

"But if you start looking, your searches might alert others as to where he is. He's on the streets for a reason. I don't know the reason, but one thing is dead certain—he doesn't want to be found."

"It can take some doing, but Black Raven has the capability. If I know just a few things about him, I can find out more. And if I can identify the root of the problem, we can work forward from there."

"I'm not sure..." A line appeared between her eyebrows. The line he longed to touch and smooth out, while telling her he'd find a way. "I don't think so."

"Let me think about what I can do." He glanced at his watch, as he considered his options and made a mental checklist of Pic-related things. One of which included finding a way to get eyes on the kid when he made it to the corner of Chartres and Conti, so that Gabe could find him later. "It's three-thirty. What do you say we return to your house? I'll run you through a workout, and then you can get ready for the opening."

She shook her head. “No.” She put the key back in her pocket. “I can work out after the opening. I’ll need the stress release. For the next two hours, I know a couple of places where I might find Banjo Richie. I want to see what he has to say about Jake.”

“Is Jake called Harmonica Jake?”

“No,” Andi said, “I think he’s just called Jake. He’s a cute kid, Gabe. Looks even younger than Pic.”

“You don’t know Jake’s real name, or where he’s from?”

“He wouldn’t tell me, even if I asked.”

“So, Jake’s got a tattoo of a dove on his neck. He roams the streets of the French Quarter playing a harmonica. And he looks even younger than Pic?”

She nodded.

“Well, even if Jake isn’t missing from the streets,” Gabe said, “there’s something wrong with all of this. Because like Pic, Jake is damn well missing from somewhere, and—” He stared at the door through which Pic had just walked out of the restaurant. “—someone should be looking out for these kids.”

Chapter Nineteen

Andi

Sunday, February 14, 6:45 p.m.

God, please let this go by quickly.

A chilly, damp breeze blew along Royal Street as Andi walked towards the gallery. In the distance large Bevolo lanterns, with flickering gas lights, flanked the gallery's doorway. Gabe walked in stride with her, on her right. Not Agent One, Agent-Whatever-the-Hell, or even Agent Hernandez. *Gabe.*

Wearing a black sports coat over a white shirt and black pants, he looked more like a well-heeled date than a security guard. Agent Four, the bald agent, was dressed the same, except his sports coat was navy blue. Weapons were discretely hidden. Their comm devices, for the moment, were pocketed. Though the earpieces were virtually invisible, Andi had requested they not wear them at all. The other two agents were already at the gallery.

Focus on the warm, beckoning flames of the gas lanterns. The same lights that have lit the way along Royal Street, for years.

Earlier, as they'd walked to places where Andi thought they might find Richie, who'd been nowhere in sight, she'd appreciated Gabe's steady presence. His intuitive ability to know what was capturing her attention, what could be cause for alarm. His nearness, his close attention to her, didn't bother her. Nor did it irritate her. It felt...right. If she was honest with herself, having him near her felt more than right.

He's positively irresistible. And I need to...go with it. But I have to remember, it's momentary. Fleeting. He'll be gone soon enough. One thing is certain—I wouldn't be walking down this street, going to my first art opening, without him.

As was the norm on Sunday evenings, Royal Street was closed to vehicles. The street and its wide sidewalks were crowded with people making their way in and out of antique stores, art galleries, restaurants, and bars. A sheen of dampness, the result of heavy humidity, slickened the grayish-green flagstone, making walking through the crowd in heels more treacherous than usual. She was out of high-heel practice, and her Christian Louboutin peep-toe, black suede pumps were brand new and too smooth on their red bottom to have a good grip on the flagstone.

Wistful notes from a violinist, the hired musician for the evening's event, reached the street. She alternated her focus on the gallery doors, only ten yards or so away, and the uneven sidewalk as she pulled her terra cotta colored shoulder wrap closer. With a deep breath, she mentally thanked Taylor, who'd brought the cashmere wrap for her to wear, along with the pumps, the form-fitting, black Donna Karan dress, and the Chanel clutch purse.

Andi hadn't dressed for a night out since before the kidnapping. But putting on the new designer shoes and beautiful cocktail dress didn't make her feel more like her old self. It made her feel like an imposter. Her attire for the night no longer mattered, though, because she couldn't do this.

"You okay?" Gabe's voice was both reassuring and concerned.

She glanced up, into his eyes, where concern matched the twinge of worry in his voice. "Fine."

"You sure?" Just a few inches away, he seemed solid, reliable, expectant. "Because you're not walking."

"Yes. I'm sure."

He cocked his head in the direction of the gallery. "Then shall we continue? Or would you prefer not to do this, after all? Up to you."

Her peep-toe pumps felt like they were made of lead. Though she was willing her feet to move in the direction of the gallery, she couldn't. "I've made a mistake. I have to go ho—"

Her words trailed as he leaned in close, his face just a few inches from hers.

"Lots of noise out here. You're whispering. Can't hear you." The evening's humidity carried his warmth and the aroma of freshly-showered, spicy-soapy scented skin as he turned his ear to her.

When she didn't say anything, he looked at her. Catching a glimpse of something in his eyes as his gaze lingered on her lips, her cheekbones, she was momentarily at a loss.

She'd seen enough slow, lingering gazes in her life to know what they meant. But then again, he was being paid to guard her, and his lingering regard indicated he was trying to do just that. He was anticipating that she was about to turn and bolt, and that's exactly what she felt like doing. She wanted to get her ass out of there, as fast as a jackrabbit in a field overrun with hunters and dogs.

"Decision's yours. We can turn and leave, or we can go in. But," he said, holding her gaze and giving her a slow nod, "you can do this."

She felt her doubts eroding as she stared into his eyes. His gaze had a power that infused her with the strength and optimism he conveyed, dispelling her worries with just a glance, a word, a smile.

She didn't want to have to tell Pic that she'd had an anxiety attack and couldn't attend. "I think I can handle twenty minutes. Tops. No more. If I can just make myself walk there."

"Want me to carry you?"

"Not funny."

"So you say, but you smiled. I saw it. At the idea of me carrying you into the gallery, I saw a tiny smile, at the corners of your—"

"Stop teasing me."

He alternated his gaze between his watch and her eyes, then gave her an encouraging nod. "Think in minute-by-minute increments, starting now. We'll walk in, then step to the left. Brandon and Taylor will be in a receiving line with us. Signal me when you decide to leave, and we're out of there. All you have to do is nod hello to the people who approach. Between Taylor and me, no one will notice if you're not talking. We'll do enough chatting for you—"

"But you don't even know these people."

"In case you haven't noticed, Captain, I received more than my share of the gift of gab. Shall we go in?"

She drew a deep breath and managed to take a step in the direction of the gallery. "I can do this."

"Yes. You can." His full smile carried a million watts of warmth. Enough to enable her to step toward the gallery doors.

One step, two steps, three. *Almost there.*

On her left, the first of the gallery's plate glass windows revealed a crowd. The hum of multiple conversations spilled from the open doorway. The violinist's music stopped for a few seconds, then resumed. There were more people than she'd imagined, even though Taylor had called to report that the gallery was full. Andi paused in mid-stride, trying to collect herself before taking the final few steps.

"There she is," someone said. "What do you know? Taylor said she wo—"

"You sure? She never wore her hair that short. She doesn't look at all like she used to. Poor thing."

Pity, in the whispered words, hit her head-on. She'd mistaken the crowd on the sidewalk for the usual Royal Street tourists. But these people weren't meandering, and their tasteful, conservative yet stylish clothes, weren't clothes of the average tourists. On women, Andi spotted Missoni, Chanel, Lagerfeld, Jimmy Choo, and Louboutin. The men wore slim-cut sports coats. Some wore bright bow ties, a standard among men in Andi's former social circles.

They stood in clusters, holding champagne flutes, wine glasses, and cocktails. Andi drew in a deep breath. Gabe bent to her, his lips near her ear. "You can do this. Walk in."

Her heart jackhammered in her chest. The flight part of fight-or-flight adrenaline started winning. Not that many would notice. Really. Maybe they'd talk, but so-the-hell what? They were already talking about her. Already looking at her like she was pathetic.

Why not really give them something to talk about? Turn. Leave.

"Doesn't look at all like she used to," a male voice said. "Such a tragedy."

"Sh. Not so loud, Tom," a female voice hissed. "Jackie. You sure that's her? She looks so different."

"Of course, I'm sure. We're friends. Or we were friends. Before..." The female voice was familiar. "Andi?"

Turning in the direction of her name, Andi recognized the auburn-haired speaker. Jackie Clements. Wearing black Chanel from head to toe. She'd gotten married two years ago, and had a baby four months earlier. Andi had been invited to events that had marked the occasions. She'd sent gifts, but hadn't attended.

She watched in slow motion as Jackie stepped forward, her arms extended. Others on the sidewalk seemed to step closer, too. Fear turned them into a blur of faces. "Andi! My gosh, honey, you look absolutely wonderful! Congratulations! It's so great..."

Don't touch me. Please. Don't hug—

Gabe stepped slightly in front of Andi. He moved obtrusively enough to stop the friendly hug that Jackie intended, but he wasn't so pushy that he was rude. Reaching forward, he took Jackie's right hand in his. "Gabe Hernandez. It's nice to meet you."

Gabe beamed one of his gorgeous smiles at Jackie, and with every bit of the so-smooth Southern graciousness that Andi had once possessed, Jackie shifted her attention to Gabe.

"Jackie. Jackie Clements. Andi and I made our debut together." She returned his smile. "Hernandez? Are you from Baton Rouge? There's a Hernandez family there. They're a large clan of liquor importers and distributors, with distilleries in Central America."

Jackie's questions were shorthand in New Orleans society-talk for 'where do you come from,' 'what do you do,' 'who is your family,' and 'is your money new or old.' Odd, that the absolute shallowness of the mindset had never struck Andi before. Even odder, that it took being an outsider for her to even recognize that mindset.

Was I like that? Before the kidnapping, did I do that? Oh. Hell. Of course, the answer is, yes.

"No. I'm from Miami. I'm just here tonight to celebrate a wonderful artist and help a great cause. It's nice to meet some of Andi's friends." He glanced at Andi, his eyes lingering, seemingly assessing her panic level, as she stood there, mute. Returning his attention to Jackie, he let go of her hand, then reached for the hand of the woman on Jackie's left. "And you are?"

"Cora Lambertson. Andi and I went to high school together. We were besties, before I went to Ole Miss. It is so nice to see Andi and her art. And really nice to meet you. You said Gabe, right?"

"Yes. And this is Nathan Marks. A friend and collector."

Agent Four, on Andi's left, reached forward and shook the hands of the women.

"We've missed our Andi so, so much—" Cora continued, as an unseen hand squeezed Andi's left shoulder, from behind. Andi jumped, turned, and had to fight the impulse to punch the person who'd dared to touch her. Struggling for composure, she drew a deep breath and kept her arms firmly at her sides.

Boisterous and loud, the man said, "Andi, do you remember me?"

She gave an automatic, faint nod. Pre-kidnapping memories swirled in her mind. She and this man had made the turn together at Galatoire's. Making the turn was a New Orleans tradition of lingering over cocktails after a long, indulgent lunch. When people made the turn, afternoon faded to evening and black-suited waiters re-set the dining table with fresh white cloths for dinner, sparkling crystal, and heavy silverware. Galatoire's had always been happy to feed another meal to the diners who lingered. She'd been a part of the tradition more times than she could count.

And what, exactly, was I going to do with my life?

She remembered sitting across from him and saying, *'Yes, sure, another bottle of Veuve Cliquot.'* Then, with go-cups full of champagne in hand, she and this good-looking man, whose name had escaped her, had moved the party a few blocks away. They'd gone to a balcony room at the Royal Orleans Hotel. Wisps of memories carried soft music, evening light slipping into the well-appointed room through shutters, fine linen bed sheets, and the patter of falling rain.

Yes, now I remember exactly who he is. He'd just recently moved to New Orleans, and was busy buying up real estate. I remember him in bed. At first, he'd been a gentleman, but then—not. I didn't plan on going there twice. That day, shortly before Victor Morrissey brought hell to New Orleans, is one that is best forgotten.

"Martin Blanda," he continued, as Gabe reached forward and shook his hand. Martin glanced at Gabe, then kept talking to Andi. "I'd love to acquire some of your pieces for my new hotel."

"Thank you. Please, talk to Jacques. The Stapleton Gallery represents my art now."

More people, some she recognized, some she didn't, and another person she remembered sleeping with, pressed forward. Blanda's voice faded as someone else said her name. Dear God, she wasn't even inside the gallery, and the crush of people was suffocating her.

Instead of running away, she lifted her right hand and found Gabe's arm. With her left hand, she clasped her purse and her right hand, trying to keep her arms from shaking. Hands occupied, she looked up at Gabe and leaned into the pillar of strength that he alone offered in the sea of swirling faces and words. "Can't."

"We're late. Let's go in, shall we?" he said with ease, ignoring what she'd said. He gave her a slow nod and a gentle smile of encouragement as his eyes searched hers. She nodded slowly, then held onto him with all of her might.

Chapter Twenty

Concierge

As I make my way between milling sycophants and hangers-on, there is a pause in conversation that fills the gallery. The collective energy in the room changes as the artist with the tragic past appears in the gallery's doorway for her first public appearance.

Her blunt dark hair, gleaming in the gallery's mixture of LED spotlights and chandeliers, perfectly frames Andi's beautifully flushed face. Looking slightly fragile and more than a little uncertain, she stands still for a moment and glances up at the tall man who is glued to her side. He gives her a nod, then she looks at the crowd with a hesitant, vulnerable-looking smile that doesn't quite make it to her forest-green eyes.

Taylor Morrissey is at Andi's side in a matter of seconds, and they take position just a few feet from the door. I look through the partygoers to see that Andi's hand remains on Tall-Dark-and-Menacing's arm, just as it was when she paused in the doorway.

Yes—menacing, because I'm not fooled by his smile or his striking good looks. I see the intent way he's sizing up everyone in the room, the way he's positioning himself in a barely disguised, protective stance.

Who is he and what is he to her? I thought she was living the life of a cloistered nun.

Everything about him, the way he leans into her, the way he looks at her, the way he's glued to her side, says *'touch her and you're dead.'*

I have news for him though, and it's a headline: I WILL TOUCH.

People gravitate to her now, just as they did prior to her kidnapping. It isn't simply her beauty or wealth. Or that once deliciously cocky, witty personality. She's now attained fairytale status in this small city that's replete with snobbery. A princess who lived through tragedy and torture. Her fabulous paintings are a tangible counterpoint of rare triumph over the basest of evil. Yet the joyous light that once flooded her eyes isn't there any longer, and that makes her...positively irresistible. I love broken ones. The ones who try, so valiantly, to fight the darkest of demons.

I'm the monster who teaches them to not even try.

I watch her confidence grow as she talks to partygoers. Her chest is mostly hidden under the rust-colored wrap, which makes her eyes even a darker green. I don't have to see the outline of her breasts to know their delicious, full shape. I memorized every inch of her with my eyes, fingers, and mouth. I know her dress cups a perfect, tight ass. I take a swig of vodka while memories of the sweet-salty taste of Andi as her legs fell open for my mouth ignite flames in my body. *Godfuckingdammit, but vodka is a poor substitute.*

I clench my jaw against the mind-twisting pull of desire. She looks my way for a second, but it's like she's looking right through me, without seeing me. As though I don't exist.

How dare she look at me like I'm just another meaningless face in this goddamn crowd of art-aficionado-society-gawkers?

The suck-ass truth is that she was rejecting me before Victor Morrissey kidnapped her. Rejection isn't something I'm used to experiencing. I get everything I want. Everything. Everyone. Every way. Every minute, of every glorious day. My business is an example of how good I am. I conceived it out of thin air, I made the necessary contacts, and I've taken it to a level that was positively unimaginable just a few years ago. I've earned my title. I'm not merely a broker, or a concierge.

I'm THE Concierge.

Reminding myself of what I am makes me feel better, as I smile politely at one partygoer, and nod to another, as camera flashes go off around Andi. The violinist is now playing "It's A Wonderful Life." Yes, it certainly is. Today's transactions with the Butcher have made this day one of my most profitable. My reapers are once again on the streets, prowling.

A potential asset provided trouble with brass knuckles last night I heard. From the bruises, broken teeth, and raw anger he's caused, my money says he'll regret it. As long as they keep the assets coming in, I give my reapers discretion as to how to do their jobs. They're professionals, but they wouldn't be in this line of work if they weren't...like me.

They're not used to serious resistance; they're taking it personally. They'll find him again because we know him. Interesting—he's a friend of Andi's. I know this because the same reapers who work the streets here are also tasked with keeping an eye on Andi, so they recognized him.

I'll use him to my advantage.

Besides, the young man with the brass knuckles sounds like a prime specimen. Blond hair. Blue eyes. A gorgeous man-boy, with all American looks. He'll fetch prime dollars.

As I look at Andi, my broken beauty, I realize it's simple. I want her. I will have her. I'm done with the waiting game I've allowed to play out for thirty one months, one week, and two days since Victor Morrissey stepped in and robbed me of her. Add a few more days to that tally, and that's the amount of time it's been since I was in bed with her, as I laid the framework for future bliss.

My future bliss. My bliss comes with fear. Fear—it fuels my dreams. Fear-I revel in it. Fear-I crave it. I was gaining Andi's trust by giving her pleasure. That I also received pleasure was merely a bonus. I'm typically a master with delayed gratification, and I practiced it with Andi. My real thrills were to come later, but Victor Morrissey forced a detour in my plans.

Not a roadblock. Merely a detour. And really, all he did was prime the pump. Because now, when—not if—I get my hands on her again, she will experience a depth of fear few can imagine.

She and Tall-Dark-and-Menacing are a beautiful couple. He looks at her with hungry eyes. Like he's imagining ways he'll screw her. Her moist cunt? Her tight ass? Her full-lipped mouth? She gives him a look that says...*yes*...any way you want to do me will work.

A threesome, anyone? Goddammit, but I'd love to orchestrate that fuckfest. I'd eat her pussy while watching her suck him.

Thank God I had the foresight to prep my fake Andi. She won't be the real thing. But soon...

Soon. I try to focus on one of Andi's paintings—*Knockin' on Heaven's Door*. A street musician, playing a guitar. Jackson Square. The Cathedral in the background. Blue sky. The painting is great, but I don't give a damn about it.

"I've never noticed the Saint Louis Cathedral from that angle, have you? Someone at my right shoulder is looking at the painting that's next to the one I'm staring at, while I imagine how Andi will taste in my mouth. "It makes me want to see this exact view. I want to be standing...on Chartres Street, where she was standing to paint it. It's as though she was yearning for peace, but unable to get closer to the Cathedral."

Whatever. Yearning. I can tell you about yearning.

Swallowing my irritation with more vodka, I turn to the speaker. She's so close, her shoulder almost touches mine. Graying-blond hair, neatly coiffed in a twist. Tasteful tortoise shell eyeglasses. Staring at the painting as though it will reveal the mysteries of the universe, she sips her champagne.

Fuck off, bitch. I'm thinking and plotting here.

The woman alternates her glance between the wall of paintings and me, assuming I'm at the opening, as most people are, for chitchat about Andi and her spectacular paintings. Or just to get a chance to see the beautiful-society-girl-turned-tragic-recluse.

I get my rocks off by hiding in plain sight. I love it so much that I manage to refocus, as I should, on the party. On being what these people want to see. As the sounds of multiple conversations swirl around us, and violin music—"La Vie En Rose"—lends a wistful air that captures the feeling of Andi's paintings, I mentally place this woman. I know her, but not well. Her family is enmeshed in the fabric of New Orleans's elite society. Her husband, a quiet man, stands on her right and nods hello to me.

I return his nod. "It is a fantastic first show. I'm looking forward to many more."

They move away. I risk a glance at Andi, who isn't looking at me. Instead, she's glancing at Tall-Dark-and-Menacing. For a moment, he stares right at me. His piercing eyes convey a look that I cannot decipher.

He means nothing. Whoever he is, he will not get in my way.

I turn back to Andi's paintings. I stare at her rendition of the St. Louis Cathedral, while I imagine my tongue tracing the scars that Victor Morrissey left on her back. I imagine what those creamy thighs, perky breasts, and yes, even her beautiful, wet cunt will look like when I'm through. My plans for her will make Morrissey's work look like child's play. When she begs for mercy...I know just how to give it to her. My brand of mercy. And I will. Give it to her.

I will.

Chapter Twenty One

Andi

Bright lights, the din of many conversations, and the clashing aromas of expensive perfumes assaulted her as she and Gabe walked into the gallery. The steely strength of his arm kept her moving forward, as they navigated through the crowd. A hush fell. Heads swiveled to watch her progress. Her steps faltered.

In a subtle cloud of gardenia-scented perfume, Taylor, wearing a black Escada woven jacket with a slim-fitting pencil dress, leaned in to kiss her cheek, as Brandon squeezed her shoulder.

Gabe's fingers tightened over hers. He leaned down and whispered, "You're doing great. Almost where we need to be. Minute by minute, remember?"

Taylor eyed Andi's death grip on Gabe's arm. "You're pale. You okay?"

Andi tried for a 'yes' headshake.

Taylor's eyes grew more concerned.

"Step to your left," Gabe said. "Against the wall. We're only six paces from the front door. We can be out of here in no time flat."

Taylor and Andi followed Gabe's instructions.

"I'm fine," Andi managed to say, focusing on Taylor. "Really. Fine."

"Give me your party smile," Taylor said. "It's like riding a bike. You know how to do it."

Andi plastered a smile on her face, the kind she used to use when posing for photos at fundraisers that had bored her to tears.

"Good," Taylor nodded. "Now do it like you mean it."

Andi drew a deep breath, and softened her features, as someone called, "Ms. Hutchenson. Mrs. Morrissey. A photograph?"

Turning in response, as Gabe pivoted to her side, Andi was blinded by a brilliant flash, followed by several more in quick succession as the press and Stapleton's PR photographer gathered together, each calling for a shot.

She spotted Samuel Kincaid, the Director of Hope House, standing to the side of one of the photographers. She waved him over so that he could get in a few photographs. With Kincaid at her side, she tried to smile while changing positions for the cameras, all while hoping she wasn't grimacing. The attention was unwanted now, but she certainly knew how to play the game. Before the kidnapping, she'd been miffed if she'd attended an event and not been one of the featured photographs, on websites and in society pages.

"Andi, it's great to see you," the cameraman from Southern Lifestyles Magazine called, as Jacques Stapleton wedged himself between Taylor and Andi.

"You look gorgeous." He gave Andi a nod, then posed for the cameras. "It's great to see you." Stapleton's steady smile and probing glance made her stomach twist. His glance was her undoing, prompting a flood of memories of the time she'd spent in his bed. Dear God, did I even think about what I did? I gave so much of myself...away.

"Your art just might be my find of the year," he said, before turning to talk to one of the reporters.

With Gabe and Brandon, both tall men, momentarily blocking the partygoers from reaching her, she managed to breathe. As she loosened the death grip she had on Gabe's arm, the smile that he gave her warmed her from the top of her head to the soles of her feet. The comforting heat of his body, pressed along her right side, felt...right.

No. Not right. Incredible, because he's making me forget I'm where I don't want to be.

"You two are doing a great job of looking like you're on a date, by the way," Taylor leaned in, keeping her voice low. "But now, you'll have to offer a few more hello's, because the crowd is moving in. Just look at everyone, imagine them naked—"

"Oh God. Why did you say that? That is part of the problem," Andi interrupted, muttering, "Damn. Did everyone I ever slept with come out tonight? I can't believe I was so...loose. What the hell was I thinking?"

"We talked about this yesterday," Taylor said. "Don't beat yourself up. You were bored, restless, and young—"

"Sounds like I belonged in a mini-series."

"A lot of people in their early twenties do the same thing."

"But I know what plenty of these people *really* look like without clothes, and it's making me ill."

Hearing Gabe's low chuckle, she glanced at him. With her high heels on, her eyes were at his chin level, where it was easy to see the genuine humor in his smile.

"Great," she growled. "Can you at least pretend you're not listening to us?"

"Sure thing, Aphrodite."

Andi pinched under his arm, where most people had an inch or two of soft flesh. Not him.

His smile broadened. "If you intend to hurt me, you'll have to try harder."

Taylor took Andi's clutch out of her left hand. She moved forward to lift the wrap from Andi's shoulders.

"No," Andi said. "I want it on."

"Okay." Taylor handed the clutch to Judith, her party planner and secretary. Judith pressed a drink into Andi's left hand. "The next few minutes will go by in a blur. And one warning—Jacques and Sonja are being persistent about seeing your other paintings ASAP. I've tried to discourage them, but they will press the issue with you."

Crap.

The semi-private group expanded by two, as her brothers, Phillip and Stone stepped into it. They both had dark hair and dark green eyes that matched Andi's. Phillip, two years older than Andi, had premature gray at his temples. Stone, two years younger, had a full head of dark, tousled hair that was the same shade as hers.

"So proud of you, baby sis." Phillip touched her cheek with a quick kiss.

"Makes two of us," Stone said, sipping on a cocktail as he gave Andi an analytical once over. "You look fabulous. Doing okay?"

After she assured them she was fine, they stepped away. With Taylor on her left, and Gabe on her right, time flew by in a blur of faces and nods, smiles, and comments.

"OMG, honey, you look amazing." Sarah Hanes, in sleek black Chanel, blue eyes asking questions she was too couth to voice, smiled a saccharine smile. "Fabulous to see you out. Let's make it a trend. Please come to lunch next week. Stephanie, my oldest, is marrying a Koch. You know—those Koch's. That Harvard tuition is paying off. She met him there. It will be a super show. You're on the list, of course, for all the events."

Momentarily stunned at the woman's lack of tact, Andi could only nod.

Was I ever so shallow that I wouldn't have seen how rude that name dropping was? Yes. I was. Just two and a half years ago.

"Wonderful. Your work is evocative," a tall man with glasses and blue eyes pulled Andi's attention from Maria and Taylor. "I'm Stan Lovett, Director of Contemporary Southern Collections with the Met. I look forward to seeing more of your work. I'm glad I came by. You've got a rare talent."

"Thank you," Andi said, thrilled and flattered.

"Fabulous," a thin woman with long, jet-black hair said. "Your paintings are remarkable. I'd like to interview you. Maybe next week? Tuesday morning? We could do it here, after you replenish the gallery with new work. It would make the cover."

Andi nodded to the woman, whom she didn't recognize, then leaned towards Taylor for clarification as the woman moved on, pausing in front of Gabe.

"New art scene reporter for NOLA Living Magazine," Taylor whispered in her ear. "Wow. She did say the cover, right? Impressive."

Andi whispered, "Not going to do an interview."

"I know. Don't worry about it for now."

"I'm so proud of you," Simon Maissen said, as he parked himself in front of their tight group. With jet black, soulful eyes, and wavy black hair that fell over his forehead, Simon had been her favorite teacher at the art academy. "You've far exceeded my expectations, even though I knew you were talented. You paint with a rare, ethereal magic."

"Yes, and they're all sold, as I knew they would be." With her arm entwined in her husband's arm, Sonja Long and Doctor Walter Long stepped forward.

Urbane and sophisticated, with thick silvery hair, and glasses, Walter was as tall as his wife, who wore high heels that showed off her long legs. With sleek, platinum blond hair, ice-blue eyes, and high cheekbones, Sonja's beauty was stunning and classic.

Simon, squeezed out by the Longs, stepped closer to Taylor. Gabe, on Andi's right, was in a conversation with two women she didn't recognize. They looked perfectly content to stay where they were, gazing into his eyes, and nodding their heads.

"Your art is amazing, Andi," Walter said. "And, if I might add, it is nice to see you looking so well. I'm hopeful your appearance here tonight means we'll be seeing more of you."

Jacques slipped through the crowd to insert himself in their small circle, lifting his champagne glass in a mock toast to Andi. "Every piece is sold. And there's a strong interest in future work. We're compiling a waiting list."

"I'd say a thank you is in order, Jacques. From you, to me. I have an eye for great art. And you, Andi," Sonja said, her glance steady and lingering enough to suggest her mind was on far more than the current moment, "are a great artist."

As Sonja made small talk with Jacques, Dr. Long's frank glance in Andi's eyes made her wonder whether he knew that she'd once been intimate with his wife. It also made her wonder whether Sonja's claim that her husband hadn't cared about his wife's female lovers had been true.

Andi's mind went back one particular afternoon with Sonja. Her tone had become insistent, almost hypnotic, as one of her well-manicured hands had slipped under Andi's blouse. The other had slowly made its way up her thigh. Which meant Andi's brain had been on pause and her body in overdrive, because if there was one thing the old Andi had enjoyed, it was the anticipation that came with good sex.

'Walter's sex drive is dwindling. He's not getting younger and I'm in my prime. As long as his is the only penis in my life, he's fine with what-and-who-ever I do. Come on. It's a harmless way to spend an afternoon. I want you. Don't you want to try me?"

Now, Sonja was so close, Andi could smell her heady perfume. *Shalimar*. The heady, exotic scent brought more sudden, vivid memories. Dim lights. Silky, soft, sweaty skin. Sexual interludes that had been all feminine, but hard-edged. Sonja's avid and demanding mouth. The feel of the woman's supple and lush body sliding along her own. Sonja's full breasts, the nipples forming hard peaks in Andi's mouth.

Sonja's blue eyes shifted to Gabe, whom she gave a lingering glance before refocusing her attention on Andi. "From the moment I saw your painting at Taylor's home, I knew we had to get your work in the public eye. Now the only question is, how fast can you deliver more material to Jacques? Tay's indicated you have more that are ready—"

"Sonja," Taylor interrupted, "I believe I said Andi would decide when to submit additional paintings."

Sonja refocused her attention on Andi. "Well? You do have other pieces available now, don't you?"

Andi tightened her grip on Gabe's arm, and he brushed his fingertips along her fingers. "Tonight's enough for a while."

"Hm. Evasive. You've become a true creative soul," Sonja said. "Tay's told me that you're one hundred percent dedicated to your art and you're devoted to the cause of helping the street people. I love to hear that. All great artists need a backstory. It will make the art world pay more attention."

Sonja's use of Taylor's nickname wasn't lost on Andi. When had they become such good friends? And was there more than just friendship between them? Had Sonja pursued Taylor, like she'd once pursued Andi? There were few secrets between Andi and Taylor, but Andi had never told Taylor that she'd slept with Sonja. For more than one reason, it just seemed like something better off unsaid.

Tay wouldn't go there. Would she? No. Absolutely not.

Sonja glanced at her watch. "This ends at nine. Why don't I go to your studio afterward and take a look at whatever else is ready? Tonight's a perfect time," Sonja added, "while we're together and high on your success."

"That's an excellent idea." With an enthusiastic nod, Jacques added, "I'd particularly like to see some of your sketches of the street people. Taylor told us about them. Really, darling, now isn't the time to be timid. The art world is clamoring for more. I'm here to help you give it to them. Remember—our other galleries will also exhibit your work. My mother just called in from Paris to suggest a New Orleans-to-Paris show. Sister cities, and all that."

"I have the feeling that what's here is merely a delicious appetizer," Simon said, reinserting himself into the conversation. "It's rare that I have a student with such an aptitude. I'm not sure my skill as a teacher did you justice."

"You're too humble. Your lessons are in every canvas I create," Andi said, meaning it, as his dark eyes held her gaze. Despite her lack of a serious work ethic in her pre-kidnapping days, the *en plein air* painting skills Simon taught had become ingrained while she was in his classes. It was those lessons that she'd drawn upon when she returned to painting as a method of coping with the traumatic stress of her kidnapping.

"Hello, Andi," John McCaskey said, as Sonja and Simon drifted away.

Great. I haven't thought about sex for years, and tonight, my past sexual exploits are dancing before my eyes.

John had blue eyes and a killer smile. Tousled waves of blondish-brown hair fell over his forehead. In his early forties, he was good-looking, in a perpetually boyish, carefree way that belied his reputation as a skilled cardiovascular surgeon.

Andi had dated him. Which meant that she'd slept with him. More than once. Not that she'd slept with everyone she'd dated, but there'd been no compelling reason not to sleep with John, who she'd actually liked—out of bed and yes, in bed. In the first few months after the kidnapping, John had called her. He'd left messages. He'd even sent flowers. She'd sent a thank you note for the flowers, but hadn't taken or returned his calls. "Your paintings are spectacular. I'm on Stapleton's waiting list."

"Thank you, John."

"I'm thrilled to see you out. Let's get together soon. Are you free for lunch? Next Wednesday?"

Before she could answer, Gabe extended his right hand to John. "Gabe Hernandez. And you are?"

"Doctor John McCaskey." John shook Gabe's hand.

"Well, John, I don't know how you guys do it in New Orleans, but where I come from, it isn't polite to ask ladies out on a date when they're so obviously on one."

John arched an eyebrow. "Didn't mean to offend. She's certainly capable of saying no if she's not interested. Andi, I'll call you tomorrow to see about Wednesday." He gave Gabe a nod, then walked away.

"Really?" Andi glanced at Gabe.

Gabe gave her a shrug. He leaned in, so that his lips were at her ear, and whispered, so close that his breath felt warm and moist. "Just playing the part, Chief. And by the way, I'm figuring out your tells. You blush. Breathe in longer. Your voice changes when you're talking to someone with whom you have a history. Like that guy. Your voice gets higher—"

She drew in a deep breath, taking in a strong dose of Gabe's delicious, spicy scent. As she looked into Gabe's eyes, caught a glance of his broad shoulders, and squeezed harder on his rock-hard arm, her body clamored for sex. Impossibly, and with an intensity that surprised her. "It does not."

"Tells are subtle. You probably don't even realize you're doing it," he said, his voice low, as a lull in the partygoers gave them a chance to talk. "Plus, you squeeze harder on my arm—"

"Like this?" She moved her fingers to the inside of his arm, squeezed through the fabric of his sports coat and shirt, and gripped a roll of flesh on the underside of his bicep between her index finger and her thumb. She pinched as hard as she could.

He chuckled. "Way more subtle than that. It isn't just you. I'm watching them, too. I'm a paid observer, just doing my job."

"I really didn't sleep with everyone here," she whispered. "You do know that, don't you?"

"Yep. By my count, only seven."

Hah. Off by two. "Not correct."

"Now you're asking for it." With a devilish gleam in his eyes, he whispered, "Martin Blanda. That black-haired guy across from me, wearing a brown sports coat, whose name I didn't catch. John McCaskey. Simon Maissen. Stapleton. Long, and not the male part of that couple."

"Stop!" Mortified, she pinched his arm harder.

"Ouch," he complained, readjusting his arm.

Andi leaned in closer to Gabe and dropped her voice, once again, to the lowest of whispers. "No one knows I had a thing with Sonja. Especially not Taylor."

"I had money on one of the Longs. Took a guess." He chuckled. "Thanks for clearing that up."

His teasing was exactly the kind of thing she would have done...before. Bawdy jokes with friends had been something she'd loved. His enjoyment of her discomfort, and ability to sense that she could handle a joke or two at her own expense, made her so damn grateful that he was treating her like a normal person, she felt like tip-toeing and planting a kiss on his cheek. It was a move the old Andi would have done in a heartbeat.

But I'm not the old Andi any longer.

With that thought, ever-present waves of Victor Morrissey-inspired reality crashed around her with a turbulent force that sucked away her momentary joy. Her thoughts returned to the dark, confined mental space in which she lived. Where the walls pressed in on her. Where anxiety stole her breath. Where living through each minute became an accomplishment.

His smile flat-lined. "You okay?"

"I'm different now. You do understand that, don't you?"

He studied her eyes, her lips, tracing the line of her jaw. In his eyes, concern replaced lightheartedness. "Yes. Understood. Perfectly."

"I'll be ready to leave in ten minutes."

"Got it, Boss." Eyes serious, he added, "Your secrets are safe with me."

"So, are Sonja, Jacques, and I on for a private showing later this evening?" Simon, her former art teacher said as he stepped in front of her again, drawing her focus.

"Of course, we're on," Sonja said, sliding an arm through Simon's. "Why wouldn't we be? Let's move forward while interest is high."

Oh hell. How do I get out of this?

"We have other plans for the evening," Gabe added, covering her hand on his arm with warm fingers that felt a lot more personal and intimate than they should have been. Still, she was grateful that he articulated the need for the pass, because it took the pressure off her. "However, we can certainly adapt our plans, if Andi would prefer to have you all over to her house."

"No," Andi said, adding quickly, "not tonight." *I'd rather die. I'm barely making it here.* A certain amount of graciousness was in order, though, because were it not for Sonja, Andi wouldn't be standing in Stapleton Gallery, and her paintings would probably forever be on the third floor of her home. "But I appreciate that you've all helped me shed light on Hope House."

"If not tonight, then tomorrow." Sonja said.

"Andi, now is not the time to be hesitant," Jacques added as he returned to the group. "You're this gallery's hottest new artist. We can't afford for these walls to be empty. If not tonight, may Sonja and I come to your studio tomorrow?"

She nodded, reluctantly. "Four o'clock?"

Jacques smiled. "Perfect. If your sketches of the homeless people that Taylor told us about have the ethereal qualities of your paintings, they're going to set the art world afire."

Chapter Twenty Two

Gabe

One second they were joking, then she said, '*I'm different now.*' With those three words, everything changed. Her smile disappeared, her eyes became unreadable, and she seemed small in a gallery overloaded with pretentious people. The clash of too many perfumes and booze became cloying. Worse, whether the partygoers were in front of her art, at the bar, or talking to a friend, their eyes lingered on her as though they were watching a curiosity.

When the ten minutes was up, as he leaned towards her to say, *'let's go,'* she glanced at him with a hard to decipher look in her eyes. Sad? Anxious? Whatever. It was unacceptable. "I'm ready."

She'd been silent as he and Tyre walked with her down Royal Street. He'd tried for small talk, to no avail. At eight thirty, they crossed the threshold to her townhome. In the foyer, she slipped off her high heels and hooked them onto a finger. The height adjustment made her seem even more vulnerable.

"Ready for that workout we skipped earlier?"

"No. Thank you." Back straight, head held high, she continued towards the stairs.

Tyre, stepping into the security room, glanced at Gabe. Voice low, Tyre whispered, "A typical dismissal, sir."

No shit. Too bad for her. I'm not a typical agent.

"Just one hour." Gabe called after her as she climbed the stairs, not wanting her night to end on a low note. "It'll be over before you know it."

Come on sweetheart, work with me here.

Halfway up the stairs, her face averted, she kept climbing. "I'm not really up for it."

"We need to build on what we started yesterday." It wasn't quite bullshit. Especially for her, now, as she stood on the second floor landing and looked down at him with an absent-minded glance that seemed to be more focused on the nightmares that played in her brain than anything in the real world. "Daily workouts are the only way to improve on that hesitation thing."

Her pause was so protracted, Gabe figured she was about to give him a resounding no. Again.

"Okay. I'll change."

His profound relief was a sure sign he'd crossed the boundary line into doing things he hadn't been hired to do. But he wouldn't waste time worrying about it. Interacting with her on a personal level, trying to take care of her emotionally, as well as physically, and it mattering so damn much to him that she let him, was just another turn in the path that had been set from the second he'd opened her file.

As he entered the bedroom that he'd claimed on the second floor, Gabe's watch vibrated with an incoming call from Marvin Paquin, a private investigator who frequently worked with Brandon's local law firm.

"Hey Marvin," Gabe said as he answered the call. "I'm going to get Ragno on the line for a conference call. You guys have met before, right?"

"Yep. Via telephone on some of Brandon's more difficult jobs."

Ragno picked up immediately, but asked him to hold for a few seconds. As Gabe waited, he undressed, and pulled workout gear from the dresser where he'd unpacked. The conversation with Pic earlier that afternoon had Gabe's gut telling him he needed eyes on the kid, because serious trouble was brewing. Before leaving the restaurant, a fast bathroom break for Gabe had included a call to Brandon for local assistance. Brandon had suggested placing a hiring call to Marvin Paquin. From what Pic had told Andi, he was heading to the corner of Chartres and Conti Streets to play music on a street corner. Marvin's eyes had been on Pic shortly after Gabe called him.

Throughout the late afternoon and early evening, Gabe had received reports from Marvin. At the last text message, which Gabe had received while at the gallery, Pic was in a line waiting to get into a shelter.

"Okay," Ragno said. "I'm back. How did she do at the opening?"

"Fantastic. You have a few minutes to talk with me and Marvin?"

"Sure thing." Through his earpiece, he heard her clicking on her keyboard. It was an indication of multitasking, which Ragno could do like no one else. After Gabe had talked with Ragno about what he'd discovered in Andi's journals, her concern for the client had spiked. It hadn't abated throughout the day, and Gabe's interaction with Pic, which Gabe had told Ragno about, had Ragno even more interested in the job. She'd told Gabe that she needed to be kept in the loop, and that's what he was doing by including her on the call.

"Hello, Marvin." Ragno's voice slipped into her matter-of-fact tone. "Good to work with you again."

"You, too."

"Did Pic make it into a shelter?" Gabe asked.

"Nope," Marvin said. "He tried two. Going to be in the low forties, upper thirties by morning, as the front comes through. Shelters were full early. Now he's in the Bywater, heading away from St. Claude. On residential streets. No cheap hotels or shelters in the direction he's heading that I know of."

"That's near where he said he got mugged last night," Gabe asked. "Right?"

"Yeah. He's three blocks from there."

"Any idea where he might be going?" Ragno asked.

"Nope. And he's not getting anywhere fast. Hacking up a lung. Every hundred yards or so, he sits on the curb with his head on his knees. I could be two yards from him and he wouldn't notice me. He wouldn't even notice a second-line parade right now. He's too sick. Shivering, for God's sake."

"You're close enough to see that?" Ragno asked.

"With binoculars, yeah. I'm two blocks away, on foot, behind a hedge. He's sitting on a curb, under a streetlight, with his guitar case and backpack on the ground. Arms folded at his stomach. Bent, like he's fighting off a good puke. Oh hell, he's vomiting. Look, I know this neighborhood. It's fighting turf for a few gangs. At any moment, some assholes could give him trouble. If the guy he clocked last night with those knuckles is looking for him now, this kid's good as dead."

"That's why you're there, Marvin. Cover him," Gabe said. "Andi would die if he got seriously hurt."

When Gabe had told Marvin that Pic was a friend of Andi's, Marvin had said that it *'tore Brandon up what his brother did to her.'* And then, he'd said to tell her *'not to worry 'bout her friend'*. At that, Gabe told Marvin that Andi didn't know about the job. He'd explained the kid was skittish, didn't want help, and he'd freak out if he knew he was being tailed. Andi didn't need to know how worried Gabe was that the thugs Pic had fought with the night before had a brass-knuckle inspired vendetta.

Pulling baggier shorts over his impact protection shorts, Gabe asked, "You're okay with keeping eyes on him through the night, assuming he's got nowhere to go that's indoors and safe? I've got two agents on rest. If needed, I could send them out."

"No need for that. I've got reinforcements. Plenty of 'em. Brandon told you about my team?"

Gabe chuckled. “Yeah. Two sons, multiple cousins, and relatives in almost every utility and city agency.”

“Yeah. Sometimes we get resourceful. Pic’s standing. Walking towards the river. My son’s trailing me, three blocks away, in an SUV. I can call in someone else if we need a break. My thinking is, you should let me intercept him. I’ll be diplomatic with him.”

“No. No contact. Give me hourly reports. More frequently if needed,” Gabe said, pulling on a t-shirt.

“Gabe, we’ve got to do something more,” Ragno said.

Gabe thought about the instant fight and wariness in the kid’s eyes. “Not yet.”

“Yo, Gabe. I haven’t worked with you before, but I’m agreeing with Ragno. I’m no softie, but watching this kid hurts. It’s like watching a stray dog, lost in traffic, and not helping. Sure you don’t want me to drop a hundred bucks or so and help him get a room for the night? Hell, he’s so pathetic, I’d take him home.”

Gabe thought about it. Once he figured out the right approach, he’d go the extra mile for Pic. Pic had saved Andi’s life, which was a fact that meant Gabe owed him a big one. But it was a fact Gabe wasn’t supposed to know, because he only knew about Andi’s suicide attempt through reading her journals. The fact that the knowledge was forbidden sure as hell didn’t mean he was going to ignore it.

For now, Marvin’s offer was tempting, but there was no telling how Pic would react. “Nothing yet. Eyes on him, watch his back, and protect if needed. Keep the reports coming.”

By nine p.m., Gabe was in the workout room, dropping two yoga mats to the hardwood floor. Positioning them parallel to each other near the treadmill, he dropped a couple of towels within easy reach.

From the doorway, Andi said, “I’m not sure I’m up for this.”

Heartbeat accelerating by just looking at her, he drank her in. Snug white tank-top. Black micro shorts that barely covered an inch of her thighs. Not much else. Just creamy skin, gentle curves, and big eyes that revealed uncertainty.

Gabe tried not to focus on the sliver of abs that showed between her tank top and her shorts. Or her long, creamy-skinned, lean legs. Her lips carried a hint of the reddish lipstick she’d worn for the party. The makeup she’d worn was almost gone, but she looked even prettier. She had her tennis shoes in one hand, hanging from her index fingers. A pair of socks were balled in her other hand.

"Really not sure about this," she emphasized.

"Doesn't mean you shouldn't do it. Put on your shoes. Tyre?"

"Yes, sir."

"I'm going silent. Yell up the stairs if you need me."

"Will do."

He pulled off his earpiece, but left his watch on. The watch would receive texts. It would also vibrate if Marvin or Ragno called, and he'd then pick up the earpiece. He set the earpiece on the kettlebell shelf as Andi walked to the blue mat, sat down, facing him, and shook out her socks.

The underside of her foot had a delicate arch. He wanted to run his thumb along it, feeling the softness of the ivory white skin. Her ankles were slender. In silence, she slipped on her socks, then put on her running shoes. All the while, seemingly unaware that he couldn't rip his eyes from her.

When she was through, she folded her legs, lotus style. She leaned back on the mat, let her neck and head drop back, placed her palms flat behind her and arched her back for a good stretch. It was impossible not to stare at her breasts, as the tight t-shirt and thin jog bra underneath accentuated the outline. Small-ish. But full. Teardrop shaped. Full on the bottom, the peaks of her nipples sitting high.

She lifted her head, then rolled it in a circle. Glancing up at him, she asked, "Well?"

Stop staring. Asshat.

"Sprint intervals, push-ups, and sit-ups." She extended her legs straight out, hugged them to her chest, then extended them again. She did a few side to side stretches, but when she was finished, her butt was still planted firmly on the mat.

"Get up. You're first on the treadmill." As a matter of self-preservation, he would do drills as she did. Self-preservation, because if he stood there and watched her workout for an hour, after the not-so-subtle air of sexual innuendo at the party, he'd be fully erect in no time. Baggy shorts over compression shorts, which had a built-in cup over his goods, were great for concealing his growing erection. Still, there was only so much the shorts could hide if he went full-fledged hard. She'd see it.

As she stepped on the treadmill, he programmed it to start with a thirty second walk/jog, then pick up speed for a ten-minute run. The whisper-light essence of lavender and rose encircled him as he stood beside the machine.

Okay, now I'm hard. Hell. I should've gotten laid before this job started.

His erection meant trouble, because she had enough going on in that beautiful head of hers without seeing how much she turned him on. Plus, he was working. She was an important client. One who tended to be damned irritable when things didn't go her way.

Sleeping with a client had pitfalls. The obvious one being that it was against the rules. The written rule—Black Raven Rule 1.2(A)(1)—was that professional decorum was to guide client/agent interaction. Meaning—sex with Andi wasn't a company-sanctioned option.

The unwritten rule among the handful of agents who got away with bending rules and crossing boundaries, was that if it did happen, the job damn well better result in client satisfaction. On every job, the client periodically filled out job performance and satisfaction surveys. JPSS for short. It had numerous questions regarding whether the agents had maintained an air of professionalism.

Notably absent from the JPSS survey was whether the agent was good in bed. Orgasms did not count for job performance scores, no matter how astounding they might be. Which meant he had no business thinking about what it would feel like to run his fingers along that slash of skin above the waistband of her shorts, and grip her narrow hips while he kissed her. He'd pull her close, so close...because given what he knew about her, and what he felt for her deep in his gut, their first time would be damn important. Monumental might not be an understatement.

Whoa! Is a first time a foregone conclusion?

Getting on his knees on the second mat, and lifting himself into a palms-flat, toes-down, plank-ready position for push-ups, he prayed that the answer was yes. If only for the sake of his penis.

I'll figure out the rest later. But I damn well can't do anything until I learn the proper way to be intimate with a victim of sexual assault. It's not like I can talk to her about it. Because I'm not supposed to know.

"I can't run this fast," she said, one and a half minutes into her interval.

He glanced up at her. "You did last night. Actually, you ran faster."

"That was last night." She leaned forward to adjust the control panel.

"Do not lower the speed."

She undid the settings he'd fixed, until she reached a slow jog.

"If you're going that slow, at least do it on a higher incline."

She ignored him. On his fifth sit-up, he assessed her. She stared straight ahead, barely breathing heavy, as she went at a fast walk. "That's not going to cut it. It's almost zero exertion for someone in as good a shape as you are. We walked faster on the way home from the gallery, when you were wearing six-inch heels."

"But I'm tired."

"Work with me here. I'm trying to give you a good workout."

Bullshit, because this has nothing to do with exercise and everything to do with getting that flat, dead look out of your eyes.

"Look—" She put the treadmill on pause, and looked down at him. "This was a mistake. I don't have the energy—"

"Sure you do," he said, reaching for his toes, gripping the tips of his running shoes, and pulling his upper body forward so that his chest flattened on his knees and his forehead touched his shins. "Focus. Put your mind on exercise, instead of wherever it is right now."

"Easy for you to say." She restarted the treadmill at a snail's pace, and refocused her attention forward. "Count this as a warm-up."

"What you're doing isn't a warm-up. It's more like a cool-down. Pick up your pace and elevation and get your ass moving."

She ignored him.

This version of Andi, different than any he'd seen before, bothered the hell out of him. Her funk was a heavy, dense fog, obliterating her personality.

But she's here, on the treadmill, trying to work through it. For that, I'll give her a gold star.

"Mental stamina's as important as what we do with our muscles. We're trying to eliminate the hesitation in your sparring. You'll need focus for that. Weakness begins in the mind." He flattened himself on his back, then stretched his arms above his head as much as they could go, and started with a slow sit-up, lifting one vertebrae at a time. He knew from reading her journals that she didn't like pity, so he wasn't going soft on her. "If I have to stand up to fix the settings, the incline I set is going to be pretty damn high. You're going to be flat out running."

She flashed him a look of annoyance, which he took as a solid sign of improvement. "Stop being such a hard ass."

He didn't reply immediately. As he tried to think of a way to jolt her out of her funk, he did another sit-up, another arm pull from his toes, and then flattened himself out on his back again.

Hell. Be direct. She's sick of people soft-shoeing around her. Her journal said as much.

Intentionally stepping out on a very thin limb, he said, "If you want to talk about whatever it was about the party that's hit you like a sucker-punch in the gut, I'm all ears."

She shot him an annoyed look. "I damn well didn't walk in here for a therapy session."

Ah. There's my Andi.

"Couldn't agree more, P.T.B. Besides, last I checked, I'm not a psychiatrist. So, start working out and I'll stop acting like a therapist."

Her brow furrowed. "P.T.B.?"

"Power That Be."

She rolled her eyes. "Andi is shorter. And uses less brainpower."

Yeah, but I'm not supposed to call you by your first name. Your rule, which you pronounced last night. Something about us not being friends.

Averting his head to hide his smile at the undeniable sign of progress, he stood and walked over to the treadmill. As he reached in front of her for the incline button, a beep signaled that her interval was over. "I'm adding four treadmill minutes on the back end, since you just wasted these four. Keep going at this rate and I'll keep adding more time. We'll be here all night. Or, you can just quit right now. Stop wasting your time."

Sparks flew from her eyes at the idea of abandoning the workout. He knew she wasn't a quitter. If she had been, she'd have figured out another goddamn creative way to kill herself and she'd have eventually succeeded.

He glanced at his watch. "It's five after nine. Which is it? Quitting time, or time to start exercising?"

Arms folded, jaw clenched, she said, "I'm not quitting. I'm here to exercise. If anyone is leaving my exercise room, it's you."

"Well, obviously you're not going to do anything worthwhile on the treadmill. So, if you really do feel like working out with any effectiveness, get on the mat. Face down for push-ups. Or, just do whatever the hell you want to for the next hour and see how you feel at the end of it."

"Cocky ass," she said.

"You're one hundred percent right."

Despite her grumbling, she got on the blue mat, face down, and started doing push-ups. He bit back a smile. "Thirty of those, then thirty sit-ups, then repeat the set while I'm on the treadmill. I'll instruct you as I watch your form."

Cranking up the speed on the incline, he counted out her push-ups as he ran. "Five. Six. Seven." When he saw her arms start to shake, when she could barely push herself off the ground, he said, "Drop to your knees or you won't make it to thirty."

Instead, she laid herself flat, face down. Her shoulders started shaking. He heard her sniffle, and realized...*Oh hell!*

He hit the pause button, jumped off the treadmill, and put one knee down on his mat.

"Go. A-a-away." Muffled words, but the meaning was clear as a bell.

Leaning towards her, but giving her enough space so he didn't crowd her, he pulled her towel close to her hands, then rested an elbow on his knee. "Hey. It's okay. You're alright."

"I can't force..." She drew a deep breath and her shoulders shook more. Still face down, she continued, "...myself to do push-ups. I s-s-suck at them on a good day. Oh God. What the hell?!" Sniffle. Sob. "Dammit. I can't stop crying and I don't cry in front of people. Damn. Damn. Damn."

"It's okay," he said, leaning forward so he could hear her whisper. "I could tell you were in a funk. I thought a workout would make you feel better. I'm sor—"

"Don't." She turned her head in his direction, flattening her right ear on the mat. Her gaze found his. "Don't say sorry. Please." More tears welled and dripped out, unchecked. "Normally, I'd have loved for you to coach me through a vigorous workout."

"I was being a hardass, though." *Because I'm turned on, and I'm trying not to be, and trying not to show pity, because I know you hate it.* "Sor—"

"Stop saying you're s-s-sorry. I hate sympathy. It's a c-c-close cousin to pity. I can't stand either of them from other people, because I obviously have enough on my own." A steady stream of tears was flowing. "I should've been able to work out."

"It was an apology. Not sympathy."

She nodded. "But now I have you worried about me being too sensitive to handle what you were dishing out. And you're going to treat me like I am different. And that's what I hate. I should've been able to shake this feeling of...of...oh crap." She gave him a pained glance, then turned her head from him, pulling her towel close, fisting it as she wiped her nose and eyes. "You can go now. I won't be exercising. I need a few minutes to...be alone."

Instead of leaving, he lay down on his mat, flat on his stomach, and turned his head to her. Each sob, each sniffle, wrecked his gut a little more. Thankfully, his erection had subsided, as a solid flood of concern filled his mind.

After a few minutes, she turned to him. "Why are you still here?"

That question, he could answer honestly. "Don't think I've ever walked out on someone who was crying."

"Now would be a good time to start."

"Nah. I'd rather stay, if that's okay with you."

She shrugged. "Suit yourself."

He shifted so that he was in a more comfortable position, lying on his side, his right hand in front of him, propping him up. She shifted and lay on her side, staring at him for a moment, then sniffed. More tears fell. Her cheeks were kissed by a delicious shade of cotton-candy pink that traveled down her neck, to her chest. He wished he had the courage to ask her if she wanted a hug. Or a shoulder to cry on.

To hell with seeking permission. He could just reach for her and see where that took them. But he didn't want to shut her down. So he stayed still, breathing in her soft fragrance of lavender and rose, and using his willpower to keep from reaching for her.

"I didn't realize the party would make me feel so bad. It kind of came at me out of the blue, too, when you and I were joking about sex."

Aw hell. Goddamn idiot. I should've known better. "I didn't mean to make you—"

"No, no," she said, shaking her head, as more tears flooded out of her eyes. "It wasn't you, or what you were saying. Well—" She sniffed. "Maybe it was. But it wasn't your fault. You see?"

"No." He matched her low whisper, with his own soft voice. "Totally confused."

"It's because that's the kind of joking I used to do. Before the kidnapping. I had no hang-ups, not even about sex. Especially not about sex. I'm so different now, and the party reminded me of all the parts of me that are dead. I'd love to be that girl again who loved life so much that she'd try anything. My lack of professional drive might have given me too much time on my hands, but I was having f-f-fun, Gabe. I used to l-l-l-laugh." Tears flowed in earnest. She took a moment to catch her breath. "All the time. I was happy. I used to smile, l-l-like you do."

Aw hell. I've got to touch her.

He reached his hand out and used his index finger to swipe a lock of hair out of her eyes. "This okay?"

She nodded.

Working silken strands through his finger and thumb, he tucked the errant skein behind her ear, then ran his fingertips down her neck, along her collarbone, and down her left arm. Gently, he retraced the imaginary line. It was barely a whisper of a touch. In fact, it was absolutely the lightest touch he'd ever used on a woman, but it electrified him. Electrified her, too, he could see, because goosebumps that pebbled her skin pressed at his fingertips, despite the warmth of the room. He was so goddamn screwed. He knew this moment was going to be frozen in his mind forever.

She met his eyes, with a slight and wobbly smile. "My father. Brandon. Phillip. Stone. Pic."

"Yes?"

"I've just counted on one hand the men who I've consciously allowed to touch me since...." More tears flooded her eyes. "Then."

Hell. She just put me in the category of friends and relatives. Not exactly where I want to be. But still, I'm in a galaxy far away from being Agent Number One.

"Oh God. Why can't I stop crying?"

"Because—"

"Rhetorical, Gabe."

"But it ended with a question mark. I could hear it in your tone." She chuckled, as he traced a line down her forearm, and back up, with whisper-soft touches that fueled another erection. "I've got all night to listen."

With the towel hiding her face, she said, "Do you always say just the right thing?"

He chuckled. "Nah. Sometimes I get it absolutely wrong, *ma'am.*"

At hearing the forbidden word, she laughed out loud. She shifted herself onto her back, then sat up and hugged her knees to her chest. With her movement, he let his hand fall away, reminding himself to take it slowly.

"I've been in mourning for the old me for two and a half years, and tonight was officially the funeral."

He could see that more tears were building. Having nothing to say to make her feel better, he stayed silent.

"Problem is, I don't know what or who I am now. I don't want to be like the old Andi. I was just as shallow as some of those people, and I don't want to be like that again." She glanced at him, her eyes brimming with tears. "But where does that leave me? If I'm not like my old self, what the hell am I supposed to be like?"

"Is that one rhetorical?"

She chuckled, despite herself. "Yes, but if you have an answer, I'm all ears. Do you have any bright, optimistic ideas on how I should fix myself, because trust me, I've gotten lots of advice. Nothing seems to work. I'm tired of overthinking the issue. Overthinking everything. Give me your idea. I'll throw it on the pile of useless advice I've gotten since that asshole kidnapped me."

He shrugged. "From my point of view, there's really nothing to fix. Just try being you for a while. Stop trying to fix anything."

"Being me? Exactly as I am?"

"Yeah. Isn't that who you're being right now? In this exercise room? With me?"

Her eyes welled with more tears, but she nodded.

"Okay, so go with it. Tonight's pretty memorable, right?"

As she nodded again, he gave a slow nod, intended as encouragement. He wiped a tear from her cheek, hoping like hell their conversation would ultimately make her feel better.

"From this point forward, if you're uncertain, go with that. If you're miserable, go with it. If you're scared, happy, bitchy, or—" He paused. "—crying. Overthinking. Whatever. Just be you."

His words prompted her to grab her towel and bury her face in it. She cried hard, with her shoulders shaking, her breath heaving. "Surely someone's told you this?"

She kept her face buried in the towel for a long minute. Long enough for him to worry that his honesty wasn't going to help her. After a while though, she lowered the towel and glanced at him. "If they did, I haven't heard them. Everyone else tells me to stop doing things. Stop worrying. Stop obsessing. Stop thinking about what happened. Lose the anxiety."

He gave her shoulder a gentle squeeze, then rested his hand there, dammit, because he wanted to hold her. Comfort her. "How's that advice working out for you?"

"Obviously not well."

"Then try it my way for a while. Be totally natural. Don't filter anything out. Sort of like you've been with me for the last day and a half. I suspect I've gotten a strong dose of the real you. Be that natural with everyone."

"What if no one likes me?"

"Never going to happen."

She dropped her hands, turned to him, and frowned. She looked pretty, even with a red nose and eyes that were filled with tears. "It could. I'm scared no one's ever going to l-love me, or hell, even like me, if I'm just the 'me' I am now."

Are you kidding me?

"Couldn't possibly be true," he said.

She narrowed her eyes. "How are you so sure?"

Well, buddy, that's a direct question. Answer it. But be careful. Don't scare her.

He reached for the edge of the towel in her hand. Rubbed the terrycloth between his fingers and cleared his throat as he thought through how to start, because he hadn't quite imagined he'd be laying his cards on the table so soon. But in the face of her abject misery, it seemed like the only move to make. With his pulse racing, every molecule in his body became aware that he was experiencing a moment of his life that he was going to remember until he died.

"I think one day, someone's going to see one of your paintings. Like *Knockin' On Heaven's Door*. And he's going to be captivated by it. Immediately. The world's positively going to start swirling around him as he studies it. He's going to wonder how an artist created something so magical and compelling out of paint and canvas, because just looking at it makes him feel the emotions he feels when he hears that song."

Her head was resting on her knees and she was still hugging her legs in close. Instead of crying, her eyes had dried and she was studying him with full attention. "I don't know who purchased that painting."

He stared at her for a long second, then shrugged, as he let the edge of the towel fall from his fingers. "Yeah. You do."

She stopped hugging her legs so tight. He continued talking in the abstract, because it was easier that way and because he could tell by the intense interest in her gorgeous eyes as her gaze fixed on him that she was drinking in every word. "Because he'll see more of your paintings and be positively mesmerized, because he's tried for years, to be creative. And he can't. Just can't do it. He's going to be so amazed by your talent, he'll lose his breath when he sees your art. Then he'll see photos of you, and meet you in person, and he'll know...that the paintings are only the beginning of your magic. Seeing your creativity was only the first wave of the magician's wand for him. The abra before the cadabra."

She gave him a small smile.

"The ball of fire shooting into the sky before the glittering fireworks explode in the night on the Fourth of July." He ached to reach for her, but didn't. "It's going to take him a while to realize what's hit him. A while to realize that what's magical in the paintings...is you."

"A while?" There was a light tease to her voice. More skepticism. "How often do you make up this kind of stuff for women?"

"I'll answer your questions in order. About two days. And never before." He paused. "May I continue? Because I haven't yet made my point."

That earned him a smile.

"All he'll know when he first sees you...is that he needs to know more. With one eyeful of you, as you stand in your mudroom, with sunlight glinting off your hair, with two hundred percent of your attention focused on your paintbrushes, he'll be hooked so hard, there will be just about nothing you can do to persuade that poor guy that he's wrong about you."

The teasing and skepticism faded from her eyes as she listened, her gaze locked on his as he went deeper. "After a few minutes of talking to you, and seeing the 'you' that exists behind those gorgeous eyes of yours, he'll be into you so much that watching you pull exercise socks on your lavender-painted toenails becomes the high point in his day, second only to hearing you voice his name for the first time. He'll want to see if he can make you smile. Want to touch you. To hold you. Want to see what's going to transpire when you embrace the idea of being you. Because his gut is telling him it's going to blow his mind."

The room was silent for a long minute. He watched her breathe. Watched her think about what he'd just said. "That is the most wonderful thing anyone's ever said to me. Thank you."

He chuckled. "And here's my point. The best thing is all of that has nothing to do with the woman you were before your kidnapping, and everything to do with who you are now. See what your post-kidnapping self is capable of inspiring?"

More tears fell, but these were different than the earlier ones. She wasn't sobbing. It was as though his words had delivered the caress of reassurance he had intended. Through her tears, she gave him a soft smile. A real one. Slightly sad, but a smile nonetheless, and it sent his heart rate into the stratosphere. "How could you possibly be so optimistic? So...hopeful. About me?"

"I'm wondering how could I possibly not?"

"I'm too...needy for someone like you to feel like that."

Her words were like distant storm clouds. He drew a breath, glanced deeper into her eyes, and decided he'd weather the storm fine. "I get to decide how I feel and whether I'm interested. Not you."

"But I'll just drag you down with me, and—"

"I decide what is good for me. You focus on being you. Understand?"

She stood quickly, wiped at her eyes with her towel, then looked down at him. "My head isn't quite together, in case you hadn't noticed."

He nodded. "I think your head is more together than you're giving yourself credit for. And no matter how much time you take, it'll be worth the wait."

She walked to the doorway, then turned back to him before leaving the exercise room. "I'm going upstairs to paint for a while."

"Great idea. You get homemade chocolate chip cookies for your efforts this evening. They'll be ready in twenty. You can eat them with reckless abandon, which you'll want to, because I saw the store-bought brand you have in your studio. Trust me. These are better. Tomorrow's workout will be extra rigorous, since you wimped out tonight."

"I thought they have no calories, due to your rule about chocolate and Valentine's Day."

He laughed. "So you paid attention?"

"Of course."

Standing in the center of the doorway, he watched her draw a deep breath. "I'm glad that *Knockin' on Heaven's Door* found a good home. It's abstract, but I was painting Pic. You know that, don't you?"

"Figured as much."

Cocking her head to the side, she asked, "Where are you hanging it?"

"Home."

Her brow furrowed. "I don't know where you live."

"Don't think that matters. Frankly, I think I've just told you everything about me that you'll ever need to know."

She laughed. "Where do you live, Gabe?"

"Right now, home's a condo in Miami. But I'm building a house in Georgia, near one of our training facilities where I teach. It would've been perfect there, hanging above the mantle."

"Would have been?" Luminous eyes studied him.

"Yeah. Don't think I can put into words why that might have changed."

Because I'm going to hang it wherever we are. I first saw you Friday afternoon, when I opened the client file. In the stratosphere I've been living in since I saw you, the hours have amounted to light years. My home will always be with you. Don't ask me how I know this. I just do.

Chapter Twenty Three

Pic

Monday, February 15, 12:05 a.m.

The funny thing about leather was that it was hot as hell to wear in the summer, but when he needed it to be really warm, like fucking now, it didn't do shit to help. Pic wore one pair of jeans, two t-shirts, and he'd even pulled on two sweatshirts under his bomber jacket. He had the hood of one of his sweatshirts pulled up, over his head. The scarf the lady on the bus had given him was wrapped around his neck, covering his mouth and nose. Except for an extra pair of jeans tucked in the bottom of his backpack, with a couple of t-shirts, he was wearing all of his clothes. And he was still freezing.

It had taken his last scrap of energy to climb the levee, walk across the crest, then go about ten paces down. With the berm rising behind him, no one would see him if they drove on the street that paralleled the levee. Once he saw that no one was there, he collected a few rocks. Sitting cross-legged, he ignored moisture that immediately seeped through his jeans and wet his ass.

I'll rest here for a minute or two, then get up.

Clouds concealed the moon in the dark sky. Thick swirls of fog were lifting off the river. A big ship glided by, its foghorn sounding in droning blasts as it made the bend in the river. The temperature seemed to be dropping, but maybe that was just a trick the humidity was playing. Tonight brought the suck-ass reality home that humidity made every temperature feel more extreme.

He had to get somewhere with cover, someplace that wasn't so obvious, because he had no doubt the two assholes from last night were on the lookout for him. A brass-knuckled punch wasn't just a punch and the one he'd thrown was awesome, even if he did say so himself. He'd landed a royal fuck-you-and-your-whore-of-a-mother kind of punch. Not easily forgotten. And that guy whose cheekbone and lip were never going to be the same, looked like the kind that could make him pay for it.

Another five minutes, and I'll get up.

His ears were so stopped up, sounds from the outside world were muted, but on planet misery, where he'd crash landed, a steady whump-a-whump-a-whump pounded in his head. His nose felt like it was being squeezed and pushed out from the inside. Because his teeth felt pressurized, like at any moment he'd be able to spit them out, shivering hurt. Yet he was so fucking cold, he couldn't stop his jaw from moving and his teeth from clacking together. Coughing up the fluorescent green slime that filled his lungs hurt, because now his back hurt, as if someone who knew how to throw fists had used his back for a punching bag.

He knew of a few great hiding spots along the Mississippi River levee, and this wasn't one of them. He was too exposed. There was the hidey-hole that he'd been sleeping in when he saw Andi climb into the water. Maybe someone had covered it in the six months he'd been in Austin, but he doubted it. Also, a little closer in, there was an old abandoned wharf with crawlspace under it. The river level was low enough that the rocky area would be dry. There were also a few spots in Crescent Park, which was about a mile away. But he didn't have the energy to make it to any of those hiding places.

I can't sleep here.

It wasn't a good place to be still. A pair of red eyes approached him, crawling through the winter-short grass. Another pair followed close behind. Pic reached for the pile of rocks he'd collected, and threw one. Using his left hand, because his brass knuckles were on his right, his aim might've been slightly off. It was too dark for him to tell whether he'd made contact. If the rat made a noise, Pic didn't hear it. But the two pairs of red eyes were no longer coming at him, and that was all he gave a damn about. He eyed his pile of rocks. Should've picked up more than ten.

I'll shut my eyes for a minute. Only a minute.

He pulled his switchblade out of his front jeans pocket, closed his left fist around it, and leaned back. Eyes closed, he gave in to the pain and shivering. Gave up being on high alert for rats. His backpack became a rock hard pillow. Turning on his side, he curled into a tight ball by pulling his knees into his chest. The position gave him the illusion of being warmer.

He thought about Monica. She hadn't showed up to play with Tank and Honey, so it was a damn good thing he'd been there, 'cause they made more money when they had a guitar player. Monica hadn't been at either of the two shelters he'd tried to get into. No one knew where she was, but she had a doctor's appointment at the LSU free clinic on Monday at two. According to Honey, Monica wasn't going to miss the appointment, because the clinic gave her meds and vitamins for the baby.

I'll go to the clinic then and talk to her there. Hope she's okay now. Warm.

After a while, he dreamed. His fingers slid along guitar strings. His mom's voice sounded beautiful, as they sang one of her favorite songs. "Iris," by the Goo Goo Dolls. In his dream, he played it so well even his idol, John Rzeznik, the lead guitarist, would've been proud. As a matter of fact, John Rzeznik was there, singing with Pic and Aubrey Rose, nodding his approval.

Something nudged at his back, bringing suck-ass reality home with one dull thump. Opening his eyes, he froze. He was disoriented. Didn't even know if the thump had been real. Decided it wasn't, 'cause that was easier, considering the dream had put him on the couch, in the living room of their doublewide, and he'd been baking an out-of-the-box cake for his mom's birthday. The whole place had smelled like chocolate. Learning the song on his second-hand guitar had been her birthday present. The dream had been more of a memory than a figment of his imagination, because that had all really happened. Well, all of it, except for John Rzeznik being there. That night, the song, and the chocolate cake—those were some of his last good memories before Clarence entered their lives and decided twelve-year-old Pic was the best thing to fuck in West Virginia.

Okay, so I feel like shit. I'll take it all—every single bit of my sorry-ass existence—over Clarence. Or anyone like him.

The amplifier in his backpack was the hardest pillow imaginable. He'd laid his guitar case in front of his face. *Still there.* A ship, with bright lights that made it look like a floating building in the dark night, coasted downriver.

Thump.

His back felt blunt pressure as something bounced off him.

What the fuck!!!

He could jump to his feet from a lying down position in two seconds flat. He'd practiced the defensive move a million times, rising out of a deep sleep and coming up, ready for a fight. But his cold had him hamstringed, and he was slow. He tried to sit up, to turn to face whatever or whoever was messing with him, and stand. Three simple actions he should've been able to do, in rapid-fire succession.

He managed to sit up and turn, but he was slow, because it made him want to puke. As he got to his feet, he dropped the knife that he'd been holding, even in his sleep. He stumbled, moved sideways on the sloping ground, and had to pause for his cold-clogged brain waves to catch up to his spinning head. Heart pounding, the whump-a-whump-a-whump sound of blood rushing in his head picked up its pace.

A large man stood ten feet away, his hands up in the air, a universal sign of peace.

I'm not falling for it.

Darkness concealed the guy's features, but his shadow said huge. Tall. Broad shoulders. Wearing black, but there was enough light for Pic to know that the guy's face wasn't covered.

Pic thought about diving for his knife. One quick glance at the ground told him he didn't know where it had landed in the long grass. "Come any closer and I'll kill you."

"It's Gabe, Pic. I met you this afternoon. With Andi."

"I don't care who you are. One step closer, and you're dead. I mean it." Despite his words, a small measure of relief registered, then it was immediately erased with suspicion. "Is the fact that I met you supposed to make me feel better? What, you came out here in the middle of the night, looking for me? You a homo looking to get laid?"

"Yes. Yes. No." Gabe lowered his hands to his sides.

"Huh?"

"Answers to your questions. First two were pretty obvious, but I guess the most important one is the last one, though I certainly don't know what gave you the impression I'm gay. Not that you can tell by looking at someone."

"Dude! What is with you? Shut the hell up! Turn around," Pic coughed, "and leave."

The asshole had the nerve to chuckle loud enough that Pic could hear it past the pounding in his head.

"But you haven't let me answer your question. Really answer it. In a way you can understand. I came here to help you."

"Yeah. Right. I'm goddamn used to men like you. Bet you thought I'd be happy to blow you for twenty bucks. Thought you'd be able to fuck me for a fifty. I've been offered more help than you can imagine. Help always comes with a steep price. I'm not willing to pay it, so I'll give you the answer I've given to every goddamn queer who comes my way. You ready for it?"

"Actually, you can stop your rant—"

"The only way I'll ever look at your sorry ass cock is when I slice it off and shove it down your goddamn throat. It'll be the most memorable blowjob of your life, 'cause you'll be giving it to yourself. Now turn around and get outta here."

"Now that you've gotten that off your puny chest, I can assure you that you'll never lay eyes on my penis. Stop the lame-ass bullshit and goddamn listen to me." Gabe paused, and before Pic could say anything, the guy continued. "Aw, hell, Ragno, I am being nice. Are you listening to this punk? He threatened to slice my cock off, which is an indication of how thankful he is that I came out here to help him. I should've just knocked his ass out and carried him there. Your idea about self-determination was misguided. He's irrational."

Pic glanced around. He only saw one man. He'd known the agents who Andi had hired were always mic'd. The devices were tiny, but he'd seen them in their ears. What he hadn't known was that the mics were so sensitive, they'd pick up his end of a conversation when he was standing ten feet away from the guy. Yet another great reason to stay far away.

"Who the hell you talking to? An imaginary friend? A fucking fairy friend for a fairy who's scared of the dark?"

Gabe laughed. "Yeah, kid. I'm shaking here, I'm so afraid. You should be so lucky to have a friend like Ragno. Look, I know you feel like crap."

"So why are you here? Never mind. Don't tell me." Pic sniffed, coughed, and bent his knees, putting his hands on his thighs. The crouch was a compromise, because what he suddenly wanted to do more than anything was lay back down and sleep. "Because the answer's no. To whatever. Go the hell away."

"I'm not leaving you here. You're sick, Pic."

"Gee. And you're brilliant, Steroid-man. Glad to see you still have three brain cells left." *Hell. Hell. Hell. How freaking cold is it going to get?* "And by the way, you shouldn't sneak up on people. Could get you killed."

"I didn't sneak up on you. I called your name before approaching. Yelled it a few times, as a matter of fact. You were in such a dead sleep, you didn't hear me. Then I had a dilemma. Walk up to you and nudge you awake, and bear the brunt of your scared-as-shit clumsy moves, or figure out some other way to get your attention."

Pic glanced at Gabe, as the man's words sunk in. He had on gloves and a leather bomber jacket. He didn't look like he was freezing. And his light eyes, even in the darkness, were nice-guy eyes. Luring him in.

Not gonna happen.

"I didn't want to have to knock you on your ass," Gabe continued, "so I decided rock throwing was a great way to get your attention. Know how many rocks I threw that hit your back before you got up?"

Pic ignored him. He reached for his backpack, slung it on his shoulder, and found his knife. He slipped it back into his pocket, then reached for his guitar case. Gripping the handle, he stood and started climbing to the top of the levee.

"Six. Let that sink in. You were so dead to the world, it took six rocks to get you on your feet. Imagine what those guys from last night would've done to you in that time. And I don't think they'd have been offering you cash for anything they'd planned."

Six rocks? No way.

"Fuck you." Pic climbed to the crest of the levee, and paused to catch his breath when he made it to the top where there was a path worn in the grass by joggers and bikers. He had no idea what time it was. Didn't matter, anyway. A van crawled along the street that ran parallel to the levee. It passed under a streetlight.

Two men were in it.

Shit.

For a second, Pic froze. Knowing he needed to run, yet unable to move.

"They're with me," Gabe said, his voice low. Reassuring. "Matter of fact, they've been following you ever since you were on the street corner playing with Tank and Honey."

"No way."

"Yes. Way. You didn't notice them when they were virtually in your shadow the whole time. That's how oblivious you are to the world. They told me you were spending the night outside and that you were looking pretty damn sick. That's why I came out here to take you to Andi's guesthouse. And I'm not lying about how hard it was to wake you. I thought you might've died. I was worried about how I was going to break that news to Andi. Come on. Get in the SUV."

"No." Other than that one SUV, no cars were in sight. The neighborhood streets running perpendicular to the levee were quiet—no cars moving, no people in sight. Pic's legs felt rubbery. He managed one step, heading downriver. Another step. One step more.

Gabe fell into step with him, an arm's length away. "Where the hell are you going?"

"None of your business."

Six rocks? Two men following me? Really? I'm going to get my ass murdered. Or worse.

"You can barely walk, you're so goddamn sick. You're a sitting duck for predators, and you and I both know the guys with the stun gun from last night are looking for you. I'm betting by the time they're through with you, you won't even be able to complain about whatever it is they decide to shove up your ass. You've maybe got twenty more steps before you pass ou—"

"Look, dude—"

"It's my turn to say shut up. Because it's cold and goddamn miserable out here and talking to your sorry ass on this levee in the middle of this night is the last place I want to be. After this afternoon, I was wondering why you've never taken Andi up on her offer to live in her guesthouse. My money's on the fact that you're running from something bad. Something as bad as I could possibly imagine and trust me, I've imagined, and seen, a lot."

Pic stopped walking for a second. Needed a breather. He would've told Gabe to fuck off, but the words got lost in a cough, then another, then he was hunched over, facing Gabe, his back to the river, and coughing like his lungs were coming out of his chest.

"And maybe, just maybe, you did something. Maybe you broke the law, and you don't want to pay the price for it. You know what? I don't give a damn what you're running away from and I don't have any magical answers to fix your life. But if Andi wants me to help you, I will."

Pic managed to stop coughing long enough to say something. "Newsflash, asshole. I'm not looking for help from you!"

Yelling at steroid man came with a steep price. More coughing. He bent over, and tried to get a good cough out, as Gabe muttered some things he couldn't make out, presumably to his imaginary friend. Pic would've paid attention, but he was trying to make his current cough the cough that would end all coughs. But it only brought more out. The green shit that filled his lungs like glue had solidified and wouldn't come up. But it sure hurt his ribs like hell and, with each cough, he felt as though his throat had been sandblasted.

"I know you're not looking for help. But a man has to learn when he needs it, Pic, and right now, you need it as much as anyone I've ever seen. You need meds, and you have to get out of this wet weather. People die from this kind of shit. I bet it's pneumonia, but—" He gave a shrug, and a headshake. "—what do I know? I'm not a doctor."

Pic had walked maybe fifteen yards. He needed a breather. He dropped to his knees. And so did Gabe.

"I'm also betting that the fact that Andi's got security surrounding her 24/7 is one big reason why you haven't accepted her offer. You're afraid of exposure, and someone who's afraid of exposure certainly isn't stepping into the middle of a security ring. Am I right?"

"Okay. You win. You're brilliant," he spat out, as the world started spinning. *Fuck. I'm going to throw up again.* "Now go home and jerk off."

"Nope. Not done yet. Here's where I make a promise to you. I don't care what started the rolling avalanche of bad shit that led you to live on the streets. Whether you did something, or someone else did something. Andi has her reasons for wanting to protect your sorry ass. And I'm damn well going to respect that. So I promise you–wherever your home is–Black Raven will not send you back there."

From his kneeling position, Pic glanced up at Gabe. His vision blurred, and played a trick, 'cause he saw two of the huge guy. *Six rocks?* He thought of the men from the night before.

"I'll go," Pic muttered, as blackness closed in on the edges of his vision. "For tonight."

"There's one caveat," Gabe said, getting down on one knee and snapping his fingers in front of Pic's face. "Listen to me, kid, because it's important. If you do anything that hurts Andi, in any way, I will personally see to it that you regret it." The guy was leaning forward, so it was easy for Pic to see that the nice-guy look was gone from Gabe's eyes. It was replaced with a grimness that promised deep fury. Coming from someone who was so cool, calm, and disarmingly chatty, the sudden shift to hard-ass was shocking. "You understand me?"

Pic nodded and, despite the murky clouds that were building in his brain, he felt a common bond with the guy. "Yeah. Got it. But it's not necessary to threaten me with that. I'd die before I'd hurt her. Before I'd let anyone hurt her."

Some of the lightness returned to Gabe's eyes. "Glad you feel that way."

Gabe nodded, stood, and extended a hand.

Pic tried to stand without Gabe's help, but the weight of his backpack and the guitar was suddenly too much. He let Gabe help him up, then let him take the guitar as they headed down the levee, to the waiting SUV.

"I was listening to the story that you told Andi about last night. I got the sense you were holding something back. Something worse than the version you gave her. And I know that's the real reason you're agreeing to go with me right now. Am I right?"

"Yeah," Pic mumbled, too worn down to argue.

"Well? What was it?"

The gentle downward slope of the levee suddenly seemed like an insurmountable obstacle. He didn't have one more step in him. He could barely put one foot in front of the other, because his knees weren't holding up his legs. Or his body. And Pic wanted to tell Gabe, because it was scary as shit. Scarier than a gun. Scarier than...anything. "A syringe. Dude had a syringe."

"You sure?"

"Positive. Once I saw that syringe in his hand, I knew I was fucked. But a car alarm went off, and they stopped moving on me. It gave me a chance to get away. They hesitated when the alarm went off, and I didn't stick around. I ran, and I guess they did too. I know they weren't after my things, because I left them all on the ground. I went back after a few minutes, hoping they'd at least have left my duffel. I was shocked as shit to find my guitar there, and my duffel, right where I'd left the stuff. The syringe tells me they wanted me."

Pic shut his eyes, and as the earth reached up to swallow him, he felt strong arms close around him, keeping him from hitting the ground. For the first time in years, Pic felt safe.

Chapter Twenty Four

Andi

Orange and blue flames licked the edges of the paper before jet black-rimmed holes appeared, then spread. Andi had been sitting cross-legged in front of the library's fireplace for almost an hour. Despite the fire's heat, her warm sweatshirt, and thick leggings, she was cold.

It was after midnight. Outside, the temperature was making a newsworthy plummet. Last she checked, it was thirty-eight degrees. Positively frigid for New Orleans at any time during the winter, and especially so in February.

But that wasn't the reason her internal thermometer was nosediving. Her deep inner chill was due to Victor Morrissey and his gift from hell that kept on giving.

The burning log's crackles and pops sounded loud in the otherwise quiet house. It shouldn't have taken so long to finish the task, but watching flames eat her words had become hypnotic.

The despair that had inspired her words was far better as a memory than a current feeling. With each fresh stack of pages that she placed in the fire, her gaze caught phrases before they were incinerated.

'I can't get the sour taste of him out of my mouth.'

'A blowjob for a devil.'

'I have no hope.'

'I'm going to kill myself. With Dad gone, there's no reason not to.'

'Pic says, See You Tomorrow. And I say, 'Yes'. Though I don't mean it.'

As her eyes absorbed that last line, she breathed deeply, smiling as she savored the crisp, comforting essence of burning pine logs. Because now she meant it.

Please God, keep Pic warm and safe tonight.

Tearing her attention from the burning words, Andi reached for a fresh stack of pages. She placed the stack in the fire, then put a fresh log on top. As the pages burned, she ran the edge of her box cutter along the spine of the final journal. She slid the empty leather binding to the pile on the library floor. She made two stacks of paper, and fed the fire the first one.

Only one stack to go.

When she'd come down from the third floor, at midnight, the door of the guest room Gabe had claimed was shut, without a sliver of light underneath. She had guessed he was inside, sleeping.

She'd gone into the package room for the box cutter. Across the hallway, two agents had been at desks in the security room, munching on Gabe's delicious cookies. Neither agent was Gabe. When she'd first set the fire, then sat on the floor with the journals and her box cutter, the bald-headed agent had appeared in the doorway of the library, nodded to her, then drifted away.

Now, footsteps sounded on the hardwood floors in the center hallway. She assumed they belonged to one of the other agents. Instead of glancing at the doorway, she remained focused on the fire, as she fed it the last stack of pages. Over the last couple of years, she'd gotten used to the patterns that came with having the agents in her house. They came with soft footsteps, they paused for a second, and they went. But she'd heard footsteps approach, and she hadn't heard them go away. And the time between then and now was too long to be the short pause for their visual check.

Heart pounding, she turned and saw Gabe standing in the wide doorway to the library. Wearing a black leather jacket, and black clothes, his hair was slick with moisture, as though he'd been outside in the rain for a while. Puzzlement killed the usual light in his eyes. "You okay?"

"Fine."

"What are you doing?" He jutted his chin at the pile of black journal covers.

"Those are journals. Well, they were. Those are just the covers."

"You're burning the pages?"

Clearly, he was searching for more of an explanation. She stood up awkwardly. Her legs had stiffened. "Yes. I'd never reread them and I'd never, ever, allow anyone else to read them. Destroying them seemed like the best thing to do. It's a cleansing, of sorts. I'm taking your advice. Being me. It felt right to do this. Tonight."

He walked to her. The muscles in his jaw were set, and his eyes were impossible to read. It was as though he was holding something back, or searching for more of an explanation. His seeming reticence puzzled her, because she knew enough about the man to know that he was nothing if not intuitive.

In the face of his silence, she continued, "There's no reason to keep them. They're just an example of me wallowing in self-pity. Tonight, after we talked, I realized the journals were holding me down, the words memorializing things I'd prefer to forget." She shrugged. "It occurred to me that shredding would've been less work, but I was cold. Burning the pages seemed a more fitting ending. Not the cover, though. I would think burning leather would smell a little like..."

Drawing a deep breath, she fought for the words. "The odor of burning skin." She shuddered. "So I didn't throw the bindings into the fire. Dammit, Gabe, my rambling indicates I'm having a problem, here. You're looking at me like...I don't know what, and whatever it is, you don't get to look at me like that. Like you're worried about God knows what, because I really should just be your job. Not a worry."

As her words trailed off, they stood in silence, eyes on each other. The only sounds in the room were the crackle and pop of the fire. He looked like there were about a million things he wanted to say, and he damn well seemed to be weighing each one.

She figured he was just surprised. Justifiably surprised. It wasn't every night that someone came across another person having a bonfire with journal pages.

Then he suddenly shook it all off. Instantly, the serious man in black became Gabe again. He smiled slightly and an easy-going light filtered into his eyes. He gave her a slight nod. "It's just that Agent Marks gave me the latest status report. He said you were burning pages of books in the library. I wasn't sure what was going on. And this is really something I didn't expect. But—" He shrugged, his gaze on her. "You look fine to me."

"I am. And if you don't mind my rambling—"

"Not at all—"

"I need to say what's on my mind. All those things you said in the workout room were wonderful. I love your idea of me just being me. Ever since I walked out of there, as a matter of fact, I've been thinking about it. The very idea is empowering. Me. No filters. So that's what I'm doing now. Burning the journals, because they needed to go. And I'm glad I'm seeing you, because I wanted to tell you, you're free to go too. If this is getting too weird for you, leave my job."

He arched an eyebrow. "Do you want me to leave?"

She shook her head. "No."

"Good. Because I don't want to leave. Like I told you before, you can always get rid of me in a professional capacity by firing me." A bemused smile played at his lips. "But that no longer means you'd be getting rid of me. In the meantime, I'm happy to be here. Thrilled, as a matter of fact."

"I'm not sure you're understanding how weird this could get. I've never even known the agent's names, for God's sake. And I don't blame you for being puzzled at what I was doing.

Still, why should I explain what the hell I'm doing in my own house? I should be able to burn my journals if I want. I should be able to burn the goddamn place down without explaining myself. Not to you, or any of the other agents. So I want to make myself goddamn clear here—I don't plan on explaining my behavior to anyone."

"Okay. No explanations for any behavior. No matter how strange. Got it, Head Honcho. Understood, Andi." He arched an eyebrow. "That cover everything?"

Sighing in exasperation, she leaned forward to pick up the covers so she could trash them. "Yes."

"Good. Because I've picked up strays all my life, and, if I do say so myself, I hit the mother lode tonight. I've set him up in the guesthouse. I figured he'd be more comfortable there, without you hovering over his every cough. After all, the kid's been living on the streets. Used to being on his own."

His words registered, igniting a wild, impossible hope. She dropped the journal covers on the floor. "Seriously?"

The corners of his eyes crinkled with his broad smile. "Yeah."

She wanted to kiss him. In gratitude. In appreciation, because, dammit, he looked so pleased with himself for giving her something he knew she really, really wanted. She'd never met a man with his brand of chivalry, nor had she met anyone with his kind of persuasive power. "How on earth did you pull off this miracle?"

"Truth is, he's really sick and he wanted to be here. We arrived about twenty minutes ago. I got him settled, and I contacted a doctor friend of Brandon's, who works from time to time for Black Raven. He's used to calls at odd hours. He's on his way."

She ran past him, down the hall, and through the mudroom. Hands shaking, she couldn't unlock the back door fast enough, but Gabe was there to help. She'd forgotten to put on shoes, and almost slipped on the damp bricks of the courtyard that separated her house from the guesthouse. Gabe righted her by gripping her arm, then she was in the guesthouse. Momentarily still, with her heart pounding, she was surprised to find the first floor dark. And quiet.

"Upstairs." Gabe said, flicking on a light.

Andi took the steps two at a time. The loft-style bedroom, with its adjoining bathroom, made up the entire second floor. Slowing when she reached the top stair, she froze, drinking in the sight that she thought she'd never see.

The bedside lamp, and the one in the corner, were both on, illuminating Pic. He was sprawled out on his back on the queen-size bed. Someone had removed the white-linen covered duvet and folded it on one of the two chairs in the corner. The quilt and top sheet were folded down, but Pic wasn't under them. Sound asleep, he was barefoot and fully clothed, as if he'd only been capable of making it as far as the bed before running out of juice.

Andi's heart squeezed at the sight of his flushed, sweaty face. Without his defenses up, he looked so young and vulnerable.

"He fell asleep before I came to get you," Gabe, at her side, whispered.

Turning to him, she blinked back happy tears. She stepped closer, and lifted shaking hands to his arms. Pressing her palms on his biceps, steadying herself in his warmth, she tried to control the roiling emotions that had her almost sobbing in joy and gratitude. Resting her forehead against Gabe's chest, she breathed in deeply. The scent of the fresh outdoors that surrounded him mingled with the aroma of burning wood and paper that was on her. Drawing strength and calmness from him, she took a few more breaths and lifted her face. "I'll never be able to thank you enough."

He touched an index finger to her cheek and caught a happy tear, as his eyes drank her in. Voice gruff, he said, "You just did. To date, that might be the best thank you I've ever gotten." He gestured with his head to the bed. "Make some noise on the way over. Try not to startle him."

She froze. "Maybe I shouldn't wake him."

"He's got to get up before the doctor gets here, and he's sleeping pretty deep. Don't want him to open his eyes with a stranger in the room, when he might not even remember where he is."

As she hesitated, Gabe did a slight knock on the wall. Then another, this one louder. Groaning, Pic turned to the sound, but his eyes remained closed. Approaching the bed, she saw that his black eye was a solid blob of swollen, purplish black flesh. Over his cheekbone, it faded to a dark greenish-yellow, matching a hue she used to paint the moisture-fed slime that grew on bricks. The side of his face that wasn't bruised was flushed pink with fever. Each breath was ragged and harsh. His exhales caught, then rattled. His long blond hair was damp.

Gabe rapped harder on the wall.

Pic opened his eyes. He tensed, then started to sit up. When he focused on Andi, he let his head fall back on the pillow. "Hey, you."

Kneeling at the bedside, she touched his forehead. He felt unnaturally hot on her fingertips. "Hey."

"Thanks for sending the big guy out for me. It's freezing out there."

She squeezed his hand. "I didn't send him out. Big guy did that on his own."

He glanced at her, then looked over her shoulder to Gabe.

"No kidding?"

Andi smiled. "No kidding."

"Damn. Don't tell him I said this," Pic said, giving Andi a weak smile, and dropping his voice to a whisper, "maybe he's not so bad after all."

"Send him up," Gabe said, his voice loud enough to carry.

"What?" Pic asked, his gaze bouncing over her shoulder, back to Gabe.

Andi heard the front door open and turned in time to see Gabe point to his ear by way of explanation to Pic. "Talking to one of my agents. Doctor's here. Benjamin Cavanaugh."

She nodded. Ben was the older brother of a high school friend. She'd danced with him at a few debutante parties when he'd been in his medical school years. He'd always been nice. Polite. Thoughtful. "I know Ben."

One dark eyebrow gently arched as Gabe looked at her. As though he remembered their cocktail party conversation and was wondering exactly how well she knew the doctor.

"It's really a small town," Andi offered by way of explanation. Otherwise, she kept her expression blank. No tells.

Let him wonder.

Pic slowly shifted himself to the side of the bed and swung his legs to sit up. Eyes glassy, he looked at Gabe. "No questions, right?"

His question and his tone conveyed an implicit trust, signifying a sea of change from their first meeting had somehow occurred. Gabe nodded. "Nothing more than about how you're feeling right now."

Pic bent over in a fit of coughing. "Easy answer. I feel like a pile of shit that's been stepped in."

Slightly balding, and with more of a paunch than Andi remembered, Benjamin Cavanaugh came into the room in time to hear Pic's comment. He chuckled. "Then I'm in the right place. Hi, Andi. You look well."

"I am, thanks. Nice to see you again," she said.

Carrying a black leather satchel, he crossed to the bed and introduced himself to Gabe and Pic. Andi moved aside so the doctor could take her place. He pulled a chair up to the side of the bed, next to the bedside table. Then he sat down, facing Pic, with his satchel to his side.

Wondering whether she should exit the room, or stay, she decided to leave. Gabe gave her a slow headshake. He whispered, "Let the kid decide."

Standing beside Gabe, she turned in time to see Pic, with his shoulders squared, frowning as he sized up the doctor. His dignity was somewhat ruined by the hacking cough that doubled him over.

She had a profile view of Ben, who ignored the suspicious look from his patient as he leaned to the side and opened his bag. As he rifled through it, he said, "I thought I'd tell you a few things about me before I start the examination. Okay?"

Pic watched as Benjamin wrapped his stethoscope around his neck. "No need for an exam. I just need cough medicine. Maybe something for this headache."

Benjamin nodded. "Sounds like a solid start. But I thought you might like to know that while I'm focusing on your cold, or whatever it is that's got you sounding so bad, you're free to tell me anything that's on your mind."

"I didn't know doctors came out in the middle of the night."

"Well, then, you're probably wondering what kind of doctor I am. I'm an internist. I run a private hospital and also work with the doctors at Ochsner Hospital. If you've got a problem I can't handle, I'll get another doctor here. I work from time to time for Black Raven, the company Gabe works for. Which means, I know how to make people better without asking too many questions." His tone calm and reassuring, Ben talked as he pulled out a few pill bottles and placed them on the bedside table.

Some of Pic's discomfort seemed to ease as the doctor spoke. Casting a wary glance at the pill bottles, he asked, "What's all that?"

"Ibuprofen, antibiotics and steroids."

Pic glanced at Gabe, a slight smile on his face. Gesturing with his chin to the pill bottles, he asked, "This the kind you take, Muscle Man?"

Gabe chuckled. "I'm not even going to answer that."

Benjamin glanced at Gabe. "I certainly hope he doesn't, unless he's sick."

"I don't, Doc. Pic's just being a prick."

As Gabe turned and went down the stairs, the doctor continued talking to Pic. "I'll decide whether you need the meds after the examination, but I'm betting the stuff that's coming up when you cough is green. Right?"

Pic nodded. "Fucking neon, man."

"Well, these pills will help you get over it. Because what you have is more than just a simple cough. My ears can tell me that. I want to tell you, also, that you're not the first person I've helped under similar circumstances. And the reason I do this kind of work, aside from the financial reward, is because I like helping people in need."

Gabe returned to the top of the stairs, with a glass of water in his hands. He walked to the bedside table, placed it next to the pill bottles, then resumed his position near the stairs.

"I'm here to make you feel better physically, and I'm not going to ask you questions about anything else. But I'm betting there's a bit more trouble in your life that I can't fix. I'd leave that to Black Raven, if I were you. And its agents, like Gabe."

As Cavanaugh paused and let that sink in, Andi bit back a smile. Damn, but Gabe was good. She wondered how long the coaching session between Gabe and Cavanaugh had lasted. "You understand that between Andi and Gabe, you're in good hands, right?"

Pic nodded, looked like he was going to say something, then instead started coughing. Andi stepped into the bathroom and brought out a box of tissues. She placed it next to the bed. Pic reached for it, taking three out at a time, and blew his nose. "Thanks, Andi. Look, Doc, I appreciate all the information, but right now, I'm just trying to stop coughing. And I'm not in anybody's hands. I'm just here for the night."

"You need to be here for more than just one night if you want to get better." Benjamin pulled out a bottle with dark red liquid and handed it to Pic, "That's cough syrup. The measuring cup on top's a full dose. You can take a full dose every six hours. Not more than that. Before you take it, though, do you know if you have any allergies to medicine or food?"

Pic placed the measuring cup on the night table, then pressed down on the childproof cap. “Beans. Hate ‘em.”

Gabe chuckled.

Andi’s draw dropped. *Does he not know what an allergy is?* “He asked you about allergies. Not food preferences. There’s a difference—”

Pic gave her a slight smile. “Joke, Andi. Mom was allergic to peanuts, but I could eat them. Just not around her. I don’t think there’s anything I’m allergic to, Doc, though I haven’t had to think about it in a while. Can’t remember being allergic to medicines or food.”

“Take a full dose. It’s going to make you drowsy. Which gets me to my final point, which I want you to focus on before you start falling asleep. I suspect it’s been a hell of a long time since you’ve seen a doctor, and there might be things other than this cold that are bugging you. You can tell me about any concern that you have. And no matter what happens tonight, I’m returning tomorrow for a recheck. Probably in the evening. So, if you’re not sure about telling me something tonight, you can tell me tomorrow. Understand?”

“Just the cold, Doc,” Pic said. “All I’m looking for is to feel better. Can’t remember when I felt this bad.”

“I promise you’ll start to feel better soon. Now, at this point I’d normally ask everyone else in the room to leave. But I want to make sure you’re okay with that.”

Pic glanced at Andi, then Gabe, with wide eyes and a quick headshake. His wide-eyed moment of panic was replaced with narrow-eyed skepticism, directed at Cavanaugh. “I’m not getting naked for you.”

“There’s no need for that. Though I’d like for you to take your shirts off. Normally I’d be doing a chest x-ray with someone if they sounded like you do, but I might be able to avoid getting you to go to my office if—” He lifted the business end of the stethoscope and wagged it in the air. “—if I can listen close and figure out what’s really going on in those lungs of yours.”

Pic frowned as those words sank in. “You going to give me a shot?”

“Probably. Maybe two.” Benjamin nodded. “I’ll decide after I listen to your chest.”

“Arm or butt?”

“They’ll hurt less in your hip.”

Pic glanced at Andi and Gabe. “Clear out, guys.”

Chapter Twenty Five

Concierge

As I left the Gallery opening, I received news that our reapers had pulled in three light-eyed, fair-skinned, blond females from homeless encampments in San Francisco, Boston, and Oahu. Before the reapers get paid, they conduct at-home pregnancy tests, hoping for bonus money. None of these new women are pregnant.

I can fix that.

With acquisitions this good, my partner and I conduct an immediate assessment. We won't waste these assets on our organ donation line. Even homely white women have a high market value in the sex trade, but that comes with a host of variables. Flat out sales are fast and expedient, though leasing is an option for select clients.

And then there's our breeding program, through which we lease the women when they're pregnant and sell the babies for adoption when they're born. Our breeding program is unsurpassed, and the benefits, in both remuneration and entertainment—*mine*—are off the charts. Infants are the cream cheese icing on my carrot cake. In some depraved, impoverished areas of the world, babies can be purchased for as little as two hundred dollars. That's not ever going to happen here. Healthy white babies in my world-wide black market fetch anywhere from seven hundred and fifty thousand dollars to a cool one million.

Acquisition assessment meant postponing my playtime. Eve, the pregnant girl we'd scooped up on Friday, was unusual. Rarely do acquisitions come in so perfect and so pregnant. Eve had been ready for placement in a matter of hours. Usually it takes weeks. Sometime months. And some of them never manage to get pregnant, even though our stud program is designed to guarantee results.

The project at hand is how to make today's acquisitions fetch top dollars. In the sex trade, a fair-skinned female will always bring in money, but a beautiful, blonde with double D tits, pretty teeth, and skin polished to perfection will bring in a hell of a lot more.

Our business thrives on more. More money. More of the illusion of perfection and exclusivity. I'm the Concierge, and I sell quality. I don't sell ugly. I sell fucking fantasies—literally—and evidently, my clients don't fantasize about making it with someone who looks better with the lights off.

My partner and I meet in our office for a few hours of work. He settles into his desk chair with a tumbler of scotch. He loves this part of our work. I used to love it, but my restlessness now infects everything I do, and as I look at him, I realize I'm more than bored with him.

Our desks face each other, and the wall of video monitors is to my right. My partner powers up his desktop computer, while I leave mine alone. The screen saver of Andi, painting in Crescent Park, taken a few days ago by one of my reapers who I pay to keep tabs on her, suits me just fine.

We're intertwined in more than just business matters. He cannot exist without me. I established that fact on day one with the mind-fuck I pulled on him. I'm the dominant one in this relationship, and I take dominance to a new level. He has no idea of the calculated moves on my part that went into our first, seemingly by-chance meeting. When we met, I already knew I'd establish myself as the Concierge. I had the imagination required for the start-up of what's now become our one-of-a-kind enterprise. My partner had the seed money, necessary skills, and most importantly, the desire to make me happy.

On his own, he was deviant enough for me to turn him into a mini-monster. I nurtured his deviant side. I also brought to the table ideas, determination, ambition, and enough contacts to make those first few critical sales. Ours is a partnership with roots in the depths of hell, fed by the devil himself.

Using video monitors, we start a head to toe analysis. First up, the Hawaii-Kai woman. The reaper's camera does a slow pan from head to toe. She looks to be about twenty. She's drugged and can barely keep her baby blue eyes open. She's lying naked, spread-eagled, on her back.

"Why does everyone have tattoos?" my partner grumbles, as he starts typing, creating a file for this acquisition. Each medical procedure goes into a flow chart that outlines the steps from acquisition to sale. From a drawer, I pull out matches, a fresh box of long tapers, and light the first one.

"Put her down for laser work. That tat's got to go," I say, as the camera shows a crude, black, peace sign on her shoulder.

"Great bone structure," my partner says, typing, as the camera scrolls in for a close-up of her face.

"High cheekbones. Square jaw. Nice. Strong shoulders. Fantastic hips," I add. "Right amount of softness. A little too fat on the thighs. Liposuction needed."

"Agreed." He types for a few seconds.

"Not too much, though. I see her as a curvy platinum blonde. We'll feature her as a Marilyn."

My partner stares at the video monitor, then nods and resumes typing. "Fantastic idea."

"With enhancements, she'll qualify as top shelf merchandise," I say. "We'll do a video auction. Platinum blond hair, red lips."

"Lips need filler. And her face and arms, even her chest, will need post-laser peels and bleaching creams. Too much sun exposure." He types more.

I sip on ice-cold vodka, and light another taper, creating a mini bonfire of dripping tapers on my silver tray as I keep one eye on the wall-mounted monitor. "Tits are way too small. Hell. They look like bananas. Implants needed. Desperately."

"Yes," my partner chuckles. "C?"

"No," I say, threading my index finger through the delicious, warm wax puddling on the silver tray that I use for this purpose. "You know better than that. Double D."

"But that's too large for her hips." The whine in my partner's voice annoys me to no end.

"Hell," I snap. "Milo?"

Milo is our Hawaiian reaper who is delivering this potential beauty. "Yes, Concierge?"

"Take a rest for a couple of minutes."

The camera goes from live to a still shot. I mute the audio and glare at my partner. "Don't start whining. We've been through this before. You can't turn every woman into your goddamn fantasy girl."

"Why the hell not?" he says, with a marked frown. "I know what's waiting for you in your bedroom. And I know what you did last night."

"Goddammit, you sound like a whiny teenager. If you're going to claim this acquisition as yours, go ahead and do it up front."

"Look who's talking," my partner says. "The woman you burned last night wasn't supposed to be reduced to organ donation, for God's sake. Do you want the analysis of how much it cost to prep that woman? I have it right he-"

"Not no, but fuck no."

He clicks a couple of times, then glares at me. "She spent six weeks at our clinic. Those resources could have been dedicated elsewhere. I estimate the value at sixty three thousand dollars. With the improvements we made, she had the potential to bring in a cool one point two million, while now, at best, she'll bring in seven hundred thousand. Because we can't deliver her alive, and we certainly can't deliver that body anywhere. We'll have to harvest her organs and dispose of the rest."

"Save it. I'm not going to fight with you about money."

His glare intensifies. Like I'm supposed to give a rat's ass about his moods. "How many times do I have to tell you that putting out cigarettes on someone's back will lead to trouble?"

"You're paranoid," I say.

"One hundred and fifty burns!"

I raise a brow, mocking him. "You counted? Sounds like someone really needs to get a life."

"You're obsessed with Andi Hutchenson. With what happened to her in her kidnapping."

I glance at my screensaver, which has changed to another picture of Andi, this one as she stares at the sky above the Saint Louis Cathedral. Truth is, I've always had a thing for candles and flames during sex. When I learned what Victor Morrissey did to Andi's back, I was riveted. I've wanted to touch those scars for two and a half years now. At this point, the wait is killing me.

"Not a goddamn newsflash. Come on. You know that. And you're not mad about the money. We have more than enough of that. So what if my fucking costs us a few bucks? I'm goddamn bored. You understand what I mean when I say bored?"

I pause, letting that sink in, because my boredom threatens his very existence. He lives terrified for the day I decide to terminate our partnership, both of which are constant threats I use against him.

"You know I get restless when I'm bored," I say, putting a cajoling pout in my voice. I know he can't resist it. "And we certainly have the capability to cover my tracks. So where's the harm in letting me have some fun?"

He glares at me, but underneath the glare, I can see that I'm winning. Of course I am. Because he likes what our millions can buy him. And he especially likes the unfettered access he has to doing anything he wants, at any time, with any one of our assets. And even more than that, he craves the opportunity to touch me.

Which I allow, but sparingly. Truth is, I'm flattered that this man, who has a predilection for platinum blond, very young, females with perfectly proportioned bodies and equally beautiful sixteen year-old-boys, is obsessed with touching me any way I will allow it.

"You're just upset I didn't invite you to play," I say, because I have his number.

His cheeks become flushed. He's waiting for an invitation. Dear God, why is everything so goddamn easy? The only thing in my life right now that isn't easy is my obsession with Andi. And that's about to change. I study him as my taper burns, reading my partner's sour expression, wondering whether to goad him further.

Nah, I decide. *He's cranky enough tonight.*

Lucky him, I decide to back off, and offer a carrot, rather than a stick. "When we're done here, why don't you join me tonight?"

He relaxes a little. He gives me an eager nod. "Thank you."

"But you have to stay silent. In the corner. No touching me or her. Unless I tell you. And then—" I pause. "You can only do what I tell you to do."

He takes a deep swig of scotch and nods.

"Say it."

"Yes, Concierge," he says, his voice gruff, as he imagines watching me do the things I like to do, which he knows I plan to do with my Andi doppelganger.

"Are you getting hard?"

"Yes."

I smile, and this one's real. Because even though I love a warm, moist pussy, there's nothing wrong with a good, stiff cock, either. Of course this makes me bisexual, but I've never really bothered with labels. Like I've said a million times, about the only thing I won't fuck is a corpse. That's actually something my partner likes to do. I prefer to do it with the living. And my favorite ever was Andi, and trust me, that says a goddamn lot.

Maybe that's what I'll do tonight. I'll let my partner do me while I have my first delicious taste of my faux Andi. She'll be good for at least a few nights, if I'm careful. So having my partner in the room to please me isn't a bad idea at all.

My partner has a nice, smooth cock. When he's aroused, it's wide and heavy, and he enhances his erections with drugs. I pretend that I'm doing him a favor whenever I'm on the receiving end of it.

"Yes, what?" I keep my voice stern, keenly aware of my partner's deep-rooted need to be subservient.

"Yes, Concierge. Thank you."

I nod, and gesture with my head to the video screen. "Back to work." I reconnect to Milo. "Show us her teeth."

As expected, they're chipped, with yellowing wear and tear that's consistent with methamphetamine use.

"Caps," I say.

My partner nods. "With procedures thus far, we're at two months out. Meanwhile, we'll monitor ovulation."

Because no matter what she looks like, and no matter what we can get for her in a straight-out sale when we feature her as a Marilyn, she's worth more to us as a potential baby maker.

When cosmetic procedures and surgical enhancements are complete and our assets are healing, we move the product to the farm where we can oversee the mating program. Though we do it the old-fashioned way as frequently as possible, we don't leave things to chance. We make sure we have an ample supply of sperm and, when the acquisitions are ovulating, we do a variety of artificial insemination techniques in addition to plain old fucking.

In the early days, we sold sperm. We learned it isn't worth the trouble, even on the black market. A shot of ejaculate, no matter how it's packaged, brings in about one thousand to fifteen hundred bucks. And that's if the sperm count is high enough. Which means I can't hook male acquisitions to a masturbator—a glorified milking machine that simulates the feel of a pulsing vagina—watching porn while shoving libido enhancers down their throats, for days on end. Also, end users of sperm are particular about ejaculate that's infected with HIV and STDs. In the population segment where my product comes from, that's a problem.

Rather than waste time and effort selling sperm, it's better to impregnate females, lease them while they're pregnant, and when the baby is born, sell that. Then impregnate mama again, and start the lease process all over again. I have fifteen clients, world-wide, who I keep almost continuously supplied with pregnant women.

We finish with our future Marilyn, then turn to the Boston beauty. Finally, at two a.m., we turn off the video image of our San Francisco blonde. We're done with work for the night.

My Andi look alike awaits. And this one sure better live up to my expectations, because if not, there's only one place I'm going next. I'm bored with waiting. Bored with being bored. I want Andi.

And what I goddamn want, I get.

Chapter Twenty Six

Andi

Monday, February 15, 2:15 a.m.

Andi climbed the first flight of stairs in the main house, debating whether she'd try to sleep in her bed, or on the couch in her studio. She'd lingered in the first floor of the guesthouse as the examination had taken place. The doctor had diagnosed a severe respiratory infection. Definitely bronchitis, bordering on pneumonia. He'd given Pic a couple of shots, and gave her and Pic, whose eyes were heavy and closing as he listened, instructions for medicine.

Now, with Pic sound asleep, she was exhausted, but that didn't mean sleep would come. Too many things had happened in the last twenty-four hours. To avoid a bad bout of night terrors, she needed to paint for a while. Needed to soothe herself, which was what she'd been trying to do when she'd had the bright idea of burning her journals.

When she reached the second floor landing, she saw light spilling from the open door to Gabe's room. His voice was low, but his words were audible as she approached the doorway. "Doc, I know it's late, but would you mind drawing it when you get home?"

Silence.

"Great. Once you do, take a few photos, then either email or text it to us. I'm texting you now, so all you have to do is reply and it'll come to both me and Ragno."

Concern for what he was talking about bloomed, as she looked at him. With his back propped against a mound of pillows, Gabe wore black shorts, and— *oh God*—not a damn thing else. Miles of broad chest, rock hard abs, and long legs graced the mahogany wood sleigh bed. Bare feet, crossed at the ankles, rested on the white linens, since he'd shoved the covers to the foot of the bed. His iPad lay on the sheets, an oversized phone was next to it, and a laptop sat on his thighs. Just looking at all that golden satin-smooth skin, and inhaling the musky-sweet scent of a freshly-showered male, made her breath catch in a way that reminded her of how long it had been since she felt full-fledged desire.

It came back with a rush.

Damp, dark hair was going every which way but flat, presumably from the rubbing he'd done with the towel that was slung on the floor beside the bed. Muscles, from his neck to his shoulders to his belly, rippled as he leaned forward and typed on the laptop keyboard. His abs were tight and ridged, without a roll where his navel met his shorts. Tight, tawny skin accented every bulge, every ripple that signified pure, muscular strength.

I want to draw that chest. The way his neck meets his broad shoulders and the slight striations in the trapezius muscles. Good God, that six pack!

Forget drawing. I want to touch him. When he's like that. I want those arms around me so badly, I can feel them. The warmth of his skin. His rock-hard strength, which inexplicably comes with the most magical of light, beautiful smiles.

Remembering the conversation they'd had in the workout room, she guessed that he'd welcome any move she made. Just what move she was ready for, though, was the issue.

She didn't think she'd made a noise, but as she virtually salivated over the splendor of Gabe in all his almost-naked glory, he glanced up from his laptop screen. With a nod and a smile, he waved her over.

"Doc. Ragno—Andi's here." Full attention on Andi, he lifted a bicep-bulging arm and ran his fingers through his hair, smoothing it. "How's Pic?"

She nodded and tried not to lick her lips as his arm fell back to his side. "Sound asleep."

"Guys—you heard that?"

He was silent, looking at her as he listened to them.

"Okay. I'm going silent. Then knocking off for the night. Thanks, Doc. We'll be on the lookout for that email, and we'll give you a report on Pic in the morning. Ragno, call me during the night if you find anything." He glanced at Andi. "They're gone. It's just us now."

"I'm not sure how long Pic will stay here," she said, from the doorway. "He's still worried about Monica. She didn't show up anywhere yesterday that he could find her, which has me worried about what I saw on Friday. Though I didn't tell him about that, because I don't want to worry him. But I can't stop thinking that the girl could have been her."

Gabe shook his head. "Don't jump to that conclusion. You couldn't really describe her for me the other day, remember?"

"I knew she was female, though. She was walking towards the river. Away from me, so I didn't see her features. And I knew her dress was loose. The kind a pregnant woman would wear.

And I told you on Saturday that I thought she had blond hair, right? It's not my imagination playing that trick now, right?"

"You did tell me that on Saturday. But you also said most of her hair was covered with a scarf."

"Old Navy. Not Muslim. I remember exactly what I told you, because those details are clear to me. But that's exactly the way Monica would've worn her hair. I have a sketch upstairs of her, with a scarf tied in her hair like that. I did it two months ago."

"But you didn't recognize her on Friday. If she had seemed familiar to you, that fact would have been something that you remembered before now. Besides, there is nothing we can do about it right now, okay?" He paused, with an eyebrow raised.

She nodded, reluctantly.

"Chances are," he continued, "Monica will show up somewhere she's supposed to be tomorrow. And if concern for her is going to be what makes Pic leave, we'll figure out a way to find her, okay?"

"Thank you."

"Just doing my job, Andi."

"I know it's above and beyond, so..." As her voice trailed, she realized, once again, she was staring. Not at his physical beauty, but the depth in his eyes as she searched for the meaning of his words. While profoundly grateful that he was willing to take on tasks that most would look over, she wondered, with a sinking heart, whether he was looking at her as one of those tasks. Whether she was something that he thought he could fix. He arched an eyebrow, waiting for her to continue. "So, thank you. Again. Meds are due for Pic in five and a half hours." She glanced at her watch. "At seven."

"If you'd like, I'll handle it so you can sleep."

"No. I'll do it. I heard part of your phone conversation. What were you asking Ben to draw?"

Lifting the iPad and phone, he patted the bed next to him. "Come see."

The surreal-ness of the moment wasn't lost on her. But he was so damn natural about inviting her in to sit with him, that any issues she could've had—and there were about a thousand—fell away. As though she hadn't spent the better part of the last two and a half years erecting impenetrable walls between herself and the normal world, where people shared things like lives and beds, she walked towards him. She stepped up with one knee, then the other. She pulled her legs up and under her, as he moved over, repositioning the pillows behind his back as she faced him.

He handed her his iPad, his fingers brushing hers as she took it. His eyes lingered, and he gave her a slight smile, suggesting that maybe, just maybe, he felt the same jolt of electricity that she did at the touch of his fingertips.

"Pic ever mention someone named Aubrey to you?"

She shook her head. "He's never mentioned anyone to me, other than the people he's met on the streets. At first, I tried to ask questions about his life before here. He wouldn't answer."

Gabe pointed to the iPad. "We might not need to ask questions."

On the laptop screen she read, '*Aubrey. A Cross. Two doves, crying. Blue sky. Clouds. A doorway. Open. Flowers. Roses. A ring of some other kind of flower (?). Color. Blue. March 3, 1982. November 7.*'

"What is this?"

Gabe held her gaze, silent. After a few seconds, he pressed his watch, typed a few more words on his laptop, pressed enter, and pushed the laptop away. "I take it you've never seen his chest?"

On the day Pic had pulled her out of the river, he'd been wearing a t-shirt. He'd stripped it off, but turned from her when he'd pulled on his sweater. She'd thought he was being modest. Ever since, even on the hottest of summer days, he'd worn a t-shirt, at least. "No."

"Then you haven't seen the tattoo over his heart. Ben studied it as he examined him." He pointed to the iPad. "This is how Ben described it to me."

Andi put the iPad on the bed. "I have a problem with having Ben spy for us. He's a doctor. It's...wrong."

"The only way we'll help him is by knowing what happened to him."

"I know that, but...Pic trusted Ben. Dear God, if my doctors repeated what I've told them, or what they saw when they examined me, I'd want to kill them."

"Cavanaugh won't be repeating it to anyone else. He's told me, and I've told you, and it ends there."

"Ragno knows."

"Yeah." He gave her a nod. "But in my world, that goes pretty much without saying. I don't do much sleuthing without her. She's a cyber expert who, when necessary, will hack through databases to figure out what the clues I'm finding mean. Trust me, Ragno doesn't repeat things."

"Is she listening now?"

"No. When I say I'm going silent, like I just did, I mean it. That was as much for you as for them. I wouldn't say that, then have her eavesdrop. Well..." He frowned. "To be honest, I might, but I won't do that to you. It's just me and you now."

"It still feels distasteful. Plus, it's a breach of doctor patient confidentiality. What kind of doctor does that?"

"A damn good one, according to Brandon. And apparently this doctor understands one of Black Raven's guiding principles—that sometimes, to really help someone, rules have to be bent."

She couldn't help but glance at the iPad screen again. "Clearly, Aubrey was important to him. People don't permanently wear the names of meaningless people. As was March 3, 1982, which isn't his birthday. He's way too young for that date to be his."

"Yeah. You're right about that. He's too lanky. His eyes, when he's not being a hard ass, seem almost innocent. As though he's wondering how things went so wrong, instead of accepting it. Wondering comes with youth. Acceptance would mean he's older. And he's barely got facial hair, but he's got some. He's sort of where I was at seventeen. My body was still too busy growing tall and dealing with muscle mass for the hair to come out on my face and chest." He gave her a disarming smile, and sat up, straightening his magnificent shoulders, cocking his chin, inviting her gaze. "Then, look what happened by the time I was twenty."

Dark chest hair complemented his tawny skin. Just the right amount of curls accented the tight brownish-pink nipples on his superhero-worthy chest. And just like the stuff of dreams, the dark hair trailed down, like a tantalizing arrow, to his waistband. With the ridged, tight abdominal muscles as a backdrop, the pathway to heaven provided by his body hair gave a solid indication that what was below the shorts would be scrumptious. "By the time I was twenty, I had to shave twice a day to avoid a shadow."

And what were we talking about? Not licking this man's nipples. Or slipping my fingers under that waistband, right? Right?

Glancing at the iPad, she refocused. *Oh. Pic's tattoo.* "It might not be his birthdate, but it's an important date to him."

"Maybe because it's important to Aubrey, whoever she might've been. So we're working one scenario that March 3,

1982, might've been the birthdate of a woman named Aubrey. Ragno's implementing searches as we speak. Social Security Administration. Birth records of individual states. Tax records. School records. Arrest records. You name it."

"How?"

"Black Raven's brand of cyber searching. Designed by the world's foremost cyber genius, Richard Barrows. Because of him, we've got the world's best data compilation and assimilation program. We've labeled different aspects of the programs different names over the years. Shadow Technology. Jigsaw. The technology is growing. The processors are learning."

"You make it sound like a person."

"It is. But smarter. Better. Our special brand of artificial intelligence. And now you know one secret as to why Black Raven is so successful. Because every agent in the field has a think tank behind him. Every variable of every job runs through our endless world of cyber intelligence. What we know, and what we can figure out, is almost limitless. Now, if you repeat what I just said," he said, smiling, "I'll have to kill—"

"But Shadow Technology and the fact that Barrows now works for you was in the news. It isn't secret."

"Media outlets were speculating," he said. "We've never publicly acknowledged that we use it, nor have we explained the parameters, which grow every day. You can ask Brandon about it, if you don't believe me. But don't say I told you. Brandon is legal counsel, which means he knows everything. The lawyers always know where the bones are buried."

Gabe shifted his attention to the laptop screen for a second. He typed in rapid fire clicks, focusing on the screen, then hit enter. "Okay. Let's get back to Pic's ink and what Ragno's doing with it. From the million or so Aubreys that Ragno might identify using that full date, she's going to run additional scenarios."

"Such as?"

"Assuming Pic is 17, 18, or 19, she'll comb through important dates in the lives of all those Aubreys. For every one of them who had a baby boy in the relevant time frame, she'll work variables. For example, if Pic is 18 today, then he would've been born in 1999, and a woman who was born in 1982 would have had him when she was 17."

Andi drew a deep breath. "I wouldn't have been ready to be a mother at 17."

"Yeah." Gabe frowned. "And I wouldn't have been much of a father at that age, either. Pic might've simply been the fall-out from a young woman who didn't have the right resources to raise a kid."

"I get it. If we know who Aubrey was to him, and if she was his mom, maybe we'll figure out his real name. And if we know Pic's real name, then we'll maybe be able to figure out what went wrong in his life."

"Right. It's old-fashioned investigation, enhanced by our cyber-capability bag of tricks. Black Raven can do in hours and days what most investigators or law enforcement agencies would take weeks to accomplish. We can search and assimilate pretty quickly. The likelihood is damn strong that once Ragno stretches her legs on this—" He gestured to the iPad. "—we'll know what went wrong in his life. And once we know that, we'll figure out a way to help him."

"But he trusts us to play by his rules."

The seriousness in his expression made her breath catch. It revealed a river of emotion that ran deep, fueled by a rock-solid determination and confidence in his ability to get answers. Forget his chest, his shoulders, his smile, his eyes.

This.

This rock solid desire to help someone, with urgency and confidence that he's doing the right thing, no matter how he has to do it, is the sexiest, most irresistible thing I've ever seen.

And dangerous.

Please God, don't let him feel like he has to fix me. Because he'll die trying.

"Someone broke the rules with him. My suspicion is it's going to take breaking a few to help him. And he might never have to know that it started tonight, with Cavanaugh telling us about his tattoo. But if we have to tell him, I'll take the heat." He gestured to the iPad. "What do you say? You okay with this? 'Cause I can call off Ragno, if you'd like me to."

Considering the idea, she drew a deep breath. "I'm not sure—"

He leaned forward, so that his face was closer to her. "You're whispering. What was that?"

She inhaled the fresh scent of soap and woodsy maleness. Because every fiber in her, every nerve ending, and every molecule, suddenly started singing a silent chorus of *hallelujah,* she forgot what she was saying. Goosebumps rippled along her arms, and her breath caught. Any reservations she had about him disappeared, as her nipples hardened, peaking with an intensity that shot straight between her legs. Lifting her face to his, as she thought *'kiss me,'* she said with her last bit of logical sense, "Don't call her off."

"So you're okay with us using the information in the tattoo?"

She answered his question with a nod, because when she opened her mouth to say the word, nothing came out.

Oh God, please touch me.

His slight smile, the default one he always wore, faded. His eyes turned serious, as his pupils dilated and his breath caught.

Yes, yes, yes!!!...I'm finally ready for some good old sex. Now.

She squeezed her thighs together against the delicious throb that, until now, had been a distant memory from a different, long-ago life. Now it was welcome, and she let it guide her into closing the distance between them. Pressing her lips to his, thinking he might need more than a hint as to how fast she could proceed, she pushed hard against his mouth and sighed as he opened his lips to her.

A heady groan sounded from deep within his chest, as though his body wanted hers as badly as she wanted him. It was a delicious sound. Deep. Feral. Male. Her nipples puckered and her toes curled with pulse-pounding desire.

"Oh," she whispered, as he opened his mouth, sliding his tongue along her lips. A surge of moisture between her legs told her that her body remembered what to do and was doing it with great gusto. Breaking the kiss, she drew a deep breath. "Oh, Gabe. I want this so badly."

Fill me. Make me feel alive again.

He leaned forward into the kiss, and their teeth scraped, as he reached around her and pulled her closer with one of his big, strong arms. His power should've felt good, but while her body shook with delicious anticipation, she froze. Unexpectedly and out of nowhere, passion fell away as spine-tingling fear charged through her in an adrenaline-fueled rush of hot blood that ignited sizzling fight-or-flight nerves.

Worse than freezing on him, she yanked her head back from his kiss, slapped away his hands, then pushed at his oversized chest with both palms.

Thank God, he instantly comprehended the message. With his hands flattening on the mattress, he pushed himself away from her.

"Understood," he said, voice soothing, his hands raised above his shoulders. "Message received. Loud and clear."

She drew her knees up to her chest and rested her forehead on them. She would've leapt off the bed and run out of the room, but she was still quaking with fear that she knew was irrational. Her legs wouldn't carry her.

After a few more seconds where the only sound in the room was the two of them, breathing heavily as they regained their equilibrium, he asked, "Hey. You okay?"

"No. I'm sorry," she whispered, all sexual urgency gone. In its place, breath-stealing fear raced through her. Diminishing. But it was real, and still there. "I guess it's just been so long. My body wanted way more than a kiss just now. And then I freaked out."

"Glad I read the signs accurately. Sorry I was going from zero to ninety in fifteen seconds flat."

"That's what I thought I wanted. But I haven't done it since…you know." His nod told her she didn't have to say more. "And when you reached around me, to pull me closer, I just felt like…"

And I'll never tell you what I felt like. I will get past this fear. That someone will hold me down and torture me. With sex. With fire. With my mouth, as his goddamn cock choked me. And I was too scared to bite it off, because each time I tried, he burned my back with a cigarette. And it hurt. Goddamn it, but the pain was excruciating.

"Hey. Tell me what just went through your mind. You're shaking. I want to help."

Eyes squeezed shut, forehead on her knees, she breathed deep, then pushed those thoughts away. "I don't know. I need my brain to catch up with my body, I think."

"Then we'll just take it slow," he said, in his endlessly optimistic tone, as though confident it would work out—whatever 'it' was. But his tone was gruff, reminding her that he was a man and he was aroused.

Opening her eyes, she lifted her forehead from her knees. One quick glance at his shorts—because there was no way to resist looking there—told her she'd guessed correctly. Thin exercise shorts didn't do much to conceal what looked to be an impressive erection. *Yes—God had built him to scale.* Every delicious inch of him. How could she want him this badly physically and yet have her brain kick in to negate the need?

He chuckled when he saw where her gaze landed. "And that answers any question you might have as to where I'd have been happy to take that kiss."

"How can you sound so okay with what happened just now?"

He laughed and shifted his hips slightly away from her. Pulled a pillow over his lap for cover. “I look on the brighter side of things. And I know your brain’s going to catch up to your body one of these days.”

“Maybe we should just do it and get it over with. If I don’t think too much about it, it might be okay.”

He shook his head. “Nah.”

“Why not?”

“Because I’m not ready, either. I don’t think either one of us is ready for our first time together. I think it’s going to be so good, we’re both going to be damn glad we waited. Hey, here’s an idea. Let’s pretend we’re in high school. We can be hot for each other virgins.” His arched-eyebrow and questioning grin stole her heart. “You game?”

She laughed. “That’s ridiculous.”

“Great. I’ll take that as a yes, because it might give us something to work with, to get your mind off of wherever it just went. Think back to when you were a virgin and let’s proceed from there. Not tonight, though. I’m really pretty tired.” The light in his eyes revealed the lie for what it was. Gratitude at his graciousness flooded through her. “Next time, I’ll move forward with caution.”

“Caution’s good.”

“How’s this? You be as cautious as you want, and I’ll be content to wait. You can do whatever you want. And I’ll let you guide me.”

She understood where he was going, but reality’s misery was starting to seep in around the edges of the warmth he gave her. “What if sex is never an option for me?”

“Then we’ll figure it out. In the meantime, let’s take it slower than—” He gave her a small, knowing smile. “—well, a lot slower than we did just now. Okay?”

She nodded, hesitant. “I never needed slow before.”

“Days. Weeks. Months. I don’t care how long it takes.”

“Given what just happened, it might take years,” she said.

“By the way you said, *‘oh Gabe, I want this so bad’*, I’m betting it’s a lot less than that.” He shifted further away, grimaced as he stood, and walked to the bathroom. “If you’re as tired as I am, why don’t you sleep with me? Nothing scary about sharing a bed when all we’re doing is sleeping, right? I’ll set my alarm for 6:30, and we can go check on Pic together.”

Another wall crumbled, because it seemed like a great idea. She stayed frozen in place, though, because there were some logical concerns. “But your men will look for me, right?”

"Nah. That last email I sent was that I have the upstairs. If you're in bed with me, I'll know where you are. If you decide not to sleep with me, I'll feel that, too, and let them know to be on the lookout for you. They're keeping an eye out on Pic with the cameras, so we know if he leaves. Plus, the door of the guesthouse that leads to the street is locked, and we have the key. Every hour or so, one of them will listen at his doorway and make sure he's okay. They know not to startle him."

He placed his laptop and iPad on the bedside table. Gesturing with his chin, he said, "You'll have to sleep on this side of the bed, though. I need the side closest to the door."

He went into the bathroom and closed the door. Through the thick wood, she heard water running. After a few minutes, as she debated whether to stay or go, the toilet flushed. She eased herself to the side of the bed he'd indicated, as the running water stopped. He opened the bathroom door, smiled when he saw her, then turned off the overhead light.

"I need to leave a lamp on," she said, slipping under the sheet, and gesturing to the light that sat on the bedside table next to her. "Is that a problem?"

"Not at all."

The bed creaked as he slipped under the sheets, then turned on his side to face her. Pressing his head into his pillow, he shut his eyes, indicating that clearly the decision was up to her and he wasn't going to try to influence it in any way.

"What if I have night terrors?"

He opened his eyes, gave her a shrug, then shut them again as he said, "Then I won't have to go far to help you. Last night, I had my hands all over you as you screamed. I tried soothing you by touching your forehead, rubbing your arms, gripping your hands. I know it's not what conventional wisdom says to do. Also knew it was against your rules. But I just couldn't let you suffer. And, when you held onto me, and leaned against me, I figured I was doing the right thing. And then I carried you to your bed, and tucked you in, even though I knew you'd fire me if you figured that out." He opened his eyes. "That okay?"

Speechless, she nodded.

"Good." He shut his eyes, and nestled his head further into the pillow. "Because I'm damn well going to do the same thing if you scream in your sleep tonight. Good night, Sandy."

Andi slipped beneath the sheet. Being three feet away from a semi-naked man, knowing nothing was going to happen except sleep, when they both damn well wanted it to, was...odd. Reassuring, but odd. "Sandy?"

Eyes closed, with a deadpan expression on his face, he said, "A name for the virgin cheerleader of my dreams. It's been a while since I conjured up this fantasy, but I'm picturing you as a teenager, and a short cheerleading skirt works. Beautiful, smart, intuitive, sassy, snappy. A little quiet. In my fantasy, I'm crazy about her, despite her vow of celibacy. I know she's hot for me, because she's horny as hell. I know one day, I'm getting to home plate, so I can wait as long as it takes. As long as I don't have to walk around with a case of crippling blue balls."

"Oh," she whispered, "there is that, isn't there?"

"Nothing for you to worry about." He opened his eyes and gave her a serious look. "I know what to do about prolonged anticipation. I was once a teenage virgin. There's one tried and true way for alleviating pressure." He lifted an eyebrow. "When I have a really good fantasy going, it's a lot like riding a bike, and I just took one for a quick spin."

"Gabe! Are you just telling me you gave yourself a hand job?"

He opened an eye, and chuckled. "Didn't I tell you earlier that even your feet are a turn-on for me? What do you think's going to happen when you kiss me? It's been a long time since I had to do it twice a day, but I'm good for that in this fantasy. You good with playing along?"

"In this fantasy, you're a virgin, too?"

He laughed. "If that'll work for you."

Andi leaned her head back, conjured up an image of a virginal Gabe, the very first time he slipped into her and started feeling the wonder of sex. Her eyes popped open. "Can we at least be college freshman?"

"Unlikely either of us were virgins by that age, by any stretch of the imagination, but okay."

"But I just thought of you as an underage boy, without chest hair, and that isn't who I want to be sleeping with."

"Okay, we're college freshman," he said. "Which means my dream virgin cheerleader is really, really horny."

"Hm," she said. "And you're on your way to being the star quarterback."

"Can it be basketball?"

Closing her eyes for a moment, she thought about the basketball players she knew in college, and nodded. "Sure. Why?"

"Because that's what I played in college. Not football. I was a guard."

"Yum," she whispered. "Those uniforms are easier to take off. And a guard? So appropriate. How's about this, Brad. Until you, in our fantasy, I've only been naked with a girl."

"Oh, Goddammit, Andi—"

"Sandy," she corrected him. "That a turn-on for you?"

"Hell, yeah. For Brad and Gabe. As long as I don't have to think about Sonja."

"But don't you want to know more about that thing with Sonja? And I'm Andi now, not Sandy."

He shook his head. "All I really care about is that you've decided you like men more now. And that it's in your past."

Andi drew a deep breath. "You know, you're the only person who knows. Other than me and Sonja. Before her, I had one other experience with a girlfriend. Tipsy fumbling, amateurish, at best. Not fulfilling. Experimenting with same-sex relationships was a fad in college. Sonja, though, was a different story. No one's ever seduced me like that. It lasted a couple of months. It wasn't like we had an emotional commitment, though. At least, I didn't. It was all about sex, and I was always a bit uncomfortable about it. And then," she added, shrugging, "Victor Morrissey came along."

And he'll always be a part of my life.

"Thank you, Gabe, for giving me a few moments where I forgot him."

"There will be plenty more." His eyes serious, he held her gaze. "If you let me."

"Play Brad again."

He softened his features and smiled. Innocent. Sweet. Eager.

She laughed. "Okay, so let's build this into the fantasy. You decided when you were twelve, you were going to wait until marriage. You're focused on basketball and your schoolwork, and you're really, really shy..." She started laughing.

His brow furrowed. "What's funny?"

"I don't think you've ever been shy a day in your life."

"I'll play shy if that's your fantasy."

"It sure is. We've had a crush on each other since the first day of class. And we've gone weeks without even kissing. But now—" She put a bit of turned-on breathiness into her voice. Sort of a tease. "I don't know how long I can go on without—"

"Don't talk like that," he growled.

"Like what?"

"Voice low. Sexy. Whispering. Hell. I don't feel like spending the entire night in the bathroom."

She yawned, nestled her head further into the pillow, and pulled the sheets up to her chin. In the space under the sheets, his warmth spread to her. She shut her eyes as waves of exhaustion lapped at her. “Glad you like it.”

“Oh. You haven’t told me what you thought of my cookies. You ate them, right?”

“All four of the ones you brought up to my studio. And two more later, before I started burning the journals. Best chocolate chip cookies, ever.” She opened one eye, glanced at him, and saw that his were shut. “What makes them so good?”

“Not telling.”

“Those aren’t chips, are they? More like chunks.”

“Recipe’s a secret. I’ll never tell. Go to sleep, Sandy. I can go a few nights without sleep, but right now I really need a few hours of shuteye.”

“You sprinkle flakes of sea salt on top?”

“Stop asking.”

She took a long look at him before shutting her eyes, as well. “Surprising. Magical. Transcendent.”

He chuckled. “High compliment for a simple cookie. Thank you.”

I wasn’t talking about the cookies. One day, when I have courage, I’ll be clearer that I’m talking about you. But someone as wonderful as you shouldn’t waste his light on me. The dark void in me will absorb it all, until you’re left with nothing.

Chapter Twenty Seven

Gabe

Monday, February 15, 7:10 a.m.

"No way. I'm leaving as soon as I take a goddamn shower."

Pic's reaction to their reminder that the Doctor had ordered him to rest, in a real bed, for the next few days was about the same as if they'd told him to check himself into the notoriously rough Orleans Parish Prison with a tattoo on his forehead that said, *'my ass tastes like skittles.'*

Given the instant *'fuck-that-shit'*-laced argument the kid offered in reply, Gabe almost asked Pic whether he'd been raised by wolves. He bit back the words. He didn't need to ask the question, because the answer was obvious. Not wolves. Something worse. Wolves took care of their pups.

"Take that shower," Andi said, worry and strain apparent in her curt tone. "We'll talk about it after."

"Turn around," he muttered, pulling the top sheet closer to his hips. He attempted to stand, then sat down hard.

"Dizzy?" Gabe asked.

Andi reached for him, but he waved her away as he started a solid round of coughing. When he could speak, he raked his fingers through stringy hair. "Come on, guys. Turn around. I don't want either of you looking at me in my underwear."

"Don't lock the door," Gabe said.

Pic shot him a wide-eyed glance.

"In case you pass out in there, I don't want to have to knock down the door to help you."

Gabe and Andi accommodated him by turning around, glancing at each other as the bathroom door shut. Andi's worried frown as she turned and stared at the closed door showed deep concern. She loved this kid. A lot. So much that the impenetrable outer shell she normally wore was nowhere in sight.

The shower started running. There was a knock-thump, as something fell to the ground. She glanced at Gabe. "Maybe you should check—"

"That was a bar of soap. Maybe shampoo. I'm not going in there. I told him not to lock the door. He hasn't. He'd have made a lot more noise than that if he'd fallen. If he passes out, we'll hear him. Relax, Mom."

Trying to reason with the kid had been almost as surreal for Gabe as waking up in the same bed with Andi. Around four a.m., she'd become restless in her sleep. He'd been on instant alert. Holding his breath, wondering if her night terrors would start, he'd reached out to her and touched her hand. She hadn't awakened, and she hadn't had night terrors, but she'd shifted towards him. Her movement made him feel like he could conquer the world. When he woke a few minutes before his watch vibrated with an alarm, she was only inches from him, curled towards him while sleeping. He'd stayed still, breathing in her lavender and rose scent, watching her chest rise and fall with sleep, until it inspired an erection so stiff that he'd almost limped to the bathroom. Presenting a unified front as they reasoned with Pic ratcheted up the surreal quality of the morning.

Andi straightened the sheets and blankets on Pic's bed while they waited. Lifting the pillow to fluff it, she frowned at finding the kid's brass knuckles and switchblade that he'd placed underneath.

Gabe met her worried glance with a shrug. "That's a habit he'll probably have for the rest of his life."

The water turned off. "Hey," Pic said through the door. "Can one of you hand me my jeans?"

In a few minutes, he was sitting on the side of the bed. With his jeans on, and the t-shirt that he'd slept in covering the tattoo the doctor had drawn for them, Pic coughed, then inhaled for another round of argument. "Look. I really appreciate you coming out for me last night, and Andi, thanks for wanting me here. But I maybe have a couple of more hours of sleep in me, and that's it. You two just don't understand." He paused to cough into his arm. "I can't lay around all day."

"Temperature isn't climbing above forty-five today, then dipping again tonight," Andi said, repeating an argument she'd raised earlier. "You'll just get sicker. The doctor's worried you have pneumonia. Don't you know how serious that is?"

"I appreciate the concern," Pic said, "but whatever I've got doesn't really matter. I gotta be at the corner of Chartres and Conti at ten."

"The doctor almost put you in the hospital last night," Andi said. "The only reason he didn't was because we promised to keep with his strict order for bed rest."

"Lying in bed all day is for rich people."

As Andi shot Gabe a concerned, *do-something* glance, Gabe almost chuckled. Because the truth was, he was loving every second of this job.

Because everything feels so right. Like I'm in the right place, at the right time.

The minute that thought crossed his mind, the hair on the back of his neck stood on end. On a professional level, he'd experienced the 'right place, right time' feeling before. The feeling that the stars were in alignment typically materialized when things were about to go sideways.

So he wondered why he had that feeling now. He had a goddamn handle on this job, which wasn't going sideways. Variables for a sideways screwup weren't there. Sure, there might be odd things happening in the periphery, most notably someone going after Pic with a syringe in hand, a fact Gabe hadn't yet mentioned to Andi.

Despite that oddity, the Black Raven job—his job—involved keeping Andi safe. Which he was damn well doing, and now, even Pic was off the streets and safe. And even when Pic chose to walk out the door, he'd be safe. Gabe was on that task, because the kid was that important to Andi.

"Can you give us rest for a full week?" Gabe asked. "I get what you're trying to do, but you need to let the meds take effect."

"Nah," Pic said, with another cough, turning pale yellow as his mouth filled with crap from his lungs. He spat in a tissue. With a grimace as he wiped his mouth, he added, "I already feel better."

"You're lying, because that wad of baby-shit-green goo that just came out of your lungs is only the beginning of your cold breaking up."

"You don't know how I feel."

"So, how about eggs and bacon for breakfast?" Gabe asked. "Or sausage. Maybe some bread with lots of butter—"

Pic winced. "Man, stop talking about food."

"Why? I think I'll cook in the kitchen downstairs. The whole place is going to smell like food when I'm cooking fat, greasy pork links—"

"Enough already," Pic said. "Just the idea of sausage makes me wanna puke. I'm not hungry."

Gabe folded his arms and arched an eyebrow. "Tough guy like you, living on the streets, always ready for a fight. How high does food rank in your rules of survival?"

Pic's cheeks flushed bright red, replacing the yellow. He shot Gabe a marked frown.

"I bet a smart guy like you has trained yourself to eat at any opportunity that presents itself. Especially when you know there are two guys on the streets looking for you, thanks to your brass knuckle punch. When was the last full meal you managed to hold down?"

"All right, dude. You win." Pic fell back on the bed then turned on his side as he swung his legs up. "Damn, but this bed feels awesome. I'll rest for a few more hours."

"Nope. If I win, I win more than a few hours. I get a full forty-eight hours out of you," Gabe said. "Besides, the rule is you need to hold down food for forty-eight hours before going outside in the elements."

Pic shifted to his side, and narrowed his eyes as he studied Gabe. "Who says?"

"Black Raven Rule 15.2.3," Gabe said. "Which I've adapted to you. Rule says sick agents who are puking their guts up need to hold down food for forty-eight hours before returning to the field."

"Really?" Andi asked, a slight scowl indicating her disbelief. "You have rules like that?"

Pic laughed. "He's bullshitting, Andi. Sounds like my mom telling me to wait an hour before going swimming. Believed that till I was eight."

"One day, I'll show you both the handbook. For now, why don't you tell us what's so urgent, and maybe we can find a way to give you enough peace of mind to at least sleep through the next few days?"

Pic nestled his head further into the pillow, and glanced at Gabe with eyes that, touched with a bit of sleepiness from the cough syrup, seemed so honest and pure, the expression torqued Gabe's heart. With none of the street-tough, cocky attitude he put on for show, the kid's lopsided smile and big blue eyes made Gabe feel a hot blast of urgency behind getting this kid on the right track. If Pic lived on the streets much longer, a good person was going to disappear. Permanently.

"Need to work, man. My cash is low. I spent a big chunk of money on that bus ticket, and I need to build it up again. This is the pre-Mardi Gras stretch. Last season, in the week before Mardi Gras, I made over a thousand bucks. It cushioned me for a few months."

"Okay. I get that." Gabe cringed inwardly that such a small amount of money meant so much to the kid. "But I have a feeling your living expenses aren't going to be the same now as they were in the past, if you'll just accept a bit of help."

As a frown crossed Pic's face, Andi added, "I'm hoping you wrap your mind around the idea that this place is yours for as long as you need it. It's time for you to think about the rest of your life."

"Andi, I usually go with just a few hours at a time," Pic said. "And I don't want handouts."

"I know that," Andi said. "Look. I'm all for charging rent. If you want me to start an accounting of what you owe me, I'll happily do it. We'll work out details later."

"But it isn't just me I'm worried about today," Pic said, sitting up, shaking his head as though trying to will away the sleepiness. "Sure, I'd love to lay around all day. But Tank and Honey need me to play the guitar. Monica and her guitar were part of their threesome. If she doesn't show up again this morning, it's just the two of them. Tank isn't all that much on vocals. He plays a tambourine, while Honey sings. They need the money as badly as I do, and they won't bring in the big bucks if they don't have a guitar player. Without Monica there, I'm it."

"Okay, that's fair," Gabe said, getting an eyeful of the worry in Andi's eyes at Pic's mention of Monica. "Nice of you to be so concerned about your friends. Can you estimate how much they'd make if you were there today?"

"Today they're going to start early. At ten. So upwards of two hundred dollars. More if it's really crowded."

"Holy crap," Gabe said, "really? Maybe I should pick a corner and start playing."

"You gotta be good, dude." Pic gave him a roving head to toe glance. "What? You play guitar and sing between dumbbell sets?"

Gabe chuckled. "Trust me, if I sang on Royal Street, no one would give me money." He paused, thinking. "Would you rest easier here if I made sure Tank and Honey made that kind of money each day this week?"

Pic nodded, but a frown played at his lips. "I guess so. But how?"

"One of my agents goes to their corner and drops money in their hat a few times," Gabe offered. "Simple enough."

Pic's eyes flooded with gratitude, which was quickly replaced with worry. "Not sure when I'll be able to pay you back."

"Don't worry about it for now," Gabe said. "Besides, Andi's paying for this. It'll be in her accounting that she's doing for you."

"Can your agent let them know I'm safe?"

"Sure."

"Like I told you guys yesterday, everybody's looking out for each other."

"That isn't a problem."

"Well, that will take care of them. But I need to see whether Monica shows up to play with them. Can your agent check on that, too?"

Gabe nodded. "Sure. Corner of Chartres and Conti, right?"

"Yeah. If someone beats them to that corner, they'll be further down Chartres. At the first spot they can grab towards Esplanade. And if Monica doesn't show to play with them," Pic said, frowning, "then I need to go to the clinic and see if she shows up for an appointment. I was going to take the bus over there today. Monica has an appointment at two. It's for her and the baby. Honey says Monica's waited weeks for it, and wouldn't skip it."

A worried glance appeared in Pic's eyes, matched by concern that flooded Andi's eyes. Gabe knew that she was worried that what she might have seen on Friday was Monica's abduction. He hoped he was able to dispel that concern sooner, rather than later. "Okay. You describe her for me, and I'll send an agent there."

"No. I need to talk to her," Pic said, blushing bright red. "I want to tell her some things I should've said before I left for Texas."

"There's no way you can go sit at a crowded hospital clinic and wait for someone to show up," Andi said. "You might pick something else up. Or spread your germs to sick people."

"Nothing you say will keep me from there," Pic said.

"I'll go in your place," Andi said. "She'll come back with me."

Pic's jaw dropped. Gabe focused one hundred percent of his attention on her and tried to keep from looking stunned.

"But you never go anywhere," Pic said, saving Gabe from having to voice that very thought. From her file, Gabe knew it had been years since Andi had left the boundaries she'd established as her safety zone.

"What are you talking about?" Indignation crept into Andi's voice. "I go places all the time."

"French Quarter. Marigny. Bywater. Treme. Tell me when you last went somewhere else," Pic said. "In a car."

"Just because I haven't done it lately," Andi said, her cheeks flushing an adorable shade of red, "that doesn't mean I can't. Nothing's been important enough, and I know how important Monica is to you, and how important it is to me that you stay here. I know it won't be easy, but I'll have Black Raven with me."

She glanced at Gabe, slipped her hands in the back pockets of her jeans, and her voice fell to a soft, hopeful whisper. "And I'll be perfectly safe. Right?"

"Right," Gabe said, so proud of her he wanted to reach out, pull her to him, and hug her tight.

She gave him a small smile, then refocused on Pic. "Monica knows me, Pic. If she shows, I'll tell her you're here and that you're worried sick about her. I'll persuade her to come home with us so the two of you can talk. I'll tell her she's welcome to stay here, if she'd like. If it makes you feel better, give me a note and I'll give it to her when I see her. Okay?"

Pic's eyes were locked on Andi. In his gaze, Gabe saw thoughtful consideration. He was looking at Andi as though he absolutely understood how important it was that she do this for him. For that, Gabe loved the kid.

Come on, Pic. Let her do this for you.

"Yeah. Thanks," Pic said.

Andi drew a deep breath. For a moment, the air in the room was heavy with the sea of change that had taken place.

"So we'll wake you again when it's time for your meds," Gabe said. "Maybe by then, you'll be hungry."

As Andi and Gabe walked towards the stairs, Pic said, "Don't know how I'll ever thank you guys enough."

Andi turned, and shrugged. "Just get better and stay here while you do."

Gabe smiled at the kid. "For now, just focus on that."

As they left the guesthouse, they had two hours before the nine thirty a.m. meeting with his agents. Pausing in the courtyard, Andi glanced at him with worried eyes. "Friday's girl," she said. "She could have been Monica. If I saw what I think I saw."

Mist fell in the cold, damp air giving a surreal, otherworldly look to the stone and brick courtyard. Micro drops caught on Andi's dark hair and eyelashes and sheened her cold-flushed skin. Gabe wanted to kiss the moisture on her eyelids, especially when he saw the worry build in her expressive eyes. Instead, he shoved his hands into his pockets to prevent himself from wrapping her in his arms. It would be too much, too soon. He got it, but damn, he'd never met a woman who needed loving more than Andi Hutchenson.

"We'll go to the clinic at two, and in all likelihood, Monica's going to be there. Okay?"

"Okay."

"Come on. Let's go inside. It's freezing out here."

As they walked through the mudroom, on the way to the kitchen, she rested a hand on his arm. "You're really good with Pic."

Inaction made his heart swell. Instead of doing the multiple hands-on things he wanted to do, like tracing a finger along the side of her face, he could only focus on the expression in her eyes. So serious. Stubborn. Determined. Thoughtful. "You thought that was good? I was struggling. I'm thinking we should've practiced on a puppy first."

Her brow furrowed. "What?"

"That's what couples do, isn't it? Get a puppy before they have their first baby?"

Her eyes changed with a look that was somewhere between annoyance, surprise, amusement, and—maybe—hope. "You have a way of putting things."

He chuckled. "And I think you like that."

Uncertainty clouded her eyes. "I should tell you we're not a couple. The fact that we slept together doesn't mean...anything."

"You know it does." He spoke honestly, his eyes intent on hers, with his heart forming the words instead of his brain, hoping like hell she didn't start backtracking. "And I sure as hell hope I'm not reading all of this wrong."

"This?"

"Me. You. Us. This. Because last night, sleeping with you, as you curled towards me, meant more to me than any sex I've ever had."

Like the splash that came with a penny hitting bottom in a wishing well, it took a few seconds for her to absorb his words. Pink flushed her cheeks as she held still, her gaze intent as she studied him. He waited, heart exposed.

"You're not joking, are you?"

"Not a joke in me right now."

She drew a deep breath. "Are you trying to make me fall in love with you?"

Of course. It's no fun to fall alone.

"Not trying at all," he said, matching her low whisper as he leaned forward to hear her better.

"What am I going to do with you?"

Forcing himself to keep some distance, he realized how hard it was going to be not to crowd her, not to inadvertently spark the fear that festered within her from the sexual trauma he was supposed to know nothing about. He swallowed, hard, and shoved his hands deeper into his back pockets. “My virgin cheerleader could kiss me.”

A frown line furrowed her brow, but a gleam lit her eyes. “Hey, Brad, you’re supposed to be shy.”

“That’s why I offered the kiss as a suggestion, Sandy, instead of just stealing one.”

On tiptoe, Andi planted a kiss on his mouth as he bent his head down to meet her. Digging her fingers into his biceps, her breasts brushed—too lightly—against his chest. A moan formed in her throat, and sounded delicious as it escaped her lips. At first, it was just a brush of two pairs of lips. He held still, praying for more. No. No. And, no. Her call. Her speed.

Fighting the urge to pull his hands out of his pockets and wrap his arms around her, he groaned as she applied more pressure. He parted his lips slightly, tasting her as she slipped her tongue over his, while sizzling electric sparks shot down his spine.

Their breathing fell into sync as he absorbed her small sighs and angled his head to adjust for their height difference. Her fingers tightened on his upper arms. The kiss was tender. Sweet. Innocent. But it lasted long enough for him to enter another dimension, as he focused on the sweet taste of her mouth, the silken glide of her tongue, the softness of her lips.

Each second the kiss lasted brought a fresh blast of promise, as each moment became about the meandering journey to getting there. If this kiss was anything like what lay in store as they worked up to cruising speed, the meandering path to ‘there’ sure as hell had advantages. Wherever ‘there’ might be didn’t matter, because his world had faded to nothing but her.

Chapter Twenty Eight

Andi

"Something's wrong," Pic said, digesting the news that Monica hadn't showed up for her appointment.

"You don't know that," Andi said, watching Pic pace the floor of the small bedroom.

"Yes. I do." He went to the chair where she'd folded his clothes and pulled on his green sweatshirt over the t-shirt he'd slept in. "And I need to find her."

What if I did *see her being abducted on Friday? And when, exactly, should I tell Pic about what I saw on Friday?*

She had renewed that conversation with Gabe as they'd been in the car on the way home from the clinic. It hadn't taken much persuasion from Gabe for her to know she shouldn't tell Pic anything about Friday.

It would worry him needlessly. Because I don't know whether what I saw, if I saw anything, has anything to do with Monica.

"Not today." Andi exchanged a long glance with Gabe, while placing a reassuring hand on Pic's arm. "You're too sick to roam the streets, looking for her. Let's sit down and rationally come up with a plan to find her."

"Good idea," Gabe said. "This is our problem now, too."

Pic made a U-turn, and faced them with a look of hope that belied the depth of his fear. Eyes bouncing from Gabe to Andi, Pic asked, "You'll both help me?"

"Yes." His expression was Gabe-style serious, meaning there was only a hint of his full smile. His gaze held the reassurance that everything would be okay. "The way it works is this—you're important to Andi, so you're important to me."

And now we're a threesome. We didn't even need that puppy.

"Finding Monica is important to you," Gabe continued, "so finding her is important to both of us. You feeling well enough to sit downstairs on the couch for a while?"

"Yeah. Sure," Pic said.

"Good. I want you to look at a few maps of the area. Flag every single place she might be. And I want you also to think about that kid, Jake, you mentioned yesterday." Some of the panic left Pic's eyes, as he listened to Gabe's smooth voice. "Andi and I tried to find Banjo Richie yesterday, but we couldn't. So give me places where we can look for him, too."

It wasn't just that Gabe's voice was calm, or that his plan seemed logical. It was the rock-solid earnestness with which he spoke that sounded so authentic, imparting the solid message of '*hey kid, don't panic. You're not alone.*'

Dear God, but this man's good.

"After you come up with the areas, give me a list, in order of importance, of people who might know where Monica, Jake, and Richie are, and then list where those people might be."

"You can't just approach these guys and start asking questions," Pic argued. "They're on the streets for a reason, and they don't talk to strangers."

"I know that," Gabe said. "So you're going to tell me the best way to approach them. That's another list for you. Black Raven calls this sort of research local knowledge, and for this project, the local knowledge has to come from you. See how much work you have to do while you recuperate? To develop an organized approach, it's going to take you a while. Especially since the meds you're on make you groggy. Meanwhile, over these next couple of days I'll keep checking in with Tank and Honey to see if Monica shows up with them."

Pic shoved some hair behind his ears, then folded his arms across his chest. "But it's the week before Mardi Gras. Nobody's in their normal places. Even the foot traffic changes."

"He's right, Gabe. Everything's different until Mardi Gras is over," Andi said.

"There's nothing we can do about Mardi Gras. We'll just have to work around it." Eyes intent on Pic for a few seconds, he said, "We'll have to stay calm, and go at this slow. I might not get to implement your direction until after Mardi Gras. By then, you'll be better, and you'll be able to go out with me. We can't rush this."

Pic nodded. "I get it."

"Monica's young and pregnant. It seems logical to me that she might just have gone home," Andi said. "Do you know where that is? Perhaps Gabe could have someone check there."

Pic shook his head. "She wouldn't go there. Not in a million years."

"Put it on the list, anyway," Gabe said.

Pic shook his head, and Andi knew where he was going with it. "I promised her I'd never tell. And there's some promises you just don't break, ya know?"

As Gabe frowned, Andi wanted to tell him not to push. Not on this one, and not now, because she knew Pic took promises seriously.

"Chief?" Gabe glanced at Andi, and pointed to his ear mic. "Tyre's at the front door. Sonja Long and Jacques Stapleton are here. Fifteen minutes early. Would you like them to freeze outside for a while, or would you like for Tyre to let them into the vestibule?"

Nervous adrenaline raced through her. "Vestibule. But not one step further until I'm there."

"Tyre. Got that?" Gabe lifted a hand to Andi, gesturing to the stairs. "Pic, I'm sending an agent in with a tablet. How are your internet skills?"

"Let's see. I polish them on a nightly basis. My brand new laptop—" He gave a sarcastic frown. "—complete with touchscreen technology, is in my backpack, right next to my iPhone 7 Plus. All wifi ready, with unlimited data."

Gabe cringed. "That bad, huh?"

"Yeah. Never held a smart phone. I haven't typed on a computer since the last day I attended school, a few years ago. I do know about the latest and greatest through advertisements and commercials I see on televisions in homeless shelters, but an iPad isn't likely to be in my near future."

While Andi's heart tumbled at the reality of Pic's life, Gabe smiled. "Then you're going to have the time of your life. Wait till you see how easy it is to download action flicks and video games. As you start to feel better, I'll teach you how to use maps and satellite technology so you can show me the places I need to look for your friends. Marks. You've been paying attention?"

He paused.

"Great. Go upstairs, into my room." He followed Andi to the stairs as he gave Marks instructions on getting his iPad ready for Pic to use.

Andi headed downstairs with him, Pic on their heels. After making sure Pic had everything he needed close at hand, she and Gabe returned to the main house. In the mudroom, she drew in a deep breath.

"You okay?" Gabe asked.

"Nervous."

"We've been through this. They're going to love your work."

They had been through it, because on and off, during the day, she'd been increasingly worried about the four p.m. meeting with Jacques and Sonja.

"I don't like the intrusion. In my home. They're from my past life. I'm better now. Really. I know I'll be seeing people more frequently. But even now, I think I'm going to have a hard time relating to people with whom I was once so...open."

"Oh," he said, arching an eyebrow. "That."

"Yeah," she said. "That. But it isn't that I slept with them both. And dear God, how terrible, that I can joke with you about sleeping with others, yet not...go there with you."

He shrugged. "We've known each other three days. Not that long—"

"Trust me. The way I behaved before, three days, in some cases, was a lifetime."

"I'm not worried about it. Because I'm feeling like I'm in line for an exclusive. Loving the anticipation of being your best, and I'm going to have fun working on persuading you I'm worthy of being your last."

She laughed, then any lightness she felt over Gabe's joke—*because that had to be a joke, right?*—faded as a few more seconds ticked away. Didn't he understand that she wasn't going to let them have a future? That all they had was these few days that he was on her job? She wouldn't allow him to get lost in her darkness. Not in any lifetime she could imagine. Given the clear look of sincerity in his eyes, she shook herself.

Focusing on the problem at hand, she said, "I don't know if I'm ready to be an artist yet."

He shook his head. "Not following. Because you're already one hell of an artist. It's who and what you are. Your talent is unmistakable. It shows in every canvas in this house."

Looking into his crystalline greenish-blue eyes made some of her uncertainty fade. "Thank you, but the fact that they want to decide what's gallery worthy—"

"Oh. Got it. You're worried they're going to start making business decisions you have to live by."

"Yes. And dear God, what if they—or anyone else—assume I'm the same sort of person I was before? Because the idea of all that casual sex is revolting to me now."

"One thing at a time. About the sex," he offered, smiling. "Set them, or anyone, straight. Fast. But we both know that's not why Sonja and Stapleton are here today. You're that good of an artist, Andi. Sonja's here to make sure she gets her finder's fee. Or whatever other accolade Stapleton's giving her."

"Not making me feel any more comfortable."

He chuckled. "It all gets back to my advice last night about being natural. Remember our talk?"

She nodded. "Being natural. Being me."

"Then quick. Are you comfortable with giving them ten more paintings?"

"Sure."

"Fifteen?"

She nodded. "But that's it. For now."

"Can you think of fifteen you're willing to give Stapleton?"

She did a quick mental check of the two hundred or so that were hanging in her house and were stacked against the walls of her studio upstairs. "Yes. Sure."

"Then, that's it. You set the terms. And do what comes natural to you. They need you more than you need them. They'll know that the minute they walk in and have their lights knocked out when they see your work. You hold the power. You have something they want, something they can't get anywhere else."

She nodded her head. "Okay."

"Want me to stay with you?"

"Please."

He flattened his hand in the small of her back. "Let's do it."

Waiting in the vestibule, Sonja looked her usual sleek and sophisticated self in head to toe black. An ivory-colored overcoat was folded over her left arm. She was typing a text on her cell phone. Jacques wore brown slacks, a beige turtleneck, and a navy overcoat. He was saying something to an agent, whose back was to Andi. Over the agent's shoulder, he gave Andi a nod, his voice trailing as she and Gabe approached.

By the time she hung up their coats, they were standing in front of paintings that hung on the largest unbroken wall in the foyer. Sonja had a bejeweled hand pressed dramatically to her chest. Jacques, head cocked slightly to the side, studied one canvas, then the next. A smile played at his lips. Their reaction made her forget, for a moment, her nervousness.

Gabe had assumed a position of unobtrusive security guard. From the base of the stairs, with his back to the wall, he shot her a full-beam smile, eyes alight with gloating.

'Told you so,' he mouthed.

The paintings that had captured Sonja and Jacques's attention were five of a series, in varying sizes, with slight changes in angle. She'd started the series by standing outside the Royal Orleans Hotel on Chartres Street, and looking down the street at the Saint Louis Cathedral.

"These are stunning," Sonja said. "The whole is even better than the parts. I wasn't aware you painted some of your canvasses in a series. I'd have insisted on that presentation in the show."

"Amazing," Jacques said, his attention fixed on the canvasses. "I have chills. You're it, Andi. You're the real deal."

The daytime blue of the sky painted in the first of the series had morphed into an evening sky with Prussian blue tones for the final painting. In the studio, she'd imagined that the street was alight with flames from gas lanterns. Flickering light played on puddles on the street and the flagstone of the sidewalk.

"The passage of time. Exceptional. You painted the first and second outside, right?" Jacques asked.

She nodded. "Two different days."

"And then you did the others in the studio?" Sonja asked.

"Entirely."

"I'm not sure which I like better. And that we have options is amazing. For purists, we have *en plein air*. For others, your studio embellishments. Rarely do artists bridge the gap from outside to inside so exceptionally. The colors. The brushstrokes. The depth. Good God, on this final one, the lantern light playing on the rain water." Jacques reached into his pocket and pulled out a phone, which he lifted and readied for a photograph.

Andi drew a deep breath. "No."

Jacques, hand poised in midair, arched an eyebrow as he looked at Andi and not Gabe. "The photos aren't for distribution."

"Please," Andi added. "No."

His dark eyes slid over her. He threw an exasperated glance at Sonja, then glanced back at Andi. "You know you can trust me."

"Of course." She fought to keep her tone conversational, and not fall into a whisper. "Otherwise, you wouldn't be in my house."

Gabe, who'd been standing close to the stairs, stepped a few feet into the foyer, and came to a stop at her side. "Ms. Hutchenson said no photographs."

Jacques kept his eyes on Andi. "I'm simply trying to get a handle on inventory."

She cleared her throat. "These are paintings, in my home. Not your inventory. I'll show you the paintings I'm offering for sale. Then you may leave."

"This might work best if it's a collaborative effort." Sonja's voice was cool.

"You both might want to forget anything you knew about me. I'm different than I was in the past. This is how I'll collaborate. Let's go upstairs, to my studio. I'll show you the paintings that the Stapleton Gallery may offer, starting tomorrow. You may set the price. All of my proceeds are to benefit Hope House. If you want to continue this, in two weeks, I'll have fifteen more. Not one day before."

"Fair enough," Sonja said, her blue eyes sharp, a small smile playing at her lips. "I like the new Andi. Lead the way. We can't wait to see what you'll offer to your eager collectors."

In the studio, they gawked more. But Jacques didn't attempt to take pictures again, and Sonja had nothing but praise for what she saw, as Andi indicated the canvasses she planned to have ready to send to the gallery the next day. The tour of her studio ended near the sketches.

Andi turned to go to the door where Gabe stood, but they didn't follow. Stapleton had paused, gazing at the wall where several sketches hung. "Oh my. These are amazing."

Sonja picked up a sketchpad from the table. "May I look?"

"There's no point. They're not for sale."

Sonja smiled, opening the sketchpad. "Everything's for sale. It's only the price that requires determination. Besides, I'm really good at persuading people to do things they never imagined doing." She gave Andi a small, lingering smile.

Drop dead, bitch. I know what you mean, and I'm no longer a pushover. That was the old Andi.

Andi glanced at Gabe. His face remained a study in blankness, but, as his gaze caught Andi's, a hard edge was visible in his eyes. Yes, he'd caught Sonja's hidden meaning.

Andi wanted to grab the sketchpads from their hands, uncomfortable with them touching the drawings that were so deeply personal to her.

"These are homeless people," Sonja said. "Invisibles. Right?"

"In that case," Jacques said, "lack of releases wouldn't be an insurmountable obstacle. They're not likely to know, and they were outdoors, in public, right, when you did these?"

"Those factors don't matter," Andi said, annoyed that they had so little regard for those they deemed invisible. Their very invisibility was what drew her to the homeless kids. "I wouldn't do anything without a release and it's really academic, anyway. Because they're not for sale."

“Your paintings are insanely good, Andi. But these sketches are incredible.” Sonja held the tablet so Jacques could see what she was looking at. “Look at how much expression she’s put in these eyes. Through shading.”

Andi’s throat caught when she saw the beautiful blonde who Sonja had been studying, with a small scarf wrapped around her head, featured in the sketch that had caught Sonja’s attention. *Monica.* Sonja flipped past the sketch of Monica, and paused at another one. *Honey.*

“Interesting, isn’t it, how these people cluster together. They seem to use the pretty blue-eyed blond girls to collect the big dollars,” Sonja said, flipping through the sketchbook as she spoke. “I read an article that said either a pregnant girl or a puppy can guarantee a panhandler upwards of two hundred fifty a day in high traffic areas.”

Looking over her shoulder as she turned the pages, Jacques shrugged. “Capitalism works just as well for the lower levels of society as it does everyone else, I suppose. One would think all the social services provided for them would be enough. Many of them go home to a nice apartment at the end of their day. They’re no more homeless than you or I.”

“No wonder we can’t get them off the streets.” Sonja paused, turning pages, her head cocked to the side as her eyes scanned the next sketch.

It took everything Andi had not to snatch the book from Sonja’s bejeweled fingers, and tell them she had no interest in submitting any of her work to the gallery. She didn’t like either of them. How in the world had she ever spent time with either of them?

“Oh look,” Sonja cooed. “You even drew the dog with this one. I love the way you treated the fur, I can practically feel how soft it is. This is exceptional.”

“In reality, we need about a hundred more Hope Houses,” Stapleton said. “Problem is, these people need to want to be off the streets. And most of them are just too damn lazy to get real jobs. We all know their cars are parked around the corner when they’re sitting under the interstate, panhandling, with those desperate looks on their faces.”

“Really?” Andi asked. “My sketches inspired this discussion?”

Stapleton and Sonja glanced at her, puzzlement in their eyes.

"I'm afraid I don't know what you mean," Jacques said, his gaze drifting downwards as he flipped a page. "I need to have these in the next show. They're amazing."

They reflected her past back at her, showing her a warped mirror image of who and what she'd once been. Shallow. Superficial. Uncaring. A part of a world that existed in her remote years. A world where she never would have noticed someone like Pic.

I'm better now, even though I'm broken.

Andi politely but firmly removed the sketchpads from their hands, then indicated the door as Gabe stepped back to allow passage. "Let me be perfectly blunt. Your conversation confirmed my decision. My sketches won't be offered for exhibition or for sale. Our business is concluded."

Chapter Twenty Nine

Gabe

Thursday, February 18, 7:30 p.m.

"Andi, you take Vitamin C, right?" Gabe asked, as Pic doubled over in a cough. The three of them were downstairs in the guesthouse, waiting on Dr. Cavanaugh. Gabe was on the couch with Pic, using his laptop and iPad to teach Pic how to incorporate data points onto satellite maps.

She sat across the room, closer to the fireplace and its crackling flames. She nodded as she glanced at him, then quickly returned her gaze to her laptop screen. She had her feet tucked up under her and her laptop balanced on pillows on her knees. He'd thrown together a pot of soup with a rotisserie chicken and vegetables he'd gotten from the grocery store. Simmering on the stove, it filled the air with homey, savory, mouthwatering goodness, waiting for Pic to get hungry.

Both Andi and Pic had blankets covering their laps, though the small, cozy house seemed plenty warm enough to him.

"Up the dose. This kid's still a walking petri dish." But he was a hell of a lot better. From Monday evening, on, Pic had resigned himself to resting. After setting up a user account for Pic on his iPad, and making sure all of Gabe's Black Raven work was locked away, Gabe had taught Pic a few preliminaries of how to use the iPad. He'd pretty quickly mastered how to access video games and live streaming action movies.

Pic now gripped the iPad like it was the best thing he'd ever held, but, because he was feeling better, he was insisting on hitting the streets on Friday to look for Monica, who hadn't yet made an appearance with Tank and Honey. Gabe had an idea for an end around.

As Pic coughed more, Andi's gaze took both of them in before settling on Gabe. Fresh worry wrinkled her brow. "What about you?"

"Yeah. Black Raven's power blend, with mega C." He glanced at a red-faced Pic, who was finally through coughing.

"Oh. A power pack," Pic said, his tone mocking. "Complete with steroids?"

Gabe threw a pillow at his head, which Pic deflected and threw back. "No steroids. And don't mock it, because I'm not the one who's sick here, am I? As a matter of fact, I'm starting you on it tonight. Now—back to work. The program auto-assigns pins for people, or whatever search components you're integrating into maps. List search components, in this case, people. As the program assigns pins, you insert them in the map, then type notes for each pin. Start with Banjo Richie."

Because I'm going out there tonight and I want to find someone who is damn well findable.

"Okay, I've got the concept, but where do I start the list to get the pins?" Pic turned the iPad so Gabe could see it.

"Touch—" Gabe leaned over, pointing to the map's search bar. "—there. The keyboard materializes, then you type the names. Once you do that, you'll be able to drop the colored pins. The document is live. Meaning whatever you type is materializing on mine. Andi, I'm emailing a link so you can integrate with us. I'll text a pass code."

"Okay." She didn't glance up from her computer.

The prompt that said that Andi had accessed the document didn't come. "Andi?"

"Yes?"

"Email plus text."

"Yes. Give me a minute to check out." She shot him a wide smile as she picked up her cell phone. In a second, his phone dinged with a text from her. *'Banana Republic. Urgent shopping trip. For Pic.'*

Andi-inspired warmth flooded through him. He wrote, *'I've got the map thing with Pic. Ragno's sent me an email. I'm forwarding it to you. A drawing of Pic's tattoo. Enhanced. Study it. Do a stream of consciousness email to Ragno & me. Anything u think of. Especially anything Pic may have told u. Ever. Ragno's been working on this for the last few days, but we need info to make sure she's in the right place. No matter how small—anything you've got might help.'*

Ragno's searches had turned up troubling information. He hoped deeper digging would lead them in a different direction. Gabe glanced at Pic, who was staring at the wonder of satellite map technology depicting areas where he'd walked for the last two years.

Glancing at his laptop screen, Gabe saw the first few green pins appear as Pic placed pins on the map. "These pins are for Richie?"

Pic nodded.

"Leave notes for each pin. Likely times he'll be there, what he'll be doing."

"Geez!" Pic tore his eyes from the screen. "Maybe paper would be easier."

"Nah. Not when you see the end result. You're a quick learner, so keep fiddling with it. We need to do it this way to auto-integrate our search results into the maps. I'll communicate with an analyst in Denver as I go to the places you flag—"

"As we go—"

"You're not leaving this house for two more days—"

"No way—"

"Guys, don't start that again," Andi said. "Pic. You're not leaving—"

"But Andi—"

"Come on." She frowned. "Don't make us the bad guys when we're just trying to help you."

"But I don't freaking want to sit around here for days on end. As nice as it is," he added.

Gabe looked at his laptop screen. Pic had dropped about eight pins in a three-block stretch. He snapped his fingers for the kid's attention. "Hey. Focus. So Frenchmen Street's a prime hangout for Richie, or are you making mistakes and dropping pins where you don't intend to?"

"No mistakes. He hangs there at night, trolling for work. Prime time is between ten thirty and three in the morning. From Snug Harbor, up and down the street. Anywhere music's playing. He's a stoner, which means he's got commitment issues. Everybody knows he's unreliable, so they don't hire him in advance. So he goes to the bars when he feels like, and sees if any bands want to pick him up for a set."

"How likely is he to be on Frenchmen tonight?"

"Pretty likely," Pic said, touching his laptop screen and dropping a few more green pins for places Richie might be. "Tourists come here for Mardi Gras, so even a stoner like Richie knows this is the time to make money."

Gabe eyed the short stretch of Frenchmen Street that was now littered with green pins. "I'll go there around nine and let you guys know what I find."

He saw it in their faces before they said a word—Andi was debating whether she should or could go, and Pic was about to insist, again, on joining him. "I'm going alone. Pic—you haven't eaten much of anything but crackers and apple juice. I get twenty four hours of inside rest after you hold down your first full meal. With protein."

He softened his tone with Andi. "And there's no need for you to go. I'm not going to subject you to crowded bars and drunks, especially when this guy might be nowhere in sight. You said it yourself—you didn't want to be outside from today until Mardi Gras is over."

"But you don't even know what he looks like," Pic said.

"I'm an investigator. I can find anyone. I found you, right?"

"But you knew what I looked like."

"True," Gabe said, "but how many guys walk around with banjos?"

Pic laughed. "More than you think. This is New Orleans. At Mardi Gras. People walk around with all kinds of things. And he doesn't always carry it. Just like me. Where's my guitar right now?"

Gabe frowned, because the guitar was in a case, in the corner of the room. Okay, so maybe Pic had a point. "Yeah, but you're not trying to get a few hours work with your guitar right now, are you? Besides, Andi's got about five sketches of the guy in her studio. I've got a pretty good idea what he looks like.

"That's good, because no one's going to point him out to you. People like the guy. He looks out for others, and you look like an oversized cop. A mean one."

"I'll smile."

Pic rolled his eyes. "Then they'll think you're stupid and rob you."

"You're underestimating the value of the almighty dollar."

"Doesn't matter what you pay."

"I seriously doubt that."

"He won't talk to you if I'm not with you," Pic said, digging in for an argument as he stared at the iPad screen and dropped green pins along Claiborne Avenue and beyond.

"We'll see about that," Gabe said. "Quick, think of a reason why he should tell me about what happened to Jake and where Monica might be, if he knows."

Pic stared at Gabe for a second, his eyes thoughtful. "Okay. Why?"

Gabe lifted his phone, and turned on the video. "Now tell him your reason."

Pic turned his head. "No photos, dude."

"I'll delete it after I talk to Richie."

With a frown, and a firm headshake, Pic turned his back to Gabe.

"I promise I'll delete it."

Pic shrugged and turned to face Gabe. "Okay. But I want to see you delete it."

And this is why the pile of shit Ragno's searches are screeching towards can't be true. He's trusting me. And he cares about these people. He's not evil. He's good. I know it.

"That's fair." Gabe lifted his phone again, and pressed the video switch.

"Hey, Richie," Pic said into the phone. "This guy's helping me. I'm sick as a dog. Been staying at Andi's house. Tell Gabe about what you said happened to Jake. Maybe it's related to what happened to me. And Monica missed her clinic appointment on Monday. It's driving me crazy. So if you've seen her, can you let this big guy know? Later, dude."

Shutting the phone, Gabe eyed the plethora of green dots on the map. "More bars where musicians play?"

As Pic nodded, Gabe typed a text for Marvin. '*You free for a couple of hours of work? At eleven-ish? Need to go to some local haunts. Find someone.*'

"Yeah," Pic said. "These pins along Claiborne and Orleans Avenue are in Treme. This one—I'll put a double pin on it—has really good food. The old lady who owns it, Clothilde, serves gumbo and roast beef po' boys all night. Food's pricey, but—" Pic smiled. "—she likes me and Richie. She'll feed us for free if we play for an hour or so." His expression turned serious. "This neighborhood's rough. You shouldn't go there at night alone."

Gabe laughed, as Agent Tyre's voice crackled through his earpiece. "Sir?"

"Yes?"

"Doctor Cavanaugh's here."

The doctor and Pic went upstairs while Gabe and Andi remained in the living room. After the exam, the doctor and patient returned downstairs. Pic resumed his position on the couch and refocused on the iPad. Gabe had briefed the doctor on how hard it was to get Pic to stay off the streets. Playing the part of stern but friendly physician well, Cavanaugh reported that Pic's lungs had started to improve. He emphasized the need for Pic to rest and remain inside. It was too damp outside. Humidity wouldn't help his lungs.

"Okay," Gabe said. "You heard the doctor. I've got enough pins on the map for one night. What about a bowl of soup?"

At eight-thirty, after soup and a fresh dose of cough medicine, Andi left the guesthouse. Gabe stuck around until Pic was in bed, fighting off sleep, and clutching Gabe's iPad. Gabe assured him he'd wake him if he got any news on the street, then went looking for Andi in the main house. He found her in her studio, painting, with all the lights on and the heat turned up.

Leaning against the doorjamb, inhaling the pungent smell of oil paints, he took in the sight of her, paintbrush in hand as she focused on the mostly blank canvas on her easel. She wore fluffy white socks, black yoga pants, and a baby blue, oversized sweatshirt. He'd love to slowly unpeel those layers and—yeah. That.

Over the last few days, the Sandy/Brad thing had settled into long kisses. Petting, like he hadn't done since his teenage years. And the night before, they'd even gotten on the couch and watched television for hours, as they nestled into each other and got cozy. It had always been his favorite kind of date, and he'd found his perfect woman for it. Finally.

As she glanced towards him, some of the deep concentration that she was directing at the canvas left her face. As she lay her paintbrush on a table, her smile melted his heart. "Is he asleep?"

Gabe nodded. "Almost. Trying hard to watch *X-Men Origins, Wolverine*."

She chuckled. "I'll check on him around eleven. It'll be time for his meds then." She stretched her arms above her head, shifting her head from left to right in a neck stretch. He fought the urge to go to her. Take her in his arms. Help her work any kinks out of her shoulders. Her neck. Her back.

No. No. And, no. Give her space.

To his disappointment, she remained near her easel, twelve feet away instead of crossing the room to him. "I don't think you're getting your iPad back," she said, lifting a tube of oil paint from the table near her easel, and opening it.

"Doesn't matter. I ordered one for him. Should be here tomorrow."

"I texted photos of the sketches I did of Richie to you."

"Got 'em."

She gave him an eyebrow arch. "They're not for distribution."

"Understood." He thought about the email reply Andi had sent after looking at the artist's rendering of Pic's tattoo, which Cavanaugh had said was spot on. "So you think the name in Pic's tattoo could be Aubrey Rose?"

She nodded, squeezed a blob of reddish oil paint onto her palette, then stared at it while she talked. "It's a guess. Based upon the rules of monograms."

"You lost me."

"That's because you're not a Southern woman, with monograms on everything since your first onesie." She squeezed out another blob, then glanced at him with a big smile. "Have you noticed my AH monograms?"

"Yeah. Impossible to miss." The letters AH were embroidered on towels in the bathrooms, scrolling across pillowcases, embossed on the stationary at her writing desk, and even stamped in lavender ink on the notepad on her kitchen counter.

Best thing is you won't have to change any of it. See? My last name starts with an H, too. Keep yours or take mine. Choice will be yours.

Oblivious to where his thoughts had gone, she continued in a matter-of-fact tone as she replaced the tube on the table. "It's a matter of proportionality. Pic didn't put the woman's full name, but the size of the rose is the size of the A in Aubrey. Sort of like when there are only two initials in a monogram, like mine. My A is the same size as my H. Just a guess, though. Plus, Aubrey Rose is such a beautiful name." Her gaze settling on him, she asked, "Why? You know something?"

"Not yet." *Because I'm not liking what the searches are telling me.* "There's something else. Cavanaugh called me tonight, after he left. When he was examining Pic, he noticed something he didn't see before. Vertical scars. Two. One on each wrist. Faded, but visible. Cavanaugh says they're consistent with a suicide attempt, a few years ago. You know anything about that?"

All color drained from Andi's face, which he took as a solid confirmation of Cavanaugh's hunch. *Aw. Hell. Hell. Hell. That's why the bond between them is so strong—a fact I'm not supposed to know anything about. It isn't simply that Pic saved Andi that day when she tried to drown herself. It's because he'd tried it too. And that's bad, in light of what Ragno's figuring out.*

Suddenly, she felt more remote than simply the twelve feet separating them. It was as though the distance between them was a deep, frigid body of water. The strength of the water's current was the importance of the lie he was telling her by not admitting that he knew details that she'd never revealed to anyone. To him. Importance was growing by the second. And there was only one anecdote for lying, and that was the truth.

The whole truth.

As Andi stood there, silent, struggling with her private memories and her equally private knowledge about Pic, his gut screamed, *'Now's the time, dumbass! Tell her now that you know everything, that you read her journals. Own your mistake. Ask for forgiveness. Embrace the suck.'*

He cleared his throat, and started, "Look, Andi—"

"I know, Gabe."

Maybe he'd have kept going, but the softness of her whisper snuffed the rest of his words. Her own memories were enough of a struggle. He didn't need to add to it. She cleared her throat and when she spoke again, her tone was firm and unwavering. "To help Pic, we need to know who he is. But how could that fact—whether he'd attempted suicide—help you identify him? Apart from Cavanaugh giving you information, aren't most medical records protected?"

He shifted gears, grateful for the reprieve. "Not from Black Raven. As a matter of fact, in this day and age, no cyber data, even medical records, is protected from anyone with a bit of know-how. If Ragno goes with an assumption that Pic is closely connected to an Aubrey Rose, and birth records indicate that an Aubrey Rose gave birth to a male in the time frame we're guesstimating for Pic's birth, and she takes that and combs through databases for a minor affiliated with an Aubrey Rose who was hospitalized for a wrist slashing—"

Shaking her head with a look somewhere between annoyance and confusion, she interrupted him. "Isn't hacking like that criminal?"

That isn't the half of it. That's only the official, Black Raven-sanctioned hacking. Goddammit, but I'm in trouble.

"Black Raven only does this sort of work on a need-to-know basis." His gut twisted with an inward cringe. The company line sounded as lame as it ever did.

Her features shifted to disgust. "I hate to think you do that kind of stuff."

If only you knew.

"We protect, Andi. And the only way to do that effectively is to know the enemy. Inside and out, and especially their secrets." By the way Andi was reacting to this mild, watered-down taste of the darker side of Black Raven, he couldn't find the words he needed to tell her about his much more intimate invasion of her privacy. His brother Zeus's prophecy—that one day Gabe wouldn't be able to fix the damage he created by ignoring boundaries—was coming to pass.

The truth—*'Hey Andi, I picked the lock to your secret room and read your journals'*—seemed like fighting words in light of the bonfire she'd orchestrated the night before. Her scowl now made it perfectly clear that he was going to be on the losing end of that fight.

As I should be. Okay. Decision's made. I can't tell her. Not now. Maybe never.

"I'm done with giving you information about Pic," Andi continued, gripping another tube of paint, and squeezing out a small blob of dark greenish paint next to the reddish color. "I know I said to keep going with Ragno's searches for information leading to Pic. And I know I analyzed the tattoo. But nothing more. Sorry." As she looked up and directed her gaze at him, the hard look in her eyes and solid set to her jaw indicated she was anything but sorry. "I won't betray a confidence. And just to be clear here, I'm not confirming or denying whether Pic ever mentioned anything about a suicide attempt to me. I'll figure out a different way to help him."

He nodded. "Understood."

"And I think you should also find a different way." She lifted her palette knife and started working the two blobs together. She glanced at him. "Stop digging. Accept him for who he is now."

At least he could be honest about this. "I'm not going to do that. I'm going to find out what went wrong in his life—"

"For what reason? Help him now, the way he is now—"

"I don't believe that I can, without knowing what went wrong. I'm going to figure it out, and I'm going to fix it."

She studied him for a few seconds. "You can't fix everything, Gabe. Some things break, and can't be put back together. You do understand that, don't you?"

As he locked glances with her, the storm cloud of worry in her eyes made him pretty damn certain she wasn't simply referring to Pic. She was talking about herself. "I absolutely understand that some things are better left alone. But I know when I should exercise my power to try to make things better. And with Pic, I need to figure out if that's a possibility."

His words did little to alleviate the worry in her eyes. But she lifted her paintbrush, and he took the action as a dismissal. One that he was damn grateful for, because he felt that he either had to tell her what he knew about her, or end the conversation. "I'll be back in a few hours."

Once in his bedroom, he typed a text to Ragno. *'Andi won't confirm or deny whether Pic tried suicide.'* He paused, thinking about Andi's initial reaction. Then he added, *'Assume it happened, though.'*

Her reply came fast, as he grabbed his jacket. *'Already did. Massaging data now. Not liking results. I'll run programs with alternate scenarios. Maybe drop Rose from Aubrey (?). Let's talk after I assimilate data. Budapest team needs my attention. You have eyes on Pic?'*

'Yes.'

'For now, you have to assume Pic's a danger to Andi.'

'Instinct says he's not."

When she received that text, Ragno called. "I know you don't want to believe it," she said. "But I know what my research is telling me. Due diligence requires us to keep Andi secure, which means we look at him even closer now. If this pans out, he's the sort of person we keep from our clients. Not allow in their guesthouses."

Heart heavy, Gabe knew exactly what Ragno was saying. He also knew the likelihood of Ragno's research leading to an incorrect result was damn slim. "Keep looking. Modify the other variables. There's got to be another plausible scenario for his mother's death out there. Or maybe we've misidentified him, and we're looking at the wrong Aubrey. We need to find more facts. This can't be right."

"I'm on it," she answered.

Tyre and Stevens were in the security vestibule. Gabe paused in the doorway to pull on his jacket. "I'm heading out. I have you both on audio. Keep me informed as to both Pic and Andi. If she goes to the back house, go with her. Do not leave her alone with Pic."

Chapter Thirty

Concierge

Thursday, February 18, 10:00 p.m.

Drawing out the anticipation, I walk around the bedroom, lighting long, elegant, cream-colored tapers. I'm ready for another night with the woman splayed out on my bed, face down, arms and legs tied to bedposts.

My faux Andi.

Close enough...for now. Yeah, the bedpost thing is a cliché. But it works.

After weeks of work, she's a dead-ringer for my fantasy girl. My stylist came in today and spent a few hours on retouching. She got the new haircut just right. Dark, choppy hair, the ends touching her shoulders. Waves bending towards her face. A bit of makeup, but not too much. Tonight she's wearing lingerie similar to what Andi wore our second time together. A thong and sheer brassiere. Both creamy white, with black lace accents.

Makeup on her body almost hides the bruises I left on her last night, when I taught her a few things. Her new name. The proper way to address me. How she was supposed to damn well enjoy it when I touched her.

Let's say this bitch wasn't exactly a quick learner.

"Hello, Andi," I say, shivering in anticipation of her reply.

I wait.

She's supposed to whisper, 'Hello, Concierge,' in as close to Andi's breathy bedroom voice as this semi-literate, once homeless person we scooped off the streets of San Francisco can muster. Despite the drugs we've administered, her luminous dark green eyes, fringed with dark lashes, are wide with panic and fear.

"You're crazy!" she screams, her arms and legs straining against the silk ties that bind her. "Let me go, you sick fuck."

"Not the correct reply." I struggle to keep my voice calm. "Have you forgotten your lessons, Andi?"

In answer, she screams again. Loud. Shrill. Deliciously ugly in all its terrifying glory. But not the right mood for this night. Her yells wind down to three words that she repeated over and over again last night. "I'm. Not. Andi."

I clench my jaw in frustration. I wanted three more nights of play. Then I planned to get to the serious stuff—the things that warrant this kind of terror. Let's just say this bitch is screaming for all the wrong reasons.

Trying to soothe myself, to keep the beast within tamped down, I calmly light one more taper, then walk to the bed. When my knees touch the mattress, she turns her head to me and spits. Her slime flies through the air and lands on my thigh. It leaves a cold trail as it drips down my leg.

I backhand the bitch.

From the corner of the room, my partner, who is supposed to be silent and still until I damn well order him to do something, ignores the rule I've set. "I told you she'd need Rohypnol tonight."

My blood boils at the sound of his voice. I don't even bother to glance into the shadowed corner where he's standing. "I don't like when they're comatose. It's boring. And you don't want me to be bored, do you?"

"No, Concierge."

Good answer, dickhead.

The mention of my name, which I drilled into faux-Andi's thoughts last night, brings a fresh batch of screams from her. She strains against the silk ties, which are doing nothing but getting tighter. "You people are crazy."

"You don't know the half of it, bitch."

I walk over to the chest of drawers, open one, and pull out a carton of Camel cigarettes. There's a sparse warning label, right below the camel, that says 'smoking kills.'

Yes. It does. And so do I.

From his corner, my partner says, "Concierge, we paid too much on this one's enhancements for you—"

"On your knees before you address me."

"But—"

"On. Your. Knees." I open the carton of cigarettes. "Or out the door." I would order him to strip, but he's already naked. Through the shadows, as he drops to his knees, I can see that his cock is full and erect. His brain might be trying to interject reasoning into this night, but his cock is giving me a solid salute of approval.

I have this man by the balls. He loves to watch me have sex. Whether I'm doing it with men or women, and no matter how I do it. He also loves to watch me torture my sex partners. And the *coup de grace* for him is fucking women he's watched me kill. Which is yet another reason why I own him. From the size of his erection, I know that he knows he's in for a goddamn treat. Because the end is coming for the bitch who is laying on the bed, and my partner is practically salivating at the thought of shoving his dick into faux Andi's dead body, marked by whatever way I decide to enjoy my time with her. I reach for a pack of cigarettes, tap it against my hand, then slip my thumb through the cellophane wrapping.

"Concierge, may I speak?" he asks, his head bowed, his voice subservient as I light my cigarette from the flame of a nearby candle.

"Yes." I take my first drag of a cigarette, inhaling the acrid smoke deep into my lungs. "Lift your head and look into my eyes."

"We paid too much for this one's makeover for you to destroy her tonight. Because tomorrow, you're going to want another one. We don't have another one close to being ready for you. Your obsession for Andi Hutchenson has become insatiable. I don't want you to be bored."

I walk over to him and lean down to run a finger over the head of his penis, touching a drop of moisture that's beading there. I lift my finger to his lips, running the bead of liquid along his lower lip before slipping my finger into his mouth. "I agree. She needs to last at least one more night for me. That's why I'm not burning her tonight."

His relief is palpable as he sucks the taste of himself off of my index finger.

"You are."

His eyes widen. I pull my finger out of his mouth, and kneel on the floor in front of him. I take a deep drag of the cigarette and blow the smoke in his face. For a second, the only sound in the room is the whimpering, mewling cries of the woman who has now disappointed me. "But first, I have to make a phone call, and I want you to listen carefully. Because if you don't agree with everything I say, I'm leaving you."

"Please don't say that."

I look closely into his eyes. I see misery. But I want fear. "And I mean it this time. I will create a new life. One that doesn't include you."

"I will die without you."

"Yes. You will. Our business will be over, and the best days of your life will be a memory. You'll be so miserable, you'll kill yourself. And I will not show up for your funeral. I'm that goddamn bored. And what I don't want—" I draw back a hand

and slap his face as hard as I can. "—is for you to goddamn tell me I can't have what I want. Do you understand me?"

His eyes are full of tears. Not from the slap, but because he believes my words, which are delivering his worst nightmare. And yes, this man gets aroused by being dominated by me. His cock is so goddamn big and hard and straining that even I'm getting turned on by it. But I don't let on. "If you don't say 'yes, Concierge,' I will get dressed and leave right now."

Ah. There's the fear I want to see. In his wide eyes. In the beads of perspiration that ball on his forehead. "Yes, Concierge."

I walk over to the dresser. My cell phone is next to the carton of Camels. Because New Orleans is fertile hunting grounds, my best reapers are here now, working the Mardi Gras season with the ones who are always here. My reapers here know the depth of my obsession with Andi Hutchenson. They're the best of the best, which makes them pretty goddamn evil and extraordinarily valuable to me. They're worth more than their weight in gold, and when they deliver Andi to me, they're going to have the payday of their lives.

I call my most trusted reaper. He'll direct the others as needed. He answers on the second ring. "Find a way to bring her to me. And then you'll get to retire wherever it is you might want to be."

His confident chuckle sounds beautiful. "Was wondering when we'd get to this. Given how restless you've been lately, I figured the time was coming soon. I have a plan."

"Involving her friend with the brass knuckles?"

"Yep. And I also want bonus money for him."

"Don't get greedy."

"Yeah, but this kid's beautiful. Tall. Blue-eyed. And once we have him, we'll be one step closer to Hutchenson."

"Don't wreck his face. Or damage his body too badly."

"Giving him to you will be revenge enough. We've been looking for him. Rumor on the street is that he's staying at her guesthouse. One of our local contacts has been friendly with the kid. He'll create a misdirection for her security team. Distract them. Draw her out. Then we'll get her. Here's my idea..."

Chapter Thirty One

Gabe

Thursday, February 18, 11:00 p.m.

Gabe walked to the corner of Royal and Barracks, where Marvin waited for him in an SUV, as they'd planned. The dark-headed man knew his way around the streets and the foot traffic. With Marvin driving, it took about an hour to hit most of the bars that Pic had flagged along Esplanade Avenue and Treme.

At a couple of places, friendly manager/bouncer types seemed happy to earn extra cash by being on the lookout for Richie. A twenty thanked them for their time, with the promise of a hundred bucks if they called with Richie's location.

He and Marvin polished off bowls of seafood gumbo at Clothilde's. As a brass band played "Mardi Gras Mombo," Gabe's phone vibrated with a call from one of the managers. They jumped in the SUV and headed to Fat Cat Alley. There, the manager took them to a small backstage room. He pointed to a tall, lanky guy with stringy hair, high cheekbones, and a red bandana tied flat around his forehead. Exactly as Andi had sketched. And as Pic had predicted, Richie wasn't holding a banjo.

Hell-bent on collecting his hundred bucks, the manager blocked the doorway behind Gabe and Marvin. The guys who were getting ready to go on stage with Richie eyed Gabe and Marvin. Grabbing their instruments, they eased around the manager, who pointed at Richie. As Gabe slipped the bill into his hand, the manager said, "You. Stay. Answer this guy's questions."

Distrust apparent in his steady, focused blue eyes, Richie squared his shoulders and gave Gabe a head to toe look over. "What the fuck do you want?"

Gabe lifted his cell phone and pressed play on the video of Pic. As it ended, Gabe lowered his hand and answered, "Just a conversation."

Richie's shoulders slightly relaxed. "I told the kid that eye was going to become blacker than black. I was worried about him, till Tank and Honey told me where he was." There was no slurring of his words. He stood perfectly straight. About six feet tall. Thin. Without a hint of bloodshot in his eyes. "You a cop?"

"No."

"You sure?" Richie arched an eyebrow. "Not even a Fed? 'Cause you look like you could be DEA. And if you are, I'm not saying a goddamn word to you."

"Not a cop. Not NOPD. Not DEA. Not any official agency, anywhere."

While one hand adjusted the bandana on his forehead, Richie pushed straggly blond hair back behind his ear with the other. "Is Pic in trouble?"

"Not from me. Come on. You saw the video. He just wants to find Monica, and I want to talk to you about his friend, Jake. Pic says you were looking for Andi to talk to her about Jake. Andi hasn't seen Jake, and now she's worried. As is Pic. I'm here for both of them, hoping you have something that will lead me to Monica and Jake."

"You one of the security guys that's always around Andi?"

"Yes."

"Why haven't I seen you before?"

"Arrived in town a few days ago."

"I get why Andi's not with you, but why isn't Pic here?"

"He's sick. Like he said. Want me to replay his message for you?"

"Nah." Richie shook his head. "You talk like you're from somewhere else."

"Miami. Does that matter?"

Richie rolled his eyes and folded his arms. "Dude, if you ain't from here, then you don't get it. It doesn't matter where you're from. You won't understand these crazy-ass streets, and how easy it is to mistake something weird for normal."

As Richie spoke, Gabe saw Pic's mannerisms. Of similar height and straggly build, they had the same street-tough wariness. Chest out. Shoulders squared. Head cocked to the side. Gabe had heard 'dude' enough from Pic to understand that a certain segment of the population still used the word. Gabe guessed he was staring at a person from whom Pic had picked up some of his tough-guy persona.

"Well, the good news is I'm from here." Marvin's voice, thick with New Orleans-style drawl, boomed through the small room. "And neither one of us is a cop."

Richie glanced at Marvin, his shoulders relaxing with relief. "Problem is, I was really stoned the day I saw what happened with Jake. Wouldn't blame anyone for not believing me."

Marvin shrugged. "We don't care about how stoned you might've been."

"Okay. I'll give you a few minutes. Gotta go onstage in a bit, though." Richie's blue eyes reflected the gravity in his serious frown. "You talked to anybody else about the street scene?"

"Not yet," Gabe said. "But I will. So shoot straight with me."

Richie frowned as his eyes crawled over Gabe, from head to toe. He let out a big sigh, as though internally, he'd made a decision. "There's weird shit happening."

Richie's comment set Gabe on high alert. Richie had the weather worn look of a guy who'd seen it all, and Gabe bet his barometer for *'weird shit'* was a helluva lot less sensitive than the norm.

Marvin asked, "Tell us about it."

Richie shrugged. "A handful of people are missing right now. Rumor has it six, maybe seven that I've heard about. Though you never know with homeless people."

"You're not homeless?" Marvin asked.

"Nah," Richie chuckled. "I just act like I am. I hang out and eat at the shelters, because the price is right. Sometimes I'll sleep at a shelter, too, if I'm hiding out from a lady friend."

"What makes you think Jake's missing," Gabe asked, "as opposed to up and gone? As in, he decided to leave New Orleans. Moved on, elsewhere. Like Pic did. He went to Texas for six months. I'm sure some people here missed him, and might've wondered where he went."

"Dude, I know what you're saying—" Richie gave a firm headshake. "—but that isn't what happened to Jake."

"Why not?" Gabe asked. "Why do you think he'd tell you he was leaving New Orleans? Does the kid have to report to you?"

Richie shook his head again, slowly this time. "One, we're friends, and Jake would've told me if he was planning on leaving. And two—" He drew a deep breath. "—'cause I'm pretty much sure I saw him get taken last Wednesday."

"Pretty much sure?"

"Yeah. I think I saw Jake trying to fight off two guys who stuffed him in the back of their van. Which strongly, sure-as-shit implies to me that Jake didn't decide to take a leisurely stroll down I-10 and hitch a ride to see where the grass might be greener."

"You think?"

"Look. I'm not gonna lie. I've been trying to persuade myself otherwise, 'cause I was pretty wasted. But I wasn't the only one to see it. At least one other person was there. And he's talking about it. Saying he's going to go to the cops if Jake doesn't show up soon."

"What had you taken?" Gabe asked.

Richie's brow furrowed in a frown as he glanced at Gabe. He folded his arms over his chest. "What the shit does that matter?"

"Some drugs have more hallucinogenic properties than others."

"Look. I'm thirty. Since I was fourteen years old, I've been high on something. I know what's a hallucination and what isn't."

"You high now?" Gabe asked.

"No. Stone cold sober."

"Why?" Marvin asked.

"Because," Richie's eyes leveled on Gabe, then Marvin. "Because I'm beating myself up, ya know? If I saw what I think I saw, I just sat there, like a dumbass, when I should've done something to help. I help these kids, man. They come here, and they're lost. Sometimes they need someone to talk to, even if it's just a loser like me. Look, I'm not much, but I'm a hell of a lot better than most of the adults who are the reason these young people are on the street. By my guess, the average age of the kids I've befriended is seventeen, though they all say they're older. And most of them are scared shitless of the cops, 'cause they don't want to be sent home."

"Did you go to the cops after you saw the incident with Jake?"

His frown deepened. "Nah. And not just because I think they're mean-spirited assholes who are all on the take. Which most of them are. Truth is, they'd assume I was out of my mind, just like you're doing." He shook his head, then sighed, dropping his arms to his side, and giving up his defensive posture. "Look. I was two days into a spice high, that I chased for a while with some rotgut vodka I bought at the same gas station that sold me the spice. You ever did spice?"

"Nah. Synthetic marijuana isn't my thing," Gabe said.

"Mine, either," Marvin said.

"Well, I wouldn't recommend starting. Stick with the natural herb. Hell—go organic if you can. Best shit's coming from California these days."

Marvin chuckled.

"Good to know," Gabe said.

"The spice I bought was laced with something that had me so high, I needed help coming down," Richie continued, "so I took a few Quaalude's, about an hour before it happened. At first,

I didn't even react. But the guy who was standing next to me saw it, too."

"Saw what?"

"Two guys, wearing masks, jumped out of a white van, and hit Jake with a stun gun before shoving him into their van."

Holy hell.

"Say that again," Gabe prodded, as the hair on the back of his neck stood on end. Richie repeated what he saw, then gave them a few more facts that were the stuff of urban legends. It would all have been easily dismissed, but for a few key similarities Gabe couldn't ignore.

"The guy who sold me the lude was right next to me."

"What's his name?" Marvin asked.

Richie shook his head. "Don't be mistaking me for stupid, bro. You're not getting his name out of me. And there's no way I'll go to the cops, either. He won't, either. But he's sure as shit telling everyone he knows. Trust me—it's better not to be on the radar of the cops around here. They're some frustrated motherfuckers. Can't do anything about the real thugs, so they come after people like me. But you can tell Pic that Monica isn't one of the missing ones. At least not like Jake is."

"How do you know?" Gabe asked.

"Because I know where Monica is. Hiding out is different from being missing."

"Who is she hiding from? And why?"

"Now if I told you that, then I'd be spreading her business, wouldn't I? And I'm not that kind of guy."

Gabe stared into Richie's eyes. "Look. I'm not asking you to help me here. I'm asking you to help Pic. The kid's sick. In fact, he's lucky he's not in the hospital. I'm trying to keep him off the streets so he can get better, but he's going crazy with worry over her."

"He's not the only one. Dude who got her pregnant sure wants to get a hold of her, as well. That's why she didn't show up at that doctor's appointment. I told her not to go. Because if you and Pic knew that she was supposed to be at the clinic, I can promise you, the baby's daddy did as well." Richie drew a deep breath. "Look. Why don't I come over and talk to Pic?"

"Easier if he could simply call her."

"She doesn't have a phone."

"Do you?"

"Nah. Mine's on the fritz. Too expensive to fix. French Quarter, Marigny, Treme, Bywater. These neighborhoods make up the oldest village in the good old U.S. of A. People walk places. Some people live their whole lives within these neighborhoods. People talk face to face here. Where else does that happen these days?"

Gabe glanced at Marvin, who nodded. "Accurate."

"People who live on the streets here are used to communicating the old-fashioned way, and—" Richie's grin was broad, and he opened his arms wide in a 'look-at-me' pose. "You're looking at part of the pony express. Look. I'd like to check in with Pic. See how he's doing. I'll get a message from him to Monica. That way he'll stay put and get better."

Gabe nodded. "Sure. Eight a.m.?"

"Hell no. I'll be asleep by then. Let's see. Bar closes at three thirty or so. I told the manager I'd stay and help the cleaning crew. It sucks cleaning toilets at Mardi Gras, but the pay is good. I'll pass by Andi's around five thirty a.m."

"You've been there before?"

"Not inside, dude. But everyone knows where she lives. You know, we street people look out for her, too. Just like she looks out for us. From far away," he said, shrugging, "but it works."

Chapter Thirty Two

Andi

She heard Gabe coming up the stairs. As he paused in the doorway of her studio, she shivered as she took in the darkness that seemed to surround him—not only in his black slacks, turtleneck, and shoes—but in the deep, deep concern in his light eyes. "Want to help me think through some things?"

"Sure."

He walked over to her, and opened his hand, revealing a small plastic bag. "Here."

"What's that?"

"A spare earpiece, for you to use. This is the best way to have a three-way. Ragno's going to call when she gets a break, somewhere in the next ten or so minutes. We'll bring you up to speed on Ragno's research, and the three of us are going to put our heads together."

Andi put the paintbrush down. The gravity in his eyes told her he was worried. If he was this worried, her scarf, sweatshirt, and fuzzy socks weren't going to be warm enough.

"You found Richie?"

"Yeah. I want to talk it over with you and Ragno." His eyes met hers for a second. "If you feel up to it."

"Yes," she said, without hesitation.

"There are also things that Ragno's uncovering on Pic that you should know. I know we're not exactly on the same page, but I hope you'll hear us out, then agree we need to do a bit more digging."

"I've been thinking about what we were talking about earlier. I know you're right. I know we need to dig into the facts. I just don't want to lose his trust."

He drew a deep breath. "I promise you that we will figure out a way to help him, and we'll build up his trust."

"Okay," she said. She breathed in deep, hesitating, then deciding to go forward with the question Gabe had asked earlier. "He did attempt suicide. Before he came to New Orleans."

"After you and I talked, we assumed he did. According to Cavanaugh, those scars are too telling. I'm going to be honest here. One part of me wants to protect you from all of this. I'd love to keep you in the dark. But I respect you too much not to let you know what I'm hearing."

"Thanks," she said. "Don't think I'd like you too much if you kept silent."

She opened the plastic pouch and poured the device onto her palm. It felt weightless. Three clear filaments, of varying lengths and thicknesses, were attached to a silver tube that was a little larger than a grain of rice. "Wow. So small."

"We're working on making it smaller." Gabe removed his, then showed her how to insert the device into her ear. "It receives and transmits when paired with our watches. It'll pick up your voice and voices within a few feet of you. Receiving and transmission functions work through each filament. The longest filament wraps around your outer ear. It keeps the thing in place. Insert the shortest filament first, before the device. It picks up vibration in your bones as you speak. Use your little finger to push it into your left ear. You're left-handed, so assume that's your dominant side for hearing. Get it into the canal as far as it'll go."

"Not sure how."

"Trick is to push it in while you're hooking the outside line to the back of your ear, and keeping the medium-length one out of your ear."

She followed his instructions, then turned her head to the side so he could see. "Feels weird. Like this?"

"Not exactly. You barely have it in."

"Can you fix it?"

And wrap your arms around me while you're doing that, because I'm freezing. You're suddenly a little too good at giving me space. I'm not that fragile. Not with you, at least.

He closed the foot or so of distance between them. She felt his fingers running through her hair, smoothing tendrils down as he pressed the filament along the back of her ear.

"It tickles," she whispered.

He leaned in, kissed her cheek, then slipped his finger into the neck of her sweatshirt, and pulled the band. "Damn. Did my chokehold give you this bruise?"

Since Tuesday, he'd increased her workouts to two a day. And he'd been encouraging her to take her self-defense moves out of the exercise room. It was all about building confidence, so she could fight past her tendency to hesitate. *Think. Then implement. If you have to, play possum while you plan your attack. Then come up with a plan, and implement it. Try to fake me out. Try to shock me. Try to hurt me.*

He'd encouraged her to make sneak attacks on him, and on Thursday morning, she had managed to surprise him with a kick that almost made it to his groin. He'd moved to the side, then gripped her in a chokehold, which he then taught her how to fight her way out of. They'd ended that with a marathon kissing session as they had once again become Brad and Sandy, driven by pure lust, yet hampered by virginal restraint.

"Probably. Doesn't matter, though. I'm still going to kick your ass one day. My goal is to knock you flat on your butt, when you least expect it."

"That's big talk."

"Not just talk. One day, I'll do it."

He chuckled. "I have no doubt you could do it to ninety-nine percent of the people you encounter. But not me. Not in this lifetime. Keep trying, though."

As she inhaled his scent—deep, musky male and lingering pine from the soap that he used—he drew her to him. And suddenly, it wasn't about the mic or the bruise. She knew it, by the way his breath caught, by the meandering feel of his touch, by the way he pulled her closer.

"This mic isn't live now, is it?" She tried not to groan. She shut her eyes as his warmth and strength enveloped her.

"No," he said, his voice a harsh whisper into her ear. "Audio's off. I'm listening to my agents, but they can't hear me. I control your device from my watch. Ragno's calling in a few minutes. She's assisting agents in Budapest and working with a team in Kosovo. She's a master multi-tasker." She felt his lips on her neck. "So, that's a long way to say we're alone. Is this an okay way to kill a few minutes?"

"God, yes." She shifted closer to him, leaning into his chest. She pressed her head into his fingertips, focusing on how it felt for him to apply whisper light touches along the back of her ear, neck, and jawline. "I haven't been able to get warm tonight."

"Your scarf's in the way." He unraveled it, let it fall to the floor, then bent his head to her neck.

"Yes," she whispered. "It is."

Focusing on her right ear, which wasn't wearing the mic, he planted kisses along her earlobe, and down her neck.

"This too much for you?" As he spoke, the moistness of his breath chilled the path that he'd kissed. In a good way.

"God, no." She shivered. Not from cold, but from sizzling sensations throughout her body, originating with the touch of his lips, his fingertips, and his strong arm now loosely wrapped around her body. "Your arm around my back, feels like...heaven.

God." Bending her head to his chest, she inhaled. "You smell so good."

"This call's going to..." his words trailed as he opened his mouth, pressing his tongue along the path that his lips had blazed, from her earlobe down her neck, "take a few minutes. Think we should..." she felt the smallest of nips along her earlobe, a gentle nibble with the edges of his teeth, "take this to the couch?" His lips closed on the area that he'd bitten, sucking gently.

She couldn't move. She could only lean into him, and nod, with her palms pressed into his chest as she arched into his kisses.

She was suddenly in his arms. He walked over to the couch, and sat down. Sitting sideways in his lap, as he kicked off his shoes, there was no mistaking that he was as aroused as she was. His erection pressed into her right butt cheek. Long. Thick. Straining against her. She shifted away.

His eyes locked on hers. "Sorry."

"Don't be," she whispered, feeling very much like the awkward virgin she'd been pretending to be. "I'm almost there, Gabe—"

"My problem. Not yours. But I can't do much about it getting between us."

"I don't want to keep getting you so hot and bothered."

"Please. Get me hot. Bothered. I don't mind at all."

"This Brad and Sandy thing has to be wearing thin for you." *God knows it is for me.*

"Not at all. You like when I kiss you," he whispered, moving his lips closer, to her neck again, "right?"

"Yes." She sighed as he applied pressure with his lips to the sensitive spot where her neck met her ear, then gave up on avoiding his erection.

"Then we're going to keep having moments like this until you're ready." He gave a hoarse chuckle. "And that will just have to be in the way."

She lifted herself up by using his shoulders and her arms, then shifted her legs so they spread around him. Crossing her ankles around his back, she gave him a smile. With her legs open, and her center pressed against his erection, she wriggled her hips closer. "Brad, you're really," she whispered, rubbing herself against him, "really big."

Eyes lidded, his lips wet from the soft tongue action accompanying his kissing on her neck and ear, he groaned. He bent forward, his lips working at her earlobe again. "Yeah," he whispered. "You're making me harder."

"I like this PG-rated dirty talk."

He chuckled, hoarsely. "Can I tell you that even with fabric separating us, I can feel how hot you're getting? Wet. Is that how you like PG-rated?"

"Yes," she whispered, closing her eyes, bending her head against his shoulder. Feeling human again. Feeling alive. And not wanting to spoil one precious second of it. "And you know, I've been thinking. I've got hands, too. I could help with some relief..." She reached for the waistband of his jeans, undoing the button, sliding the zipper down.

He groaned, then caught her hands, stopping her. "Mm. Not now. Like I said, Ragno's going to... Aw. Hell. Here she is." He moved awkwardly around her, shifting his hands and arms and touching a button on his watch. "Hi, Ragno. Give me a minute."

He touched his watch again. Drawing a deep breath, he lifted her chin in the crook of his finger. "She's on mute. She'll give me a few seconds. But not much more. For all she knows, I was on the toilet."

Andi laughed. "Did you really say that?"

"Sure. Sex, showering, and toileting are usually the only three things that keep me from answering her right away." He kissed her lips, pulling the zipper up, and buttoning. "And she's a female. She usually doesn't want an explanation, so we're good. You okay?"

Andi nodded as she pressed her lips against his. His evening stubble felt sharp against her chin. Rough. Perfect.

"Oh yeah," he groaned, then lay his head, with a thud, on the back of the couch. "Our time's up. Ragno will be refocused in a heartbeat on a live fire situation in Pakistan or some other remote area of the globe if I keep her on hold too long. Ready to meet my best friend?"

"Sure."

"Here goes," he said.

"About damn time. Was just about to drop you." Through the mic, Ragno's voice—distinctly feminine, slightly rushed, and more than a little annoyed—came through, as though she was sitting on the couch with them. "Do you have any idea how many jobs I'm working? While running more scenarios than I care to admit for you? It's walking like a duck, Angel, as I've said for the last two days. I'm delivering a 'come-to-Ragno' moment with this call. By the way, what the hell are you doing over there that you had me on pause for so long…"

While Ragno continued, Gabe lifted Andi's chin with his index finger. "Sound okay?"

"*Sound okay*? What the hell—"

"Andi's on the line with us," Gabe answered.

After a few seconds of total silence, Andi said, "Hi, Ragno. Nice to meet you."

"You too. Sorry, Andi. You certainly didn't need to hear my rant. Agents normally don't surprise me with three-way calls that include the client. Usually, with Angel, I know exactly what he's up to. I might be a bit slow on the uptake, but now…" She paused. "Good Lord. That's why you sound like that, Gabe. I'm getting it. All. Loud and clear."

"Come on. I'm not that readable." Gabe swung his legs up onto the couch. Lifting the blanket, he gave Andi room to reposition herself. She draped herself over him—her legs stretched out inside his, her hips right below his waist, and her chest against his. A perfect fit. He covered them both.

"To me, you are." A teasing tone told Andi that Ragno had guessed exactly what was happening between them. Or maybe, there was no guessing involved. She glanced up, and threw a questioning glance in his direction.

With a shrug, he mouthed, almost silently, "She's got ways."

"Speak up, Michael Gabriel Hernandez. No whispering if we're having a three-way."

"Sorry Ragno," Gabe said, "I was saying you have ways of knowing things. Andi needs to know that I can't keep secrets from you, and even if I tried, you'd figure it out. That's why you two needed to meet now."

"Yes. All true. And just in case you're unaware, Andi, this is big. You're the first woman, friend, girlfriend—you label it—that he's brought home to Ragno, ever! Sorry, Angel. I thought she should know. Yay. Special moment. Let's mark it. Andi, usually, with Angel—"

"Love his nickname," Andi said.

Ragno laughed. "Only I get away with it. I'm not referring to sweet, innocent cherubs, by the way. Gabe's named after two Archangels, which makes him damn powerful. And like the Archangels, our man here is tasked with mighty deeds. Trust me, he's got the power to complete them. Don't let that smile and his jokes fool you. There's a hell of a lot of depth to him. And by the way, while we're off task, Angel, Zeus is looking for you. Evidently your brother and Brandon are communicating, because Andi and Taylor are communicating. You fill in the dots. Zeus said you haven't returned his call today. Let's just say our Polaris is getting a bit miffed that you're not responding to his light beam."

"His message didn't say anything was urgent," Gabe said. "I'll call him in the morning."

"As a matter of fact, while you had me on hold, he sent me a text asking if I'd heard from you. And you know how he gets when you go non-communicative. He starts asking me questions. And Andi, just to clue you in, although I figure out 99.99999 percent of what Gabe's up to, I don't spread it around."

"Good to know," Andi said.

"Tell Zeus I'll call him later. And I'm not hiding anything, so answer away."

Silence. No words, no typing. Andi wondered whether the mic system had stopped working. With her index finger, she touched her ear. The external filament was still there. With her pinkie, she felt for the device.

"Really?" Dry sarcasm was apparent in Ragno's cryptic answer, which confirmed that the mic was firmly in place. Her one-word answer also indicated to Andi just how much their words were merely the tip of a deep connection between the two of them. "Pardon my bluntness, Andi, but Angel, are you really ready to discuss with Zeus and his partners whatever is happening between you and this favored client?"

Gabe shifted under Andi, kissing the top of her head. "Okay. Got it. And I'll handle that end of it." Andi felt his chest rise and fall with a deep breath. "Back on task, Ragno, before you get called away. I want to run a couple of things by you and have you bring us up to speed on what you're finding out about Pic."

"Andi, you okay with knowing details?" Ragno asked. The concern in her tone prompted Andi to sit up. She braced herself, as Ragno continued. "I feel like I already know quite a bit about you. I've worked the corporate end of your file since the job began. Can't help but feel protective. Not that I'm second guessing Gabe, but I'm not sitting beside you. And, to be honest, Brandon, Sebastian, and even Zeus, will be pissed as hell if we do anything to traumatize you. You're one of our most important clients."

"I'm fine," Andi said, "Gabe's right. I want to know."

"Okay. Gabe, you go first. Tell us about Richie." Ragno's tone went from that of a concerned friend to a professional, efficient job controller.

Gabe stood, letting the blanket pool softly down onto Andi's lap. Eyes on Andi as he spoke, he visibly shifted gears from enjoying the moment to becoming all business. Shoulders straight, he stood tall. "Richie's off. Admitted pothead. Uses synthetics. Gas station crap. Sometimes boosts that with alcohol and Quaaludes. At best, his credibility sucks. That being said, he seemed sober when I talked to him with Marvin. It was good I had Marvin with me, because Richie wasn't giving me a damn thing. I needed local flavor to give him reassurance."

Andi could hear Ragno's keyboard clicking. "I'm cross-referencing that Marvin was helpful in our New Orleans files."

"A bit of good news. Richie says Monica's fine. He knows where she is. He's going to deliver a message for Pic later this morning."

"That's fantastic news," Andi said.

"Yeah. Pic's relieved. Other than that, though, it isn't so great. Richie saw two men," Gabe continued, "wearing black, features concealed either with bandanas or some other type of mask, snatch Jake off the streets. Right before his eyes. Early evening. Much the same way Andi said she saw two guys snatch a blond-haired girl off of Esplanade on Friday. Both incidents involved a nondescript panel van. Andi saw black. The Jake incident involved a white one, according to Richie."

Chills ran along Andi's spine as Gabe spoke. She reminded herself that she was safe in her studio, the place where she felt most at home in the world. She shivered. Tried to shake it off. Drew a deep breath. Even pulling the soft blanket up under her chin didn't warm her.

"You okay?" Voice soft, more than a little concerned, he reached out and laid a gentle hand on her shoulder.

Fighting off the waves of terror, Andi nodded.

"Is she?" Ragno said, "because the worry in your voice spoke volumes."

Gabe's gaze was thoughtful, as he kept his eyes on her. He let his hand drop from her shoulder. He ran it through his hair. The dark waves he pushed back sprang back into position on his forehead. "You sure?"

"Yes. Don't baby me."

He nodded. "She's good."

"Andi, can you talk a bit throughout this call? Obviously, I can't see you. I need to know you're handling all of this."

"I'm okay, Ragno," Andi said, forcing herself to speak in something above a whisper. Drawing a deep breath, she added, louder, “Really. I’m fine. I want to know. Would this work better if we did a video chat?”

Gabe shook his head, no, as silence fell on the line.

“Bad idea?” Andi asked, not understanding the extended pause.

“Maybe one day I’ll do a video chat with you,” Ragno said. “But not today. Let’s move on. Gabe—panel van similarity. Andi saw black. Richie saw white. Also, Richie saw two men, faces concealed, which is consistent with both the Pic and Andi incidents. What else did Richie give you?”

“Something I can’t brush off. One of the men who abducted Jake had a stun gun,” Gabe continued. “Richie was dead certain of it. Described it as square, black, plastic. Gripped in his left hand. He said the guy used it and Jake collapsed. So, with the stun gun and the panel van, Richie gave me two facts on the Jake incident that provides commonality between Pic’s assault and the incident Andi witnessed.”

“Did Richie see a syringe?” Ragno asked.

Drawing a deep breath, Gabe shot Andi a concerned glance. “He didn’t offer that fact—”

“Wait,” Andi said. “A syringe?”

He sat down hard on the couch next to Andi.

“Hell, Gabe! You and Pic didn’t tell Andi about the syringe?”

“Obviously not,” he muttered. He glanced at Andi, his lips drawn down in a frown. “Sorry. I didn’t know about it at first. Pic told me about it Monday night, when I found him on the levee. It’s a big part of the reason why he agreed to come in with me. It scared the crap out of him. And I figured it would do the same to you.”

“Don’t do that again.” She tried to wrap her mind around the implications of men going after Pic with a syringe in hand. “Don’t keep things from me. I don’t need that kind of protection. Understand?”

He nodded. His tone soft and gentle, he said, “Understood. I erred too far on the side of caution. Crossed the line between protection and overprotection. I’m usually better at such judgment calls. Forgive me?”

She lifted her face to his, touching his lips with hers. “Yes.”

“Okay, now that that’s settled, back on task, you two,” Ragno said. “Was Richie close enough to see something as small as a syringe?”

"Not really. He said he was about forty feet away." Leaning back, into the couch, he lifted an arm, and draped it over Andi's shoulder.

Nestling into his side as she absorbed his warmth, her gaze settled on the far wall of her studio, on the sketches that hung there, above the table where her sketchpads lay. Pic. Monica. Tank. And other people who lived on the streets of the French Quarter, Marigny, and Bywater. People most others ignored. In the expressions that she'd sketched, she saw a silent plea: *See me. Help me.*

"And I didn't ask him about a syringe. For the same reason I didn't tell him anything about what Andi saw or about what happened to Pic. I'm not sure what to make of the guy. Not that I get a bad vibe off of him. Truth is, I don't. His heart seems to be in the right place. He's so goofy, I actually liked him. So much so that he told me he'll stop by to see Pic in the morning, and I told him that was fine. The kid's stir crazy. I figured seeing a friend would help, even if the friend's got a bit of baggage. On top of the commonalities with the stun gun and the panel van, there's something else that Richie flagged. It's weird."

"What?" Ragno asked.

"Andi saw a blond woman abducted. Pic's a blue-eyed blond young man. Jake's also blue-eyed and blond. Richie says rumor has it on the streets that five to six other young people are missing. All homeless. I asked him for descriptions. All of them have light-hair and light eyes. The Jake incident was a week ago Wednesday. Andi's sighting was Friday. Pic's assault was Saturday night. What does all of this give us?"

"Coupled with two sightings of panel vans, two sightings of stun guns, and a syringe," Ragno said, "I'd say that gives us either an odd bunch of potentially criminal coincidences or, possibly a predator who likes fair-haired people no one misses when they disappear. My mind is churning, like I know your minds are. Not going to run with the speculation, though I just did. We need more facts. Andi, are you okay?"

"T-terrified." She forced herself to keep her eyes on the sketches on the far wall. Their cry of *'See me. Help me'* became her focus. "But a hell of a lot better than I've been for the last couple of years. Keep going."

"Like you, I see too much evil," Ragno said, sounding pissed. "And it infuriates me. Let's continue, Gabe, because I know where this is leading."

"Yep. I know you do. I've got knowledge of interest to local law enforcement. Possibly even the Feds. Question is, should I go to the cops, when the cops in charge of this district are certifiable assholes? Last Saturday's obligatory courtesy visit to NOPD Officers Jack Spagnoli and Cal Thompson clarified their 'don't call us' message. And anything I know, if I know anything at all, is based on three things: One–Andi, who the cops don't believe, two–pothead Richie, whose credibility is beyond questionable and, in any event, won't talk to the cops, and three–Pic, who based on everything you're finding, Ragno, cannot go to the cops. Even if he was inclined to do so. And that's where we need to bring Andi up to speed on Pic's background."

"Yes. Agreed. And that's where I'm getting back to the walks-like-a-duck moment." Her voice softening slightly from the matter-of-fact, curt tone, she continued. "Because Angel, as much as I know you and Andi aren't going to like what I've found, there's no other scenario. His fingerprints sealed the deal—"

"You analyzed his fingerprints?" Andi shot Gabe a questioning glance.

"Had to," Gabe said, "because of what we were finding. Over the last few hours, Ragno and I have tried like hell to rule out this bad news."

"Don't worry, Andi. Nothing we're doing will ping law enforcement databases. Agent Marks lifted Pic's prints off a glass. I took them, and searched databases for similarities. And I'm damn glad I did," Ragno continued, "because if Pic is in any way a component of the story you'd need to tell the cops—

"If I go to them now, he is," Gabe said, "Undeniably."

"Then you're not going to the cops," Ragno said. "Not for a while, at least. I need Andi's authorization to get a team to Mapleton, West Virginia. Delicate subject, Gabe and Andi, but I'm thinking about billable hours. I'm happy to work as much as I can on this, and I know you are, Gabe. But to do this job properly, we need more resources from cyber and field divisions. We need to figure out the story behind what I'm finding. To do that, we need manpower. Face to face time. Interviews. Andi, you know how expensive Black Raven hours are."

Andi straightened her shoulders. Side pressed against Gabe, she dug deep within. As she focused on the sketches, she found bracing strength.

I see them. With Gabe's support, I can help. I'm so much more fortunate than Pic. I have resources. I have...so much more.

She turned to Gabe. "Please stop talking past me. Give me details. Let me assess how to proceed."

"It's rough, honey," Gabe said, tone soothing. Hesitant. Concerned. Protective. But not patronizing.

"Oh, hell. Look. I'll have to drop our call in three minutes. Budapest job is going south. Andi, can you handle bad facts in a nutshell version?"

Andi drew a deep breath. "Yes."

"The young man you know as Pic is Lucas Tanner McShane."

Andi's hands shook at the mention of her friend's real name. Feeling as though she was finally getting to know him, she realized that maybe Gabe had been right. They needed to know the story of what went wrong in Lucas Tanner McShane's life, and how he became Pic, a young man who lived on the streets of New Orleans.

"Lucas was born to Aubrey Rose McShane. He just had his seventeenth birthday. On January 23."

Dear God. He's so young. Her eyes rested on a sketch of Pic. From across the room, the lifelike gaze that confronted her said '*help me*' in a way her young friend would never voice.

"Aubrey Rose left the father's name blank on Lucas's birth certificate. Hospital records indicate there was a brief moment when she considered putting baby Lucas up for adoption. Evidently, she changed her mind. I've got data on the number of places where Aubrey Rose and her son Lucas lived. Sending an info package later tonight. Aubrey Rose took any odd job she could find. Mostly, it looks to me like she worked as a stripper, who tried like hell to make a living as a piano player. Her life was a colossal struggle."

"Was?" Andi asked.

"Aubrey Rose was murdered a little over three years ago. November 7. The date on Pic's tattoo without a year." As Gabe's arm tightened around her, Ragno asked, "Are you sitting, Andi?"

"Yes," she whispered.

"Gabe, I'm in the investigatory files of the Mapleton, West Virginia police department. Photos confirm what I deduced. Which is why you're not going to the New Orleans Police Department or any other law enforcement agency with anything related to Lucas, aka Pic. And why I need Andi's authorization to send a team to Mapleton."

Any hesitancy over prying faded, because the young man who'd saved her needed help. Real help. *I'm finally getting the chance to repay the favor.*

"Okay. I authorize all the manpower needed to help Pic. As long as I have control over what's done with the information..." she added, glancing at Gabe.

He nodded. "Absolutely."

"Understood," Ragno said.

"Then you've got the green light from me to send a team there."

"Good. I know you both want more information on this. Gabe, I know you're still trying to figure out if there's any wiggle room in this bad news. Andi, I'm sorry to deliver this, but I don't know any other way to tell you and my research is unassailable, though Gabe is trying to figure out if I could possibly be wrong."

"Just tell me."

"An outstanding warrant indicates that Lucas Tanner McShane, the young man you know is Pic, is wanted for the murder of Aubrey Rose McShane, his mother."

Chapter Thirty Three

Andi

"No." Fighting a chill, Andi hugged herself. "That isn't possible, Pic is kind, compassionate. His mother? No. He wouldn't..." The words stuck in her throat like sand.

"Andi, we'll work through this. One of Gabe's many strengths is great investigative instincts. No truth is ever buried for long with him," Ragno said, then fell silent for a few seconds. "Gotta go. Gabe, I'll check in later. Files are on their way."

Andi stood, yanking out the earpiece. Gabe held out his hand. She dropped it in his palm. The concern in his eyes made her shiver.

She walked back and forth across the room, pacing. "Pic talks about his mom. And when he does, he talks about her like someone he loves. Or loved. Come on, Gabe, you've heard him talk about her. Right?"

He reached for his laptop and cell phone on the coffee table. "Sure have."

Andi went to the easel and picked up her scarf from the floor. Draping it around her neck, she gave him a penetrating look. "So what does your gut say?"

Snapping open his computer, he leaned back on the couch with it settled on his lap. "There's something sideways with this whole situation. Don't know what it is. Yet. But I'm going to find out." Shifting his tone from worried to calming, he added, "Just because someone's wanted in connection with a crime, that certainly doesn't mean he committed it. We'll figure this out. This actually isn't a terrible development, because—"

"Oh. For the love of God. Really?" Turning on her heel, poised in front of the coffee table, she waited for his gaze to lift from the laptop screen. "You can even find a bright side to this?"

"Of course." He typed a short burst, glanced at the screen, and then returned his attention to her. The corners of his lips lifted in a shadow of his habitual smile, but his expression was more pensive than happy. "Now we have plenty of solid clues pointing to what went wrong. Right?"

Her exasperation evaporated. "I guess."

His smile drifted away. Worry replaced the optimism that had briefly lightened his eyes. "Things sometimes get worse before they get better."

Shivering, she returned to aimlessly pacing, as Gabe typed. To her easel with her work in progress; there, the painting of the footbridge at Crescent Park held no interest for her. She made a U-turn back to Gabe and the couch. She thought about joining him, then reconsidered. Watching him work at his computer, as though he was tackling a project that he enjoyed, was going to drive her nuts.

She crossed the studio, to where the sketches hung, and stared at one of Pic she'd done a year earlier. He'd been sitting with Monica. She'd captured happiness in his beautiful eyes, using a light touch with her lead pencil. And more. To her, the sketch captured his innocence, and it now tore at her heart. *Am I always seeing things that don't exist?* Swallowing the grit of worry from her throat, she asked softly, "Can I be so wrong?"

"If it helps, I'm right there with you. I don't think that kid would hurt a flea. Unless threatened. Then all bets are off."

"Running certainly makes him seem guilty, doesn't it?"

Relief overcame her when Gabe gave a firm headshake. "Not to me. It makes him look like a scared kid. People are innocent until proven guilty beyond a reasonable doubt." Fingers clicking on the keyboard, he talked as he typed. "We'll figure this out. I promise. Corporate could do some of this for me, but I want to be more hands on. So right now, I need to mobilize a couple of agents to Mapleton. Reviewing the data Ragno's pulled together, looking for available agents who have the skillset required to finesse an investigation in a small town, and bring them up to speed, is going to take a few hours."

"And you can't do it if I keep interrupting you."

He gave a slight, thoughtful smile. "I'm knee deep in data. Ragno gave you the highlights. We're sparing you the nitty gritty details. If we want agents to hit the ground running by midmorning—"

"We do."

"Then I've got to get this going now. Trust me, Sandy," he said, his voice deepening, "I'd love to return to what we were doing before the convo with Ragno derailed us."

The heat of a blush burned at her cheeks, but work was more urgent. "Mobilize the agents. Work. My offer still stands." She paused, then lowered her voice. "You can collect anytime, Brad. And, you've really opened the floodgates. Next time, you might get lucky. We might get...quite a bit further."

He gave her a long, hungry gaze. "Never thought I'd get hard hearing another guy's name, but hell. Anytime you say Brad, I'm ready. I have a few hours of willpower in me, but that's about it. Don't use that voice again. Please."

"You started it. Brad."

"Stop!"

"What?"

"That voice. Whispery. Deep. It screams sex."

She chuckled. Clearing her throat, she removed the huskiness from her voice. "How's this?"

"Better. But stay over there. I need every inch of the thirty feet separating us right now."

Her heart smiled. "Feet firmly planted."

"Good. Stay that way, but show me that sketch."

She turned it to him.

He studied it for a second. "Do you have any where his eyes are blue?"

"No. I usually don't use color. That's why Sonja's comments the other day were odd, when she was looking at the sketches. At first I was wondering what made her think of blue-eyed blondes and pregnant women when she was looking at the sketches of Monica and Honey—"

"You didn't say that then."

"I know. But it's stuck with me, in the back of my mind, ever since. At the time, I was just plain annoyed with her and Jacques in general, so I didn't focus on it." Andi shrugged. "She explained it away by saying she was just giving her cynical view of the world. He said something about capitalism. Do you remember?"

"No. Frankly, I was mostly focusing on what in the hell you saw in either of them."

She shuddered. "I can't imagine being with people like that now."

"I'm sorry for the reason behind the change, but I'm sure glad that part of you has changed. Mind bringing that to me?"

She walked across the studio to him, holding out the sketch. He took it from her, then growled, "Now back away."

All playfulness evaporated as he studied Pic's face. He drew a deep breath, reached for his phone, and snapped a photo. "Pic's file needs the right cover photo. I'm guessing he's never let you take an actual photo of him?"

"You're guessing correctly."

"Then I'll use the sketch. I want the agents to have the correct first impression." He clicked his laptop a few more times, touched his watch, and said, "Hello, Lamonte. Glad to hear you're available for Operation Lucas Tanner McShane. We'll shorten it to Operation Pic, which is the name we know this kid by." He paused, silent as he listened for a few seconds. Then he chuckled. "Not all men are egocentric assholes. I'm happy to serve as a save call. I'll give you a minute to get rid of him. Tell him it's urgent."

He shook his head while glancing in Andi's direction. "Why do women have such a hard time saying, *'Gotta go. Good night?'* Lamonte's a bad ass. She's shrewd and her field skills are on a par with any of our best agents."

And her body count is damn high. She's got no qualms with inflicting Black Raven-style corrective action and expedient justice. That's why I'm using her. Pic wouldn't have murdered his mother. Not now, and not a couple years ago when he was Lucas. He ran from something evil. I have a strong feeling we'll be headed in a direction that's going to require a special brand of ingenuity. If I can't get there to deliver it, Lamonte will do it. Without flinching.

Keeping his full rationale to himself, he said to Andi, "Lamonte's on a date that sucks and feels powerless to end it."

Andi shrugged. "Used to have the same problem myself. It's one of the many benefits of not dating."

"Glad you feel that way," he said, giving her a full beam smile. "Remember—dating's hell. Not something you ever want to do again." His smile drifted away. "Everything okay, Lamonte?" He listened. Chuckled. "I'm sending data now. Cyber division's sending more. Ragno's my alternate contact." He paused. "Want your brainpower to help come up with leads as you get ready for your flight. Cover photo is a sketch of Lucas Tanner McShane. Calls himself Pic. Call me back once you settle in with the files. Want to talk with you about it and about who your partner will be."

He stared at Andi, a thoughtful expression on his face. "This will be okay."

"Are you talking to me?"

He nodded. "Yeah. Lamonte's offline. We will believe in innocence until proven guilty. Won't assume the worst. Databases provide a fabric. Texture, though, requires real life, hands-on investigating. My agents will go to the trailer park where he and his mom lived. The school he attended. We're looking for nuances. Like all the things I didn't know about you, until I got here."

"Or I could just try to talk to him about it."

"Yeah?" Skepticism filed his eyes. "And what would happen?"

"He'd run."

"Give me a day or two with agents in Mapleton. Lamonte will be there first thing in the morning, and I'll send another agent to join her. She'll pick up and follow any scent she can. Which gets me back to what my gut's been telling me. You know him as well as anyone. Is there anything that you might have heard from him about his home that you haven't already told me? Even something seemingly unimportant?"

She glanced at the easel, and drew a deep breath. "I think he had a counselor. Or some kind of help. After his suicide attempt. And they were poor, so it was probably through a service provided by the hospital he went to."

"Beautiful," Gabe nodded, clicked a few times, and focused on his screen. "That's exactly what I'm looking for. An avenue we probably would've stumbled upon once Lamonte gets to Mapleton, but it's better to get going on it and do cyber groundwork in advance." He typed a fast burst, then glanced up at her. "Give me more. Anything he said. Context, if you don't have details."

A paintbrush that she didn't remember picking up was in her hand. She squeezed hard on the lacquered handle. She bit the inside of her lip, and remained silent.

Here's your context—when I tried to kill myself, he told me I needed to talk to someone. He was pretty damn insistent about it. And he used this believe-in-tomorrow phrase, which sounded like psycho-babble to me. So I assumed that he'd talked to someone. But I can't tell you that, because my suicide attempt is something you'll never know about.

In the face of her silence, Gabe stopped typing. "He talked with you about his counseling?"

Is this how I want to start a relationship with this man? Withholding a vital piece of myself before this show even gets on the road? And is that sad bit of my history a vital piece? And are we starting a relationship, when I know I'll have to push him away. He can't handle my darkness.

Damn damn damn.

She gave Gabe what she hoped look like an *it-was-nothing* shrug. "Not exactly. It just seems logical."

He nodded. Started typing again, as though her answer satisfied him. He stared at his computer, reading for a while. Every now and then, he typed a few fast bursts.

"What are you doing now?"

"Scrolling through manpower. Looking for an agent to partner with Lamonte. Normally, corporate does this kind of stuff, but I pull my own teams together when I have the time."

"While you're doing that, I'll sketch the scene I saw last Friday."

He narrowed his eyes and rested his hands on the laptop. "Not sure you should force your mind to go back there. Think you can handle it?"

I have no idea. "I'll make myself. If I try," she said, lifting the Crescent Park canvas off the easel that stood closest to her work table, "more details than I was able to tell you on Saturday might come to me."

"That how it works?"

She clipped a clean piece of sketch paper to a blank canvas. Turning to the table where her oil paints were laid out, she moved them to the side to transition the work place for sketching. "Sometimes. Normally, after spending hours outdoors, focusing on a scene, my mind's eye can recreate details that didn't make it to the canvas while I was outside. That's why I paint my scenes in a series, with some paintings created in my studio. It's the reason my outdoor time's so precious to me."

He typed, then the clacking of the keyboard stopped as his gaze returned to her. "Keep going. I'm multitasking. Lamonte's in the file. Asking questions. I can answer her while you and I talk."

Pretending that their conversation wasn't of monumental importance, she made sure the lead points of her different sketch pencils were in a precise line. "It's my...therapy, I guess. Visuals that become imprinted on my brain while I'm outdoors enable me to get through my nights. Recreating the sights on canvas, drawing and painting from normal images of a regular day, the images that exist in my mind, requires focus. That kind of focus, on something other than my memories, enables me to calm the anxiety that's plagued me ever since my kidnapping. Sounds crazy, right?"

Please say no. Because I just explained my life to you. I'm better, but this —this fighting to hang on—will forever be my normal. And it suddenly matters whether or not you think I'm batshit crazy.

Holding his cell phone and laptop in the crook of his arm, he rose, then advanced on her with the stealth of a jungle beast. He lifted her chin in the crook of his finger, as warmth and contentment filled her. “Sounds like the most logical thing I’ve ever heard. Smart. Brave. Amazing.”

His understanding filled her with an intense longing to open herself to him, both physically and mentally. She couldn’t imagine what it would be like to have one person on the planet who knew every dark corner of her soul. And accepted her anyway. Damaged. Screwed up. Afraid. It would be a relief to share what she’d held inside her like a cancer since her kidnapping.

But if she did, he’d realize how broken she really was. And he might never look at her the same. She managed a small smile. “Really? All that?”

“Yeah. All that,” he whispered, touching his lips to her forehead. He stepped back, placed his hands on her shoulders. “But maybe your tried and true method won’t work for what you saw last Friday. You weren’t painting then. So you weren’t as focused. And whatever you saw was upsetting to you. So if you try to recreate it now, it will have the opposite effect of what painting in your studio normally does for you, right?”

Of course he was right, but that didn’t matter. “I need to try. And I’ll be fine. If it becomes too much, I’ll stop.”

“Promise?”

“Yes.”

He nodded, though his eyes held more than a bit of uncertainty. “I’ll be downstairs. If I stay up here, I’ll stop working. And what I have in mind for the best way to spend the next few hours certainly won’t be helping Pic. When you stop painting, come downstairs. I’d love if you curled up next to me while I work.” He bent his lips to hers, gave her a lingering kiss that sent her into a world of warmth, light, and promise, and then stepped back at the exact moment when desire started overtaking her senses. “And I’ll just have to find the willpower to keep my hands off you until I’m at a breaking point on Operation Pic.”

Chapter Thirty Four

Pic

Friday, February 19, 4:45 a.m.

"Hey, kid. Get up."

As the bedroom lights snapped on, Pic opened his eyes to see Gabe in the doorway. He wore jeans and a tucked-in, long sleeve t-shirt with the Black Raven logo on it, and his hair was standing up, as if he'd just rolled out of bed. His Glock was holstered at his hip. Without a smile, and with stubble darkening his cheeks and chin, Gabe looked more serious than normal. And tired.

Spaces between slatted shutters, closed on the outside of the guesthouse, revealed no light. "Richie's here?"

"Yeah. A little earlier than he said he'd be. I let him in. Told him to help himself in the kitchen. I'll go back to the main house while you guys catch up. How are you feeling?"

"Better." With the covers firmly pulled up to his shoulders, Pic inhaled, then waited for a cough that didn't come. "Progress. Finally."

Lifting one hand from under the covers, he gestured to Gabe with a swirl of his index finger. Gabe rolled his eyes, then turned around. "You're more modest than a girl. It's weird. Any particular reason?"

Letting the sheets fall back, Pic got out of bed, reaching for his jeans, which he'd tossed over a nearby chair. "Yeah? So?" He pulled on the jeans, and zipped them. "And it's none of your fucking business."

He immediately felt bad for treating Gabe, who really seemed like a good guy, like a shit. Yet it was his fallback when he felt pressured and uncomfortable, and he'd certainly never held back before. Modulating his tone and getting a grip on his pissy attitude, Pic added, "Finally feel like I can breathe again. Knowing Monica hasn't disappeared is a huge relief, I gotta tell you. Richie can give her the message that I'm outta my mind with worry about her. She'll find me. Or want to see me. I'm sure. Well, pretty sure."

Gabe's late-night news that Monica was not missing and that Richie would get a message to her for him made Pic feel better. He worried about his friends, and Monica, being pregnant, and out on the streets, worried him the most. As his stomach grumbled, Pic was damn glad to feel that his body was cooperating with his good mood. “And you’ll be happy to hear that I’m starving.”

“Ecstatic over that newsflash. I’d be doing cartwheels, if I’d slept at all. There’s lots of stuff for you to eat downstairs. Fruit. Muffins. Bread. Peanut butter.” Gabe, his back to Pic, leaned against the doorframe, lifted his left arm and straightened his hair.

“What kept you up all night?”

“Not for you to worry about. Or as you’d say, none of your fucking business. See how much nicer my way of answering was? You dressed yet?”

“Not yet.” Pic slipped on a t-shirt. “You can turn around now.”

Gabe turned, and leaned against the doorframe again, this time facing Pic. “I cook a hot breakfast in the main house at our morning meeting time. Walk over at nine-thirty if you’re hungry. Pancakes, eggs, and bacon.”

“Damn,” Pic said, reaching for a sweatshirt. “It’s freezing.”

“Got colder overnight. Rain’s predicted. I adjusted the thermostat when I walked in. Don’t know why it was so low.”

“Andi did that. I was hot when she came into say goodnight. Bet I can make better pancakes than you.”

Gabe arched an eyebrow. “Really?”

“Yeah. Sure. Used to cook all the time.”

“You didn’t have a parent around to cook for you?”

Aw. Fuck. I stepped into that one.

“Well?” Gabe prodded.

“Nah. Loser who should’ve been my dad wasn’t around. Mom worked a lot.” Pic smiled, covering the instant, deep pain at the thought of mornings with his mom. Most mornings had been more bad than good. He’d learned at a young age never to knock on Aubrey Rose’s bedroom door to wake her up for breakfast, because he never knew who was in there with her. But there had been mornings when it had just been the two of them, and those had been the best mornings of his life. “She said my banana pancakes were the best she’d ever had.”

Gabe’s eyes were serious as he gazed at Pic. “Remember that promise I made to you on the levee the other night?”

Pic pursed his lips. Stayed silent for a second, as he pretended to think. “That I’d never have to lay eyes on your cock? Aw man. Please tell me ya aren’t taking that one back. ‘Cause I’ll still slice it off and shove it—”

“Nah. That promise still stands—”

"Good, 'cause this is creepy with you looking all serious and shit."

"Cut the crap. I'm not joking. I'm talking about the promise that I wouldn't send you back to wherever you came from. Andi wants to help you. And so do I. So anytime you want to talk to either of us, just do it."

Hope flared. Starting from his feet, traveling up his legs, and sizzling up his spine, lighting the way to his brain. But the path to his mouth was nonexistent, because Pic had obliterated it.

In the face of Pic's silence, Gabe's thoughtful stare became more intense. "For us to help you, you'll need to talk about what the hell it is you're running from. It would be a damn shame if the only side of your story that no one ever tells is your side."

"What the hell is that s'posed to mean?"

"You're smart, Pic. Think about it. Whenever you're ready, start talking. If not today, maybe in a week. Or in a month. A year. I don't care when, but don't wait too long. Because the streets are going to kill you. Find me before that happens. I'm your safety zone. Understood?"

As he stared at Gabe, he knew he was looking at his best, and maybe his last, chance out of the life he'd fallen into.

Please help me. I'm so tired of running.

Pic didn't have the voice for the first word. Plus, he heard Richie rustling around downstairs. Now wasn't the time or place, and the moment came and went without him saying a goddamn thing.

"Pancakes. Nine-thirty. Get rid of Richie well before then. Whatever you do, don't bring him to breakfast. Andi's had a long night." Gabe's intense gaze let those words sink in. "Richie looks like the kind who'd stay as long as we let him. I think he'd be too much reality for our girl."

They went downstairs together to find Richie in the small kitchen. He'd taken off his leather bomber jacket. His bandana was firmly in place on his forehead. He had a plate on the counter, and was slathering peanut butter on a slice of bread. His face lit with a broad grin when he saw Pic. "Dude. You got a sweet gig here. Please tell me you're not so stupid that you're thinking of leaving." He peeled a banana. Using his fingers, he mashed it on top the peanut butter. "Ever."

"Yeah. It's great." Pic grabbed a banana from the fruit bowl on the counter.

"Richie," Gabe said. "You know how to find me. Keep me informed."

With a squeeze bottle of honey in his hand, Richie nodded at Gabe. "Likewise. And if you need me tonight, I should be back at Fat Cat Alley. If I'm not there, I'll be at Clothilde's. Thanks for the food."

"Thank Andi next time you see her. Pic, Agent Tyre's in the courtyard if you need anything." To Richie, Gabe said, "Courtyard's the only way out." He gestured with his head to the door of the guesthouse that led to the sidewalk. "It's locked. Five different ways and there's no key around here. It stays that way."

"Fuck," Richie said, his eyes on the door as it clicked shut behind Gabe. "These guys are serious, aren't they? Two of them greeted me at the gate, then he showed up. How many are there?"

"Four. Gabe introduced me to the team yesterday."

"I always saw two with Andi, but never thought there were more than that. Guess it makes sense. Shift has to change. They always packing, even when they're in the compound?"

"Yeah. Especially when they let in lowlifes like you. And I'm pretty sure the big guy had his shirt tucked in so you'd see it. He's uptight, but not that uptight."

Richie went to a window that overlooked the courtyard, used his index finger to give himself about an inch of a view, and said, "Yep. There's one out there." He shut the drapes, took a bite out of his sandwich, chewed for a while, and walked back into the kitchen. He sat on a stool. "Creepy to be under lock and key, huh?"

"Nah." Pic bit into the banana as he leaned against the counter. "They're here for Andi. They're not worried about me. And trust me, I'm damn happy to be here. Been too sick to care that I'm locked in." He jiggled the last of the banana in the air. "Other than soup, this is the first thing I've eaten in days. Right now, I'm just thrilled not to feel like puking."

Half the sandwich gone, Richie studied him as he chewed. "Glad to hear you're feeling better, because you look like shit. That guy might've broken your cheekbone when he decked you."

"That's the least of my problems. Man, when Gabe found me, I passed out." Pic swallowed the last bit of the banana. He opened the fridge, eyed its contents, then reached for a glass and poured orange juice into it. "Want some?"

"Nah. Any beer?"

Pic turned back to the fridge. "No. How about apple juice?"

Richie made a face. "Not without vodka."

Pic opened and closed the kitchen cabinets. "Sorry. No booze here. Thanks for coming. You'll get a message to Monica for me?"

"Yeah. Sure." Richie gave Pic a slow grin. "But wouldn't you rather give her the message in person?"

His heart rate immediately accelerating, Pic swallowed a large gulp of orange juice. "Think she'd want to see me?"

"Hell, yeah. After I saw you on Sunday morning, I told her you were back. She's been jonesing to see you. I was looking for you to tell you that. Gabe finding me last night saved me searching for you today. I'm damn glad, because I sure as hell don't have time to play matchmaker."

"Tell me where she is. I'll go by later today."

"Really?" Richie stretched, then rotated his neck, giving Pic his trademark grin. "Later? Why not now?"

Like a soft breath of wind gently blowing soap solution through a bubble wand, the reasons formed. And just as easily as bubbles burst and disappear into nothingness, the reasons why Pic shouldn't walk out the door now evaporated as he looked into his friend's questioning eyes.

He was staring at his grisly, street-wise friend, who smelled of bar smoke, stale alcohol, and peanut butter, but Pic was remembering Monica, one of the last times he'd seen her. They'd been in Crescent Park, and it had been a hot August day. She'd made a wreath of green clover stems and small, white pompom shaped flowers. She was wearing it in her blond hair. She'd been sitting so close, he could smell the fresh greenery as the breeze carried it to him. Together, they'd been daydreaming about one day having enough money to get a place together.

"You said you're feeling better," Richie prodded.

"Yeah, but it isn't even daylight yet." Glancing at the draperies, where a narrow slit would have shown daylight but now only revealed darkness, he added, "And I'd have to at least let Gabe or Andi know I was leaving. Which means waking her or bugging him."

"Why? You answer to them now? Like you're their kid? Or are they prison wardens?"

"Nah. It isn't like that." *But it is. Isn't it?* "It's just that they'd be worried if I left now. Like I said, I've been really sick. Promised them both I'd stay put for a while. Not go out on the streets."

"Monica's at my place. You know–off of St. Claude."

"Thought you lived on North Prieur Street. Off of Esplanade. Behind the dry cleaners."

"Nah. I moved since you were last in town. I'm a few streets away from there now. It'll take you fifteen minutes or so to walk there. Max twenty. Spend a few minutes with her, then get back. You'll be back in an hour. Before anyone misses you. Come on," Richie said, standing. "Let's go."

It had been six months since he'd seen the first girl who'd ever made his heart race, and he had a lot of talking to do with her. And the fact that he felt like he couldn't go to her suddenly wore thinner than snakeskin. "Okay. I'm going. But help me think of a way to do it. Because if I leave, that guy in the courtyard's gonna alert Gabe, then Gabe'll be here in a second, and ask me where the hell I'm going, and then he's going to argue with me until I end up staying." *And fuckitall, but the big guy could argue.*

"Aw hell. There's no way out. It'd just be better if I wait till this afternoon, prove to both Andi and Gabe I really am feeling better, and tell them I'm going. Gabe might insist on going with me—"

"Dude, if you wait till later, you could miss out on seeing her."

Heart pounding with that dose of reality, Pic asked, "What do you mean?"

"Meaning she's not staying in New Orleans too much longer. I told her I'd give her the bus money out of here. Up to her when she leaves, though. I doubt she's gonna stick around on the wish that she might see someone who's too sick or too much of a wimp to come to her when he's got an opportunity."

"Fuck!" Pic paced through the kitchen. "Tell her to stay. Don't let her leave. Tell her I need to talk to her. Tell her—"

Richie shrugged. "Look, I'm tired. Bedtime's fast approaching. Last night was good, but there's five more nights of Mardi Gras and I've got a lot of work to do between now and then. Whatever you have to say to Monica will definitely mean more coming from you—"

"Then help me."

Together, they came up with a plan. A half hour later, Pic was punching his brass-knuckled hand into the other, as he jogged down a quiet, residential block of Kerlerec Street with Richie's banjo on his back. About five feet ahead, an orange cat ran across the street, turned to look at him when it pounced onto a stoop, then puffed itself up into a fat ball in the lighted doorstep of a pink cottage. Even with the hood of Richie's sweatshirt pulled over his head and the leather jacket zipped up to his chin, Pic was freezing.

Richie's tennis shoes were about a half-inch too small, and the big toe of Pic's left foot nudged against the tip. Each inhale brought the stale scent of Richie's barroom-soaked clothes. Each exhale was a vapory plume. Morning light was breaking the blackness in the night sky, but the streetlights were still on. In the five blocks that he'd walked from Andi's house, Pic had only seen two cars, and those had been on Esplanade.

Focusing on the route that Richie had given him, Pic repeated it to himself. Cross Esplanade—done. Turn left on Kerlerec—done. Take a right on Bourbon. With houses crammed together, this stretch of Bourbon Street looked nothing like the barroom and strip-club stretch that was on the other side of Esplanade. It was quiet. On Mardi Gras day, even the predawn hours would have people on the streets. But right now, there wasn't a soul in sight.

As Richie had reminded him, Bourbon became Pauger Street about a block or so over Esplanade. The fact that Pic had gotten confused about the most direct way to get to Urqhart Street had cracked Richie up.

'Dude-you've been in Texas too long. If you go up Esplanade the whole way, you'll be going way out of your way. The streets all bend with the river. It causes directions to go haywire if you go off track. I'm happy to stay here a couple of hours or so, but no longer. So hurry up, take the most direct route, and get your ass back here.'

As long as he lived in New Orleans, Pic swore he'd never get used to the bendy streets or even the naming system, which Pic sure as hell knew better than most people. So he followed Richie's directions, step for step. Once on Pauger, he'd cross over Saint Claude and go the few blocks to Urquhart Street, take a right, then go a few more blocks before getting to Richie's place.

By his guesstimate, when Bourbon became Pauger, he had twelve more cold blocks to go. When he got closer to Saint Claude, there'd be more cars. But right now, he was in Sleepyville, where there weren't barrooms and the smaller houses in the cramped neighborhood were nothing like the ornate stretch of mansions in Andi's stretch of Royal Street. Fat drizzle drops started and then it was raining, hard. In a few seconds, he'd be soaked, but he didn't care. Because in just a few minutes he'd see Monica.

Given what had happened to him the weekend before, he was on high alert. He was focused forward, going at a slow jog that was almost too ambitious for his gunk-filled lungs, when a black van pulled alongside him.

Fuck!

He stopped dead in his tracks. Hesitated a second. Turned. Glanced into the driver's side window. The driver—with a black and gold New Orleans Saints baseball cap over his ski mask—did a military salute as another guy climbed out of the passenger side.

Fucking hell!

Pic shifted, swiveled, and turned. He leapt into the street, and ran towards Esplanade. It was the way he'd come and it was a busier street. More cars. More likelihood he'd see someone who might deter these assholes. Two men, about ten yards away, stepped out of the shadows and blocked his path.

"Sure hope you're wearing your knuckles now, because we have ours," one of the two called. Calmly. Low tone, but high on threat.

"Yeah. We've got a green light as long as we don't break your pretty-boy face."

Pic didn't waste his breath on words. With two of them ahead of him and one so close behind him that he could almost feel his breath on his neck, Pic swiveled and leapt for the sidewalk on the opposite side of the street. He ran in the opposite direction, and realized the van had been backing up to their position. He ran like his life depended on it.

How the hell am I going to fight off three men?

Someone did a flying tackle from behind. Pic yelled as he went down. Or he tried to, but horror drowned his voice. What started as a yell came out as a breathy grunt of fear. He landed in the middle of the sidewalk, face down, with the guy on his back.

One of the men grabbed his arms and pulled him over so that he faced the sky. The guy who had landed on Pic's back rolled off and grabbed his feet. As he struggled against the two of them, he realized the only sound in the street was his heavy breathing, his grunts, and the low engine hum of the nearby van. Another of the men moved over him with shiny silver duct tape, sealing his mouth. As Pic looked down, the needle-end of a syringe captured his attention. He twisted to avoid it. Turned. Jackknifed his abdomen, but couldn't break free.

He felt a prick in his neck and immediately started feeling woozy, as though his limbs were too heavy to move.

"Hurry," one of the men said. "Get him in the van."

They lifted him, walked a few steps with him, and threw him inside. He landed with a thud on the hard floor. Richie's banjo, which had been knocked loose from his shoulder, landed with a thud next to him. The doors closed. "This one's pretty. Even with the black eye you laid on him the other night."

The man who'd been driving—the one with the baseball cap—came into view and looked down at Pic, as he said, "Tom. Get into the driver's seat and get us out of here."

Pic looked straight up, because he suddenly was too loaded to move his head. As he felt the van move, he watched three men study him.

"Great looking," one of the men said. "Blue eyes. Square jaw. Tall. What do you think? Concierge will pay us ten thousand apiece?"

"At least. He was worth the extra effort. He's so pretty, I'm betting Concierge will use and abuse him for a while before selling him," another one answered.

Concierge? What the fuck?!

"Yeah. Plus he'll go in the sperm pool before he gets sold."

Pic's stomach roiled with oily terror twisting his gut. As he wondered what in the living hell he'd fallen into, he realized whatever they'd shot into him had paralyzed him. Feeling like he was weighted to the floor with the force of invisible lead, he couldn't move his arms or legs. He could hear. He could see. But his vision was tunneling while their words became garbled. He fought to stay conscious. At least awake, he had a shot of escaping. Passed out, he was as good as dead, or worse. Sounded like dead would be preferable.

Run run run.

Not a chance in hell. Pic couldn't move so much as a finger. His heart pounded hard enough to feel every painful beat. Panic and fear seeped like black tar into his every cell.

Pic felt pressure at his belly. Heard the slip of the zipper at his fly. Felt the pull of his jeans as someone drew them down his legs. "Now that's what I'm talking about. Concierge will want to see this one fuck. And be fucked."

Help me. Someone. Help me.

Bathed in icy sweat, he felt shudders racking him from the inside out.

Help.

Me.

His pleas were silent. And hell, even if they weren't, there was no one to hear or give a flying fuck about him now.

Andi...Gabe...God. Help me.

"Concierge and I have a special deal on this one," the baseball-capped guy said. "You'll get paid your normal rate for a choice fair-haired male, and I've got bonus money for each of you. Big bonus money."

"Why's that?"

"This kid isn't simply merchandise. He's bait. By taking him, we've created a distraction for the security team that surrounds something near and dear to the Concierge's heart."

"There's a heart in that chest?"

Pic heard a harsh laugh. "Good point. Here's what's going to happen now. Regular operations are called off. We need to get ready to move in and get the prize. Once we deliver, we're winning the lottery."

Chapter Thirty Five

Andi

"Tyre, grabbing some shut eye. Going dark. You and Marks are on task until the a.m. meeting."

Andi heard Gabe's voice as he climbed the stairs to her studio. From the doorway, he gave her a lingering glance. "All good up here on the upper floors. Ms. Hutchenson will be fine until then as well. She won't need you. If there's an issue, yell. Over." He paused, then touched his watch. "That part about you was an assumption. Am I right?"

Hand hovering over the table where she'd just completed reorganizing, for the umpteenth time, sketching pencils, leads, brushes, sharpeners, and erasers, Andi hesitated, glancing at the serious set to his jaw and absorbing the intensity in his eyes as he stared at her from the doorway. Running the variables through her mind as she debated the pros and cons, there was no doubting the look in his eyes. Was she emotionally ready to take this to the next logical step? Or, would she freeze again?

God, please, no.

Somewhere along the way, her subconscious made the decision for her. She gave a slight nod. Gabe's shoulders relaxed.

"Is Pic okay?"

"Yes. Tyre reported that Richie left about ten minutes ago. Pic returned to bed. Agent Lamonte is arriving in Mapleton as we speak. Her partner will be there by noon. They're up to speed on Operation Pic."

The last time Gabe had appeared in her studio, it had been four-thirty, right before he went to meet Richie. She'd known when he returned to his room, because every now and then, she'd heard a word or two of his conversations with Lamonte, Ragno, or his men as he worked. "You had a good idea on suicide counseling resources. I found someone he talked to. Might help us get a picture of Pic's mindset before his mother's murder. Lamonte will start tracking down that lead ASAP."

She glanced at the skylights, where the inky blackness of the night sky was fading to charcoal gray. Fat raindrops pattered on the skylight, then increased in tempo so that she had to raise her voice to be heard over the cacophony. "I lost track of time."

"Five forty-five. Weather forecast says rain. Then cloudy today. Going to be in the high thirties most of the day. How's the sketch coming?"

"Come see." He crossed the room to where her easel was set up. Together, they looked at the sketch of the Creole townhouse on Esplanade Avenue.

Shading techniques gave the appearance of light glinting off the steep pitch side-gabled roof with multiple roof dormers. Clean, straight lines of decorative parapets formed its borders. She'd captured the asymmetrical arrangement of the arched openings at ground level, as well as the roughness of the brick exterior, softened by the curves of the scrolling wrought iron lining the balconies. It was when she got to the scene that should be on the right—about a block and a half down Esplanade Avenue—that things started to get blurry in her mind. She'd left that section blank.

"Nice." Gabe cocked his head. Andi smelled soap on his skin, and a fragrance that was all him. The real essence of Gabe Hernandez was fragrant warmth. Reminiscent of pine, with a trace of muskiness. "You decided to start with the house this time, rather than the street." There was no censure in his voice as he leaned closer.

"Now I'm getting to the hard part. I figured I can obsess about the oak tree that should go here," she said, pointing, "at least until noon."

"When we talked about what you saw on Saturday, you said that, at first, the tree blocked your view."

"Until I went around it," Andi reminded him. "That tree will give me at least two hours of time-wasting detail. More, if I start obsessing about the bumps, ridges, and swirls in the bark." As she stared at her third attempt at sketching the scene she'd witnessed on Friday, Andi was almost ready to admit defeat. "You were correct all along. The problem is, last Friday I wasn't on Esplanade for all that long. I had only been there for, at most, ten minutes when it happened. I was still in scouting mode. Looking for a setting I might paint at a future date. So my brain doesn't have the images to focus on," she said. "All I have is brick and wrought iron. Oak trees. And shadows from clouds racing across the sky. Those are the things I was picking up on."

He bent closer to the sketch, and narrowed his eyes. "But you've got a lot of details in the house. Even the initials in the wrought iron. MLB."

"Yes, but I've seen that house about a zillion times. The man who built it in the eighteen hundreds was instrumental in starting the New Orleans Cotton Exchange. Wealthy people had their wrought iron custom designed, often with their initials. So that detail is something I already knew. And I just spent a half hour working on all those scrolls. I'm procrastinating getting here." Andi pointed to the blank part of the canvas, which had her stomach clenched into a hard knot.

"Unfortunately, if someone asked me what kind of cars were lining the street, I wouldn't be able to tell them the specifics. I know I saw a van, but I have no idea of the model, or identifying features. And a woman. I've tried to draw her twice now, in the sketches I did earlier tonight." She lifted her arms overhead, and gestured to the two easels where the earlier sketches stood. "Each time I draw her, she looks more and more like Monica. And based on what Richie said, we know that's my imagination, not actual memories."

"Maybe step away from it for a while?"

Earlier, she'd indicated he'd get further the next time. His low tone, and the hungry, serious look in his eyes said he was damn ready to test the waters, but in keeping with his promise, he wasn't going to push the issue. The first move had to be hers. Collecting her thoughts, she turned from him and the sketch that was going nowhere. She looked at the table where she'd laid out her tools. Straightened the pencils so that the tips were all in line.

He took the pencil out of her hand. "Look at me."

As she turned to him, he stepped closer and lifted her chin with the crook of his finger. A glimmer of light shone in his eyes. A trace of a smile curved his lips. She was learning to appreciate that even though he was easygoing and endlessly optimistic, Gabe was always thinking. The currents in this beautiful river of a man ran deep. Really deep. She lifted her face to him, and then his arms closed around her. "This okay?"

The weight of his arms, pulling her into his solid chest, felt better than right. It made her uncertainty a fleeting thing that quickly receded. "God, yes."

The first touch of his lips brought instant warmth. When his tongue slid along her bottom lip, sparks turned the warmth to fire. She wanted more. Everything. All of him, inside her. Locking her hands behind his neck, pulling herself up, she arched into him as she opened her mouth to him. Nipping at his lips when he pulled back to breathe, pressing harder against him when he moved too slowly, she encouraged each movement from him and demanded more.

"Wow."

"More," she whispered into his mouth, reaching for his hand, and pulling it to her breast. He got her not-so-subtle hint fast. Lifting both hands to her chest, he kneaded her breasts. Sizzling need surged through her, even though the sweatshirt and t-shirt she wore dulled the effect of his touch. "Not enough. More."

He slid a hand under her shirts, his fingers cold against the warmth of her skin. He cupped her breasts gently, then brushed his thumbs over her nipples. His touch on her bare skin, on the hard nubs of her nipples, ignited more than sparks. It was as though a wildfire ran through her body. There was no stopping the desire that the flames fueled. While one hand took possession of her breasts, she felt him tug gently at the waistband of her sweatshirt. "On or off?

"Off." Within seconds, the sweatshirt was off. Underneath, she wore a t-shirt.

He tugged at the bottom of it, arching an eyebrow. She gave a nod. He lifted it, slowly. She wasn't wearing a bra. He stepped back for a second, drawing in a breath as he got his first eyeful of her bare breasts. Her nipples, stimulated by his hands, were hard peaks. "Beautiful."

Leaning down, he placed his mouth on her left breast as he cupped them both. One long kiss there, then another on her right. He opened his mouth, drew in the nipple, and sucked in her flesh. Yearning need pulsed hard between her legs, radiating everywhere.

"You know that thing we have," she said, shivering, "about taking it slow? Being Brad and Sandy?"

"Yeah." He shifted from her left breast to her right. Tongued her nipple, then opened his mouth wide, drawing her into his mouth as his other hand kneaded her right breast, his thumb flicking over her nipple. Groaning, she gripped his shoulders and pulled up his shirt. "Forget about it."

"Sure?"

"Yes."

"Positive?"

"Stop asking. Hurry."

"Nah." He lifted his face from her breasts, and came in close for a kiss as his hands found her chest again. "Slow is way too much fun. I'll get there. Slowly. Stop me at any point." As she melted into him, with her back against a wall, she felt his fingers trace a line down her stomach. He didn't stop at the waistband of her pants. "This okay?"

"Yes. Right now, it's..."

He kneed her legs apart as he continued kissing her. It was a damn good thing she was leaning against the wall, because her legs couldn't hold her up. He slipped his fingers into her panties, into her mound, parting her folds, then started circling her entrance. She gasped as he pressed hard on her clitoris.

He groaned as his fingers swirled into moisture that was building by the second. All pretense fell from his eyes. He gave a deep, honest and hungry groan as he slid fingers inside her. "God. You're so, so wet."

Two and a half years without sex had evidently lowered her threshold for orgasms. As he thrust his fingers in and out of her, she started coming. "Gabe. I'm—"

"Yeah," he said, as he continued the thrusting motion while pressing his thumb against her clit. "Want you to keep coming. We're only just starting."

Breaking away, he lifted her and walked over to the couch, gently setting her there. He knelt in front of her, and lifted his shirt over his head. Her hands crawled along his tight, tawny skin, stretched taut over his rippling chest and shoulder muscles.

As he peeled off her yoga pants, she reached for the waistband of his jeans and unbuttoned them. But she got no further with that because he moved his hips away. In a quick, steady move, he shifted his shoulders so that her knees were over them. As he bent his face to her mound, she froze at the thought of oral sex.

She pushed him away. He looked up, shooting her an arched eyebrow glance. "Stop?"

"Yes. But no. This is a different kind of problem." One she hadn't thought through. Hadn't had the need. Until now.

Oh, for the love of God, just tell him.

"I don't think I can let you do that. Because if you do, it begs the question of blow jobs. I used to. Before. But I can't, now. And it isn't fair, really—"

"Oh." His shrug lifted her legs with his shoulders. "Don't worry, honey. This might feel good for you, but trust me, it'll be better for me. I've been dying to taste you...and I don't feel like telling you when I first had that thought. I don't need a blow job in return."

The discussion ended when he rested his butt back on his heels, bent his upper body forward, and pressed his open mouth into her mound. Her body shook as his tongue worked through her folds. As she shut her eyes and gave into the explosions that rippled through her, she whispered, "You sure?"

"Positive." His deep voice vibrated throughout her. He took her clit into his mouth, and gently licked it as he sucked. Arching her back and pressing herself to him, she kneaded her hands through his hair. When he slipped a finger into her, she gasped. "Yes."

He slipped in another finger, swirled it, then started thrusting his hand so that his fingers went deep, deep inside of her, while his tongue and teeth worked her clit, taking her higher with each touch. "Oh God. Gabe. That feels so, so good."

Sparks sizzled up and down her body, racing along her legs, down her spine and to her fingertips. Building and building, without release. "Oh Gabe. Never. Never felt this good before."

If I did, I don't remember it.

His answering groan as he used his teeth on her clit sent shockwaves from her mound throughout her body, and still her need built. Arching into him, she was panting as she tried hard to relax into an orgasm...that...impossibly...wasn't... coming.

Frustrated, she gripped his head tighter. And still her need built. Higher. Higher, as she thrust her hips with the need for release. Moaning, she suddenly knew she needed to feel him making love to her, while she made love to him.

"Need you. Inside me. Now."

He lifted his gaze to her. "You sure?"

"God, yes."

In a matter of seconds, he stripped off his jeans. Took a condom out of the pocket, opened it, and covered himself. Her right leg was against the side of the couch, and he was lying between her thighs, his penis poised at her entrance. He hesitated, with his weight balanced on his hands.

She lifted both her legs, folding them behind his back, and arched into him. Reaching down, she gripped his shaft, shivering with anticipation. "Now, Gabe. Please."

"Going slow," he said, between clenched teeth, as he pushed the head in, but not far. "You're so..." He did a circling motion with his hips, swirling a few inches into her, then pulling out, and repeating the move. "Tight."

"That's why it feels...so...good...oh...God, Gabe... Don't need it that slow. Now. Hurry!"

He thrust hard and deep, spreading her walls with a swift, decisive move. "Oh." Low and throaty, his one word was enough of a statement. "God, but this feels great."

"Yes," she whispered, as heat and warmth spread from him throughout her body.

"Understatement. Worth. The. Wait." With his eyes on her, he started thrusting. Gently. Pulling almost all the way out, slowly pushing back in. Going deeper and deeper with each move. When she started thrusting back, he picked up his pace. Slightly. She sensed he was holding back. But they were both panting, and the need that had built into a brittle pinnacle for her started crumbling where her walls clenched hard around him.

"God, Gabe. So perfect."

Giving a long, slow groan, he buried himself deep inside of her.

She could feel that he was close, but not there yet. Pent-up tension rippled along his chest muscles and arms as he held back the need he was fighting to restrain, while her release built into an orgasm that left her breathless and shaking.

As her orgasm ebbed, she was gripped with urgency to make this as good for him as it was for her. Raising her hips, and shifting to her side so that she could spread her legs more, he sunk in even deeper.

"Oh. Yeah. That's—" he growled, pushing in deeper. "Even better."

She gasped with the heightened pleasure the shift in position brought. As another crest started building within her, she whispered, "Don't hold back."

He moved faster and faster. And then he stopped. "I'm losing control. This feels too good."

"Let go. I can handle it. I want to feel your strength."

His low groan was a magical blend of frustration and desire. When he started thrusting again, using the force she was inviting, she said, "Yes. Like that. I love how you're so deep in me."

"Come again for me." Through slitted eyes, he watched her. With the couch creaking in protest, he slammed into her, propelling himself deeper and deeper inside with each hard, spreading thrust. He filled her with a power that her body absorbed. Her sighs became constant, while his moans became harsher, more guttural. He clenched his jaw and kept pumping into her.

"Almost there," she said. "Oh, Gabe."

She lifted her legs higher, and folded them tightly in the small of his back. Her inner muscles clenched along his long, thick erection, coaxing him into a deep and powerful orgasm. Flexing his hips so that he was even deeper inside her, she felt the throbbing pulse of his release. More of a groan than words, he mumbled, "You're—we're—perfect. Together."

Afterward, they lay, panting and sweaty, on the couch, chest to chest. "Strength," she whispered. "It's like you gave me your strength. I've never felt that before. Never," she mumbled, lips parted on his rising and falling chest, "felt such power behind...the act. Everywhere. Throughout my entire body."

His arms tightened around her back, as his chest rose and fell with heavy, deep breaths. "Perfect. There's more where that came from. But sleep first."

Answer enough, because his actions as they'd made love, tender at first and then with demanding, unrelenting passion, had said it all. His need for her made her feel like a woman again. His trust that she was ready for good, hard loving, and giving it to her, made her feel capable of being desired. Capable of receiving and—equally important—giving intense pleasure.

As she chased him into deep, contented sleep, Andi felt whole. Healed. Still her post-kidnapping self, but a better, stronger version than she'd ever dared to hope.

Sometime later, Gabe's sudden jerking of his arms awakened her. He gently shifted her off of him and sat up. The sound of footsteps, running up the stairs to her studio registered. Gabe covered most of her body and some of his lap with a blanket as the bald-headed agent appeared at the doorway, then quickly backed away. "Sorry, sir. Ms. Hutchenson. We've got a problem."

Chapter Thirty Six

Gabe

Friday, February 19, 8:45 a.m.

"Tyre. Talk to me." Gabe brushed raindrops off his sleeve and out of his hair as he entered the guesthouse.

"Richie's still here," Tyre said, stating the obvious. "Pic isn't."

"Sure as hell need a bit more than that." Taking his phone out of his pocket, he turned it on as he eyed Richie, who was wearing jeans and a green-hooded sweatshirt that Gabe recognized as belonging to Pic. A frisson of foreboding fluttered along his nerve endings as Marks shut the door and followed him into the living room.

Gabe slipped his mic into his ear. "Stevens. Copy?"

Why was Pic's friend wearing his clothes? Even under normal circumstances, that would strike him as odd. But Pic was missing, and everything in him was saying something was off here. Way off.

"Yes, sir. Accessing security footage now," Stevens said, through the mic.

Arms folded across his chest, Richie tried hard to look like he wasn't bothered by Tyre, who stood in a wide-legged stance within an arm's reach of Richie. Arms and shoulders tense, the two glared at one another, looking like they were getting ready to start throwing punches at any minute.

"Details, Tyre. How did this happen under your watch? And where is Pic now?"

"Six minutes ago, this asshole came to tell us Pic was late." Tyre's face was flushed, almost the same color as his red hair. "They pulled a switch on me, and I fell for it."

The agent was about to get his ass fired for his incompetence and he had the look of someone who knew it. Pic was important to Andi. And they'd failed her. Tyre's screw-up was Black Raven's screw-up. Pic better be somewhere safe, eating a donut as he checked out girls, otherwise both the agent and Pic's weird friend were in for a world of hurt.

Richie jerked his chin in the agent's direction, but kept his eyes on Gabe. Smart move, knowing which man posed the most danger to him. "Dude, get the fuck over it. Pic'll be walking up any minute, ringing the doorbell at the gate." Richie spat out the words, then continued in a voice that was more like the nice-guy-voice that he'd used earlier with Gabe. "Ain't necessarily a big deal. Despite all the weird shit happening these days, I'd say the most likely scenario is the kid blew his curfew." He smiled. "Besides, Pic's just a teenager, meeting his girl after a few months of not seeing her. Don't know about you guys, but I'm not such a great timekeeper when my cock's hard. Are any of you?"

Both Marks and Tyre returned Gabe's glance with enough unease in their un-amused gazes to confirm what his gut was telling him. Something a hell of a lot less benign than Richie's story was happening.

"Sir?" Stevens said, in his ear.

"Yes."

"Client's headed your way."

Hell.

With Andi present, there'd be no time for damage control. Marks and Tyre had been on the night shift. Gabe had technically been off duty on Andi's official four-man detail, but he'd been up most of the night working on Operation Pic, which had taken his research to Mapleton. He'd filled Marks and Tyre in on his earlier conversation with Richie, so they were up to speed on everything he'd discussed with Andi and Ragno. In addition to monitoring Andi's property throughout the night, Marks and Tyre had combed through NamUs, the Department of Justice's database for missing, unidentified, and unclaimed persons, then correlated that information to New Orleans-related events. When Gabe was climbing the stairs to Andi's studio at five-forty-five a.m., before he'd turned off communication with Marks and Tyre, he knew that their searches had turned up a solid string of LSI-NOLA.

Last Seen In New Orleans. Maybe the events were in the range of normal for cities that attracted transient populations. But there were enough that Gabe wouldn't want his own teenage kid roaming the streets, alone.

Yeah. Maybe nothing's wrong. Maybe the kid just wanted to be with his girl that bad and maybe he's just a little late getting back. But this is too damn coincidental.

"If you'd just move aside and let me outta here," Richie added, "I'll go get him."

Not in a million years.

With a burst of cold, wind-driven air and swirling raindrops, Andi entered the guesthouse. While he'd yanked on his clothes and shoes, Gabe had asked her to stay in the main house until he sorted through whatever was going on. He hadn't taken the time to be persuasive before jogging down the stairs, across the courtyard, and into the guesthouse. So, of course she hadn't listened. He didn't blame her.

In five minutes, she'd gone from naked, warm, and wrapped in his arms, to dressed in yoga pants and a sweatshirt and jolted into a situation that she shouldn't have to worry about. She'd slipped on a pair of boots that Gabe had seen by the door of the mudroom. With her dark hair even more tousled than usual, and her cheeks flushed from the cold and running, she looked both irresistible and too worried for his peace of mind, as her gaze bounced from Richie to Gabe, then back to Richie. Gabe's stomach turned sour.

This was not the way she should be spending her first waking moments. Not today, after they'd first made love, which had been off-the-charts...*hell.*

"Richie's here. Pic left." Without her having to ask a question, Gabe replied to the concern in her eyes. "Figuring out details."

"Hey, Andi," Richie said. "Was just telling your goons that Pic went to see Monica, who was staying at my apartment. He was supposed to get back here around seven-thirty. Eight at the latest. Don't get alarmed. I'd be late too if I was seeing my girl for the first time in months."

Richie glanced at Gabe. "And I wouldn't have had to make a big deal about this, but you guys have this place locked down tighter than death row. All I'm trying to do is go to my apartment to tell Pic to get his ass back here. If I hadn't been locked in, none of you would've even known that he left."

"We'd have figured it out when he returned, though," Tyre mumbled.

"Probably. But given how easy it was to pull a switch on you," Richie added, arching an eyebrow and pushing his stringy blond hair behind his ears, "maybe not. Anyway, Pic and me were operating on the theory that forgiveness is easier to get than permission."

Brow furrowed, eyes glinting fire, Andi's glance returned to Gabe. "You said Pic was sleeping. That Richie left. What the hell happened?"

"I screwed up." Gabe owned it without hesitation. Because even though he wasn't the one guarding the gate when Pic walked out, shit flowed uphill on jobs. Any mistake belonged to the agent in charge.

"Ma'am, it was my fault. Agent Hernandez was off duty." Tyre had the sick-to-his-stomach look of a man who was ready to take what was due him. "As soon as the situation's remedied, I'll tender my resignation."

"Tell me exactly what happened." Gabe admired the restraint in her tone. The woman who had routinely fired agents on the job for far less than what Tyre had done wasn't resorting to that impulsive action, proving that she was smart enough to know that a temper tantrum wasn't going to produce the desired result.

"I know now that Pic left at five-forty-five a.m., dressed in Richie's clothes," Tyre said. "But at the time, I thought it was Richie who was leaving. They're the same height. Similar builds. The kid wore a hoodie, which concealed most of his features. He was carrying Richie's banjo, in its case, slung over his right shoulder. He even said '*later, dude,*' in the same tone that Richie used when he walked in not one hour earlier—"

"Yeah," Richie said. "We practiced that. Gotcha, huh?"

Tyre winced, as Gabe fought the urge to punch Richie's nose into the back of his skull.

"By the time I let Pic, dressed as Richie, through the gate and went to check on what was happening in the guesthouse—" Tyre cocked his head towards Richie. "—this one was upstairs, sound asleep, under the covers, facing the wall. Snoring. I saw the top of his head. Hair color's similar. Thought he was Pic. So that's what I reported. Didn't know any better until this one—" With a frown, he jutted his chin in Richie's direction again. "—came knocking on the back door to the main house at zero eight thirty-five."

Marks cleared his throat. "Sir. Ms. Hutchenson. I was in the security room. I saw exactly what Tyre's describing. To me, it looked like Richie left. Absolutely nothing aroused suspicion."

"Take a fucking chill pill," Richie said. "You've been had. Get over it."

Wrapping an arm around Andi's stiff shoulders, Gabe's mind raced down a highway that was far different than the one Richie was paving. If Pic left as observed under his own steam, and Gabe trusted Tyre and Marks enough to have faith in their observations, which indicated a voluntary departure, then the lack of a prompt return by Pic could mean nothing was wrong.

Except his always reliable gut was telling him otherwise.

Where the hell are you Pic? You wouldn't worry Andi like this. Not on purpose.

"Come on guys." Richie shoved his fingers into the front pockets of his jeans. "This sure as hell wouldn't be the first time a seventeen-year-old boy lost track of time when he's getting some puss—"

"Go to Richie's apartment," Andi said, focusing one hundred percent of her attention on Gabe and interrupting Richie's rant. Eyes alight with both anger and fear, Gabe caught a glimpse of the hell into which she was slipping. "Bring Pic back," she insisted.

But my gut's saying he won't be there. Because Pic wouldn't have done this to you. And I'm dying inside, because I know how hard you're going to take it when you realize how wrong things are. If you haven't already.

"I'll find him," Gabe answered. *Goddammit.* Forcing himself into calm, rational mode so that he could think, rather than react to the deep-from-within need to scoop her into his arms and tell her it was going to be okay, he tightened his arm around her.

"Richie," Gabe said. "I'm assuming there's no phone at your place?"

"You assume correctly."

"Address?"

Richie shook his head. "Look. I'll just go. No need for you to escort me."

Releasing his hold on Andi, Gabe took an aggressive step closer to Richie, until their chests were six inches apart. Richie was five inches shorter and probably a good forty pounds lighter. He held Richie's gaze and, to reinforce the message, squared his shoulders. He waited for the look of understanding to reach Richie's blue eyes. When he saw it, he said, "You're either going to give me the address now, or I'll rearrange your face. One. Two—"

Richie spat out an address.

"Stevens, you copy?"

"Yes, sir." Through his mic, Gabe heard Stevens clicking at the keyboard and mouse. "Location's two point one miles from here. Sending you the most direct route via text." As Gabe's watch and phone both vibrated with the incoming directions, Stevens added, "And sending an alternate route. Streets are congested. Some French Quarter Streets, including Royal, are closed today. All day. Parades start early. Eleven a.m. Official routes run along Canal, on the opposite side of the Quarter from where we are."

"Send it to Marks and Tyre. They're going. I'm staying here. With Richie. We might need to have more of a conversation."

"Gabe, I want you to go," Andi said firmly, from behind him. "And I'm going, too."

"No." *Not just no, but hell no.* He wasn't leaving and even if he was, he wasn't taking her. "My men—"

"You. Pic trusts you." The *'I trust you'* was implied, and he felt her confidence down to his marrow.

Hell. One issue at a time. Transportation and game plan—first. Andi—after.

"Marks," Gabe said, not budging from his 'in-Richie's-face' vantage point, "go get the car."

By the time Marks made it to the garage down the street, got in the SUV, pulled out, and returned to the corner, ten minutes would pass. Walking might be faster, but Gabe had the sinking feeling that Richie would do everything in his power to make it a long, slow walk, and he couldn't very well walk the man through the streets at gunpoint, although the idea held a lot of appeal.

"Would be faster to walk," Richie said, as Marks made his way out the door.

"Not asking for your opinion." If things went as he suspected, and they didn't find Pic at Richie's apartment, then letting Richie flutter in the wind–seemingly free–would probably be more productive than holding him prisoner until Pic returned.

He typed a text to Marvin. *'Available today for surveillance?'* He hit send, then said, "Tyre. Go upstairs in the main house. My room. Get my jacket and Glock."

"You'll be sorry," Richie said. "French Quarter bars are cleaning up from last night's party and getting ready for today's. By now, delivery trucks are blocking streets. Takes a lot of beer to keep the bars full. It's Mardi Gras, dude—"

"Shut up," Gabe growled. He glanced back to where Andi stood, about three feet away.

She mouthed, 'Thank you,' proving that she was as sick of Richie's bullshit as he was.

His phone beeped an incoming text. Marvin. *'Yo. Available. Gimme deets.'*

As Richie continued with a rant about how most people who lived in the area knew to park their cars and leave them parked from the Friday before Mardi Gras until Ash Wednesday, Gabe replied to Marvin via a text. He provided instructions to meet at the address Richie gave them, then follow Richie from there, wherever he went. He ended the message with an all capped warning, *'BE INVISIBLE.'*

While Gabe sent the text, Richie continued, "I'm telling you, dude. Walking would be faster. Today's when the real party begins and given that they're shutting down more streets earlier this year, it's going to be gridlock out there. If you were local, you'd know that. Everyone in the city's on the move. And up until about eleven, liquor delivery and trash trucks will block traffic in and all around the Quarter. It'll take—"

Gabe opened his right hand, reached out, and collared Richie while he pushed the guy to the wall. Feeling and hearing the satisfying thud of the guy's skull as it smacked the brick, he kept a lock on Richie's skinny neck, digging his fingers into his throat as the man gagged. Gabe added pressure from the heel of his palm into his Adam's apple. When Richie got over his surprise enough to start clawing at him, Gabe swiped his hands away with his free hand, pressing into Richie's pale, white neck harder, until his face turned bright red and his eyes bulged. "When I say something, I mean it. You understand?"

Richie managed a tiny nod.

"Don't say another word without my permission."

Gabe let go. Richie, clutching his throat, collapsed against the wall, wheezing. Leaving the guy trying to suck in air, Gabe went to Andi, gripping her upper arms as she looked up at him. "You have to promise me that you won't do anything foolish. I can't take you with me, and I don't want you to try to follow us. With or without an agent. Don't, Andi. Promise me. I can only do my job finding Pic if I know you'll be right here, safe and sound, when I get back with him."

Her jaw set. "Pic obviously isn't thinking clearly. I—"

"No." And before she argued, justified, or tried to coerce him into changing his mind, he said gently, "Not because you aren't capable of handling the crowds and craziness out there—you are." It was a bit of a stretch, he knew, but she was better now than she'd ever been since the kidnapping. Didn't matter how good she was. He still wanted her safely behind locked doors, with an agent on guard. Call him old-fashioned, but she was more than a client, and if anything happened to her... "But anyone on the streets right now could get hurt in the crowds, which are going to build throughout the day. Why put yourself into that kind of situation?"

Since her gaze told him exactly what she was about to say, despite his scare tactics, Gabe switched direction. "I won't be able to concentrate on retrieving Pic if I'm worried about you every second we're out there. Let me do my job, Andi. Stay here and rehearse what you're going to say when he walks in and you ream him out for worrying us."

She gave him a clear-eyed look. "I was about to say—before I was so rudely interrupted—I want you to be damned careful out there." She brushed his jaw with her fingertips. "And thanks for that vote of confidence, even though we both know it's not true. Go. Don't look at me with that much worry in your eyes. I'm fine. Go. Just bring him back."

Given Mardi Gras-related road closures throughout the Quarter and the traffic-congested streets that surrounded it, the straightest shot to the address Richie had provided on North Prieur Street was Esplanade Avenue. Vehicles on the narrow street traveled at a snail's pace. Gabe, in the back seat with Richie as Marks drove, felt frustration ratcheting up his blood pressure. He'd left Tyre and Stevens at the house with Andi.

The day had changed from rainy to gray. Misty, but it wasn't pouring. Pedestrians, some wearing jester's hats, more wearing purple, green, and gold shirts, while some were in business suits, filled the sidewalks. People walked between traffic and cars that filled driveways, blocked sidewalks, and took up every possible inch of curbside parking. Everyone seemed to have a cup or a can in their hand, glistening beads draped around their necks, and broad smiles that proved the gloomy weather wasn't bothering them.

"Looks like we're the only people not going to a party," Gabe mumbled, as his watch vibrated with an incoming call. His brother Zeus. He sent it to voicemail. Ragno had given him a solid clue that Zeus wanted information regarding the Hutchenson job. Given his brother's ability to ferret out details, that conversation didn't need to take place with an agent and Richie in the car.

As they waited at a red light where Bourbon met Esplanade, a woman wearing a costume of sheer rainbow swirls stepped into the street in front of their SUV.

Marks gave a low whistle. "Is she..."

"Yeah." Gabe's eyes traced blue, yellow, orange and red swirls of body paint. "Not wearing anything but primary colors."

Richie did a low catcall of a whistle. "Toto, this ain't Kansas. Friday's a little early for the body-painted chicks, but it gets earlier every year. Happy Mardi Gras."

"Why isn't the paint dripping in the rain?" Marks asked.

She smiled, winked, and turned to them when she looked inside the vehicle. Preening, in all of her airbrushed, body painted glory.

Richie asked, “Is that a pot of gold on her…”

“Can that be legal?” Marks muttered. “It’s broad daylight.”

A man accompanying Rainbow Woman, dressed in a bodysuit that was spray-painted to look like a yellow-brick road, scowled at Marks through the windshield. Too bad it was hard to take him seriously. Gabe watched two police officers on horseback cross in the middle of the intersection. Their glance took the woman in, but then they moved away without breaking a smile. “Guess so.”

“Light’s long.” Marks drummed his fingers on the steering wheel, his gaze still fixed on Rainbow Woman. Four young men wearing Roll Tide sweatshirts, stood in freeze-frame in the middle of the intersection, staring at her.

The light turned green. A woman pulling a red wagon with two kids sitting in it was three paces behind Rainbow Woman and the congestion she was causing. Which meant she and her two children were in the crosswalk, in front of their SUV, which had the right of way.

“Come on. Get a fucking move on, people,” Gabe muttered.

Gabe glanced at Richie, who was hunkered down low. Richie arched his eyebrows. His smirk sent a silent *I-told-you-so* message. Just as Gabe started to think no one in this crazy-ass city would notice if he gun-prodded Richie through the streets, traffic started flowing.

Richie’s apartment was located on a commercial property that had parking for seven cars and a storefront with a large, solid commercial sign:

A-1 Dry Cleaners.
Delivering fresh-cleaned clothes and linens to the New Orleans Metropolitan Area.

A large, cinderblock garage, with three solid doors, was attached to the storefront. A neatly hand-lettered sign attached to the front door indicated the business would be closed until Wednesday. Burglar bars covered every window. Signs that said, ‘Do Not Park Here’ were posted, ineffectually, all around the property. Parked cars were three deep everywhere.

Richie climbed stairs alongside the garage, then fished a key out of his front pocket.

“You didn’t give Pic the key?” Gabe asked.

"Nah. Monica's here to let him in." Richie bent to unlock the door, then opened it and pushed it aside.

One glance into Richie's small apartment, which reeked of marijuana and cigarette smoke, confirmed what Gabe's gut had suspected all along. Pic wasn't there. Neither was Monica. Seething, he walked quietly through the living room and kitchen, studying the place.

An old brown couch had tears in the leather. Fast food wrappers littered the low coffee table and the kitchen counter. Pizza boxes were stacked on top of a trash can. A bottle of vodka, half empty, was on an end table. In the bedroom, a mattress and box springs, without a frame, was barren of sheets. The mattress had multiple stains. Between the living room, bedroom, and bathroom, Gabe counted at least five overflowing ashtrays. There was no television. Full trash bags lined one wall. There was no art. No posters.

Gabe glanced at Richie. "Where is he?"

"How the hell would I know?"

"Not the right answer. You've got one more chance."

"Hell. He's probably almost back at Andi's by now, with Monica. And when you get there, tell him I want my damn banjo, 'cause it ain't here."

Gabe bent his knees, rotated his body in Richie's direction, and threw an uppercut that landed squarely on the scrawny guy's chest. Richie's air left his body in a solid whoosh. Gabe finished the guy off by landing another punch, this one into his right side. When Richie fell to the ground, he left him there, barely resisting the urge to kick in the guy's kidneys.

"Next time I touch you, I'm breaking your ribs. Consider that a promise. And if Pic doesn't show up damn soon, it's only a matter of time." He glanced at Marks. "Find anything that gives us a goddamn clue as to who the hell this guy really is. Because I'm betting his name isn't Richie, and if that's his first lie, then we need to figure out the rest. Papers. Bills. Checkbooks. Computers. Cell phones. Stevens?"

"Yes, sir." Stevens came through the mic, loud and clear.

"Everything okay with Andi?"

"Yes, sir. She's upstairs in her studio."

"Good. Don't tell her the kid isn't here. If she asks, say we ran into traffic issues." Gabe eyed Richie, who was still writhing in pain on the floor. "Find the owner of A-1 Cleaners."

"Yes, sir. Will do."

"Dude, you're insane," Richie said between moans. "I'm as surprised as you. That kid was supposed to come here. Monica's been here for the last week. I'm telling you, I don't know where the hell he is. Man. I can't breathe."

Gabe picked up a trash bag full of clothes. Dumped it on the floor and kicked through an assortment of rank, grungy garments. Glancing at Richie, he said, "If I'm wrong, then I'm sorry. Dude."

Chapter Thirty Seven

Andi

On the night after they found her friend Collette's body, Andi had been alone in her family's Florida beach house. Sleep had eluded her. That night, when Victor Morrissy came for her, she'd been in bed, focusing on the rhythmic crash of the nearby surf.

No! Not now. I can't afford to slip away to the world of terror. Not now.

As pain lit fire once again to the scars on her back, Andi, alone in her studio, fought to keep from succumbing to the rollercoaster ride of flashback-driven fear and horror. Inhaling deeply, with relief, she heard the thud of Gabe's footsteps rounding the second floor landing.

She focused on the doorway, where Gabe would be coming in. Soon. With the sleeve of her sweatshirt, she rubbed the liquid fear off her cheeks. Though she was sitting on the floor in her studio, her mind had been in the exact moment she had awakened to find Victor Morrissey standing over her bed. Though her fear was inspired by what she'd endured in the hours she was missing, her worry was all for Pic. Because that's what Pic was. Missing. Just as she'd been.

There was only time for her to draw a deep breath before Gabe appeared in the doorway. He caught her trying in vain not to look like she'd been crying. The floor around her was littered with sketches of Pic. She'd been torturing herself, bargaining with God, swearing that if/when Pic was found...she'd do anything.

She stacked the sketches into a neat pile to give herself time to brace for the bad news that Gabe's grim expression carried. She gulped for air as Gabe dropped to his knees beside her. "He wasn't there," she said.

With his arms wrapped around her, she felt his chest rise and fall with a deep breath. "I'm so sorry."

"Monica?"

"No sign of her. Didn't look like either of them had ever been there. But the place was such a pigsty, I can't tell. Richie's swearing Monica was there, and Pic should have been. I'll find him, Andi." Shifting so that he could cradle her face in his hands, he held her gaze. "I swear it."

Just as the man typically emanated light and warmth, the concern that he now conveyed was palpable. It was inky dark concern, cloaking all the deep golden goodness that was Gabe's essence and carrying a gravity that was wrong.

All wrong, because his concern was for her.

In it, she saw a future. His future. Their future. If they could possibly stay together. It wasn't a future he deserved, because he deserved better than someone who would suck every ounce of radiant warmth from him. And unlike the past that had caused her life to be a constant struggle against torment, the future she glimpsed was one she could prevent.

Pic first, then Gabe leaves. For good.

"I fired Tyre."

"I saw the camera footage, after you left. I made the agents show me. Reality is, Pic did a great job—"

"Reality is, it is unacceptable job performance. As agent in charge, you have legitimate cause to fire me."

"Good to know," she said. "But I'm not firing you. I wouldn't trust anyone else to work as hard as you will to find him." Softer, she continued, "Use these." Breaking away from Gabe, she shoved the pile of sketches of Pic into Gabe's hands. "For a flier. Paper the streets. Shelters. Alert any authorities who will listen. We'll fix whatever went wrong in his past. I'll pay to fly him out of the goddamn country, if I need to. Black Raven can do that for me, can't you? Let the world know Lucas Tanner McShane was here. And he's missing—"

"We don't know that he's missing. Not yet."

She saw the lie for what it was. An attempt to help her hold onto hope.

"Don't. Ever. Lie. To. Me. Again."

A pulse beat at his temple. He nodded, reluctantly. "Understood."

"Now go. Do whatever you can do to find him. Because..." she gulped for air, trying to hold it together as she sat again. With his eyes on her, she found a momentary strength not to succumb to the pull of her personal horror, "...I damn well know what happens when people go missing. GO!"

Message delivered, she gave in to the mind-suck of Victor Morrissey's legacy. Placing her head on her knees, hugging her legs to her chest, she gave in to the darkness cloying at her. This fear was too big for tears, this terror too enormous to voice.

Been there—God—done this. I can fight it. Fight it. Fight it. If I concentrate, I can.

She sensed when Gabe stood. Heard him moving about her studio. But the reach of darkness that pulled her back to the world of trauma was strong. She ignored his movements.

After some time, she felt him again at her side. "Andi," he whispered. "Lifting you."

Powerless to stop him, she felt his strong arms under her knees and at her back. Felt when he stood with her. He walked a few paces, as she turned her face into his chest and drew in a deep breath. After a long minute, where he stood still while his warmth and strength seeped into her body, she looked up. He bent his face and held his lips to her forehead, smoothing the concern and fear from her brow. "Ready to stand?"

"Yes." His warmth had oozed into her very core, and she now understood that even if she wasn't okay, even if she was anything but fine, she needed to act strong. Or he wouldn't leave. And he wouldn't find Pic, if he stayed there, trying to make her better.

I'm stronger. Because of him.

He steadied her on her feet, placing her in front of one of her easels. He'd placed five blank canvasses on each. "Focus on something good. I know you've got the images in here." Cradling her head in one large palm, he lifted her chin with the other so that she looked up at him. "In your mind's eye. You told me that's how you get through your rough days and nights. Do it now. Paint. Fill these canvasses with something beautiful, something good."

"Your eyes. They're all wrong," she whispered. "I don't want them looking at me like that. Don't want you all concerned for me. I'm fine."

"I know you are. And you will be." He gave her the slightest of smiles. With it, a glimmer of the luminous light she'd come to associate with him shone through. "Paint my eyes however you want them. I'll find him, Andi. I swear it."

Chapter Thirty Eight

Pic

Pic jerked from unconscious to conscious, between one erratic heartbeat and the next. Icy wetness sluiced his head and shoulders, hitting his skin like shards of ice. He blinked water from his vision. Confusion remained.

What the fuck!? Goddammit. So cold.

His hands were pulled taut and stretched over his head. Cold water pounded his bowed head. When he tried to step out of the water, shackles bit cruelly into his shinbones.

Soapy fingers and hands clutched his balls, switching his focus from *goddamn that's freezing*, to *what the hell?* Again. Seriously. What in the name of hell was happening and how the hell had he gotten wherever the hell he was?

Hell. Hell. Hell.

The fingers squeezed harder. He let out a long groan. Confused again, because it felt kinda good, but kinda painful. *Ouch!* But it was good pain. And then there was no kinda about it.

Because I'm that goddamn hard. I'm lit up like a ramming rod, by this sick dream? When the hand squeezed his balls again, his head shot up and an indignant oath sprang to his lips, even as nausea welled in the back of his throat and the watery view blurred and spun.

Gotta be a dream.

It felt like a million years ago when he'd asked Gabe to turn around so he wouldn't see him without clothes. Not being covered was now the least of his goddamn problems. With a filter of water poured over his vision, he made out two butt-naked women and two bare-assed men hosing him with sprinklers as they lathered him with their bare hands and shampooed his hair.

"What the fuck!? Get your fucking hands off of me!"

One of the women moved her face close to his. Wide, scared blue eyes held his gaze for a second. "Sh. They watch. They won't feed any of us if it doesn't look good. And I'm starving."

Young. Dear God. She's so skinny. She looks like a kid. WTF! And I've got a raging hard-on. From this! Men are fucking rubbing their hands, and Jesus Christ—themselves—on me.

Help.

Me.

Despite the water, the harsh scent of soap, and their hands and their bodies on him, Pic drifted in and out of consciousness. Two were fair-skinned blondes. The others were darker. Limbs were so tangled and bodies were so close, he couldn't make out features, as his thoughts swirled. They left the hair on his head, but shaved his face. They shaved every inch of his skin. Even his pubes. His ass.

There was something familiar about one of the guys. Something...about the ink on his neck. Birds. But Pic was too woozy to focus, drifting in and out of consciousness as they worked on him.

It was easier not to focus, anyway, because when he did, all he could think of was that he was naked, chained, and he shouldn't be turned on. But he was so inexplicably hard that each touch of fingers on him, female or male, had him getting harder. Longer. Bigger than he'd ever imagined he could be.

Without a doubt, if I could reach my cock, it would take me about ten seconds to jack off. What in the fuck is happening here? Am I gay?

Lips grazed Pic's cheek. Blue eyes that he suddenly knew looked into his, as the guy planted a kiss on Pic's lips. As Pic flinched away from the kiss, it registered why the ink on the guy's neck had looked familiar.

Jake.

"Pic. Wake up." Jake's lips were at his ear. "We're in hell. Do what they want. It's the only way you'll eat. Cameras. They watch. They'll dose you more if you don't. The more they give you, the crazier you'll get."

But what do they want?

Pic drifted off without asking his question. He woke up again, and realized the water was turned off. He was dry, but still shackled. He felt hands slathering his skin with lotion, and he groaned. Pressure and pain had taken hold of his body, all emanating from his groin.

One of the girls backed slightly away from Pic. The blond girl. She rubbed her breasts as she did a slow drift down to the floor, arching her back all the while.

Woozy unconsciousness took hold. When he opened his eyes again, the darker-skinned guy—not Jake—was holding onto her hips as he rammed himself into her. She was on her elbows and knees, with her ass high. Her mouth was open. She moaned as he thrust, her boobs bouncing with the action. Through it all their focus was fixed on Pic's cock, which was jutting straight up in front of him.

He'd never done anything with anyone after Clarence. No sex, no blow jobs. But he knew how to use his hands, because all guys did that, right? And what he needed, more than anything, was to release some of the pressure that was rising into his back. He felt as if a goddamn horse was kicking him there. But he couldn't, because he was tied up.

I'm going to shoot off into the air.

Before he drifted off again, Jake pressed a kiss on his lips, then bent his head to Pic's ear. "We've gotta get out of here. Try telling them you'll screw without the drugs. Fight to keep your mind clear."

Huh?

His eyes closed and his mind escaped to woozy oblivion, as snakes of pain coiled around his thighs. He felt hands on his cock and then she put her mouth there. Or his mouth. Pic froze for a second, at that thought, and then wondered whether what had closed around him was a mouth. And if the body part belonged to a guy...

Oh. No!

Panic subsided, slightly. He knew it was a mouth, because Clarence had taught him what teeth, tongue, and a throat felt like as somebody sucked him.

So maybe there's a silver lining there, right?

Too scared to look down and see whether the mouth belonged to a male or female, Pic kept his eyes shut tight. Reality was—he was so goddamn horny he didn't care. As whoever it was flattened their tongue along his shaft, Pic gave up resisting. There was only one way he knew to satisfy the urge that now burned a trail of fire from his groin, throughout his entire body.

He groaned, jerking his hips forward, instinctively going deep to assuage the cloying need. All he could do was jerk his hips forward, trying to release the pent-up energy. Hands cloyed at his balls. Fingers slipped between his butt cheeks. Bodies rubbed over him. Tongues licked him. And still, he kept his eyes closed, thrusting and praying for it to end.

Eyes closed. Eyes closed. Jesus. Please. Don't let me see this. Help me.

Finally, as he exploded into the mouth, his stomach roiled with bitter nausea. Before his orgasm ended, he felt tears running off his face.

The next time he awakened, Pic had no idea how much time had passed. Hours? Days? He was dry. His stomach was rumbling with hunger. That wasn't what worried him, though. He'd been hungry before. He could go days without eating, if he needed to. He hoped though, that what he was remembering hadn't actually happened.

He hoped that he'd lived through the worst wet dream ever. Hope that it had only been a goddamn nightmare and that he'd awaken in Andi's guesthouse, flittered through his brain. His hope faded, though, as hopes always did. His hard-as-a-rock, pounding like a steady-drumroll cock, told him that he was still living a sick fucking nightmare.

Literally.

He was naked and uncovered.

Yeah.

That hadn't changed. Flipping to his stomach, to give whoever might be watching a view of his ass rather than his hard-on, he tried to get his bearings on what he was going to see when he opened his eyes. He was on a floor. He felt wooden slats under his searching fingers. Spaces where planks joined.

Goddammit, but my balls are aching.

He stilled his breathing. Tried to listen for recognizable sounds. There was nothing he could make out. Something was wrong with his hearing, anyway. Blood was rushing and pounding through his head—the one on his neck—with the same force that it was pounding through the head that had taken control of his body.

His groin felt like it was a tire that was filled to the point of blowout. He had maybe two more minutes before he started humping the floor. His hand. Anything.

He opened his eyes. A naked girl was in the corner. She had long blond hair, big blue eyes, huge boobs, and she was leaning against the wood-paneled wall, with her legs stretched in front of her. She gave him a slight, sad smile.

"Where am I?"

"I don't know," she said.

"What do they want?"

"For us to fuck."

Oh.

Now it made sense.

Like none at all.

"Sex slavery?" He'd heard stories. Of people getting kidnapped, sold to rich old men. But thrown into a wooden cell so that he'd screw some girl? What kind of creeps were watching?

"Come here. It's time. Make it look good."

"I don't even know you."

She laughed. It sounded bitter. Like the hopeless, sad kind of laugh that came from the old homeless people in the shelters. "That's...sweet. Don't matter, though. I'll see you again in a few days. Unless you...disappear. Best I can tell, they keep a rotation of you guys going. And then you...go. Away from here. Don't know where."

"A rotation?"

She shrugged. "Only thing that matters is getting to eat. Don't ask me more, because I've got no clue. All I know, is some rooms are different. Sometimes there are props, and sometimes there's more than one of you."

"Of me?"

"Yeah. Like three guys lined up to fuck me. It goes on like that, for days. Then it stops. Then it starts again."

He read acceptance in her eyes as she relayed the facts. "How long have you been here?"

She glanced upwards at the ceiling. His gaze followed hers. Cameras. Directly overhead and in the corners.

"Come here," she said, her voice low and urgent.

He stood. Felt like covering himself, but couldn't. He walked over to her, with his goddamn hard cock on display like a flagpole. He sank to the floor with a heavy thud. She turned to him, and wrapped herself around him so that her huge boobs were smashed against him. One pressed into his arm, the other slipped forward, caressing his chest.

Her mouth was on his ear. "I've lost track of time. A few months. Three. Four? I was living on the streets in San Francisco, then woke up in a hospital bed. They gave me these tits. Do you like them?"

Pushing back, without wanting to react, he did, because her tits were huge. Hard and soft at the same time, and her nipples were stiff peaks that stole one hundred percent of his attention. *Hell.* He didn't think he could get harder, but he did. Pain shot from his balls, down his legs. It was only a matter of minutes before he'd be unable to resist what was so obviously the direction he needed to go.

"They fixed my nose," she continued. "Took off a tattoo. Some of the guys start off like you. Nice. Hesitant. But you all get mean. Then it takes longer and longer for you to get off. I think it's the drugs they give us to keep us horny." Louder, she said, "They'll give us food if we make it look good."

"Good?"

She glanced into his eyes. "They like creative. Not missionary. They're watching. I'm hungry. Please. I need to eat. Here. Will this help?"

She spread her legs wide and gave him a smile that seemed real. As she touched herself with one hand, his attention became riveted on what she was doing. One finger. Then two. Slipping inside of herself. In. Out. Faster. Faster, and he was mesmerized, because he'd never watched a woman do that. Never seen that part of a female, so close. Her lips formed an o, while her eyes were on his cock. As she panted, she lifted a hand to him. He slipped his hand in hers, letting her guide him, so that his fingers replaced hers.

Recognizing the futility of every minute where he'd ever hoped for a better existence, with a life like a normal person, Pic's stomach twisted as he touched her warm wetness and absorbed his new reality. "I've never done this before. How the hell am I supposed to make it look good?"

Chapter Thirty Nine

Andi

Friday, February 19, 8 p.m.

Stepping back from her easel, Andi studied the portrait of Gabe. The image was the best of the four attempts she'd made, but nothing came close to capturing the beautiful energy of the real flesh and blood man. Cerulean blue and Pthalo green paint would never convey the laughing gleam in his ever-changing eyes, no matter how good her technique.

Yet...she narrowed her eyes, studying the intensity.

Maybe this one's a keeper.

A wailing siren captured her attention. Normally, the townhome's thick masonry walls, sound-proofed windows, shutters, and window coverings kept street noise out of her third floor workspace. Not tonight. Sirens seemed to be the norm for the evening. She held her breath, until the siren quieted.

Sirens mean nothing in terms of finding Pic. Authorities aren't looking for him. Black Raven is. And it's been at least two hours since Gabe's last update.

To keep crippling fear at bay, she refocused on the canvas. Only one background color would capture the no-holds-barred vibrancy and warmth she was trying to create. Yellow. She'd use multiple hues, and enhance the color's positive effect by feathering the brushstrokes, so the texture reflected light.

Slow-rolling her head from shoulder to shoulder, she shrugged into the movement to ease tension in her upper back. Lifting her arm and bending it over her shoulder, she slipped the wooden end of a long handled paintbrush under her t-shirt and ran it along her scars, scratching the itching that wouldn't let up.

As the lacquered wood worked soothing magic along her skin, she heard Gabe's footsteps coming up the stairs. *Finally*. He gave her a slight smile from the doorway. Eyes serious, wearing a black leather jacket over the dark pants and shirt she'd seen him in earlier, he was in full work mode. Jaw set. Gun holstered. "Teams?"

He paused.

"Going silent while I bring Ms. Hutchenson up to speed. Still monitoring you, though. Talk to me if anything comes up." Touching his watch to adjust his mic, he studied the angle of her arm, elbow in the air, hand behind her back. "I could do that for you."

Returning the brush to the table, she shook her head. "You've got more important things to do. But thanks for offering."

"Want to update you. And given where we are, I have a question."

She'd gotten used to the way his business-like updates distilled the horror of Pic being missing into a matter-of-fact, methodical plan for finding him. Yet no matter how reasoned Gabe's approach sounded, unlike one plus one equaling two, the sum of all bits that he'd delivered hadn't equaled Pic. And the look in his eyes told her this report wasn't going to be any different.

He leaned against the doorjamb, hands in the pockets of his jeans, with his gaze crawling over her. For a moment his gaze shifted to the four canvasses, which now contained, in various states of completion, his face.

"News," she repeated. "Have surveillance cameras produced anything?"

His focus returned. "We've got more footage from cams along Esplanade Avenue. Actually, the cam from Pug's Po-Boys gives us the best view. Enough to confirm what we suspected earlier—Pic crossed Esplanade Avenue and headed downriver."

"Why wouldn't he take the most direct route to Richie's?"

"Don't know. I have ideas, but nothing firm. Yet. Video shows us he kept walking away from the Quarter. He might've taken a left, though. In the very next block. Or a right. The turn in the river makes the streets bend. He might've thought he was going the shortest route to Richie's. Or—" Gabe paused. "—he might not have been going there at all."

"But that doesn't make sense. Why would he have gone out if he wasn't going to see Monica at Richie's?"

"Don't know. We will find answers, though. We just don't have them yet."

Fighting through her concern, she moved a tube of bismuth yellow closer to Naples yellow. She glanced towards Gabe, who'd fallen silent, frowning as his gaze locked on her shaking hands.

"Stop worrying about me. I know it's weird for me to be painting now—"

His frown softened. "Not weird at all. It's a coping skill. A damn good one. Given my line of work, I've been around people who react all kinds of ways when bad shit happens in their life. From what I can tell, you're handling this just as well as anyone.

Better, as a matter of fact." His tone lightened. "Not to insult your work, though, but there's no way my eyes look that good."

She glanced at the canvasses. Then she turned back to study him for a second, deciding he really meant what he said. "You really don't know, do you?"

Brow furrowing, he frowned.

"The eyes I've painted don't come close. When I see you, I see a man who shares his warmth with the rest of the world. A man who lives with unbound enthusiasm. Courage. A man who protects the weak. Bolsters the strong. A man whose very smile is a bright, welcoming light. A man whose beautiful eyes can see people who are so lost, they've forgotten how to hope." She sighed. "All that's in your smile. But mostly in your eyes. They're absolutely riveting."

Still in the doorway, he gave her his thousand megawatt smile. "Only when I look at you."

And that's a problem. Because I'm the one person you shouldn't look at with all of that feel-good joy in your eyes. I will suck it all from you. Don't you see that? And I can't let that happen. I won't let that happen.

"News," she said.

"Just returned from the Eighth District. Talked with Officer Thompson, to see whether the cops could facilitate the process of acquiring footage."

"I'm sure he was helpful," she said, with a frown and heavy sarcasm in her tone.

"He laughed so hard, he almost swallowed his toothpick when I asked about police procedure for networking residential crime cams in areas outlying the Quarter, where most of the cams aren't networked."

"Didn't you expect that sort of reaction?"

"Yeah. But my purpose was to let the authorities know some of what we're doing, and I accomplished it. I've got a feeling. I thought I'd give them what I like to think of as a warning flare of trouble ahead. It's standard protocol on our jobs."

Eyes jerking back to him, she gave up on trying to focus on anything but his words. "What feeling?"

He eased away from the doorway and came to her. He pushed her hair behind her ear, then let his hand rest on her shoulder. "I can't read too much into it at this point. But this is how I find solutions. It's a process. I'm giving you what few details I have, while trying to keep speculation to myself until we've got facts."

The weight of his warm palm on her shoulder kept her grounded more than any painting ever had. "Keep going."

"Thompson confirmed that the official city crime cams that are in place don't work. When I told him that we were looking for a street kid who was missing, he gave me the blowback I expected. Said good luck with searching for a vagrant at Mardi—"

"Pic's not a vagrant."

"Not to us." Gabe pulled her close and draped his arms over her shoulders, around her back. As he held her, she breathed with him, letting his calmness reach into her soul. "But to the rest of the world, he is. And, given the Mardi Gras mayhem out there right now, I can't say that I blame Thompson for his don't-bother-me-with-that-crap attitude."

"Did you tell him that Monica is missing as well, and what Richie said about Jake?"

"Didn't get that far. He'd have dismissed it as speculation and innuendo, anyway. Right now, he has more urgent problems. About an hour ago, there were gunshots fired into a crowd on Bourbon Street, a block from Canal Street, right near the parade route. They've stopped the parades for a while. He's dealing with serious crowd control issues, plus a crime scene in the middle of it."

Andi shuddered. Resting her chin on his chest as their gazes met, she said, "That's why I'm hearing sirens."

"Yeah. Not our problem, though. Local neighborhood watch groups are being more receptive with the cam issue. They've gotten emails out to members, with an alert for suspicious activity. Even on normal days, it takes time for us to access non-networked security cams. A lot of them don't retain footage for more than a few hours. And—" His frown deepened. "—as my agents have heard a million times—it's the Friday before Mardi Gras."

"No one's paying attention."

As Gabe's gaze conveyed a full dose of how right she was, a flare of anxiety stole her breath. *No. Don't go there.*

"We're paying attention. Your downstairs dining room and kitchen now serve as home base for eight additional Black Raven agents assisting in legwork, plus we have a full cyber team at headquarters."

"Ragno?"

He nodded. "She's on it. With her cyber team. And then there's Marvin and his son, Billy, who have eyes on Richie. Who, by the way, has done exactly what he said he'd do. He's inside, presumably sleeping. We're watching him for a blink of anything off kilter. Hoping he'll lead us to a clue."

"If he's really a bad guy—"

"My gut says there's no 'if' about it."

"Then why would he have told Pic, or anyone, about Jake being missing?"

"Well, this is speculation, with a few facts. My hunch says there was a fuck-up. By acting like he was concerned about Jake's disappearance, Richie kept a great undercover story going. He's working for someone who snatching these kids—my theory—and has been funneling information about these homeless kids to someone for a while. But the fuck-up happened when Jake was snatched. Someone else saw it, and he's talking. This isn't a hunch—it's a fact. Guy goes by Shroom. As in Mushroom."

"Seriously?"

"I can't make this shit up. Now that we're on the streets, talking to some of these people, we've learned that Shroom is a low-level dealer. He's telling everyone that Jake was snatched. We're trying to find Shroom, now. My theory is that it would have looked damned suspicious if Richie didn't also appear concerned, when Shroom and Richie were together when it happened. So Richie started talking, and at least pretended to be looking for Jake. He didn't seriously think anyone with any authority would listen.

"Another possibility could be that the guy Pic clocked the other night is part of the bigger operation that Richie works for. That guy wanted Pic, bad. Richie delivered him and at some point, Richie's going to lead us straight to the guy. These are theories, Andi. I could be wrong. I'm working hard to figure things out. Brandon and Sebastian authorized the full court press, which I'd have insisted upon, anyway. Given that our screw-up caused this situation, we're on it even more full-bore than usual. Extra manpower is doing door-to-door canvassing for camera footage, and spreading the word at places where Pic might have gone, in case I'm dead wrong about all of this and Pic simply decided to break free from being here."

"We could only hope."

He gave her a small smile. "Hold onto that hope. Don't lose it, just because I'm running with all these other hunches. By the way, I had to talk to the powers that be about us. I was trying to skirt around it, figuring it's our own business, but I'm also on a job. And that's the reality. Details are important. So now, Brandon, Sebastian, Zeus and Ragno have an idea. About you.

Me." He touched his lips to her forehead. "This." He pulled her in tighter, squeezing his arms around her back. "Us. I simply gave an idea. Hoisted a warning flag. Didn't tell them too much."

Good. Because I don't know what this is.

Before she could say anything, he shifted to business mode, separating his face from hers, while keeping his arms draped around her. "Unfortunately, for the crime cam angle of attack, with each minute that passes, the likelihood of automatic erasure of relevant footage increases. So he might've slipped through the cam grid. While satellite footage is sometimes an option, the cloud cover, coupled with the early morning hour, makes feasibility non-existent.

"Which gets me to the second area I've implemented—real time monitoring of the periphery. We're papering the city's homeless shelters with fliers. Putting out reward money for information regarding Pic's whereabouts. We're monitoring everything being called into NOPD and Neighborhood Watch groups. Cyber division is also analyzing output from programs that we've got running through cameras that are networked in databases we've infiltrated. We have advanced facial recognition software, and to develop the composite, we've put in your sketches of Pic, plus the video I took of him for Richie last night.

"Where possible, we're doing retroactive time-based, and real-time, searches. We'll know if Pic so much as shows up—or showed up—anywhere in front of any camera that we can access. Bars. Strip clubs. Bus station. Train station. I'd also like to do this with all the sketches you might have of Jake and Monica."

She crossed the studio to her table, and started sifting through the sketches.

Gabe, at her side, continued, "Here's where I get to my question for you. It involves my third line of attack. When I'm working the parameters of a job, I imagine the possible scenario of the worst thing that can happen, then I cover that base."

With his voice quieting, becoming downright somber as he spoke, an internal chill raced through her. It had been so long since Andi had trusted her own gut feelings that she was loathe to start now. But everything in her shouted that Pic was in trouble, with the beat of a loud, insistent ticking of a metronome in her head. Illogically, but unequivocally, she knew without doubt that something terrible was happening. "Pic's in deep shit, Gabe. I just know it."

"And if he is, I'll make it work out, Andi. That's my job. We call it embracing the suck, but what it really means is accepting reality and working through it for the correct result. No matter what shit gets served on a platter. In ninety-five percent of my jobs, the worst thing never happens. But in the five percent that do, I'm ready."

She found a sketch of Jake that showed the tattoo on his neck and added it to the pile of sketches for Gabe. "So give me the worst-case scenario."

"Wanna sit down for a minute? You've been standing for hours."

She couldn't hide her shiver. "It's that bad?"

A slight nod, and hardening in his eyes, gave her the answer. "It isn't pretty. And it brings up what Lamonte's uncovering in Mapleton. So I need to tell you that, too."

Inner demons caught her breath in their death grip. Eyes shut, she focused on Gabe's warmth, the heaviness of his strong arms around her, and found light in the darkness. Drawing a deep breath, she nodded. If this man, who was trusting that she could handle the nitty-gritty facts, thought she could handle the news better by sitting, she knew she should damn well sit.

Settling on the couch, he assessed her, then, satisfied when she squared her shoulders, nodded. "It's about what you and I were talking about with Ragno. It looks like someone is snatching homeless runaways off the streets. Blue-eyed, blond, vulnerable teenagers. Any teenagers. Young runaways are one of the most vulnerable segments in our society. They readily fall victim to the predators who make the domestic and international sex trades their business. I've got a team using facial recognition software to look for Pic, and I'll add Monica and Jake, as well, in the usual online portals, because predators are tech savvy now. We're searching the dark web and encrypted sights, in addition to places like Craigslist, Eros, and Tinder—"

"Holy shit, Gabe. I used to use Tinder."

"Um. I know. It's in your file. I knew you were an active member of the hook-up generation even before I attended your art opening and met some of your conquests."

Her stomach twisted. "Never really thought about unsavory characters using it as well."

He touched the tip of her nose with his index finger. "Because you were having too much fun."

"My fun was way different than what you're talking about."

"Yeah." Voice turning even more serious, he added, "Those sites are fluff compared to some of the more hardcore sites we'll check out. Ragno, with Zeus giving the secret handshake to Government muckity-mucks, is now integrating Black Raven intel with expertise from some of the Government's best. The most sophisticated slavers, the ones who shoot for big bucks on the international market, are so heavily encrypted, it can take lots of trial and error to gain access. It's a process, with undercover agents and virtually untraceable bank accounts. In case we need to go that route, we're starting the liaison process with official task forces. Unfortunately, we've had to do this before. We know the ins and outs. Ready for your question?"

Eyes locked on his, she nodded.

"We can make up an alias for Pic before we start circulating his face among investigators outside of Black Raven, but even with an alias, it will only be a matter of time before his face pings with the Mapleton arrest warrant. Earlier I promised you I'd only use his information with your approval. Now I'm asking you for it before Ragno proceeds."

"Yes. For anything." Thoughts swirling, Andi fought against the pull from tentacles of her deep-within, downward spiral. Squaring her shoulders, pulling her legs onto the couch, she turned to face him. Keeping her voice strong, she asked, "What has Lamonte found?"

He shifted his hips, settling deeper into the couch. He turned sideways to face her, softening his tone, but kept it matter-of-fact as he reached out and toyed with her hair, wrapping a curl around his index finger. "Your idea of suicide counseling resources, and our hacking through medical records, led us to answers of what went wrong. But really, we didn't have to look too hard. Lamonte found the counselor that the hospital referred Pic to after they treated him for slashing his wrists, which occurred three weeks before his mother was murdered. We have ways of getting people to talk to us, and Lamonte was prepared to use every coercive technique in her considerable arsenal. Instead, Doctor Jonas Trimble greeted her with profound relief. He spilled his guts. He's looked for Pic, but done a damn amateurish job of finding him.

"To sum it up. Fourteen-year-old Pic had three sessions with Doctor Trimble over ten days, from his admission into the hospital for slashing his wrists until the November 7 murder of his mother. In his third session, on November 5, Pic spilled his guts. Told Trimble that he'd been repeatedly sexually assaulted, spanning a two-year time span."

Andi drew a deep breath. Gulped down some air as her insides clenched with sorrow for Pic. "Oh, Gabe—"

"I know."

Seeing worry for her appear in Gabe's eyes, she shook her head. "Go on."

"Pic wouldn't give Trimble a name. Trimble was instituting procedures to have child protective services investigate further, and possibly remove Pic from the custody of his mother, when news broke of his mother's murder. Blunt force trauma to the head. A weapon was never recovered. Evidently, as authorities arrived, one of the officers stated that they saw a young man matching Pic's description running from the scene." Gabe shrugged. "I'm guessing he kept running. Straight to New Orleans, I think, given how long you've known him."

Gabe lifted her hand out of her lap, holding it in his. "Which doesn't surprise me in the least, given what else Lamonte's pieced together based on information from Trimble and others, mostly neighbors in the trailer park where Pic and Aubrey Rose lived."

"What?"

"We strongly suspect the pedophile boyfriend was the long-time chief of police of that town. Clarence Walker. Neighbors place him as a repeat late-night visitor at Pic's home. And an after school visitor. Neighbors can even place him there, at Aubrey Rose's trailer, on the day of the murder. The body was discovered around four in the afternoon. Marge Smith, the closest neighbor, heard yelling, then it got quiet. She saw Clarence show up, yelling started again, and then there was quiet. She saw Pic run away, then Clarence left, and a patrol car came in."

Rage took hold of her gut. "That explains why Pic was so scared to tell his side of the story. Or talk to anyone."

"Yeah. And why he ran, and kept running, when he heard sirens that day. Walker ruled that town for ten years. He was asked to step down three months ago, which is one reason people—including Marge Smith—are talking freely now."

"Why did he step down?"

"Two other young men have accused Walker of repeated charges of rape. And there's noise that others are coming forward. Criminal charges are pending. Lamonte's going to visit Walker tonight. She'll continue her investigative work, because we've still got that murder warrant to contend with." Gabe paused, his jaw set, his eyes glinting with rage. "But I have a strong feeling everything will work itself out."

"How?"

"I own this problem. I'll take care of it as the situation deserves. And in that regard, Andi—" His gaze held a hardness that she hadn't imagined could be possible. "—I will not give you details."

Chapter Forty

Andi

Saturday, February 20, 2 a.m.

Flames tore at Andi's back.

Scorching, agonizing heat pressed into the thin, sensitive, skin.

Wrists bound to her ankles, the bindings forced her into a fetal position, bending her naked, exposed back. Powerless to move. Suffocating from having her mouth on his cock.

Pain was unending and excruciating. Within the swirling sea of pain and screams, the ominous click of the lighter became a cannon blast that quieted her as she braced for more. The flare of flame caught her attention, then he waved the freshly lit cigarette before her tear-drenched eyes.

Heart pounding loudly enough to block out other sounds, she braced for the sharp bite of pain as he pressed the red tip inches from where he'd last marked her.

Hold it.

He laughed when she screamed, so she tried not to. Until the pungent, sweet stink of her own burning flesh filled her red world.

One—two—three—four—five—

Find me. Find me. Find me.

Goddammit, is anybody looking for me?

She screamed until she passed out to the sound of his sick laughter.

"Andi! It's Gabe. I'm here."

Smelling salts lurched her back to consciousness.

Lighter.

Click.

Flame touching the fresh cigarette.

Burning tip, to her skin.

Hold it. Hold it. Hold it.

Smoke.

One—two—thr—

"Andi, I'm here. With you. Hold on to me."

Lifting her chin to Gabe's voice, she was able to breathe before she felt another cigarette burning the flesh along her spine. Howling, because she couldn't stop slipping away to a world where the devil tortured her.

"Wake up. Shake it off. Come on, my strong girl. It's Gabe. I'm with you."

End this.

Kill me.

Please kill me. It hurts. It hurts so bad.

"Fight, Andi. Fight. You can do this, Andi." Gabe's voice was getting closer. "You're in your studio. I've got you. You're safe. Fight it, dammit. Fight it."

I'm trying. But he's been at this for...f-f-f-forever...and it hurts so bad I want to...die. Dear God, please take me. He's too sadistic to kill me. But I want you to take me.

Dear God. Please.

"That's my girl. Hold on. To me. Like you're doing."

Let me die. This time, end it. A fresh scorching circle of torture went deep into her back. Ow. Please.

"Baby. Hold on. I'm not going to leave you. Not going to leave you. Not ever. You understand me?"

Ah. I can feel Gabe's hands. If I hold on, he'll pull me out. Pull. P-P-Please. Gabe. Please. Please. Pull me out of this burning hell.

"That's it, Andi. Breathe. Look at me."

I'm trying.

My eyes are open. Why can't I see you?

Lighter. Click. Flame—

Oh. No. Gabe. Please.

"Come on, Andi. Goddammit. Open your eyes!"

Like a mirror shattering, fear and pain crashed around her, leaving her out of breath and numb. Darkness swirled as the night terror receded, threatening to take her with it, but she held onto Gabe, who was on his knees in front of her. Her hands grasped his wrists and he pulled her forward, away from the red-laced darkness, to him.

Wrong Gabe. Worried-to-death Gabe. Worried sick for me.

Shutting her eyes, she drifted into the safety of his arms as he closed them around her. With her consciousness foggy, she felt Gabe lift her. Heard him talking to someone, as he cradled her like a baby on his lap, hugged her close, and whispered, "It's over. You're fine. It's over Andi. You're fine."

After a while, she was able to open her eyes. Shaking herself, she remembered the day. Remembered that Pic had disappeared. Remembered everything that had happened up until she decided to lie on the couch in her studio and rest for a few minutes. But after that, she didn't recall what had transpired that had Gabe whispering to her, as he tried to keep her centered.

She didn't need to recall it. The severity of her most recent night terror was written all over his face. As he lifted a hand to stroke her chin, she saw fingernail gouges at his wrists. Her nails.

Decision made.

Pushing his hands away from her face, she said, "I will not do this to you."

"Don't—"

Pulling away from him, she stood, locking her knees and pressing her palms against his chest to remain upright. "If you stick around, I'll drain the life out of you. Every ounce of joy, every positive thought. I will suck out all your happiness. You don't know what I'm fighting." She fought to find the right words, because her thoughts remained disassembled from the nightmare. With fatigue bearing down on her, standing took effort that made clear speaking difficult. "You. Don't. Know. Promise me. Pic returns. You leave. Promise me."

"Because you had night terrors at the end of a colossally bad day? Because you scratched my wrists?" He held up his wrists, showed them to her. Three-inch long gouge marks, trails of her terror, oozed fresh blood. "This is nothing. Nothing. You understand that? I'm signing on, Andi. Wherever this road might take us. Your past was part of you from the minute I started falling for you and I will not let it defeat us. Do you understand that?"

Downright drifty and woozy from the nightmare, she shook her head. "Eyes can only see so much, Gabe. Even yours. You'll never know what really happened." A little clearer, she added, "There are things that torment me even more than how Victor burned me. I...don't think I could tell you those things. Even if I wanted to. Which I don't, because you'll look at me like I'm pathet—"

He held his index finger to her lips, gently interrupting her rant. Eyes glinting with a look she couldn't decipher, he said, "I've got to tell you something."

Fresh fear jarred her. "What?"

He drew a deep breath. Looked away, then back at her, his cheeks flushed red.

"Dammit, Gabe. What?"

"I know all those things. I read your journals."

Drawing in a deep breath, she couldn't comprehend his words. And then suddenly, she did. She opened her mouth to say something, but no words came.

"Yeah. I'm not proud of it."

"But, how? When?"

"I knew there was a false wall in your studio. My rationale was that I had asked you for all the keys, and you didn't provide all of them to me. Given the enormity of the breach of trust, my excuse seems lame, now, but I was supposed to have access to the entire premises—"

"That doesn't mean you could read something so private—"

"I know. It's inexcusable. I saw a boundary and I damn well leapt right over it. And since I'm giving you one hundred percent honesty, I'm now convinced I did the right thing, because you'd never tell me those things. You'd always use your secrets to drive barriers between us. Like you just tried to do."

No words. She had no words for the enormity of what he was saying.

"I want all of you Andi. Not just the fragmented parts you allow the world to see. Yeah, I was a dick to read something that personal, that intimate. I'm sorry for invading your privacy, but I'm not sorry that I got to see you raw and real."

"But," she protested, shaking her head, thinking that she must be dreaming. Again. "This doesn't make sense. You wouldn't—"

"Sure I would. Let me remind you what Ragno told you the other night. Don't let my smile fool you. If I'm an angel, I'm a dark one. I don't just protect people, I damn well fight battles for them. And to do that, I leap over any barrier put in my way. I picked the lock last Sunday. The second day I was here. Sat in that room—" He gestured with his head to her private alcove. "—and read your secrets for hours." His gaze held hers. "I know everything, Andi. From the sexual assault that you never told anyone about, to how you were trying to kill yourself when you met Pic. Everything. And that's part of why I've fallen in love with you. You understand me? Because I understand how goddamn brave you are. On top of being captivated by everything about you at first sight, your paintings, your eyes, and even your feet." He paused, then his eyes became serious. "I understand the depth of your struggle. I'd be honored to help you fight it. Let me. Please forgive me so we can move past this."

As waves of understanding lapped at her, she realized that she was living a dream that would have no ending. Because it wasn't a dream. In the moments where she stood silent, however, the weight of untold horrors started lifting from her chest. *Someone knows. And that someone is him.* "I know you think you can handle this, but—"

"There's no 'but' in this discussion, Andi. You can ask me to leave for the rest of your life. The only way I'll goddamn listen to you is if you tell me in your heart of hearts that you want me to leave, because you don't think there's ever a possibility for you to love me. If it's because you're worried of what being around you does to me, you can keep those thoughts to yourself. Now," he said, giving her a small smile, his voice soothing, "it's two forty-five in the morning. I've got absolutely nothing new to report to you, except Brandon is on the first floor, being resident agent in charge of your job and Operation Pic while I get a few hours of sleep. Both of us desperately need some rest, so we can get through tomorrow. What do you say we stop talking and do that together?"

Give in. For the moment, just goddamn give in.

Together, they went down the stairs. By the time he stepped out of the bathroom, she'd stripped off her clothes and was drifting off to sleep. Fatigue after her night terrors was always real. Palpable. They were mind-numbing, draining events that left her sapped of energy.

Yet as he slipped under the covers with her, she curled into his chest. Pressed together, his warm closeness felt...right. As though he understood her need, on this night, as on so many nights, not to be alone. To have someone else breathing in the dark, right night next to her. To have her body enmeshed with the man who could find and conquer even her demons.

As she breathed in his scent, and felt his warmth, she wanted more. Drowsy, she lifted her face and pressed her lips to his.

His kiss was tender. Gentle. Drowsiness receded as his tongue slid along her lips, then met hers. She took his hand, pulled it to her breast, and he answered with a slight groan.

"Sleep," he whispered. "Right?"

"After," she said. "Make love to me. Please?"

"Do you forgive me?"

"I don't know," she said, as honestly as she could, then reached for him.

"Let me love you, Andi. We'll work out the rest."

"For now, make me feel something other than miserable as I fall asleep."

"Give me a minute." His mumble was gruff. He walked out of her room, then returned in a few seconds. Sitting on the edge of the bed, he slipped on a condom, then turned to her.

With his fingers, his mouth, his tongue, his body, he answered her body's cues. When the steady warmth and pulsing of his flesh filled her, his soothing heat and strength radiated throughout her body. If she'd ever shared a more intimate moment with anyone, she couldn't remember it. What they were doing wasn't about sex. The act meant togetherness, first and foremost.

Afterwards, he kissed her, while his eyes conveyed a silent promise of love, and all that the word meant. She returned his look with open honesty. "I'll only accept your love if I can return it with equal force," she whispered, as his arms tightened around her. "Only if I can give you equal, in return. And I'm scared I'll never be there. I'm worried my past will always be in the way."

Chapter Forty One

Andi

Saturday, February 18, 8:30 a.m.

Andi awakened with a start to an empty bed. She spotted a handwritten note on the end table, tucked under her cell phone.

No new developments overnight. I'm out. Brandon's downstairs. He'll alert you if anything changes. Turn on your phone when you awaken. Try to eat something. G.

She turned on her cell phone, and saw a text Gabe had sent at seven-thirty a.m. *'How r u?'*

She replied, *'Fine. Thx for your note. Don't worry about me. Call if there's news.'*

She held the phone long enough to see if the ellipses signifying an answering text appeared. They didn't. Clasping the phone for a second longer, she prayed. *Please. God. Let Gabe find Pic.*

As she pulled on a pair of jeans after her shower, she heard a knock on her bedroom door. A deep male voice, one she recognized, asked, "Andi. You up?"

"Brandon?"

"Yes," he said, through the door. "Juliette's here."

Juliette?

"Oh *hell.* It's Saturday, isn't it?" Which meant at nine a.m. it was time for her weekly allotment of pampering, courtesy of Juliette Bandeau. Last week, she'd had a massage and facial, which meant this week, she could expect a manicure and pedicure.

Through the door, Brandon answered. "Sure is."

Dressed, Andi opened the door. "I forgot."

"Don't blame you." Wearing a black turtleneck sweater and black slacks, Brandon had the same business-like look that Gabe had worn since Pic had disappeared. If he carried a weapon regularly, the lawyer typically had it concealed when he was around Andi. Now, though, the gun holstered at his hip conveyed the impression that he was operating on par with the agents, capable of dealing with danger and ready to use a weapon if needed.

"I thought you might be sleeping. I almost sent her away, but I know that my wife moves heaven and earth for appointments with her royal highness, so I called Taylor for a read on what to do." He shrugged, giving her a slightly sheepish smile as his tone turned sarcastic. "Some things are better answered by a girlfriend. Taylor told me you'd want to talk to Juliette yourself, especially since she managed to get into the Quarter this morning, with all the streets closed to traffic."

Juliette made it crystal clear to all clients of her in-home spa services that she had more than enough work to keep her busy. And she was very selective, regarding her client base. Taylor had found her based on a friend's referral, and Andi had been wait-listed for a few months before becoming a regular. Andi accepted the Juliette-style attitude—she firmly let her clients know she was doing them a favor, at $150 per hour, because she was punctual, reliable, and provided exceptional services. Most importantly, Juliette didn't gossip about her other clients. Andi took her discretion as a sign that she wasn't gossiping with others about her.

"Are you up for dealing with her, or would you like me to send her away?"

"Is there any news about Pic?"

"Not yet."

Hell. Sighing, she squared her shoulders. "I'll go downstairs."

Juliette, standing in the vestibule, wore a cream-colored turtleneck, black pants, and leather boots. Her sleek black hair was in a neat ponytail that draped over her left shoulder. She'd apparently hung her coat in the closet, and was waiting to be let up the stairs. A Black Raven agent who Andi didn't recognize stood, arms folded, in the vestibule a few feet behind her. Back to the wall, his gaze shifted from Juliette to Andi, then Brandon, as they descended the stairs. He slipped into the surveillance room, as Andi made it to the first floor.

With her tote bag at her feet, Juliette arched an eyebrow in irritation over being kept waiting. It was subtle, but unmistakable. "Are you okay?"

Over Andi's shoulder, Juliette's gaze followed Brandon as he walked through the foyer, towards the kitchen. From that direction, Andi heard the hum of voices, in low tones. Trying to focus on the fragrance of fresh coffee that filled the downstairs, Andi ignored the questions in Juliette's eyes, like *what is Taylor's husband doing at your house*, but she was too polite to ask.

"I'm so sorry," Andi offered, "I should've canceled."

She wasn't the sort of person who treated manicurists as therapists. Not even Juliette, whom she trusted implicitly. Andi wasn't about to discuss what was happening. *I can't even verbalize the horror of it.*

Eyes narrowing as she studied Andi, Juliette's cool, brown eyes shifted from irritated to concerned. She nodded with the understanding that Andi wasn't going to spill her guts. Because Andi never did.

"No kidding. I should've been smart enough to reschedule. The French Quarter, on the Saturday before Mardi Gras? Did we do this last year?" She gave a solid headshake. "I don't think so. You're a wonderful client, but not this great. I could've just as easily gotten down here on Wednesday, when the city's suffering a hangover and no one's out. Trust me, traffic's a bear out there. I had to park about seven blocks away, in the Marigny. But—" She accented her pause with a smile. "—look at the awesomeness I brought with me."

Reaching into her tote bag, she pulled out a clear plastic pouch. "New OPI colors. The spring collection, released three days ago. You're going to love this." She pulled out a color, and held it up to light that filtered in through the leaded glass transom above her front door. "Just a bit of a bluish, silvery tint, but mostly lavender, right? You know colors better than me. The name of it is, *'Don't Make Me Blue.'* How sweet is this?"

On other days, Andi could've slipped into excited-about-nail-color talk with Juliette. But not today. Not with Pic missing. With her heart feeling heavy in every direction her mind raced, OPI's new shade of lavender just wasn't going to do it for her.

"Look, I'm sorry. I'm not up for a mani-pedi this morning. Why don't you just go, and get out of here before the crowd starts building again?"

To say that Juliette had been exposed to the gamut of Andi's moods was an understatement, so she easily shook off this one. "I'm here. So let's both make the most of the situation."

"No. I'm feeling off this morning—"

"Which is all the more reason for you to use me. Come on. You've paid for this time. At least let me give you a color change. Why don't you grab some coffee while I get things ready upstairs. Once your feet are in hot, soapy water, we can decide whether you want your usual treatment or just a quick fix." She lifted her wrist, and glanced at her watch. "It's nine-fifteen. I'll be out of your hair by eleven-thirty. I promise that by then, you'll feel better, no matter what's wrong."

If only it would all be so easy.

In five minutes flat, Andi was sipping hot coffee, her feet were soaking, and a heated roll filled with lavender and rose scented potpourri was draped over her shoulders. Gently falling rain in a faraway rainforest sounded through the room. The chair was set to a rolling motion. Juliette had removed the nail polish from her fingers. Lifting her feet out of the soapy water, she rested them on a thick, plush towel as Juliette dried them.

Despite having slept soundly in Gabe's arms for at least five hours, and the coffee, once Andi settled into the comfort of the massage chair, waves of fatigue lapped at her consciousness. Putting the coffee to the side, she leaned back, shut her eyes, and stopped paying attention as Juliette moved from foot to foot, hand to hand. The ritual was quietly soothing. It didn't quite weave together the frayed endings of Andi's nerves, but it gave her breathing space.

Gabe will find him.

He will.

He will.

Juliette gently tapped Andi's left foot, a sign to put both feet in the soapy water. While they soaked, Juliette stepped behind the chair to give Andi a neck massage. Leaning forward, Andi kept her eyes closed, focusing on the feel of lush, soapy water on her feet, anticipating the soothing pressure of Juliette's fingers on her shoulders.

Instead, a wet cloth covered Andi's nose, pressed there by a strong hand. Andi gasped as she reacted, while inhaling sickly sweet wetness that could only be a drug. It was one that she'd smelled before, when Victor had needed to subdue her.

Chloroform.

Immediately woozy, with the room spinning before her eyes, Andi felt a sharp prick needle into her neck. She tried to lift her hands to claw at Juliette's hands, but her brain's signals misfired.

Andi heard Gabe's voice, using the phrase he constantly hammered into her in their workouts, 'don't hesitate.'

Too late. I already did.

Fighting to hold onto thoughts that were fading, Andi tried to fight through her dizziness and stand. With both feet in a slippery tub filled with soapy water, instead of going on the attack, she sat down hard, in the chair. She tried to scream, but couldn't hear her own voice. When she tried to get up again, Juliette was in front of her, with strong hands on her shoulders, holding her down.

Eyes shrewd, assessing, Juliette smiled. She put a hand in front of Andi's face, waving fingers in front of Andi's eyes. Her fingers became a sickening blur, as double vision gained control. "Sorry, hon. You're my golden ticket out of pretending that I give a goddamn flying fuck about other women's cuticles."

With the room swirling around her, Andi fought to keep her eyes open as Juliette lifted a cell phone to her ear. "Ready for pickup. Get your ass over here."

The other woman kept her gaze on Andi as she dropped the phone into her purse. Taking one of Andi's hands into her own, she let it fall, limp and impossibly heavy. Hands working fast, she wiped Andi's face with a warm cloth, removing evidence of whatever it was she'd inhaled. She pushed Andi's head to the side and wiped at her neck with the cloth.

As her eyes drifted closed, she saw Juliette take a blue tube of something...concealer?...from her tote. Andi felt pressure on the spot where the needle jab had been.

"Good enough to get you out the door." As Juliette prepped her for some unknown horror, Andi's brain raced through defensive moves she'd practiced with Gabe, the no-hesitation drill he'd instilled in her, time and time again. She could hear his voice. Think fast. *Act*. Think fast. *Act*. Think fast. *Act effectively*.

Waste...of...t-time.

As crippling paralysis overcame her, Andi's thoughts became fuzzier and fuzzier. Unable to think coherently, unable to move. Helpless.

"Help! Andi's had a heart attack, or something!" Juliette screamed. "She's not breathing! I'm dialing 9-1-1."

Chapter Forty Two

Gabe

"Gabe. Stop. He's not giving you anything." Ragno's voice came through his mic, loud and clear, though he'd muted her call before landing his first punch on Richie.

Damn, but she always finds a way.

Gabe ignored the intrusion. Rearing his arm back, he closed his fist, reconnecting his knuckles into the soft flesh of the man's soft stomach. "Ready to talk?"

Bent over, between full-body heaves as he emptied his gut onto the floor, Richie held up his hand and flipped his middle finger in the air, just inches from Gabe's face. Gabe thought about breaking the man's fingers, one by one, but decided against it.

For now.

"If you value your fingers at all, I'd keep every last one of them out of my face."

The pothead had slept all through Friday in his stinking shithole of an apartment, exactly as he said he would. Using a banjo that he'd picked up from a friend, he'd played with other musicians at the Fat Cat club until four a.m., exactly as he said he would. From there, Richie had gone to an all-night grill at the foot of Bourbon and Esplanade, where, according to Marvin, he'd eaten enough to satisfy a horse. Then he'd returned to said shithole, locked himself in, and had yawned as though he'd been sleeping when Gabe had banged on his door for a rise and shine visit. The smirk that had accompanied Gabe's update regarding Pic had inspired Gabe to show Richie he had nothing to smile about.

"He knows something," Gabe muttered, for Ragno's benefit, checking the time. Nine-fifteen. Which meant he'd been 'questioning' Richie for a full five minutes. "But you're right. Enough. I have another team of agents arriving in NOLA from Last Resort at noon, correct?"

"Yes."

"Have them bring Serum One." Referring to the blend of sodium thiopental, scopolamine, and amobarbital sodium that agents administered for tough interrogations, Gabe wanted to have it ready in case breaking the man's fingers didn't produce the desired result. The serum definitely wasn't something one could get at a corner drugstore. On certain high-risk jobs, it was part of the agent's tool kit. Andi's job hadn't been that kind of job. Until now.

"Gabe. Listen up." Zeus's growl broke in on Ragno's call, conveying a solid warning to *'calm down'*. His brother was at Denver headquarters, working beside Ragno. "I've dropped everyone else. Me, you, and Ragno on the call. You can't use Serum One in a domestic setting without permission from the file's originating partners. That's Sebastian or Brandon, in this case."

"Understood. I'll get it. I'm through with Richie for now." Drawing a deep breath, Gabe side-stepped the eggs, sausage, and foamy, blood-laced goo that Richie had vomited. The stink of puke, coupled with the stale smoke and musty odors of the unkempt apartment, made bile rise in his throat. He glanced at the two agents who would be taking over surveillance of Richie for the next several hours.

Their eyes conveyed a solid message that Gabe's methods were fine by them. "Cuff him. Ankles and wrists. Keep him standing. Tape his mouth. I'll be back."

"Gabe?" Zeus said. "Just so I'm clear here. Five minutes of using him as a punching bag was not warranted."

"You agree with three minutes? Or four? Do not micromanage a field agent's discretionary calls while you're all comfy in Denver." Stepping out of the apartment, onto the stairs that led alongside the garage, Gabe breathed in cool, crisp, fifty-degree air. The mostly cloudy, yet rain free day, was a hell of a lot better than the rainy, frigid weekend they'd just endured. Tamping down his irritation, Gabe kept his voice calm. "Trust my judgment, Zeus. Ragno—that goes for you too. Richie goddamn smirked when I told him Pic's still missing."

"Rein in your temper." Although his voice remained as calm as ever, underlying worry crept into Zeus's tone. "This isn't like you. You normally do with words what other agents do with their fists."

"Well, welcome to the reality of this job, Zeus. Because nothing about it is normal. Something's way off. I feel like I'm looking at an alternate reality that seems so normal, that the first wrinkle of deception—something that I could get a handle on—isn't even there. And I'm as cool as ever. Every punch was warranted. I'll let both of you know when my temper's in play. Or if I can't control this."

From the landing, Gabe's gaze crawled over the congestion on the narrow street as people got into position for the holiday. While Gabe had been occupied with Richie, Marvin had driven around the block to avoid getting stuck in front of the dry cleaners.

He reached into his pocket for his phone and typed, *'Ready for pick up.'* He sent the text to Marvin, then continued his conversation with Zeus and Ragno. "There isn't one thing that's amusing about the disappearance of a seventeen-year-old kid. Smirking was not the correct reaction. Richie now understands that."

"I'd say," Ragno said, sarcasm flag flying high.

Marvin replied, *'Gimme 5. In gridlock on Rampart.'*

'Don't bother w/ side streets. Meet u on Esplanade.'

"Justification for the file, if you feel that I need it, is that we always start where things stopped making sense. In jobs where we don't have a solid trail to point to the danger source, it's the subtleties that matter. You two know that. I know that. It's what I try to teach our agents at Last Resort, for God's sake. In plain-world speak, it's goddamn common sense." Breathing in another deep gulp of fresh air, Gabe realized he'd been holding out hope that Richie would give him something. Anything. Which now meant he had to swallow a bitter pill of disappointment.

"We're twenty-nine hours out from Pic's disappearance, and the only thing we've got is that things went off-kilter with Richie. We now know Pic didn't head here, so Richie is lying and needs to tell the truth. And speaking of things that don't make sense, no one lives off the grid like this guy. No one. Except Pic. And the other runaways we're looking for. But this guy isn't a runaway. By the end of today, Richie will be talking. I guarantee it."

After leaving Andi's, Gabe had gone directly to the dry cleaners, thinking Richie's landlord might be able to shed some light on just who the hell Richie was. They'd been unable to locate the owner, who had apparently closed each of his four business establishments for the duration of the holiday and left town. Gabe had picked a lock on a side door, and figured out the business was exactly what it purported to be—a dry cleaners.

Gabe continued, "Recently acquired camera footage from the Marigny area tells us Pic was several blocks off course."

"He may have gotten into a car. Voluntarily. Just as he walked out of the gate of Andi's house," Zeus said. "For drugs, maybe. Or, as much as you want to believe otherwise, the kid could have spent the last couple of years prostituting for mon—"

"Not a goddamn chance."

"For the record, I was listening in on the discussion between Gabe and Pic the night that Gabe found him on the levee." Ragno's voice softened. "I've never heard a clearer picture of desperation, relief, and yearning for something better. I'm solidly in Gabe's camp on this. Yes, he walked out. Probably because he thought he'd see Monica. But I don't think he would've disappeared like this. He wouldn't have done this to himself, or to Andi. Or Gabe, at this point."

"Field agents are fact finders, Zeus. Unless you have solid data to back up conclusions that override my findings and decisions," Gabe argued, trying to keep a snarl out of his voice, "stop questioning my judgment."

"Playing devil's advocate, Gabe. That's all. We don't have full video of the area in question where Pic was last seen," Zeus protested. "I've looked at what we do have. Slide by slide, second by second. You're missing coverage of several blocks at key times. There's enough gray space there to provide a route, coupled with a time lapse, where he could've simply walked out. And kept going, without us knowing."

"It would be too coincidental," Gabe said. "Plus, I disagree. We have enough footage to see where Pic should've walked, keeping pace and timing consistent, had he kept walking. The only thing that makes sense is the possibility that Richie's a connection to something bigger. So I need to make him talk. Whether he's lying about why Pic left, or where he told Pic to go, or whatever the hell, I don't know. Richie's lying. I know it like I know my name. Ragno, any luck with satellite imagery?"

"No. We've been through every potential source for the relevant area. Two things are going against us. One, it was still dark. Two, cloud coverage was heavy. All of New Orleans was covered in rain yesterday morning. So any effective imagery was blocked."

"In the meantime," Zeus said, "keep in mind one thing—Pic may have just decided to leave. Admittedly, the chances of that are low, but a teenager with a runaway history could very easily have wanted to leave a setup where there are armed guards keeping him in..."

Having explained, ad nauseum, to everyone who was now involved with Operation Pic, that they should disregard the five percent likelihood of voluntary departure that their computer models gave for Pic's disappearance, Gabe tuned out his brother. Climbing down the outdoor stairs, he crossed the parking lot of the dry cleaners. It had been half empty when he'd arrived, but now it was congested with cars, trucks, and vans. People were setting up ice chests, lawn chairs, canopies, and barbecue pits, settling in for a two-day party. A couple of port-o-potties were in the back of a pick-up truck. A hand-lettered sign said, *'$3.00.'*

"Gabe," Zeus said, "my question called for a reply."

"Answer it. However you think I should, because I stopped listening. You're giving too much weight to the voluntary departure scenario."

"Not the correct response from a field agent when you're talking to a partner."

Hell! His brother seldom pulled rank.

"Let's keep communication open between us for the duration," Zeus continued, "because..."

Continuing down the block, past a flatbread truck with stereo speakers the size of refrigerators cranked up, Gabe couldn't hear what his brother was saying even if he tried. Which he didn't. He reached Esplanade, and stepped into the back of Marvin's SUV and relative quiet. Both Marvin and his son, Billy, who had his father's full, dark hair and eyes, glanced at him expectantly.

"Anything?" Marvin asked.

Gabe shook his head and pointed to his ear. "No," he mouthed, "I'm on a call."

"Your display with Richie, from what I heard—and yes, I was damn well listening to every second of it," Zeus continued, "—has me worried.

"Where to?" Marvin asked.

"Home."

"What the hell, Gabe," Zeus said. "Did you just say that?"

"Um, Angel. Did you hear what you just said?" His brother's worry had crept into Ragno's tone.

"Yeah." Sinking into the seat, his gut twisted. Not because he'd used the H word. That he was building his dream house near Last Resort, outside of Atlanta, Georgia, no longer mattered, because his dreams had drastically changed. His greatest desire now resided far from there. Home for him, for now, and for as long as he could imagine, was with Andi.

His gut pained him because he was now heading home and was going to have to report to Andi that they had nothing. *Nothing*. And each time he had to say 'I'll find him', without anything solid to go on, his heart ached for her. For Pic.

People don't simply disappear. Not unless there's big trouble. Not when Black Raven is looking for them.

"Home? You're on a job, Gabe. Do not make me sorry I trusted that you could handle the screw-up with this client," Zeus said, "even though you're now balls-deep in the job."

Eyes on trees from which glittering Mardi Gras beads hung, Gabe thought about his brother's recent history. "You're one to talk. I can think of two jobs when you were balls-deep."

With a whoosh, his brother let out a deep breath. "Okay. You've got me on that. Which means you should damn well listen, because I know what I'm—"

"Message received. I've got more important things to do now than swallow a sour-tasting spoonful of brotherly love. So shut the fu—"

"Before you two devolve further into a pissing contest, Gabe, please listen to Zeus. Even if Richie's lying—" Ragno paused for a moment. "—your human punching-bag demonstration suggests that a bit of perspective is warranted."

"Which begs the question," Zeus said. "Just how serious is this?"

As goddamn serious as she'll let me be.

"You told me that with Samantha, you just knew. I never understood it, till now, okay? So butt out, brother. Message received. I'm treading carefully."

"She's thinking the same as you?"

Fuck me to hell. Would you just let up?

"We're not quite on the same wavelength." Gabe tried to keep his voice low, so that his personal drama didn't reach Marvin and Billy.

"What the hell are you doing?"

"It's complicated." They crossed Rampart Street, and traveled down Esplanade, along the border of the French Quarter.

"Open line," Ragno interrupted. "Brandon's calling Code Blue."

Gabe immediately sat up, alert, his eyes scanning the traffic, the pedestrians, counting the minutes and seconds it would take to get home. Code Blue meant client in peril. Since Brandon was the agent in charge at Andi's house, that meant she was in trouble.

"Medical emergency. One minute in." Brandon's voice was calm. Low, yet conveying urgency. "Andi's passed out. Not waking up. Emergency—"

Seven blocks. Esplanade to Royal and I'm there. Two stoplights. Traffic's crawling.

"...are on their way. Agents, get cars. Stat."

I can run faster.

Gabe opened the door, his feet hitting the ground before the SUV fully stopped. Over his shoulder, he yelled to Marvin. "Medical emergency. Andi. Head there."

Running hard, Gabe dodged pedestrians. *One block down.* In his mic, with open audio to Brandon and all teams listening in, he said, "I'm four minutes out. Talk to me."

"Juliette—"

"Who?"

"Spa service provider."

Gabe dodged a family of two adults, two toddlers, and two rottweilers. One dog lunged, with a growl, as Gabe remembered the detail from the client file. "Got it." He leapt away from the open jaws. "Saturday's her regular morning."

Juliette. One of the few people Andi felt comfortable touching her. The esthetician had been a regular at her home for a year and a half, and had been referred by Taylor Morrissey.

"Continue mouth to mouth," Brandon instructed someone, presumably an agent at Andi's side.

Holy shit! "She's not breathing on her own?"

Silence.

Hell! Hell! Hell! No! This can't be happening.

"Agents Stevens and Williams—mobilize vehicles." Brandon's words, efficient and terse, conveyed frustration. "As best you can."

Gabe knew it would be an exercise in futility to get to the Black Raven cars that were garaged two blocks away from Andi's house. When more agents had arrived, they had expanded their vehicle coverage. But it did little good now, with traffic and blockades. Even with permission from officials, driving on French Quarter streets meant that barricades needed to be moved on each corner.

A crowd spilling out of a busy restaurant filled the sidewalk. Gabe ran into the street, between parked cars and moving traffic. A large truck, turning at a corner, missed his left knee by an inch.

"Brandon—pulse?" He'd been a field agent long enough to know the moment that life came down to a simple number, when someone's existence hung in the balance between this world and the next.

Because Brandon was willing to relinquish control over her to medical staff, he knew they were at that moment.

"Checking."

Pain ripped through his midsection as he waited for a response. *Three and a half blocks down.* More than halfway there. In the silence that met his mic, he heard sirens. Gabe dodged a trio of musicians, instruments slung over their shoulders. As fear-fueled adrenaline surged through his body, he fought for calmness.

This will work out. It will. It will.

"Gabe, she's fading. Stay with me, honey." The concern in Brandon's voice, apparent through the mic system, turned Gabe's blood to an icy, turbulent river. "Come on, Andi."

Feeling like a part of him died with each step that he took, Gabe turned right on Royal Street. With the shift in direction, the sirens grew louder. He was momentarily grateful he was on a street that was closed to vehicular traffic, because the street gave pedestrians more room to spread out. He sprinted down the middle. Rather than go around a decorative barricade that was designed to keep cars out, he leapt over it.

"Brandon?"

"Pulse is now steady at fifty-two. Before we instituted mouth to mouth, it was dropping below fifty BPM—"

"*Hell!* Heart failure?"

"Don't know. Gabe, Ragno, teams—EMS has arrived. Our vehicles have not. Given condition, EMS control is best option. You copy?"

Which meant Brandon was overriding a basic Black Raven rule on a security detail—never relinquish physical control of a client, unless life is in peril. As the severity of Andi's condition became as much a reality for him as each breath of air that he took, Gabe found strength to run faster.

"Copy," Ragno said.

"Gabe? You copy?"

"Copy."

Two blocks left.

"Andi's healthy. Fit. Young." Jogging around a group of men who wore tight red shorts and were holding beer cans, he continued, "No medical illness. This makes no sense."

"EMS is wasting no time. She's on a stretcher. They've got oxygen, loading her in. I'll accompany her to the hospital, Gabe, if you're not here."

Through Brandon's mic, Gabe heard the paramedic say, "No, sir. No ride along. Follow us."

"Ochsner," Brandon said. "Main Campus."

"No, sir," the EMT said in a firm voice. "With the patient in this state, we need to get to the nearest level one trauma center. That would be University Hospital."

Turning down the side street, Gabe saw the ambulance, red light flashing, siren wailing. The back door remained open. A blue-clad EMT was inside, leaning over the stretcher.

"Twenty steps away," Gabe said. "I'll go with her."

Desperate for a sight of her, Gabe kept running, weaving through a crowd of on-looking pedestrians as two EMTs stepped inside and started shutting the door. From ten feet away, he watched them push Brandon away.

Through the last few inches of the open door, Gabe heard the EMT say, "Please follow us to University Hospital, sir."

The tires screeched, leaving Gabe in the middle of the street. He sucked in air, trying to regain his breath from the sprint. Four other Black Raven agents, including Brandon, looked at him with eyes filled with worry and concern as the ambulance drove away. Pedestrians made way for the screeching vehicle, then filtered back into the street as it disappeared.

"Drivers?" Brandon asked.

"At garage," an agent reported. "Talking to the NOPD. Traffic cops have the street barricaded. They're not giving us clearance for driving. We're telling them it's a medical emergency, and they're telling us they need verification, if you can believe that. They're saying that's the reason emergency medical support is staged throughout the Quarter."

"Ragno," Gabe said, his eyes glued to his last vision of the departing ambulance. "Can you get a satellite read on the ambulance? We've lost sight of the ambulance. I repeat. We lost sight of her."

"Copy," Ragno said. "All agents. Marking zero hour. Client out of our control at nine fifty a.m., Central Time."

"Ambulance turned right on Bourbon." Gabe ran, his eyes glued to the ambulance as it made its way down the street. "At last sight, it was heading toward Esplanade."

"Marvin?" Brandon, running in step with Gabe, pulled his phone out of his pocket. He grabbed Gabe's arm, as the ambulance disappeared across Esplanade, two blocks ahead of them. "Follow me. He's four blocks away. He'll get us there ASAP."

Because Andi's life being on the line was too difficult to bear, Gabe promised himself that next year, they would not be in New Orleans for Mardi Gras. For others, it might be the best party in the world. To him, it would always be a logistical nightmare.

Through his mic, he talked to Brandon as they weaved their way through meandering pedestrians. "This isn't making sense. Just like Richie's story about Pic makes no sense. Andi's healthy. Fighting fit. She's been a great workout partner for me. All week."

"Stress?"

"Yeah." Gabe side-stepped a group of three men dressed in pink polka-dot dresses, carrying white poodles, "But she's certainly faced that before. Ragno, you listening?"

"Yes," she said. "I'll contribute when I have something. Accessing satellite imagery. Cloud cover remains a problem. Also having my agents utilize cameras that we accessed previously in the search for Pic. I'm following you, though. Agree with where you're going, Gabe."

"Andi passed out when she was with Juliette, correct?"

"Correct," Brandon answered.

"Sir?" A voice broke into their mic system.

"Yes?" Brandon said.

"A second ambulance has arrived. Same company. Crescent EMTs."

Brandon and Gabe glanced at each other. A sliver of uneasiness trickled down Gabe's spine.

"Communicate with their home base. Figure out the source of the confusion."

"Who dialed 9-1-1?" Gabe asked.

"Juliette initiated the call as she yelled for us," Brandon said, glancing at Gabe as he ran. "I ran up the stairs as she provided information. I took the phone from her, assessed Andi, responded to the operator's questions, and completed the call. Then called Code Blue, alerting you."

He'd followed proper procedure. "No one else was there when Andi passed out?"

Gabe saw Marvin's SUV in the distance, doors open for them.

"Correct."

Another voice broke into their mic system. "Sir?"

Brandon responded. "Copy."

"Juliette is attempting to depart the premises."

"No!" Gabe, Brandon, and Ragno answered at the same time.

"Roger."

"Let her know medical personnel will have questions," Gabe said, his eyes on Brandon, who gave him a nod. "Or make up something else. Under no circumstances can she leave. I don't care if you have to cuff her to the dining room table."

Brandon and Gabe jumped into Marvin's car. Seventeen excruciating minutes later, Marvin pulled into University Hospital, where the triage nurse looked at Gabe and Brandon as if they were spouting gibberish.

"One at a time. What name was that again?"

"Andi Hutchenson," Gabe said.

Checking her desktop computer, she shook her head. Again. Cast them an uneasy look. "And when do you believe she was admitted?"

"I know she was admitted within the last fifteen minutes. EMT's brought her here. White female," Gabe said. "Picked up at her residence in the French Quarter. Unconscious, unless she awakened on the way here. Twenty-seven years old. Petite. Dark hair."

The dark-haired, dark-eyed nurse's stern expression shifted towards something a little more sympathetic as she listened to Gabe. "Only thing we've gotten via EMT in the last half hour was a 45-year old black man who'd been stabbed." She glanced at her computer monitor. Clicked a few keypad strokes, narrowed her eyes, and studied the screen. "I've now checked our records for the last two hours. Nothing. She's not here."

"I requested Ochsner," Brandon said. "The EMT's were emphatic they were bringing her here, saying they needed to get her to the nearest Level One Trauma Center."

"Well, from the Quarter, that would be us."

Gabe glanced behind her as double doors opened and a tall man with brown hair and green eyes came out. He sat at the desk next to the other nurse, glanced over their shoulders into the crowded waiting room, and sighed, as he muttered under his breath, "I fucking hate Mardi Gras."

Makes two of us.

Through the open doors that revealed the inner workings of the ER, Gabe saw people clad in scrubs, two patients lying on stretchers in the hallway, and a buzz of activity around a central station. All the activity of a busy ER in a crowded city. *No sight of Andi.* As icicles of fear pierced his chest, Gabe said, "This isn't possible."

The nurse arched an eyebrow. "Trust me, this kind of mistake happens. Let's check Ochsner. And East Jefferson."

"Name on the ambulance was Crescent EMT. A fleur de lis for the T."

The nurse nodded. "There are others, but Crescent seems to be the exclusive outfit for Mardi Gras staging in the Quarter. We'll call them." Eyes shifting from Brandon, to Gabe, then back to Brandon, she added, "Don't worry. We'll find her."

"Ragno," Gabe said, feeling like he had officially entered an upside-down universe where nothing made sense. "Any luck with satellite feeds?"

"Cloud cover's a problem. I'm operating with a twenty-minute lag. We were able to trace the ambulance as it turned onto Bourbon. It crossed Esplanade, presumably to avoid gridlock there. Then the clouds got in the way. I'll keep looking."

In the longest minutes of Gabe's life, Black Raven learned that Crescent EMTs had no record of the first ambulance that had appeared at the townhome. As he discovered that no hospitals in the nearby vicinity had admitted Andi, cold calmness settled into every molecule of Gabe's body. Mind. Gut. Extremities.

"Brandon, what are Louisiana EMT rules for transporting a patient who dies en route to the hospital?" The question came from Zeus, who was now remotely monitoring New Orleans area emergency room intake.

Gabe, stunned by the hard logic behind the question, had to go outside.

"Likely scenario is EMT's will engage in resuscitation procedure." Brandon slipped into lawyer mode as he answered Zeus's question. Voice calm. Authoritative. "ER physician would make the call whether to continue that effort. Louisiana does not have direct delivery to coroner's office by EMTs."

"Okay," Zeus said. "So she'll arrive at an area emergency room, alive or...

Not going there.

Clipped commands from Zeus and Ragno sent Black Raven into crisis mode. Agents were immediately dispatched to University Hospital, awaiting Andi's arrival.

Likelihood? Slim to none.

There was no logical reason why it would take an ambulance this long to reach its destination. None. Zip. Zero.

His heart thudded in his ears as he tried to suppress his overactive imagination from coming up with crazy, wild scenarios for Andi's disappearance. The other question circling his brain like acid was—had Andi been alive when they'd loaded her onto that ambulance? Or had they—whoever the hell "they" were—killed her and then whisked away her body?

But why? This makes no sense.

Zeus's team of cyber agents, operating at Ragno's side in Denver, were monitoring patient intake at other area hospitals.

Drawing deep gulps of fresh air, Gabe slid into the back seat of Marvin's car. As Brandon, in communication with Zeus and Ragno, discussed the logistics behind assembling a crisis support team at the New Orleans Lakefront Airport, Gabe focused on where things had stopped making sense. Upon arriving back at the townhouse, he stalked into the library, where Juliette sat on the couch, tapping her foot in irritation. Her face became a study of concern as she got to her feet. "How is she?"

"Maybe you'd like to tell us," Gabe said, approaching her from the doorway.

Her perky damned ponytail swished over her shoulder. Her eyes widened. "How would I know?"

"Gabe," Zeus growled into his mic. "Remain calm. At this point, all we know is that Andi became ill while this woman was giving her a manicure and pedicure."

Ignoring his brother's warning, Gabe zeroed in on her, as a spider would a fly. He walked into her body space calmly. Coolly. And continued walking as she backed up. When she was against the wall, he gripped her forearm and shoved her ahead of him up the stairs, to the guest bedroom with the pedicure chair. The foot tub was drained. Cleaned. Towels were folded, neatly. A faint trace of lavender lingered, but other than that, there was no evidence that a manicure or pedicure had recently happened.

Shutting the door, he took off his jacket. Rolled up his sleeves, and said, "Ragno. Start talking to me. All things Juliette." He nodded to Brandon, who stepped into the room and stood to the side, giving Gabe a clear sign that he wasn't going to interfere with whatever Gabe had planned.

"How dare you!"

To Juliette, Gabe smiled. For the hell of it, he made it a charming smile, as he flexed his hands. "This is how I dare."

Chapter Forty Three

Gabe

"Zero minus one hour ten minutes. Adjust lines of communication." Ragno's voice was calm and steady. "Six teams. Multiple channels on line C, for individual teams. Line A-team leaders—Brandon, Gabe, Zeus, Marks, Ace, Me. Line B—all teams. My team's monitoring all comms. Team Leaders—go to A."

Half-running down Royal Street, with Agents Stevens and Todd in step next to him, Gabe opened his mic to Line A.

"Copy that. Crisis team is fully mobilized." Ace's audio mic carried his low voice as well as the faint noise of helicopter engines.

Gabe knew Adam Cooper Evans. Ace for short. Typically quiet, he worked primarily on high-risk jobs. Like Gabe, a few times a year, Ace trained newer agents at Last Resort, which was where Ace had been at zero hour. Gabe considered Ace the best of Black Raven's best. Knowing he was on the job brought a small measure of comfort.

"Gabe." Ace said.

"Copy."

"I'm operating in just-in-case mode," Ace added. "As in just in case I need to unleash the wrath of hell as we rescue. Three choppers en route. Packed to the rotors with support. Pulling in additional resources from the surrounding area. When we know where she is—" Ace's hard, matter-of-fact tone had shifted to one that conveyed consideration of the personal drama that was unfolding for Gabe. Ace had been drafted as a team leader within minutes of Andi's non-arrival. As a team leader, data was not censored. Team leaders needed to know everything. Every gritty detail. "I've got every conceivable contingency covered. Do not worry about my end."

"Thanks, Ace."

"Gotcha. Going silent. But listening."

Engine noise disappeared as Ace switched off his audio.

Heart pounding in a chest that felt compressed by the devil's red-hot tourniquet, skin clammy with nervous sweat, Gabe struggled for focus as he ran the last block to Marvin's car. With each minute that ticked past zero hour—the moment Andi was taken—circumstances became more dire.

From Zeus and Ragno's position in the corporate think tank, he heard the reassuring, yet indecipherable, din of keyboards clacking, monitors humming, beeping electronic devices, and multiple conversations. Too loud. "Hey Ragno. Zeus." *Calm*, he reminded himself. *Just like I'd be on any other job.* "I can hear you guys thinking."

"Sorry. My bad." Zeus said, as the ambient noise of the cavernous cyber room drifted to the background. "Better?"

"Yeah."

"Admirable restraint, Angel." Ragno was clearly referencing his demeanor while interrogating Juliette.

He'd been threatening, but his actual physicality was the opposite of what he'd used with Richie, due to significant doubt about Juliette's complicity in anything criminal. And, unlike Richie, she didn't make the mistake of smirking.

"Second that," Zeus added.

"Not looking for approval. Looking for you guys to start flexing cyber muscle. Give me something helpful. And I'm not done with Juliette." Gabe, Stevens, and Todd, slid into the rear seat of Marvin's SUV. Marvin drove, while his son Billy rode shotgun.

"Where to?" Marvin asked, over his shoulder, as he eased into traffic.

"Away from congestion. We're staging. More details to follow." Brandon was doing the same thing with another team in a Black Raven vehicle, heading east of the city.

On a wing and a goddamn prayer, more details better *follow. I'll find you, Andi. I swear it. And after I do, they'll pay the price.*

As Line A remained ominously quiet, Gabe's gaze crawled along the endless stream of traffic on Esplanade Avenue. As each minute passed without Andi appearing through the door of an ER, his questions to Juliette had become more pointed. But after ten minutes of interrogation, Juliette still seemed exactly what she purported to be: a provider of at-home spa services to wealthy clients. She'd responded to questions with a mix of perfect concern for Andi, coupled with irritation that they wouldn't allow her to leave the townhouse until Andi walked through that goddamn door. And though he hadn't laid a hand on her, he'd made it perfectly clear that he'd be happy to do so. She'd responded just as an innocent person would—scared and indignant.

Although she was the last person to see Andi before whatever the hell had happened to her had happened, given her reaction, Brandon and Gabe had mutually decided that the face-to-face conversation was going nowhere fast.

They'd left Juliette with her ass firmly planted on the floor, hands cuffed behind her back, a leg of the dining room table providing a solid anchor. An agent's eyes were on her. No doubt she was continuing her tirade of how much shit she and the powerful people she knew were going to rain down on Black Raven.

Bring it on.

Cyber-support had used satellite footage to trace the ambulance to a position near an I-10 on ramp. Under cloud cover, though, it had disappeared and had not been seen on the interstate. Going on the premise that the ambulance had traveled away from the French Quarter, Brandon and Gabe assumed they needed to do the same thing.

They were in the unenviable position of a Hail Mary move—making a leap without a planned landing. They were leaving the congestion zone of the French Quarter and downtown, but without a clue as to where the hell to go from there. It wasn't the first time Gabe had launched a Hail Mary on a job. But it was his first time having so much at stake.

One break for them was that, unlike Richie, Juliette did not live off the cyber grid. Zeus and Ragno's teams were scrutinizing every Juliette-related transaction they could find, following cyber trails, putting the flesh of cold-hard facts on a life in a way that words alone wouldn't.

"Gabe—thoughts clear?" Zeus asked as he worked.

A legitimate question to an agent who had personal feelings thrown into a job that had gone sideways in just about the worst way imaginable.

Taken. I will not think about what is happening to her right now. How scared she must be. How this is her goddamn night terrors come to life. If she's alive or de—No!

"Gabe?" Zeus prodded. "Question pending."

"I'm good." *And flat out lying.*

"I'll keep asking. Answer honestly. I know how hard this is. No shame in stepping down from the helm." Zeus spoke in a professional tone that conveyed both a field-agent's perspective and a brother's concern.

"Not gonna happen. Work on answers. Don't worry about me."

"Roger. Had to ask."

"We'll find her," Ragno said. "People don't simply disappear on Black Raven's watch."

"I told myself that very same thing this morning, as I looked for Pic. Reality is different, and we all know it."

"So acknowledged. Now move on. We're better. We win." Ragno's words and tone made it clear no wallowing was allowed. "Slight bit of good news. We're getting flags on odd financial transactions from Juliette's bank account. Richard's getting crafty with encryption cracking to trace the source. Stay tuned."

"Zero minus one hour fifteen minutes," Ragno said.

"Ragno, encryption difficulty's raising red flags over there, right?"

"You bet, Angel."

"Serum One will be delivered by noon," Brandon said. "If we don't have Andi by then, I'll personally administer it to Juliette. And Richie."

"Toilet report. All checked. Nothing." Stevens, in charge of operations at the townhouse, came through loud and clear on Line A.

Dammit to hell. That would've been too goddamn easy.

Juliette's phone—the one she had handed to Brandon in the midst of her 9-1-1 call—had revealed a call origination at nine thirty-seven. Black Raven had verified the legitimacy of that call with Crescent EMT's, and no calls had been made from the phone in the hour before. On the theory that Juliette had made a dupe call to the fake EMT's who had actually arrived on site and taken Andi away, Stevens' team had torn the second floor's toilets apart, looking for another phone that Juliette might have dumped.

"Roger," Ragno said. "We're logging it."

Juliette had been alone with Andi for a full half hour before she alerted agents to the emergency. That was plenty of time to administer a drug, let it take effect, call for a pick up, and dispose of the evidence.

The toilets in Andi's house had reliable, old-fashioned plumbing. The pipes were large and capable of delivering a dismantled phone to the city sewage system. And that fact bothered the hell out of Gabe, because the system was also capable of disposing of anything, such as a syringe, used to administer a dose of any number of drugs that could have promoted the symptoms that Andi had exhibited.

What had Pic said? 'They came at me with a syringe.'

Fuck me to goddamn Hell!

"Ragno," Brandon said. "Taylor just sent you a text of every person she knows who is a client of Juliette's."

"Got it. We're analyzing payment records and phone records as we speak. Spider webbing out from there, chasing the contacts."

"Taylor says there are probably some she doesn't know about. Evidently, Juliette networks well with the New Orleans upper crust," Brandon said. "How many clients can she possibly have that are willing to pay $150 per hour for nail polish?"

"Statistics show average price nationwide ranges from $35 to $75 for manicures and pedicures. That fee puts Juliette solidly at the top," Ragno said. "She charges two hundred per hour for massages. And there are add-ons for each service. She also represents three lines of beauty products. Pricey ones. Last year's income for IRS purposes was two hundred ten thousand. But that's what isn't adding up on my ledger. She spends more than her reported income, and that's on transactions I can find. Assets are off-kilter with income. The woman lives an extravagant life."

"So where is she getting the money from?" Gabe asked, as knee-jerk, traffic-inspired irritation flared. They were on Loyola Avenue, at a point where there were three lanes of traffic. The bus station was a block up the street, on his right. Interstate ramps were ahead of them. Marvin had braked at an intersection where their lane of traffic had a green light.

Gaze focused forward, noting brightly colored parade floats, with a police escort, traveling slowly on the street under the interstate, without regard to whether anyone else in the city needed to goddamn be somewhere that didn't involve parades and partying. Just as Marvin tried to edge into another lane for an escape route, a city bus blocked them in.

"Wait. Wait. Ah. Yes," Ragno whispered. Louder, she explained, "We're partially in an account that she uses for a slush fund. Richard's working on more access, as in trying to trace incoming wire transfers. And though we haven't yet figured out the source of funds in the slush fund, it's hefty. Balance is two point three million plus some change. Slush fund is in another name. Not identified anywhere else with Juliette that I've found. Yet. That warrants a few questions, I'd say."

"I'm heading back to Andi's," Brandon said. "I'll be glad to ask her some questions."

"I'll go," Gabe said, happy to have another crack with questioning Juliette. "It isn't like I've managed to get that far away. We're blocked by parade floats right now."

"No. I'll need your team to act on any answers she provides."

"*Jesus H. Christ.*" Excitement filtered into Ragno's voice. "She uses the fund for travel. In fact, she booked a ticket yesterday for Dubai. Departing at six p.m. this evening."

His tone dripping with sarcasm, Zeus said, "Sweet. How many manicurists travel to Dubai? Vegas—probably. Grand Canyon—definitely. Dubai—odd, at best."

Pulse pounding with the damn interesting news, Gabe said, "Ragno. Tell us where she's been in the last few years."

"Working on it. Luckily, international travel records are pretty easy searches, given government watch lists, which we have access to through Jigsaw."

As Ragno talked about Black Raven's anti-terrorist cyber-assimilation program, Gabe tuned her out. He didn't care how they found answers. He just cared that they did. "Brandon. Send me Juliette's client list."

"This is what we've got so far," Ragno said, as Gabe's watch vibrated with the incoming text from Brandon. "Bhutan, Dubai, Vietnam, Maldives, Russia, Bhutan again—evidently she liked the happiest place on earth—Kazakhstan, Hong Kong..."

Gabe sat up, straight. "Holy shit. She's visiting countries that don't have extradition treaties. Planning an exit strategy?"

Zeus gave a low whistle. "And today, she's traveling with her longtime friend. Brandon?"

"I'm on it," Brandon said. "Once they drop me off at the townhouse, I'll send agents to intercept her travel companion. Zeus, how close are they? That information might prove to be a useful, truth-inspiring tool as I question Juliette."

"Analyzing relationship," Zeus said. "They look close. Partner's name is Alicia Clements—"

"Wait." Gabe's gaze absently followed the procession of floats, while his mind raced. "*Partner*? As in lesbian lover? Nothing wrong with that, but curious."

"Double checking. Hold for a second." Through Line A, he heard his brother breathing. Fingers hitting the keyboard, clicking with speed. "Bingo. Cyber profiling hinted. My eyes confirm. Two women. Both in early thirties. They've lived together for five years. They share credit cards, bank accounts, and phone plans. Alicia isn't shy on social media. Whoa. Women who are just friends don't kiss like that at Melissa Etheridge concerts. Rainbow logos. LGBT marches. Pattern of communication confirms closeness. Consistent travel together. There's no record of a marriage, but, yeah. Lesbians. Lovers. Why?"

As he listened, Gabe scanned Taylor's list of Juliette's clients. First three names he didn't recognize. Then there was one that he did, with a jolt. Muscles at the base of his neck tightened. "Ragno, send me Sonja Long's address."

"Sure," Ragno said. "But why?"

"Two whys pending," Zeus said. "Wanna tell us what you're thinking?"

As his back tensed, Gabe's mind dwelled on the tiniest sprout of a hunch that he'd ever had.

Chapter Forty Four

Gabe

"I met Sonja at the gallery opening," Gabe said. "Didn't like her."

Thinking back, he remembered the way Sonja had looked at Andi. Sonja's gaze alone had clued him into the fact that he was looking at one of Andi's former lovers, and Gabe had gotten a double dose of that feeling with both Sonja and Stapleton, when they'd been at Andi's house the day after the gallery opening. Holy hell.

And on that day, Sonja had fixated on the sketches of the homeless kids. "Sonja also had an interest in Andi's sketches of homeless kids. They made her think of how people use blue-eyed homeless kids and pregnant ones. Which seems damn odd, right now, doesn't it? Given that Pic, a blue-eyed blonde, is missing. And others. And—as Andi pointed out—the sketches were in black and white."

"I've now seen a few of those sketches. Pic. Jake. Monica," Zeus said. "They're amazing. I'm guessing any collector would have more than a passing interest. Give us a few more minutes. We'll come up with something better."

"The minute you guys come up with something better, I'll head there." Gabe shifted in his seat, hesitated over what he was about to say, and realized he didn't have the luxury of decorum and discretion. "Sure as hell wish you'd hurry up. In the meantime—" His gut twisted as he fought to keep his voice calm. "—we have to assume for a moment that Andi's been taken by someone, correct?"

"Zero minus one hour twenty minutes," Ragno said.

"Yes, Gabe, you are correct," Zeus said. No one needed to voice the obvious—that if Andi hadn't been delivered to an ER yet, the likelihood of her ever showing up at one was nonexistent. "Assume taken."

Drawing a deep breath, Gabe continued, "It was targeted and well-planned. Given Andi's net worth, there's a strong financial incentive. But that scenario doesn't make sense. Domestic kidnappings for financial profit are few and far between, and there are plenty of wealthy targets. There's also the stalker angle, which would mean someone from Andi's past has come back with a vengeance. Most likely from back in her pre-kidnapping past, since her social interaction since then has been severely limited. Right?"

"Correct," Zeus said. "And we're working that angle. Remember, though, Andi is outside all the time. Anyone could've been watching. We're analyzing all of Andi's contacts as we speak. But you've been there. Until we come up with something better, go with your gut for a while."

And hell, but now it's going to get really personal. Sorry, Andi.

"A former lover could've been watching her while she was outside, correct? All this time," Gabe speculated.

"Yes. It's possible," Zeus said, "or had someone do the watching for him."

"A former lover who is really damn obsessed with her could also plant someone in Andi's house who would be able to give information, correct?" Gabe asked.

"Yes," Ragno said. "But we did background checks."

"Other than her housekeeper, who's been in the family for years, the only regular service provider is Juliette," Gabe said. "She passed a background check when we first were hired, but she could be working for the stalker, correct?"

"Possibly," Zeus acknowledged.

"Black Raven did due diligence on Juliette, but there was no red flag. After all, Taylor was Juliette's reference. Plus, her history with Andi had her seeming so benign this morning, there was no reason to search her when she arrived. Right, Brandon?"

"Correct," Brandon said. "Until right now she was not perceived as a threat in any way."

"Taylor's a damn good reference," Zeus said. "And, I'm looking at the file. When we did our due diligence, Juliette checked out to be exactly what she purported to be. Coupled with her prior uneventful contact with the client, she is the perfect plant for someone who wanted to harm Andi."

"Yes. Until now." Gabe lowered his voice, slightly. "Which gets me back to an odd coincidence about Juliette being a lesbian. This info is for team leaders only. I figure the more you guys know about Andi's past, the more we can speculate on her immediate future." Gabe glanced around the car as he said that, then lowered his voice further. His agents were using iPads that were networked with Ragno's cyber team, and their attention was focused on their tablets. Marvin and his son were looking straight ahead. And all of them, no doubt, were doing exactly as he did on every job he'd ever been on. Listening to the team leader talk, particularly when said leader's voice got low.

Gabe shrugged off all the reasons why discretion should matter. "Getting back to Sonja, here's one thing the cyber team might take a while to figure out. Sonja is bi-sexual. Cheats on her husband. She and Andi had a thing in her pre-kidnapping days

Line A carried a few seconds of dead silence.

"Use that info with discretion. About Andi's involvement with Sonja—I guessed that fact," Gabe continued, as the procession of floats ended, and the gridlocked cars started moving. "It isn't something Andi discusses. Brandon—she says Taylor doesn't know about the affair. That's how much of a secret it is. Want to know how I guessed it? The way Sonja looked at Andi the night of the gallery opening. As if she hadn't eaten in days and Andi was a perfectly cooked steak. It wasn't simply a look of a former lover—there were others of those at the opening. It went beyond that."

"Okay. I'm not sure the lesbian thing is persuasive, but you've got a former lover, looking at her oddly, and you don't like her. I'm rolling with it," Ragno said. "You've got enough for me to agree that we need further exploration. The Longs are well-known philanthropists. A few quick searches have indicated they're wealthy enough to fund just about anything they want. Here's Sonja's address. We've got nothing else. At least, you need to have a chat with her."

"Marvin, go to..." His gaze scrolled through the text that Ragno sent. "...Saint Charles Avenue. Hell! Is that on the parade route?"

"No. Saint Charles is on the route, but the Long residence is further down. Closer to Tulane University. On a corner lot, fronting on Saint Charles. Driveway's on a private, gated street. Security for the neighborhood provided by...hold a second...Top Tier Security," Ragno reported.

Gabe knew the reputation of Black Raven's competitor. "Which means the homeowners association does not fuck around."

"If you want to avoid the entry gate—"

"I do. I want to surprise her."

"You'll have to get creative. There are no side streets. Tall brick wall encases the neighborhood, except for the two houses fronting on Saint Charles. Lucky for us, the Long residence is one of those two houses. But that means you still have to go through the guard gate. There is no rear or side access and there is a wrought iron fence lining the sidewalk. Traffic indicators suggest the most direct route is congested, but nothing like the downtown area."

Marvin glanced over his shoulder as he waited at a traffic light. "Taking Claiborne, to Broadway, then right on Saint Charles. We can be there in fifteen."

One of his agents handed Gabe an iPad with satellite imagery of the address. The photos had a thirty-minute time lag. The most recent photos, though, were obscured by cloud cover. Images from two hours earlier had a clear view. He zoomed in and out on the photo of the large residence, analyzing the best way in. Glancing at the street that led away from the Saint Charles Avenue guard gate for three blocks or so and ended in a cul de sac, Gabe looked at the dozen or so homes that made up the luxury enclave. "Ragno, send all possible intel on the property. Security parameters. Photographs. Marks?"

"Yes, sir."

"Find Stapleton. Do the same thing with him. Personally tell him that Andi is missing. Get a read on his reaction."

"Jacques Stapleton?" Brandon asked, concern underlying his tone.

"Yes. Is there another Stapleton we should be worried about?"

"Sonja and Jacques are both wealthy and powerful pillars of New Orleans society—"

"Doesn't mean shit in terms of potential for criminal activity," Gabe said. "And whoever did this has a fat bankroll."

"I'm aware. My point is," Brandon said, "rabbit trails are time wasters."

"Roger that. But if all I have are my own slim hunches, then I'm going to stampede down the rabbit trails."

"FYI—Stapleton doesn't seem to be a client of Juliette's," Ragno said. "Maybe because males are less likely to spend that much money on spa services."

"You said it, Ragno. Not one of us males."

"Doesn't make you guys smarter," Ragno said.

"Let's all back up a second," Zeus said. "I understand pursuing the former lover angle, but we have to have more than that to go after these people. Gabe, your personal involvement with Andi might be coloring your judgment a bit here—"

"If you're talking about jealousy over past history, I'm not like that." Shifting in his seat, trying to stretch his legs out in front of him, he shook his head. As though his brother could goddamn see him. "I don't care what Andi did in her pre-kidnapping days. That's not who she is now." He considered the lesbian angle, frowned, and shifted again in his seat. "Look, it's not like I don't have experience with women..." He searched for the right words.

Ragno, voice as matter-of-fact as ever, prodded him. "Your point?"

"Andi's the rare kind of woman who could spark an obsession..." He drew a deep breath, thinking of how she responded when they made love. How she encouraged him with her body. Her focus. Her sounds. How she made his world stand still, unlike anyone else. "And I'm not saying that lightly. Fact is—personal attraction taken out—Stapleton and Sonja are both former lovers of Andi's who had significant recent interaction with her. And there's a doctor who was also salivating over her at the opening."

"Another former lover?" Zeus asked.

What the hell? He may as well air all of Andi's past history. If it meant they'd find Andi, he'd keep the list going for as long as it took. "Yep. Doctor John McCaskey. Since the opening, he's called her twice and sent flowers. Ragno, start a profile on him. If anyone has better ideas for the moment on who we should be talking to, or looking at, chime in."

The line went silent.

Shit shit shit.

Something was off about all this.

Because there was also Pic. And the other kids. Could Andi's disappearance have anything to do with the kids who were missing? Jake. Monica. The others included in the faintest whiffs of the rumors that Richie had repeated? The rumors that Pic had heard? Would-be robbers going after Pic with a syringe?

His gut, and Black Raven-style wisdom, told him that the timing of Andi's disappearance and Pic's disappearance were related. Something, someone, somewhere tied this clusterfuck together. And it was up to them to put a screeching halt to it.

"Zeus. Brandon. Gabe might really be on to something." A faint hint of excitement had crept into Ragno's voice. "Sonja Long is a client of Juliette's, and there is no record that she ever paid Juliette one cent."

"People have all kinds of reasons for paying cash," Zeus responded.

"Sure they do," Ragno said. "But one big reason is to hide something. Coupled with Gabe's feelings, who, I might add, is a master at reading subtleties, the lack of a money trail is more than enough for me."

"Brandon?" Gabe asked, as Marvin picked up speed on Claiborne Avenue.

"Yes."

"Can you ask Taylor how it was that she and Andi started using Juliette?"

"Give me a minute."

Gabe leaned back in the seat, his head pressed against the headrest. He indulged himself by thinking of Andi, her luminous eyes, and her slight smile. The essence of the lavender that she wore, the way her home smelled of her. The way she looked at him like she was always trying to figure him out. How she hung on his every word—even when she was irritated with him for trying to get a rise out of her. Holding her as they slept, the way her smaller body fit into the curve of his.

The way he'd awoken just hours ago, with her nestled into his chest, her head resting on his arm. He'd stayed still for a few long seconds, savoring the feel of her in his arms. He'd been around long enough to know that sleeping with someone was different than sleeping with someone you loved. Until Andi, it was a distinction that had been lost upon him.

"Talked to Taylor," Brandon said. "Sonja referred Juliette to Taylor, shortly after Andi's kidnapping, and suggested Juliette might also work out for Andi. According to Taylor, Sonja has always been oddly interested in Andi. That's a quote. *'Oddly interested'*. Andi's become a curiosity in their social circle, though, since it's been more than two years since the kidnapping, she's no longer a constant in most conversations, except for Sonja's. I didn't tell Taylor about Andi and Sonja being lovers. But I did ask Taylor if she knew Sonja had lesbian affairs. She said no. However, she reminded me the gallery opening was Sonja's idea. So your hunch is worth pursuing. Matter of fact, I'm more than on board now."

I was doing it anyway, because I'm that goddamn good at reading people. And now, my gut's screaming at me to go to Saint Charles Avenue.

"It's one of the most exclusive neighborhoods in the city," Marvin said. "There's gonna be in-house help. Assume guarded. You not only want to talk to this woman, you'll want to analyze computers and search through records, right?"

"Yes." *I'll do plenty of searching, if I smell a rat.* "If Sonja's there, I want my agents to do recon while I talk to her." He glanced at the agents in the van, who nodded. "If Sonja isn't there, I'd prefer to simply have a look around and not seriously harm someone who might resist that action. Unless I need to. What I see will dictate my actions."

On any job, Gabe didn't want to disable collateral personnel unless necessary. One basic premise was unless a hunch was foolproof, collateral force was kept to a minimum. Richie and Juliette were directly involved. Not collateral. That's why he didn't give a shit about Richie's broken nose, cracked ribs, and whatever other damage he'd inflicted. Juliette, ass on the floor, handcuffed to a table, also wasn't a problem, because she was the last person to see Andi. Even more so now, given what they knew of her slush fund and her upcoming trip to Dubai, the fact that she was Black Raven's prisoner was A-OK. But his hunch regarding Sonja wasn't proven—yet.

"Brandon, give me local knowledge. Team—" His gaze encompassed his two agents, along with Marvin and Billy, "We have three objectives going in. One—talk to Sonja, if she's there. Two—see what's inside, whether she's there or not. Three—access computers. Objectives will evolve. Parameters—gated community, Top Tier security guards at the only entrance to the neighborhood, daylight, house with alarm system and, we have to assume, also guarded."

"Safe assumption about the guards, Gabe. I've been to social events there," Brandon said. "The Longs are serious collectors. They've got a Monet. A couple of Picassos. Other paintings I wouldn't even try to name. Sculptures. They're not using Top Tier for their home, though. They seem to use a no-name outfit for security. To a casual observer, the guards look like the real deal. To me, they look big on brawn and firepower, small on brains."

"Okay," Gabe said, mind racing through scenarios.

"Best local knowledge in the world is sitting in the front seat of your vehicle," Brandon continued. "Marvin, Billy, and their team of brothers, sons, sisters, cousins can get in any place in the city. They're damn creative."

Gabe glanced into the front seat, as Marvin stopped at a red light on Claiborne Avenue. They both turned and gave Gabe thoughtful smiles.

"They've got an in with personnel in utility companies?" Gabe asked.

"Everywhere," Brandon answered.

"Yep," Marvin nodded. "Just 'bout all of 'em."

Cable company? Nah—not enough of an emergency. Electric—that would get them on the perimeter, but it was hard to sell for the inside. Thanks to Big Brother, though, there was one sure way to get in. Emergency gas leak. Even if the homeowner didn't smell it, the gas company could access the house if it was reported. Federal regulations required gas companies to respond to reports of gas leaks, measure the grade of the leak, detect the source, and enter nearby premises for inspection. "Only thing that will work here is gas."

Agent Stevens, who was stuck in the middle of the back seat, between Gabe and Todd, muttered, "That could work."

"The drawback is," Gabe added, as the traffic light flashed green, "most people know to be wary if the gas company comes knocking. Black Raven agents wouldn't fall for this."

Or maybe we would just let them in while we scratched our balls, given the ease with which Andi disappeared from a house with agents on the premises.

"So what do your agents do if the gas company comes knocking?" Marvin asked, accelerating and shifting lanes.

"Verify emergency with the company," Gabe said. "Be suspicious. Keep eyes on workers. We have to assume the security at the Long residence is at least as smart as Black Raven."

"Vince is damn persuasive," Marvin said. "He's worked on Brandon's jobs before. Worse thing that would happen is they send us away. But you might get in a side door while we're arguing. And Vince and I can argue for one hell of a long time."

Gabe wondered whether it was worth it, because it sure seemed like an elaborate way to do something that was normally simple for him—get into a house.

Gut check, in light of parameters?

Yes. Worth the time.

Marvin continued, "Job like this will cost Brandon about seven thousand for Vince's cost—"

"He'll pay," Gabe said. "But we need to execute ASAP. Within thirty minutes. Doable?"

Marvin nodded, then glanced at his son. "Get Vince going. Give him the address. Ask him to confirm house is a gas recipient, then tell him parameters." The traffic light turned green, and Marvin accelerated.

"Two scenarios," Gabe said. "Plan A–Vince creates a gas emergency ruse, advance team gets in, figures out if Sonja or her husband are there. If either owner is in the residence, I coincidentally knock on the front door to talk to them. Once inside, I'll improvise as the need arises. Plan B–advance team goes in using the gas emergency ruse, we figure out homeowners are not there, advance team distracts whatever help is on the premises, and I do whatever it is I want to do in there."

"We can work with either scenario. This is easy for us. Like red beans on a Monday." Marvin sounded so calm and matter-of-fact, Gabe had absolute faith the man could deliver. "It's our thing. Your end's the wild card."

"I can handle my end."

"Vince confirms that the home is a gas recipient," Billy said.

Marvin nodded. "Figured it would be. It wouldn't be a New Orleans mansion without Bevolo lanterns."

"More than gas lanterns." With his phone firmly planted to his ear, Billy reported what Vince was telling him. "Usage is consistent with a shitload of appliances."

If the circumstances hadn't been so dire, Gabe would've enjoyed this moment. He could feel the anticipation of the agents sitting next to him, as they sat up straight and nodded in agreement. Gabe looked at the iPad, with the satellite imagery of the house. "House fronts on Saint Charles. There's a public sidewalk. Pedestrians. Vince can say multiple calls of gas odors. A concerned jogger. Whatever."

"Gabe—" Zeus broke into the phone conversation on line A. "We have Sonja's phone number—at least the one that Taylor and Andi use. We'll have access to phone records shortly. From there, we'll be able to determine where she is."

"No. You'll be determining where that phone is, which might not get us anywhere." Gabe zoomed in on the driveway, the front porch, and the side door of the Long residence. Scrolled over the garden beds. Looking to see if the Longs advertised the name of their company providing security on their home. "For all we know, she has multiple phones, in other names. She might be nowhere near that line."

"But we'll have a trail that will lead to her," Zeus said. "And we're employing facial recognition software on networked surveillance cameras all around New Orleans and outlying areas."

"Zeus," Brandon said, his voice loud and clear through line A. "I'm talking to Juliette, while I wait for Serum One. She's not giving me a goddamn thing, but she seemed downright frightened when I told her we'd soon be talking to Sonja. As the file's originating partner, I'm fine with whatever Gabe decides is necessary."

"Thanks, Brandon. Zeus. Copy?"

"Yes," Zeus said, grudgingly.

"Great. Zeus, Ragno—you guys in Denver keep clicking away," Gabe said. "I'm doing this my way, until you give me something better. Team—switch to line C-1." Next to him, Stevens and Brooks nodded as they made the communication line adjustment on their watches. "Team leaders—talk to me there if needed."

"Once we give him the go, Vince can meet us at the corner of Broadway and Claiborne in ten minutes for staging," Billy said. "We'll pull into the back of Carlos's Mini-Mart. Carlos will go with us."

"Gas Company Emergency Plan is a go," Gabe said. He glanced at the satellite image on his iPad. Studied the exterior of the mansion, with its symmetrical lines, leaded glass windows, and fluted columns. Thought about Sonja's ice-blue gaze crawling across Andi's face and body. She'd looked at Gabe with eyes that, in retrospect, had carried loaded questions and an unmistakable challenge.

Chapter Forty Five

Gabe

"At the Long residence," Gabe said, from the interior of the NOLA Gas Co. van, which was now parked in the wide driveway, alongside the front porch of the Long residence. The van was out of the line of sight from the Top Tier security agents working the guard gate, who'd given them the green light, after studying Vince's documentation of the emergency.

"Zero minus two hours five minutes," Ragno said.

"Anything new?" Gabe asked. The van was parked at an angle that gave Gabe a view and fast access to the front porch.

"Not yet. You'll know as we do, Angel."

From a dark-tinted side window, Gabe kept his gaze trained on Vince and Stevens. Dressed in NOLA Gas Co. logo attire, with windbreakers concealing their weapons, they talked to a man who looked like he'd fit in on Black Raven's payroll.

If we hired Neanderthals.

Tall, broad-shouldered, with long arms that were so bulky, they curved away from his body, and with a dark, thick beard, his wide-legged stance in the doorway of the elegant home conveyed a solid message: Stop!

The Neanderthal gave an emphatic headshake, and through Agent Stevens mic, Gabe heard a deep voice say, "I don't smell gas."

"Yes, sir. We understand that," Vince said, his voice carrying loud and clear through the mic. "Due to the proximity of the reports, the company has disabled the connection to this residence."

Vince gestured to the gas lanterns that flanked the front doorway, where the flames were extinguished. He then pointed to Marvin, who was also wearing a uniform as he walked through the yard, holding a square metal device, presumably doing an inspection. "We've had three reports in the last twenty minutes and my man's readings confirm it. This house is the nearest..."

As Vince continued his story about why they needed access, Stevens shoved a clipboard at the guy's chest. The Neanderthal took the clipboard in a beefy hand, pulled a cell phone out of his pocket, and made the call to the gas company that any intelligent person would've made.

Mistake number one—he dialed the number that was on the incident report.

The phone on the seat next to Gabe rang. Sticking pretty much to the script that Vince had given him, after confirming that he was, in fact, talking to the gas company, Gabe informed the guard in simple, clear terms that he was obligated to let the men in the home to measure gas levels and inspect gas lines.

"Can't they do it from outside?"

"No, sir. Only part of our work can be accomplished outside. Regulations require us to inspect from the point of entry and the interior of the house."

"This is a goddamn pain in the ass."

"Yes, sir." Gabe kept his voice calm, painfully aware that precious time was ticking away. "We will reestablish the connection after our inspection. If you do not permit inspection, we cannot restore the connection."

"Seriously?"

How dumb is this guy? Pic's right. Steroids have drained this guy's brain.

"That's correct, sir. It's a public safety issue, sir. Not to mention a fire hazard for your own home."

"You just talking 'bout in the kitchen?"

"Well, no. I'm sorry, sir, but it also includes dryers, hot water heaters, in addition to kitchen appliances. Usage indicates that the residence is fully loaded. We know this is a tremendous inconvenience."

"Yeah. No shit. You mean the hot water's off?"

Okay, he's at idiot level.

"Well sir, without gas service, your hot water heaters will not work," Gabe explained. Patiently. Calmly. "We cannot restore gas service until we know the residence is safe. Given how much of a valued client you are, we've sent several personnel there. We'll be out of your way in no time. Sir," Gabe added, "are you the homeowner?"

"What does that matter?"

"The homeowner will need to sign off on our paperwork."

"Not gonna happen. They're not here. I've got authority to sign—"

"I suggest you call them."

"I suggest you go fuck yourself."

Mistake number two—he fell for it. The line went dead, as the guard stepped back in the doorway, allowing the two men at the front door to enter the home. He would've shut the door, but Marvin, approaching the porch, was ten steps away.

As soon as Vince and Stevens disappeared inside, Gabe, Todd, and Carlos, got out of the van. As Gabe walked through the front door, through Stevens' mic, he heard Vince droning on endlessly about the dangers of natural gas accumulation.

"Sir," Stevens whispered, his hiss conveying urgency. "*Go!* Kitchen. Far rear. Two guards."

"Copy." In the doorway, Gabe's skin pebbled. His neck muscles pulling, he got an eyeful of the paintings adorning the far wall of the elegant, spacious foyer. Not Monet. Not Picasso.

Hutchenson.

And not one, but three of Andi's paintings—ones that had been hanging at the Stapleton gallery opening—were clustered together. One, he'd understand. Two, spelled excessive. Three, was one too many.

A crystal vase, filled with sprigs of fresh lavender and long-stemmed white roses, adorned a round table centered in the elegant hallway. Exactly the same as the arrangement in Andi's foyer. Exactly the same as the flowers that were scattered throughout Andi's house.

He now understood the urgency in Stevens's '*go*' command. Andi's art and the flowers had obviously touched a chord with Stevens, who'd been guarding Andi for weeks.

More than enough for me.

For the first time since Andi hadn't appeared at the ER, hope flared. He pulled his Glock out of his holster and eased the door shut. Continuing through the foyer, he inhaled the same essence of lavender and rose that had filled Andi's front entranceway while grounding himself with feeling the familiar, rough-textured handle of the weapon he routinely carried on domestic jobs. The familiar weight—30.18 fully loaded ounces—was comfortable. Reassuring. With gun in hand, his mind shifted to any-force-necessary mode.

Andi, I will find you.

He gestured with his head to Todd, signaling him to stay in step. "Coming in. On my signal, we disable guards. Ragno."

"Yes."

"We're on the right track. Dispatch more agents. Every single agent Brandon doesn't need at the townhouse. You and Zeus throw more resources on finding out everything we can on Sonja and Walter Long. Properties. Addresses. We need to know where they are. Need to know it, now."

With Todd at his side, Gabe ran to the rear of the house. He went into the kitchen, Glock in hand. "Hands up."

Time stood still as the guards decided their fate. Frozen for a split second, they both eyed Gabe and Todd, who had their Glocks aimed. Ready. The Neanderthal slowly started lifting his hands from thigh level. The other guard, smaller and younger, was faster—he raised his hands high over his head.

The Neanderthal's going for it.

Before his thick fingers touched his gun, Marvin and Stevens—along with Gabe—had weapons trained on him, while Agent Todd and Vince moved in on the second guard.

Gabe kept steady focus, aiming his Glock at the gnarly tendons of the man's oversized, hairy right hand. "Don't."

Mistake number three—his fat hand inched closer.

Gabe fired. The man's hand exploded, in a burst of blood splatter, flesh, and sinew. As he bent forward, bellowing with pain, Gabe said, "Todd. Vince. Billy. Carlos. Secure them. Make them talk. Any force necessary."

Turning, running, he yelled over his shoulder. "Marvin. Stevens. Search this place. Marvin—first floor. Stevens, with me."

Taking the stairs three at a time to the second floor, they hit a wide hallway. A rear stairway led to another floor. On the second floor, there were eight doors. All shut. "Stevens. Take the left. Todd."

"Yes."

"Anything?"

Through Todd's mic, Gabe heard the Neanderthal. Breathy. In pain. But still hanging tough. The hate in his voice was apparent, as he snarled, "You gotta hit me harder than that, you fag."

"Stevens," Gabe said. "Hit him harder."

"Gladly."

Gabe's first door led to a bedroom. Well-appointed. Clean. No Andi. Closets were full of clothes, but empty. Bathroom, empty.

"Todd. What about the other guy?"

"He swears he knows nothing," Todd replied. "Swears today is his first day on the job. The big guy is obviously his boss. Threatening to kill him if he talks."

"Separate them."

"Ragno, Zeus, Brandon. Anything?" Gabe's second door led to a workout room. Two exercise bikes. Two treadmills. A rack of hand weights. Another bathroom.

Fuckitall. Are you even here, Andi? Or am I wasting time searching when you're somewhere else?

"No," Ragno answered.

"Serum's arrived," Brandon said. "Administering now."

"Facial recognition is starting to produce results," Zeus said. "Analyzing...nothing firm, yet."

As Gabe stepped out of the second door, he saw Stevens enter the third door on the right. Gabe twisted the knob on his third door. Locked. Taking a step back, he raised his left foot and planted a solid, heel-driven kick below the door knob. With a sharp crack, the door flew open.

"*Andi*. Thank Go..."

Fleeting elation turned to heavy dread as his mind absorbed the horror of the vision confronting him. His gut tumbled down the highest cliff he'd ever climbed. Straight into the depths of hell.

He'd found her. Too late.

Naked. Positioned chest-down on the four-poster bed covered in white linens, her beautiful face, pale and waxy, turned to the door. Blindly staring, her once luminous eyes were now dull and vacant. Her mouth, slightly open. Her slender back pock marked with fresh burns.

Gabe's breath left his body as his gaze crawled over the horrific tableau. Digesting the vision, his eyes blurred, and he fell to his knees with the hardest sucker punch of his life. His heart stopped. His world no longer spun on its axis.

"No!"

"Gabe," Zeus said. "What are you...?"

Gaze riveted on Andi's expressionless eyes, he couldn't move. Couldn't grasp the reality that was laid out, across the spacious bedroom, fifteen feet in front of him. He couldn't do a goddamn thing for the seconds that it took his brain to absorb the meaning of the horror on the bed. But for her utter stillness, in the golden glow of soft chandelier light, her face was as achingly beautiful as ever.

"Holy shit!" Stevens, from the doorway behind Gabe, gasped for air. "They killed her. Oh. God."

Young agent. Could be his first death.

Forcing himself to look at her face, and not be consumed by the crimson red rage of fire that was burning his gut and blinding his vision with pulsing, molten lava, Gabe cleared his throat. "Stevens. Search the rest of the house."

I need a few minutes alone with my beautiful girl. I want to close her eyes. Cover her. Tell her...I'm sorry. Tell her how much I love her. Before this becomes a crime scene from hell.

"Yes, sir."

Too late. Too late. Too goddamn late.

"Gabe," Ragno said, not breaking professional stride with her tone. "Confirm."

"Team leaders," Zeus said, "Code Blue."

As his brother calmly called for integration of all phone lines due to a critical emergency, Gabe opened his mouth in an attempt to pull in air. Sucking in a harsh, choking breath, the cloying, heavy smell of lavender and rose filled his nostrils. His mouth. His gut. With the thick fragrances, came a sour smell of burned flesh and acrid cigarette smoke. And the stink of pain and horror.

The odors sparked anger that gave him the power to right himself. Getting to his feet, he shook off the sucker-punch of harsh reality that had felled him. Finding a forced, makeshift equilibrium in the shaky world where Andi was dead, he crossed the room to the poster bed, where black leather bindings with shackles hung loose from each of the vertical columns.

Rage building, he stepped on cigarette butts littering the hardwood floor and carpet runners near the bed. Underfoot, a waxy yellow puddle cracked on the hardwood floor. The same yellowish color as the mess of tapered candles that sat atop silver candlesticks, on a silver tray, in front of a tufted couch. "She's made-up. Perfectly. They bound her. Burned her back with cigarettes. They recreated the burns on her back that Victor Morrissey left there. Then they..." He lost the ability to speak as he glanced at the torn skin on her wrists. Eyed the same on her ankles. Her legs were spread, in a wide-V. Saw fluid stains between them, at her upper thighs. *Semen?*

He swallowed hard to keep down the bile of more anger than he'd ever experienced.

"Zeus. Ragno," Gabe said, kneeling at Andi's bedside. "Find these goddamn fuckers for me. Find them. *Now*. Brandon?"

He heard Brandon clear his throat, fighting past emotions. "Good God."

"Don't wait for the serum to work on Juliette. That bitch is a part of this. Beat the living shit out of her until she tells you where Sonja and Walter Long are."

"Copy. Working on that," Brandon said.

"Gabe. Stand down," Zeus said. What he meant was for Gabe to relinquish control to someone who could think rationally.

"No. I'm calmer than I've ever been in my life." Holding a breath, he lifted his fingers to her neck for confirmation of the obvious. "I know exactly how I'm going to kill Sonja and Walter Long. With my bare hands twisting their necks, after I burn their eyeballs out with cigarettes. Help me find them, Zeus. Ragno. Brandon. Now."

Letting his index finger and middle finger linger on her neck, where a steady pulse should beat, Gabe muttered, "No pulse."

Absorbing details as he went through rote field examination, questions started drifting past the horror. How had they accomplished so much in just two hours and change? Transporting. Torturing. Makeup. Raping. Then exiting the premises.

Gabe's mind clicked on what his fingers were pressing into. *Skin.* Colder than it should be. He studied the turn of her nose, the color of her skin at her cheekbones, and...*holy shit*...the too thin arch of her eyebrows. He felt a glimmer of impossible hope. The millions of tiny details he had absorbed about Andi suddenly seemed off as he stared. Unlike the woman on the bed, Andi had beautiful, thick eyebrows. And an upturn to her nose. A slight bump on it, too, where Victor Morrissey had broken it.

Blinking, Gabe stared at her nose. It was close, but he wasn't looking at Andi's nose. *Not her.* He almost said it aloud—this wasn't her. Then he forced himself to slow down.

Gather facts. Hard facts. Don't hope for the impossible. Don't make this wishful thinking.

Shifting his fingers to under her arm for a more accurate read of her body temperature, he touched the chilly skin under her armpit. More hope bloomed.

"She's cold."

"How cold?" Ragno asked.

"Too cold. Copy?"

"Copy. Zero minus two hours twenty minutes," Ragno said. "Even if she was murdered immediately after abduction, normal algor mortis indicates that her body temp, at a minimum, would be ninety-three degrees. Likely it would be higher."

Facts I damn well know.

Hope building, Gabe's body vibrated with a sudden flood of wild optimism. "This body is at ambient temperature. Andi shouldn't have reached this for hours." He scraped his fingernails over her bicep. Flesh-toned paste accumulated underneath his nails. Along the trail left by his nails, the skin had a blue tone. "Full-body, flesh-colored makeup is hiding blue color."

"Rigor?" Zeus asked.

Gabe lifted the hand that was outstretched, to the door. It was like trying to move a baseball bat that was stuck in concrete. "Full. Consistent with anywhere from twelve to twenty-four hours out. She's not Andi."

"Gabe," Zeus said. "Go slow."

"I did."

"I know you don't want this to be her. Are you sure?"

"Positive. Eyes are close, but the color's goddamn wrong. As in contact-color wrong, the kind of contacts that people wear over brown eyes to make them look green." Pinching together his thumb and index finger, Gabe touched her eye and pulled out a soft contact lens, revealing a dark brown iris.

A scar—almost concealed by makeup, under her armpit—caught his attention. A breast implant scar, which Andi did not have. "One hundred percent sure. Holy shit. Whoever she is, they made her up to look like Andi. Exactly like Andi. And it's like they used a goddamn roadmap of the burns on her back." He reached into his pocket for his cell phone and took a bunch of pictures. "Photos coming."

Relief that he wasn't staring at Andi evaporated, as he snapped images of the mess of raw, black-rimmed, circular burns on the corpse's back. "This is what they intend to do to Andi. Stevens. Where are you?"

"Third floor," Stevens answered. "A surgical suite. Examining rooms. No people. I'm in a huge office. Multiple monitors. Video equipment. More evidence of an Andi obsession. Need your eyes, sir."

Gabe turned from the corpse, then ran out of the bedroom, and up the flight of stairs. Found the room where Stevens sat at one of two large desks, furiously typing. On the monitor, a screen saver with photographs of Andi flashed a mosaic of stalking obsession.

Andi—in Crescent Park, painting. Andi—walking on Royal Street, with her attention focused on Gabe. Andi—in Armstrong Park, with Black Raven agents within ten feet of her, talking to Richie. Andi—sitting on a park bench with Pic. Andi—a pre-kidnapping image of her with long hair, smiling coyly at someone who wasn't caught in the image. Andi and Sonja—a side view, mouth on mouth kissing.

"I can't get in," Stevens said. "I've got some computer forensics experience, but nothing's working with this."

Blood boiling as he stared at the images, Gabe drew a deep breath. "Ragno. Have someone guide Stevens."

"Gabe," Zeus said. "Get in the van. Sending you to rendezvous with Ace."

Hope soared at his brother's words. Needing no encouragement, Gabe ran down the two flights of stairs. "Location?"

"Not yet. But soon. Brandon's gone semi-private. I'm listening, sparing the details over the lines. Serum, coupled with Trask-style persuasion, has Juliette cracking. Talking about a horse farm. North shore of Lake Pontchartrain."

"I'm in." Gabe lifted the keys from the floorboard, started the engines, and backed out of the driveway. "Where to?"

"Take Saint Charles to the River Road. To Deckbar, which is right past Ochsner Hospital. Chopper will pick you up on the levee. Traffic indicators indicate it's an eight-minute drive, max. You'll be driving in the opposite direction of the parade route."

Thank God. "I'll make it less."

"Gabe," Ace said. "Chopper landing in five. We'll do touch and go. Get your ass in gear."

"Copy."

Three minutes of driving, which included a short jaunt on the street car tracks that separated the two lanes of vehicular traffic and running a red light, got him to the River Road. "Zeus. Anything more?"

"Not yet. I'm confirming Juliette's details through facial recognition software along the route. Ragno's team, once into the Long's computers, will know a hell of a lot more. We'll have a precise location with intel. Soon. According to what Juliette's saying, this is big. Details she's giving potentially tie in with missing kids. Copy?"

"Copy."

Turning right on the River Road, his gaze on joggers, bikers, and dog walkers who were using the grassy levee at the foot of Saint Charles as a park, Gabe understood why Zeus's directions were sending him further upriver. The crowd dwindled as Gabe accelerated, leaving Saint Charles Avenue in his rear view. "Pic?"

"Nothing so specific yet. But from what Juliette's saying, it's a sophisticated trafficking ring, where people are sold into sex slavery—" He paused. "—and possibly worse. We're relocating Richie to Andi's townhouse for more in-depth interrogation by Brandon. Serum's already administered. Where are you?"

"On River Road. Ochsner Hospital is ahead of me. I see it." Glancing into the sky, Gabe saw a Chinook-47F drifting down, twin rotors spinning. He ditched the van on the side of the levee. Running up the sharply inclined slope, he ducked as the chopper landed, then ran forward. As he jumped through the open door, he yelled, "Go!"

Chapter Forty Six

Andi

Through deep, luscious sleep, a kind she didn't often have, Andi felt the delicious, wet heat of suction on her right nipple. Too woozy to open her eyes, waves of contentment washed over her body.

Gabe. Yes. Best dream ever.

As he opened his mouth to take in more of her, tonguing the hardened nub, and gently gliding the sheet off of her nude body, she turned slightly towards his side of the bed. His warm body wasn't next to her, though. No one was.

Breathing in deeply, sinking further into a soft sea of fine linens and dreamy contentment, the scent that she inhaled—a lush blend of vanilla, jasmine, and rose—was wrong.

Gabe doesn't smell like flowers.

The mouth moved away. Maybe she'd dreamed it. A susurrus of conversation teased the edges of her consciousness, but she couldn't make out the words. Confusion registered, but she was too sleepy to care, until smidges of her deep, delicious sleep flittered away. With increased awareness came a metronome beat of doom. Like the very beginning of a night terror, where she was too paralyzed to do anything about the coming horrors, it occurred to her that something was wrong. Her senses were so dulled by drugs that the thought inspired only a low-level curiosity.

Fingers replaced the mouth. Tweaking. Teasing. A lover's good morning touch. Waves of consciousness lapped at the shores of her sleep, bringing hard to grasp knowledge. As fast as the froth of a wave dissipated into the sand, the knowledge for which she was fighting slipped from her grasp. But with the next wave, more awareness swam to the surface. Wave after wave built, as she remembered that for some indeterminate amount of time, she'd been drifting in and out of consciousness.

Suddenly, thoughts that she'd been struggling to hold onto, on and off, for God only knew how long, flooded through her consciousness.

This isn't Gabe!

Fear flooded through her veins, pebbling her skin, while yanking her nerves into a taut bow. Instinctively wanting to jerk her body out of reach, she froze instead. Instead of shrinking away in revulsion, she forced her body to go slack.

Whomever had her was standing at her bedside, talking. God, she wanted to open her eyes to orient herself. But she needed to establish the 'who' and the 'where', because the moment she awakened, it would be a game changer.

Be still! Play possum. Gather facts. Formulate a plan.

With every ounce of willpower she could muster, she forced herself to turn towards whomever the hell was now cupping her breast in their hand as they tweaked her nipple. Moving as though she'd just shifted position, Andi nestled further into the comfortable bed, as though what they were doing didn't repulse her.

With her change in position, her adrenaline rush faded as quickly as it came, as the drugs once again took over. Heart, brain, thoughts, and emotions dulled by remnants of whatever the hell Juliette had given her, Andi struggled to stay awake and focus on what she knew.

Two of them? They were now—and for some indeterminate chunk of time had been—standing next to her bed, talking. The hand disappeared. A female voice. A male voice. They were talking louder now. Almost yelling. She sounded angry. He was trying to placate her.

Not a dream. Not a night terror. Not one of her PTSD-induced daymares. This was reality. Her worst Victor Morrissey-inspired fear come to life.

Eyes closed. Eyes closed. Be smart. Assess. Gather information. You've been through far worse. So far.

"She's not waking up, goddammit," the female said. "You do understand that if you fucked this up, I will kill you?"

Not easy, staying limp and still as a fresh wave of adrenaline-driven energy coursed through her. She tried to place the voices. Both were familiar, but out of context. Which was such a stupid thought, she almost laughed.

How could any of this possibly be in context?

"Don't fucking ignore me!" Tone strident, the female's manner of speaking suggested no one ever dared.

"Hard to do when you're screaming like a goddamn banshee!" the male said. "Everything is proceeding on schedule. The drugs are competing, but the anesthetic properties are wearing off."

The male voice was also familiar. Genteel. Deep. Calming, or trying to be. But he had the terse snap of a man who was losing patience. Andi felt fingers on her neck. At her carotid, gently pressing her pulse.

She knew with certainty that she should recognize the voices, but no names came to her. She drifted to sleep for a moment, then jolted awake. Almost opened her eyes, until she remembered she was trying to gather information while not letting them know that she was awake.

Stay awake. Assess. Gather information. Stay AWAKE.

Mind slightly clearer than before, taking an inventory of all the facts she knew, she remembered Juliette, injecting her neck. Juliette, calling someone, then dialing 9-1-1. It had been the wrong actions from someone she trusted, and the phone calls had been in the wrong order. The first never should have happened. Then her muscles and limbs had become limp, then locked.

As her mind had started drifting away, she had tried to tell Brandon about the wrongness, but by then, she couldn't speak. Could barely breathe. She remembered Brandon, alarmed. Yelling. A mouth, on hers. Someone helping her breathe. She remembered Brandon, saying Gabe's name. Telling Gabe what was happening. Her final thought had been that Gabe was coming. *She'd be okay. Brandon has me, and Gabe is coming.* And then she'd blacked out.

Gabe didn't make it in time. He's still coming, though. But God knows what they'll do to me before he gets here. So I've got to get myself out of here. Think about the voices. *Think, think, think.* Gabe's voice, drilled into her in their exercise sessions, reminded her what to do.

Assess. Think. When you have enough knowledge to formulate a plan, go on the offensive. Once you move, do not hesitate.

She wasn't thinking clearly, though, because there was still too much sedative in her system. As her mind drifted, she tried to focus on the heavy fragrance that enveloped her. Sensual. Female.

I know that fragrance. I know who wears it.

Sleepiness intruded. Powerless to do anything but give in, she knew that when she woke again, she would need all her senses. Because those voices belonged to people who weren't going to lay a goddamn hand on her. If Victor Morrissey had taught her anything, it was that she'd die fighting before someone had his, or her, way with her. As her mind shut down, she inhaled. And knew the name of the scent. *Shalimar.* Heavy. Sensual. Retro. Intoxicating.

Don't sleep. Think!

"Sonofagoddamnfucking bitch," the female said, tone low. Threatening. Angry. "I want her awake, and I want her awake right now."

She heard the petulant tone at the end of the sentence, heard the inflection in the words, *I want*, and knew, with certainty, who had her.

Sonja Long! Why?

"You're doing this to torment me," Sonja said, her tone drifting lower. "It never takes this long."

Holy hell! She does this often?

"Now, now, dear, you know I had to make sure the departure scenario was convincing."

That voice belonged to Walter. Answering to his wife.

What the hell?

"The sedation drugs I gave her were stronger than what we normally use, because Andi's not a no-name homeless person that we pulled off the streets. This was a riskier extraction. Give the reversal agents a few more minutes."

The gentle hand disappeared. In its place, Andi felt a firm press of fingers on her neck. She could smell someone's sweet breath, felt the warmth of their exhale, and felt strong hands on either side of her face.

Eyes closed. Eyes closed. Figure out how bad this is.

"If the Ritalin's working, why the hell isn't she awake?"

"She will be," Walter said. "And it wasn't just Ritalin. I had to do a mixture. Soon."

"But she's not even close. I didn't go through this trouble for you to turn her into a goddamn corpse. You're the one who likes to fuck dead people. Not me. And I certainly hope you got your fill last night, because my real Andi is going to be mine for a long time."

"Now Sonja, we've been through this. You won't be able to keep her as your plaything. We agreed you would only have today. We have to get rid of her. It's too dangerous. We'll have to dispose of her bod—"

"On what planet do you think you're standing? Certainly not one where you get to tell me what to do. I can, and I will, keep her for as long as I goddamn want to," Sonja said. "When are you going to learn that I get what I goddamn want? Or else I leave you. Are you not understanding that your value lies in giving me what the hell I want! As I want it. Now give her another injection and wake her up!"

"Another injection right now would be too much. For once in your life, Sonja, would you please have patience and—"

The sharp sound of flesh hitting flesh sounded loud, reverberating in Andi's head. It instilled fear that made her toes curl and goosebumps rise on the back of her neck.

"Patience? I've waited two and a half goddamn years for this moment. And I've had enough of your disrespect." Sonja's voice dropped to a low, threatening growl. "Bow your head. Apologize. Are you forgetting who you're talking to?"

"Of course not," he said, with a shift in his tone. Sounding more subservient than angry, he continued, "I'm sorry. Please forgive me, my love. She'll be awake within the next fifteen minutes. Groggy, but awake. It will take her longer to become fully alert. More of the reversal agent right now wouldn't be good for her. You want her functional, don't you?"

There was a long pause.

"Leave me alone with her—"

"But you said I could watch."

"And I changed my mind. You'll have your turn with her when I'm done. And don't hold your breath, hoping I'll agree to kill her tonight so that it'll be your turn."

"But—"

"Stop sniveling. Go in the barn and find some work to do."

"We should restrain her, especially if I'm leaving you alone with her. When she awakens, she'll put up a fight."

"No, she won't. She knows me, Walter. She loves me. Go."

"You're fooling yourself if you think she'll be happy to be here—"

"Godammit, but would you stop throwing roadblocks my way. I can handle whatever resistance she might have in her. Don't you understand I want her to be her same old feisty self? She's different now. Go. Occupy yourself for a few hours, let me coax her into having fun like we did before, then come back and watch when the real show begins."

I've landed in a freak show. He watches her with lovers?

That hadn't happened before. At least, not to Andi's knowledge. But more horrific than that, was the implicit assumption in their statements. They were going to kill her. Eventually. It was just a matter of when.

As Andi tried to comprehend the alternative universe into which she'd plummeted, she heard footsteps. Presumably Walter, following she-bitch's instructions. A door opened. And shut.

I've got to do something while there's only one of them in here.

As the thought materialized, she drifted asleep, and stayed that way. Until with a jolt, she awakened. She had no idea how long she'd been out. A fresh wave of Shalimar teased a memory, then parts of it came back to her. Slitting open her eyes, Andi took in vaguely familiar, opulent, elegant furnishings. Heavy mahogany. Cream silks. Tassels. Why did this place look familiar? Her sluggish brain tried to fit together what she was seeing to the scent of Shalimar.

Sonja!

Andi tried to breathe as though she was still asleep. Through the tiniest sliver of an opening in her eyelids, she saw Sonja, wearing sleek black pants and a fitted top, move silently about the room, lighting tapered candles at a round coffee table that was nestled between two easy chairs and a tufted couch.

It all came back to Andi with a rush. Juliette. Sonja. Walter. Through the narrowest of a gaze, Andi thought she recognized where she was. Sonja's bedroom at the Long's Saint Charles Avenue mansion. But the proportions seemed off. While the room appeared larger, the same glittering chandelier hung over the elegant sitting area that was snugged up to the fireplace. Beyond the fireplace, there were large bay windows, hung with cream silk drapes. She didn't remember bay windows in Sonja's bedroom, the last time she was there. The fireplace was lit. Lights were dimmed, but on. Drapes were drawn. Impossible to tell time of day. Or night. Drifting into the fog again, Andi tried to swim to the surface, knowing she needed to do someth....

Damn. She'd passed out again. For how long this time?

No clue.

Shalimar. Sonja...Come on Andi, focus for your life here.

Slitting her eyes again, she saw Sonja lighting more candles, these atop thick silver candlesticks at an end table. Sonja liked elegant tapers, in varying lengths and thicknesses. She liked to play with the tapers, as flames flickered on the wick. Liked to run her fingers through the hot dripping wax. Sonja had told her that she special ordered dripping tapers, made of natural, organic beeswax. When Sonja had sex, she liked to take warm wax and rub it on her skin. And her lover's skin. And the tapers themselves became...toys. In ways that had nothing to do with lighting.

Acidic bile rose in the back of her throat and waves of nausea prickled Andi's skin hot and cold as she remembered the times she'd been in Sonja's bedroom. On the sofa. On the cowhide pelt rug in front of the fireplace.

Those damned candles.

Wait...those heavy, silver candlesticks that held the tapers...would be perfect weapons. As Andi focused on the array of tapers and candlesticks, the lights in the bedroom flickered. A soft chime sounded, like an old-fashioned doorbell. Sonja, who had been bending over the candles, with a matchstick in hand, froze.

Dropping the match on the silver tray, Sonja strode to the fireplace and pressed a button on the wall. "Marcus?"

"False alarm, Ms. Long." A male voice carried over the room's intercom system. "Zone 1C-4. French doors near the garden-room bay window, at the East wing."

"I know where my goddamn garden room is. What caused the false alarm?"

Silence.

"Marcus? I asked you a question."

"Yes, ma'am. We're investigating now. Wooded area around lake. I noticed aviary activity there earlier. Probably just a bird, flying into a window, be—"

"Probably? Are you serious? Find out with certainty. I'm not paying you to sit there scratching your balls."

Wait. What? Something—or better, someone—had activated the security system? Andi's heart leapt.

Gabe. He's coming to kick your ass, that's what's happening, you bitch.

"Confirming now, ma'am."

While Sonja's back was turned, Andi flexed her hands and feet. The movement caused pins and needles sharp enough to bring tears to her eyes. Blinking them away, she kept Sonja in her peripheral vision as she visually chose a weapon. Yes. That two-foot tall, six-inched base, silver candlestick on the end table near the settee would do nicely.

I'll swing it harder than a baseball bat.

"What in the hell is taking so long?"

"Nearest guards are...there now. Yes, ma'am. False alarm. Those French doors are problematic. We've worked..."

As the guard discussed the sensitivity of the system, disappointment felt like a physical blow to her chest. Thinking Gabe was there to rescue her, like a white knight on his horse, lance drawn, was just a case of wishful thinking.

It's just you, now. Deal with it, Andi.

As long as the other woman's back was turned, Andi moved her hands and feet some more to bring back circulation. Mentally she tried to gauge the distance to Sonja. The distance to the door. The distance to the bay window and French doors that were beyond the fireplace. There were other things she could use as a weapon from the bed to the door. Plenty of candlesticks and decorative figures with some weight to them.

Mentally, Andi rehearsed her moves. Travel the seven or eight feet to the table. Grab the candlestick, then run like hell. If Sonja came at her—and Andi had to assume she would—she'd hit the bitch as hard as she could. Aim for the eyes, Gabe had taught her. Aim to crush. Break her nose. Let momentum take your swing through her face to the back of her head.

"Goddammit, would you shut up? I'm sick and tired of false alarms," Sonja snapped. "I'm paying you a goddamn fortune. For the millionth time, the system's only supposed to be visible to me when there's something for me to worry about. Do you goddamn understand?"

"And as I just explained, although I understand your frustration, the system needs to be sensitive, given the size of the property and your...needs. And you've insisted on having a personal warning system."

"Understood. Figure out a way that false alarms don't bother me so frequently. Or else you're fired. Do you comprehend that goddamn instruction?"

Without waiting for a reply, Sonja flicked the button. Glancing in Andi's direction, she frowned in annoyance, then resumed her position at the candles. When she was through lighting them, she opened a rectangular silver box. Pulled out a cigarette and lit it. Sitting on the settee, she took a deep drag, as she glanced again at Andi. "It's like waiting for goddamn water to boil. Wake up, Andi."

The red glow of the lit cigarette was a trigger, causing Andi's heartbeat to falter, and her bravado to start vaporizing. Waves of terror stole her breath as she looked at the glowing tip of the cigarette. *Stay still. Still. Be smart*. Forcing measured breathing, she relaxed her jaw and unclenched her fingers. *Stay in the now.*

She had a plan. Eight feet. Candlestick. Run like hell. Kill the bitch if she comes at you.

Andi considered talking it out, pretending she was confused about how she'd gotten there. *Worth a try, because it would buy time. Maybe she'll talk. For a while. Because she's not touching me. Not with her hands. Not with wax. Not with a candle. And absolutely not with a cigarette. Been there. Done that.*

With eyes only open a fraction, Andi focused on the heavy silver candlesticks, mentally hefting each of them. Yes, that one. At least a foot tall. Curved. Ornate, with rounded balls up the column and a square base that provided sharp, lethal corners. She imagined the coldness warming under her hands, imagined the weight of it, imagined the feel of her fingers gripping the sleek cylinder. Visualized the places on Sonja's head where the heavy candlestick would do the most damage. The temple, certainly. The nose, not lethal, but it would slow her down. A jab in the eye—definitely. She imagined the fight. Imagined the countermoves. Imagined crushing the woman's skull. Just as she'd do to Victor Morrissey if he dared to return from the dead.

I will not be a victim. I'll die first. Better yet, she'll die first. And I'll fight anyone else who comes my way. I'm going to get free.

Or die trying.

Chapter Forty Seven

Gabe

As Gabe's team moved between trees at the Long's Northshore estate, Ragno kept them informed of intel as they got it. "Data now suggests as many as thirty victims currently being held on the property. Copy?"

"Copy," Ace said.

Thirty hostages, and please God, Andi as well. Gabe's resolve hardened. "Copy. Element of surprise while searching and rescuing is of paramount importance. Anyone or any damn thing standing between us and Andi, and the other victims, is subject to instant termination."

To that end, the agents who'd accompanied Gabe and Ace in the Chinook were heavily armed and spread from corner to corner over the fifty-acre estate, which did a damn good job of looking like an upper crust horse farm. More resources were on the way. Ace led Beta team—the twenty agents charged with the search of the dozen outbuildings. Gabe led Alpha team—himself and four additional agents who were to take control of the ranch house, the security epicenter they suspected was located there, and—hoping against every ounce of hope he'd ever had in his life—find Andi.

Ragno, with her team at corporate headquarters in Denver, was overseeing everyone in real time via satellite, while Barrows and his team, through the portal provided by the computers on the third floor of the Saint Charles Avenue mansion, had accessed the cyber-depths of the illicit activities conducted by the Longs. With each keystroke, they were shedding light on a human trafficking organization of the highest, most exclusive magnitude, with a worldwide reach. So far, they'd confirmed the sickest of scenarios that Gabe had theorized since Pic's disappearance. Juliette and Richie were also providing their own perspectives as Brandon and his team continued their interrogation. As more and more facts of who and what the Longs were selling became apparent, just cause for Gabe, Ace, and their agents to use lethal force reached an all-time high.

For the security on site, who protected the Longs and their human trafficking enterprise, the future was dire. For them, potentially interfering with victim rescue, was just cause for a bullet through the brain. Until the entire estate was under Black

Raven control, each agent assumed the role of judge, jury, and executioner.

On reaching the tree line, Gabe and his team dropped to their bellies and started crawling. There were a hundred yards through fields of long grass to traverse before reaching the enormous ranch house up ahead. The morning's clouds were gone and bright, and early afternoon sunlight taunted him as he crawled. A placid pond sparkled on his left, while to the right, the land gently swelled. Terraced steps led to the house from grassy pastures. White fencing corralled gleaming horses. With the house in full view, Gabe paused to assess their next move. Taking out his binoculars, he scanned the building from left to right. The three-story French Country house glinted with gray shingles and stone. It boasted turrets, bay windows, wrap around porches on both levels and a shit ton of security. Two men were stationed at double entry doors, no doubt more in back.

"Holy crap," Willis whispered. "These guys have bucks, or what?"

Leon peered through her binoculars. "I guestimate 'round twenty mil, and that's not counting all the livestock."

"Livestock here means people, as well as animals," Gabe reminded them. "Andi." His body went cold as his heartbeat kicked up several levels.

"Look at all those horses," Evans whispered in awe. "And the house. Man, that thing must be thirty thousand square feet."

"Then we'd better hustle and search smart," Gabe responded as he readjusted his binoculars to the left of the main house. Barns. Smaller buildings, in the distance. He saw no trace of Ace or the other agents, just Long's security patrolling the main house.

Zero minus three hours twenty minutes. Feels like a lifetime since they'd taken her. Luck, you've been a bitch today. But please, don't fail me now.

He indicated the direction they would take—through the weeds alongside the pond, along a stone retaining wall near the pool, through an overgrown garden. Gabe returned the binocs to his pack. "Entry, East-side French doors by that trestle."

"No intel yet on interior of residence," Ragno said, "proceed with caution."

"No shit."

"I suspect security is on third floor."

"It's where we'd put it," Gabe muttered. "Balconies for shooting, if needed. Windows, all points around. Views of entire property if technology fails."

"Move out Alpha team. Let's show these bastards we're smarter. Better. And they chose the wrong side."

Slithering on their bellies, they made it down to the house without being detected. *So far, so good.* Gabe motioned his team to cross the stone patio. The outdoor living space had enough plants and furniture and assorted décor crap to make for good cover as they did a running crouch to the doors. Blocked by two giant shrubs in decorative pots flanking the doors, Gabe picked the first locks. His team crouched low beside him. If security spotted them now, it would be a different ball game than what they had planned.

But they'd deal with that. They'd come to play ball. Any way it was thrown at them. And they'd win. Any way. Any how.

He felt the tension in the second lock give. He opened the door. Interior lights dimmed. A faint doorbell chimed. "We're a go. Move it."

As his team slipped inside, he locked the door behind him, and ran across what looked like a sunroom filled with white wicker furniture and lots of plants. At the side of the interior doorway, he stopped on a dime. He held up his fist to his team as heavy footsteps approached. Low voices.

Two men.

His team drew weapons and scurried out of sight of the approaching people.

As two armed guards entered the room, one said, presumably into a mic, "False alarm. Must've been a bird."

As they approached the French doors, Gabe took them both out with a *pop pop* of his silencer. Eyeing their Berettas, their neat black uniforms, their comm systems, and brawn, he gestured for his team to search them. "Keys. Access cards."

On open mic, he said, "Don't underestimate security. Two down, plenty more to go. These people have the bucks and motivation to hire top notch firepower. Evans. Lane. Drag these two out of sight, then start first floor recon, without setting off any alarms until we control the system. I'm headed upstairs. Willis. Leon. You're with me."

Sylvia Leon, a multi-skilled, dark-haired agent who specialized in cyber assistance in field operations, nodded. She stepped through blood and brains to claim anything that looked like keys or keycards from the dead men. People only underestimated Leon once. Her small stature and pretty face hid a well-honed body, nerves of steel, and a razor-sharp mind. Gabe had seen her calmly lift her weapon while typing, take down two men without breathing hard, then continue negotiating her way through a complex security system.

Gabe, Leon, and Willis lightly ran down the highly polished, dark wood floor of a wide hallway decorated with oil paintings of bucolic country scenes, then, darted up a long, wide flight of carpeted stairs. Steel doors, with a keypad, suggested they'd guessed correctly about the third floor, which momentarily blocked them. Gabe listened as Leon and Ragno strategized how to dupe the system. As they talked, Leon sorted through the keys and cards they'd lifted from the guards. Gabe stared at them. Thinking.

"Leon," Gabe said, remembering the dead woman at the Saint Charles Avenue mansion and what was at stake on the farm. Sometimes, giving people a chance to surrender was warranted. But in this case, given the potential fall-out with innocents on the property, immediate lethal force was justified. "Given the strength of the encryption Ragno's encountered thus far, we're likely walking into a highly sensitive monitoring system. I don't want to give whoever is in there a chance to sound the alarm."

She nodded. "Understood."

Glancing at Gabe, she inserted a card in the lock. He held his breath. Waited. Then heard a reassuring soft click. No bell. No warning. Two men, sitting in a large, dimly lit room as they monitored a bank of screens, weren't expecting a breach as he and Leon entered, weapons raised before they turned around.

Gabe took out the guy on the left, firing a round into the center of his forehead. *Pop*. Leon did the same to the other guy as he rose from his chair, a startled look on his face.

"Willis. Stand guard."

Grabbing the slumped man by the collar, Leon yanked him out of his chair, and dropped him to the floor before sliding into his vacated seat. Willis stood guard at the door, while Evans and Lane—via their mic system—reported two hostiles down in the kitchen.

The house was at least thirty thousand square feet. A search would take a while, and until they'd gained control of the security system, Evans and Lane were taking care to avoid activities that would set off alarms. Meaning, unless Andi was sitting in a wide-open space, they wouldn't find her.

But he had to try.

Andi, where the hell are *you?*

Gabe felt the urgency in every atom of his body as he scanned the live feeds on the two dozen flickering monitors.

As he watched the changing images on the screens, Leon clicked away on a keyboard. "Ragno. Ace. Four hostiles down," Gabe reported. "Alpha team in position. Security control room. Live feeds are mostly from the out-buildings. We don't own the system. Yet."

Gabe had gambled that Andi would be in the residence, not one of the outbuildings. She'd be at the ranch house, removed from the main operation. Sonja's personal plaything. Gabe desperately sorted through the sea of video images, looking for confirmation that his guess was correct.

There were plenty of images. Buildings. Rooms. Victims.

No Andi.

His heart pounded with a loud whump-thump that battered his chest, his brain, his gut.

Dead? Alive? Hurt? Goddammit. I need to know. Now.

"Leon. Internal views of the house."

"Roger that. System feeds are currently set external. Perimeter. No internal views."

"No shit. Tell me something I don't know."

Exhibiting Ragno-esque calm and stoicism, despite the fact that she was sitting in a chair that was flanked by the bodies of two dead men, and had field agents hanging on each of her keystrokes, Leon said, "I'm creating a firewall, so hostiles who have access to this system don't see what we're doing. After the firewall is established, I can start manipulating the system and Ragno's team can immediately step in. Gabe, do not touch that keyboard."

He pulled back his hand, his eyes fixed on the monitors. "Ace. Beta team. Warning. I'm seeing multiple scenes of what could be hard core porn movies. It's what you're going to walk into and it's sickening. I've got nothing against porn. But these people aren't all...enjoying it. And some of them are really young. Operations are very active, whatever the hell these operations are."

"We're uncovering more details," Ragno said. "For context, for all agents—expect anything in the search and rescue. Barrows is now decrypting a digital ledger. We're analyzing acquisitions. Transactions. Surgeries. Drugs administered. We believe that Gabe just described part of their breeding program. Babies."

"Holy shit," Gabe said, realizing the real purpose of the farm. "They breed and sell babies?"

"That's only part of it. Richard's analyzing the codes in the ledgers and hidden documents we found on the computer at

Saint Charles Avenue. The Long's aren't just savvy, they're sick pervs. They're key players in the black market human organ trade. Zeus has opened the lines of communication with the heads of requisite governmental agencies."

Zeus's specialty—governmental liaison. He'd work out the back-end solution as he spoon-fed details in a manner that ensured that law enforcement didn't interfere with Black Raven's objective. When Black Raven uncovered high profile criminal activity in the course of their jobs, the company typically tendered information, and credit, to a federal agency with jurisdiction over the matter. Politicians called it positive public relations that provided Black Raven a license to operate as a virtual private army, while the Government claimed credit for criminal takedown. Black Raven called it goodwill capital. Given the size and pervasiveness of the illicit sex trafficking enterprise they were now uncovering, the company was going to reap enormous goodwill capital.

Which means nothing if I don't find Andi. And Pic. Both of them. Safe. Secure. Home. That's all that matters.

Interminable seconds ticked by, erasing years from his life. Should he quit tormenting himself by watching all the live feeds? Just go the hell on a rampage through the house, kicking in doors and shooting anyone who wasn't his Andi? Sounded like a solid plan.

Over the mic, Gabe heard a soft pop, pop.

"Two hostiles, dead," Ace reported. "Thirty feet east of the red barn."

"Sir, how are we coming with disabling the alarm systems?" Evans asked.

"We haven't. Yet."

"It's slow going, until we do," Evans said. "Most doors we're encountering on the first floor are locked."

"Understood," Gabe said. "Do not risk it."

They were in a catch-22; until the entire premises were secure, the agents in the house had to avoid setting off alarms. Kicking open a locked door would do just that. Two false alarms—the first caused by Gabe's entrance into the ranch house—within fifteen minutes would give them away.

"Firewall's up," Leon announced. "All security alerts—disabled. Ragno's—in." With each burst of Leon's keystrokes, the wall of monitors flashed different camera feeds. Split screens of video appeared with schematics. "Gabe. For interior feeds, focus on monitors one, two, three."

Gabe started clicking at the keyboard, muttering, "Andi, where are you?" It was a multi-layered system, but it had basic manipulation through placing a cursor over schematics. Each of his clicks picked up a different camera view and different options for zones. "Ragno."

"Yes."

"See zone options? Codes suggest door locks can be manipulated remotely. Confirm."

He heard her clicking. "Confirmed. All doors are now unlocked. You've got the run of the place."

If only I knew where to fucking run.

"Evans, Lane—wide open access."

"Yes, sir. Copy."

Gabe manipulated the schematics, clicking areas he'd spotted as he did recon on the way in. He sorted through video feeds, while keeping his gaze on the monitors.

Feed 2FE-10. Bay windows, west wing. Empty bedroom. No Andi.

Leon typed furiously, then refocused on the monitors over her station. Her harsh intake of air caught Gabe's attention. A fresh view of rooms. Multiple kids. Naked. Skinny. The monitor that had Leon's attention showed two young men, naked, erect, and waiting, while another fucked a young girl, who was on her hands and knees. She was crying. Desperately. "Leon, what building is that in?"

"Red barn."

"Those other rooms?" He gestured with his chin to the views he'd reported earlier.

"Also red barn," she answered, focusing as she typed on monitors that showed the back end of the security system. Codes. Schematics.

"Ace," he said.

"Copy."

Feed 2FE-11. Balcony room. Overlooking paddock with mare and colt. A library. No Andi.

"Barn appears to be the epicenter. You'll find most of the thirty victims there," Gabe said. "Hurry. Leon. You okay?"

She nodded, then cleared her throat, but kept typing. "Ace," she said. "There's a satellite security station at the red barn. I'm now replaying a loop on their feed of the last ten minutes, so they will not see you or your men approach. Copy?"

"Copy."

Feed 2FE-6. Balcony room. Overlooking pond. No Andi.

"Given the reporting audio lines into the system, and proximity data," Leon said, glancing up at a monitor that listed names, "I'm counting at least eight hostiles at the red barn. Maybe more. Plus—Walter Long. Basement room. End of hallway. On left. Medical examination. Copy?"

"Copy. One hostile down," Ace said. Though the mic, Gabe heard a muffled pop. "Another one down."

As Gabe's frustration built, the conversation in his mic receded. Until he clicked on feed 2FW-6.

Bay rooms, east wing.

Andi!

Thank you, God.

Elation turned to dread, because she wasn't moving.

Sleeping? Dead? Holy hell. He couldn't tell. Was this another Andi lookalike, or his Andi?

He directed the camera to pan out.

Sonja—smoking a cigarette on a settee. Her gaze on Andi. Shutting her eyes. Taking a deep drag. Leaning back on the couch. Holding in her exhale.

Andi. Easing her legs off the bed. Wary, but focusing her wide-open, gorgeous eyes on Sonja.

Relief propelled him. Lunging to his feet, Gabe started running. On his way out of the security room, he yelled, "Ragno. Leon. Feed 2FW-6. My cell. Now!"

"Copy that," Ragno said.

Heart pounding, he yelled, "Evans. Lane. East wing. Second floor." Running up the nearest flight of stairs, he lifted his cell phone and opened the feed.

Andi moved fast. Not towards a door. Not towards a window. She moved towards Sonja. Sonja opened her eyes, at the exact second Andi gripped a silver candlestick. Sonja, startled, kicked at Andi. It was an ineffective kick, barely glancing Andi's thigh. She repositioned herself, ready to lunge again.

"Holy shit, Angel," Ragno said. "Get your ass in gear!"

By the time Gabe had the door in his sight, the drama that was playing out on his cell phone video feed indicated he needed to slow down. There was no gun in sight. Sonja hadn't even picked up one of the many candlesticks that were near the couch. Instead, it appeared she was trying to use words to reason with Andi. Gabe stopped at the door. He didn't open it.

Andi reoriented herself. Determined sparks flew from her eyes as she planted her feet on the ground. Andi, with a firm grip on the candlestick, had the solid upper hand and, even more importantly, the training to handle Sonja. And the rage to make each strike count.

Evans and Lane, breathing hard, caught up to him. Eyes glued to his cell phone, making sure Andi was on the winning side of whatever fight Sonja threw her way, said, “Stand down.”

Ragno demanded, “Gabe, what the hell are you doing?”

Gabe watched Andi do a running lunge. Stepping up, on the couch and over, she squared off with Sonja.

Hand on the doorknob, he kept his eyes on the monitor. If Andi appeared to be in jeopardy, he was going in with his weapon raised for a kill shot. For now, though, he stood firmly on the other side the door and watched Andi lift the candlestick. “Letting her conquer her demons.”

Chapter Forty Eight

Andi

As she hefted the candlestick, every bit of Andi's consciousness was reduced to watching her prey. Sonja opened her eyes, breathed out a plume of cigarette smoke, and gagged as she saw Andi coming for her.

Sonja's eyes widened, an indication that she read Andi's rage accurately. But she didn't cower. Instead, a faint smile played across her lips. "Andi! Put that do—"

Kicking out as Andi came swinging, Sonja's bare foot connected with her upper thigh. Andi stumbled back, but quickly regained her footing as Sonja rolled, then leapt to her feet.

Steadying herself, she lifted the candlestick again, as Sonja screamed and rolled away.

Fight, then flight. Get out of here.

Fear fueled Andi's strength to a point where she forgot to be afraid. Her focus was Sonja, who needed to be disabled so that Andi could get the hell out of the room. She knew that Sonja couldn't be allowed to make a move towards the alarm system. Sonja needed to be down.

Dead? *Maybe.*

Definitely disabled. Unconscious.

Curling her fingers tightly around the slippery silver, Andi planted her feet. Sonja circled behind the sofa, keeping it between them. "Let's talk."

Vision tunneling on Sonja, Andi asked, "About how you plan to kill me? I think not, you sick bitch."

Sonja's eyes hardened, but her voice softened. "I'm not going to kill you. Come on, Andi. Don't be ridiculous."

Talk was wasted breath. Breath was for the fight, because no matter what Sonja said now, Andi knew what she'd heard as she'd been laying on the bed, feigning unconsciousness. With a burst of energy, Andi took several running steps. She leapt onto the seat cushion of the sofa and over the back. Sonja backed away, and Andi hesitated. She had been planning on hitting Sonja in the head.

But the idea of bludgeoning someone to death was damn hard to implement. Andi couldn't look Sonja in the eyes and swing at her head at the same time. So she aimed, instead, at Sonja's upper thigh. As she swung her weapon with the full force of her body behind the blow, the candlestick made solid, thudding, metal-to-flesh contact.

Sonja looked shocked that Andi had actually struck her, then quickly recovered and lunged for Andi. Using a move that Gabe had taught her, Andi jumped to her side. Sonja crashed to the floor, then quickly crawled forward, grabbing Andi by the ankle.

Andi stepped on the woman's hand until she let go. As Sonja levered herself upright by holding onto the back of the sofa, Andi planted her feet and readied herself to swing again. With blue eyes widening, Sonja realized way too late that she'd underestimated the rage that had a hold of Andi. "Andi, what the hell are you doing? I'm here, keeping you safe—"

"You are bat-shit crazy if you think I believe that."

Sonja raised her arms over her face, as Andi swung. Powering past the sickening crack-thud that came with the contact of metal into flesh and bone, Andi realized that Sonja's arms took the brunt of the strike. "Jesus, Andi, stop! I love you."

As Andi absorbed the full sickness of that statement, she lifted the candlestick again. Eyes wild, undeterred, Sonja stepped forward, arms outstretched, fingers curled into a claw as she aimed for Andi's eyes. Rage pushed Andi past her reluctance to hit the woman in the face. This time, Andi's swing struck the woman in the forehead.

Eyelids flickering, stunned, Sonja hung onto consciousness as a gash opened on her forehead, and blood started pouring from it. Her eyes rolled back, and then she fell to the floor.

Unconscious. But breathing. Disabled. No longer a threat. Not going to call for help. Goal: accomplished.

Run. Hurry. Before Walter returns.

Andi spun on her heel, and realized she was too late. The door was opening. With a fresh burst of adrenaline coursing through her body, she charged. Before the door fully opened, she started swinging the candlestick in an arc that would take the now bloody stick where the new threat was about to appear. But the gray-haired doctor didn't step through the door. Vision tunneling once again, her mind screamed, '*Not Walter. Not. Not. Not.*'

Gabe!

With solid strength, he caught her wrist in an implacable grip. "Whoa. I've got you."

God. Yes, he did. The candlestick bounced to the floor as Gabe yanked her hard against him. Still riding the surge of kill-or-be-killed power, her body rebelled. She pushed away from him. "Walter's coming back. We have to get the hell out of here now!"

"No. We've got him. The Long's aren't going anywhere but prison. Look at me." Gripping her shoulders, he blocked her with his large body. "You're okay. I'm getting you out of here."

On the periphery of her vision, around him, around her, she was aware that others were entering the room. "Sonja. . ."

He used his sleeve to dab at the cut over her eyebrow. "They'll deal with her."

While her mind told her to listen, her body, still in flight mode, revolted. She slapped away his hands, trying to get away. "You don't understand." When he didn't move, she grabbed his hand, and pulled.

"No, Andi. Breathe. I have you. You're safe now. We have control. Do you understand me? You're safe. Breathe for me."

Her hands, suddenly too weak to lift, started shaking. Her legs could no longer hold her, and her entire body trembled.

"Breathe in, deeply. You're safe, honey." He scooped her into his arms, supporting her. The action kept her from falling, because she suddenly lost the strength to stand under her own power. To someone else, he said, "Find Ms. Hutchenson some clothes." He cradled her against his chest, as he said, "You're safe. Come on. Try to breathe."

Leaning into him, she gulped in smoky air, as more energy left her body. "Safe?"

He lifted her chin in the crook of his fingers. "Look at me."

Focusing, on him, she drank in the glorious sight of him, the dark angel who she'd been worried she'd never see again.

"You're safe."

"She was going to kill me. Walter. They're terrible. Sick people."

"I know," he said. "But we're putting an end to that."

Energy coursed out of her body. As the world started spinning around her, she saw two agents, throwing blankets over the fire that had started in the carpet.

"Ragno. How much longer till medics get here?" He paused for a second. As she watched him, his face started to blur. "Good. Andi's in shock. Adrenaline wash-out."

"I'm not," Andi said, before her brain switched off. In mental cut-out mode, she felt Gabe cocoon her in his strong arms. Free-floating, she drifted into the safety that he offered, lifting her arms onto his shoulders, clasping her hands together behind his back as he held her. Sounds were muted. All light was gone. Only the scent of him and the feel of him informed her awareness. Male. Powerful. Confident.

Gabe.

Her final thoughts were his whisper, “Safe, Andi. You’re safe. You won, honey. You did it. No one’s ever going to hurt you again. I promise.”

Chapter Forty Nine

Gabe

"Ace. That's fantastic. Have a medic look at him, then have someone bring him here."

Heart lightening with the news he'd just received, Gabe turned and looked to where Andi was laid out on a gurney in the farmhouse living room. She'd been out for about a half hour. Ace's team had control of the farm and was implementing victim rescue. More agents were arriving. A task force of Federal investigators specializing in sex crimes was on its way. Ragno and Barrows were uncovering horror after horror in the Concierge's databases and sharing the knowledge with the agents on site.

The Concierge. Sonja Long. A conduit straight to hell. For a fee.

He lifted a warm washcloth and slid it over Andi's forehead. "Come on, honey. Wake up so I can tell you how much I love you." He'd dressed her in a Black Raven t-shirt and sweatpants, which was part of the supplies that had arrived with the first wave of additional support.

Suddenly sitting up, she gripped the oxygen mask that covered her mouth and nose, and yanked it off. Eyes desperately searching, they rested when her gaze fell on him.

"Hey, you're safe."

He watched her fear recede, as she gulped air.

"Do you remember anything?"

She nodded. "Everything. But I don't know where we are now."

"Downstairs. At the Longs' farmhouse, on the Northshore of Lake Pontchartrain. There's a team of agents triaging in the barn. You've been out for about a half hour. That's it. You had an adrenaline crash. We're thinking you might still have some of the drugs in your system that Juliette administered." He hesitated, studying her calm demeanor. "What exactly do you remember?"

Because if you don't remember, I'll take the fall out for beating Sonja within an inch of her life.

"Everything. Juliette. Injecting me. I was out, until I was here. Walter was giving me something to wake me up." She shuddered. "For Sonja. I remembered what you taught me. To formulate a plan. To think. To implement. Is she still alive? Or did I kill her?"

"You knocked her unconscious, but she's going to live. She'll spend the rest of her life in prison. You've had enough for one day, and I have some pull around here. I can whisk you away, while we're still in the process of sorting through this clusterfuck. But still, we're working with Federal agents, and they'll want to talk to you. Eventually. Will you be okay with that? Because otherwise, anything that happened up there can be blamed on me."

"Yes. One hundred percent fine. She was going to kill me."

You don't even know the half of it.

A steady whump, whump, whump sounded. As the noise built, he said, "Helicopters. Medical support." Gabe touched his ear, listening for a second. "Ace. Can you repeat that?"

"Your friend Pic's a handful. He just threatened to cut off my cock and shove it down my throat."

Gabe laughed, relief pouring through his veins. "Copy. Glad to hear he's talking his typical trash."

"There is no goddamn way he's going to let anyone give him a medical exam until he sees you and Andi and you guys persuade him he needs help. Copy?"

"Given what might've happened to him in the last twenty-four hours, I can't say that I blame him. Have a couple of agents bring him here. Tell him Andi wants to see him. We'll talk him off the ledge."

Her eyes wide with hope, Andi said, "Pic?"

Gabe nodded. "He'll be here in a minute."

"But how is it that he's here?"

Gabe explained some of what Black Raven had figured out about Sonja and Walter Long's human trafficking enterprise. He didn't sanitize it, figuring Andi deserved to know the unvarnished truth. She'd earned it. He filled her in on how the Long's profited from the sale of human slaves, how they harvested organs for black market profit, and how they produced and sold human babies.

"From what Ragno's figuring out with the Federal task force that's now involved, this has been going on for years," he explained. "One of the more extensive organizations ever uncovered. And damn sophisticated. They preyed upon young, homeless people. Runaway kids, really. We're now working with Federal investigators. Some of their victims have already correlated with missing persons in the DOJ's database for missing, unidentified, and unclaimed persons. Jake was here. A few of the others that we've identified as being last seen in New Orleans, as well."

A shadow crossed her face. "Monica?"

"She's not here. But we've found her, and if we're reading their records accurately, you saw her abduction. On Esplanade a week ago, yesterday."

She shuddered. "I knew it. That's why, when I was painting the scene, the girl I was seeing looked more and more like her."

He nodded. "Law enforcement agents will soon be implementing a takedown of the person who has her. There are potentially thousands of victims. It's going to take some time to unravel everything."

A door opened. Pic, dressed the same way as Andi, entered the living room, flanked by two Black Raven agents. Blue eyes haunted by fresh horror, he nonetheless gave a tremulous smile when he saw Andi and Gabe. Andi jumped off the gurney. "Pic!"

They met halfway. Andi flung herself into the kid's arms. He lifted her, spun her, then pulled her in, holding her close. Gabe watched the kid start to fall apart. His shoulders shook. He buried his face in her shoulder. "I'm sorry, Andi. I never should've left. Jesus Christ, but I'm so sorry."

"Don't," she said, holding him tight. "You're okay now."

After long minutes, Pic lifted his face and glanced at Gabe with eyes that were full of tears. "Hey, man," he said, clearing his throat. "I owe you an apology, too."

"You owe me nothing," Gabe said, walking across the room. Andi pulled him into their hug, and then Pic's tears started again, with chest wracking, hoarse sobs. "I don't fucking know what's wrong with me. Crying like a girl. It's just...I was so goddamn scared, and...they made me...fuck... but this is twisted." He backed away from them, his face flushed red, as more tears fell from his eyes. "They're drugging people...and there was a girl...she wanted me to...and hell...I couldn't stop...Holy shit. What kind of place is this?"

Over their shoulder, Gabe saw Steve Richards enter the living room. Steve was the Black Raven physician, who had done a preliminary exam on Andi when she'd been unconscious. "Doctor's here."

Breaking from the hug, Andi took Pic by the hand and sat with him on the couch. "Pic, we need to let Doctor Richards look at you."

"Not no, but fuck no. My clothes are staying on, and no one's goddamn touching me at this place. Or anywhere else."

Gabe thought through what he should do. "What do you say I let you hitch a ride via helicopter right now with Andi and me? We go back to Andi's place, and you agree to live in her townhouse for the foreseeable future."

He rubbed the tears from his eyes, his attention on Andi. "You still want me there?"

"Of course," Andi said.

"Because I kept thinking I'd blown the only chance I was ever going to get."

"But Andi and I agree that you have to let Doctor McCaskey examine you this evening." Gabe glanced at Andi, who nodded as he spoke. "And you have to take his advice on what you need to do."

"Like what?"

"Whatever he says, including talking about what happened here with someone equipped to help you."

Pic frowned, but the scared look in his eyes told Gabe he was going to agree. The scared look also told Gabe the kid was so rattled by whatever the hell had happened to him since he'd been abducted that he was relieved that Gabe was laying down rules.

When Pic hesitated, Gabe said, "The only way I can get you out of here is to have you released into McCaskey's care. Come on, Pic. He helped you when he examined you earlier this week. He'll meet us at Andi's. Otherwise, I've got to let the doctors here examine you, and you may be here for a while. They're implementing procedures—"

"Okay. I'll go. But first I need to know something." Despite the fear that haunted his eyes, bravado slipped into Pic's voice. "What I want to know, is whether Richie set me up. Because none of what I know makes goddamn sense. It was too goddamn convenient for those guys to find me. Besides, I was dressed like Richie. So how'd they know it was me?"

"You guessed correctly. Richie set you up. He's been working for the Concierge."

"And what the fuck, exactly, is that?"

Andi gripped Pic's hand, as Gabe gave the kid the same nutshell version he'd given Andi regarding the Concierge's operations. "Richie did some talking this afternoon once he realized we were onto him. He's been working for the Longs for years. Feeding them information on vulnerable street kids and passing along news about Andi, because Sonja Long was obsessed with her. A stalker from hell."

"But Richie was a good guy. He was worried about Jake."

"Yeah. That was clever on his part. But the reason he talked to me about Jake, or to anyone, really, is because someone else saw him in the vicinity when Jake was kidnapped. Some guy named Shroom, who we're still looking for. To keep his cover, Richie had to act like he cared that Jake was snatched. And he was goddamn convincing. Until a few hours ago."

"Monica?" Pic's voice was so hopeful, it dug into Gabe's gut.

Gabe nodded. "Rescuers are on their way now to bring her back home."

A fresh tear dripped down the kid's cheek. Gabe decided to go all the way. With the two of them on the couch, Gabe got down on one knee to keep from towering over them. Andi reached out for his hand, while Pic had a fresh look of concern on his face.

"I have some other news. I know it's a lot to absorb all at once, but there's a chopper waiting for us right now. Pic, I want you to know that when you walk off this farm, your life's starting over. You're not only leaving this hell, but your own personal hell is over. A few moments ago, I received news that Clarence Walker of Mapleton, West Virginia, killed himself at some point throughout the night. He left a note seeking forgiveness for some of his more heinous acts. One of which was killing your mother. You're free to be yourself, Lucas Tanner McShane. Whoever it is that you want to become. And Andi and I are going to help you."

The look of wild hope in Pic's eyes, coupled with the surprise in Andi's, as they absorbed the news that Gabe had delivered, made every step that Gabe had taken on the side of darkness worth the effort.

He focused his gaze on Pic, reached out, and rested his hand on his shoulder. He felt the kid start trembling, and he leaned closer, willing Pic his strength.

For a few seconds, Gabe did nothing but breathe in the pure, unadulterated wonder that oozed from the kid, reveling in it. Because for all the darkness that Gabe carried with him, every moment, every day, for all the real-life horrors that he'd found a goddamn way to smile through, there was no reward greater than seeing the stunned look of someone who, for perhaps the first time in his life, had fate take a winding, decisive twist in his favor.

Chapter Fifty

Gabe

After their second shower since returning home, Gabe toweled beads of moisture off of Andi. Swishing most of the water off of him, he wrapped her tight in a fresh towel, then sat on the vanity stool. Grabbing her hand when she would have walked out of the bathroom, he pulled her to him so that she sat on his lap. He picked up his mic and slipped it into his ear. "Marks. Status?"

"Pic's sound asleep in the guesthouse. Snoring. Lots of people roaming the sidewalks, considering it's three in the morning. Otherwise, nothing."

"Good. Alert me if anything changes." He slipped out the mic, set it on the vanity, next to the box of condoms he'd brought into the room earlier.

Andi, eyes questioning, didn't have to ask. "He's asleep."

Inhaling her fresh fragrance and warmth, he got an eyeful of the profile of the two of them in the mirrors that surrounded her vanity area. He turned the stool sideways so they'd both have a view. "Well, Sandy, this is a way we haven't done it, yet."

"Haven't you had enough for one evening?" She leaned forward, and whispered in his ear, "Brad."

In answer, he let his towel fall away, slipped on another condom, and lifted her. He undid the semi-knot he'd just tied on her towel, and let it fall to the floor, as well. As she spread her legs, draping them over the stool and his hips, he centered her on him and pushed home.

"Oh," she moaned. "God. You're insatiable."

"That a problem?"

Her body answered with a mind-blowing 'no' as she wrapped her arms around his shoulders and moved her hips to meet his thrusts. After, he carried her to bed, pulled the covers over both of them, and realized he couldn't wait till morning. He wouldn't sleep, not without having the conversation he knew they needed to have.

In the soft lamplight, he turned to his side. She did the same. Head propped on one elbow, with the fingers of his other hand tracing a line along her jawline, he said, "Do you forgive me for reading your journals?"

Her face turned serious. "Right now, I think I'd forgive you for just about anything."

"I really am sorry. And I won't overstep again. I promise. But I'm still glad that I did. Don't you think you might benefit from talking some of that out with someone?"

She gave him a hesitant nod. "Maybe."

"Well, you agree Pic needs help, right?"

"Of course. And I'll help him get it."

"And we also need to talk about that thing you were saying about wanting me to leave after I found Pic. Your idea about you, and your fears, draining all the light from me."

"I'm still worried about that, but—"

He touched his finger to her lip, interrupting her. "I have to tell you something. I've never admitted this to anyone before. It's about my smile."

"I think I know what you're going to say."

"I'm not always as my smile makes me appear."

Her eyes were serious as she weighed his words. "You're smiling now."

"Of course I am. I'm in bed with you. I'd be a fool not to be happy, even though I'm laying my heart on the line."

"I misunderstood you. That smile blinded me. Such effusive warmth. You ooze it. But now, I think you smile to light the darkness that you see. Everywhere. In other people's battles. In their eyes. In their hearts. In the way they carry themselves. You see it, and you smile through it. Why?"

He drew a deep breath. "I told you I learned to smile for my mom after my father was murdered, didn't I?"

She nodded.

"I wasn't smiling because I was happy," he said, toying with her hair. "I learned all kinds of things when my father died. Like how to be the glue that can keep a family together. How to anticipate needs of others. Back then, it was my mom and my brother. Now, it's my clients. I show them how to have faith that things will work out. How to make things work out. Along the way, I learned that no matter what crap life is throwing at you, a simple thing like a smile usually makes people feel better. If they want to be better. Believe me, with some people, my smile doesn't do a goddamn thing to help." He looked in her eyes. "It only works magic when people want it to. And you wanted it to."

"But you don't just smile. You take action."

"I try."

"Like Clarence Walker? His suicide seems too coincidental."

He inwardly cringed. "You realize that going forward, I'm never going to lie, or give you less than I know. Honesty needs to be a two-way street between us. Understand that?"

She nodded.

"So if you don't want to know the details, if they're too much for you, just tell me to sanitize it. I'm treating you as my equal, okay?

"Go on."

"Walker was a predator, of the highest order. I can show you the interview that Lamonte conducted with him."

"But why would he confess?"

"We have ways."

A frown furrowed her brow. "Ways? As in torture?"

"Sometimes. And serums that help with truthfulness."

"Show me the interview."

He picked up his cell phone from the night table. Found the file. With his heart beating hard, he played it for Andi. Five minutes in, after Walker, red-cheeked and sweating, named some of the boys with whom he'd had sex, including Lucas McShane, and explained how he'd used his billy club on the back of Aubrey Rose's head as she argued with Lucas, Andi glanced at him, her eyes wide.

"It gets uglier from here," Gabe warned.

"I've had enough. Just tell me why he killed her."

He switched off the video. "Walker knew it was only a matter of time before she turned on him. While she was originally shocked at the news at what he'd done to Pic, he knew she'd ultimately believe her son. When Pic ran out of the trailer, Clarence let him go, then framed him for the murder. He called it a win-win. After he explained what happened to her, Lamonte asked him questions about the boy he had identified, the duration of the abuse, stuff like that. You don't want to know more details, do you?"

She shook her head. "After he confessed, did he really kill himself, or did Lamonte kill him and make it look like suicide? Because what I'm trying to figure out is, what, exactly, you guys do. What you do."

I perfectly understand.

"It's complicated."

"Un-complicate it for me. Answer my question."

"Lamonte says he killed himself after writing the note."

With her gaze intent on him, she searched his face. The set of his lips. His eyes. "And you believe her?"

He nodded. "I don't second guess a field agent. If she says he killed himself, then he did."

Though she sure as hell might have persuaded him to do it. And I can think of quite a few ways I'd have persuaded the monster to off himself. I'm not going to lie to you, but please, Andi, stop asking questions.

As she sat with her legs drawn up, and the soft covers flowing over her, he waited for her to tell him his fate. She rested her elbows on her knees, and cupped her face in her hands. "Whether we have a future gets down to one simple fact: I don't want you to waste your life trying to help me get over what's happened to me. I'm not a case. I'm not a job. I'm not a problem you're supposed to manage. I'd be an endless source of frustration for you. I'd be an endless drain, because what I have can't be fix—"

"I promise, you don't need fixing. To me—" He reached for one of her hands and gripped it, tight. "—you're perfect. For so many reasons, and part of it is because you can understand the darkness that I see. There isn't one thing I want to change about you. You understand me now, like no one else possibly could. Please, Andi. Give us a chance. I love you. Just as you are. I don't know how else to say it."

She reached out for him. Ran her fingers along his cheekbone, as his world stood still. "I love you, too. And I will give us a chance. But you have to promise me one thing."

"Anything."

"That, at least around me, you'll only smile when you're happy."

He laughed. "Easy."

He pulled her close. Within minutes, their limbs were tangled, and then their bodies followed suit. Later, as he drifted off to sleep, he heard her whisper, "Gabe. You're smiling."

Pulling her closer, he whispered, "Happiest man alive."

Hello there –

Thank you for purchasing and reading *Concierge*. I hope you enjoyed it! Please help spread the word about *Concierge* by telling your friends about it and posting a review where you purchased the book.

I love to hear from readers. If you'd like to say hello, you can find me on Facebook and Instagram. You can also reach me through stellabarcelona.com, which has blogs that I update from time to time, some book related, some not. My site also has book pages with excerpts and book club questions. There is also an "Ask Stella" blog series, where (almost) any question is fair game. You can email me at mail@stellabarcelona.com and, if you'd like to keep up with news from me, you can join my mailing list on my website, as well. Don't worry—I'm too busy to send out frequent newsletters, and I promise I won't share your email address. If you'd prefer to use the U.S. mail, I can be reached at P.O. Box 70332, New Orleans, Louisiana, 70172-0332.

In addition to you, others deserve a thank you for helping me with a wide variety of subjects, such as carefully reading the raw manuscript, decorating a Royal Street townhome, the type of helicopter needed for the story, backstory for the Hernandez brothers from Miami, historic maps of the French Quarter, medical questions, reviewing the back cover copy, technology support, website design, and much, much more. Thank you to: Miguel Andrews, Drew Bevolo, Stephen J. Broussard, Esq., Denise Chopin, Esq., Wendy Dolan (Get Online NOLA), Rebecca Diamante, Richard Hernandez, M.D., Charles W. Richard, M.D., and Amy M. Winters, Esq. A special thank you is also extended to: New Orleans artist Kathy B. Richard, for answering questions about the artistic side of Andi; Diego Larguia (New Orleans Academy of Fine Arts), for graciously taking the time to talk to me about en plein air painting; and Fredrick Guess (Fredrick Guess Studio), for creating inspirational paintings of French Quarter street scenes, including the painting of the St. Louis Cathedral used on the *Concierge* cover.

Thank you again, and stay in touch!

Stella

ABOUT THE AUTHOR

(Photo at Bevolo Gas & Electric Lights, 318 Royal Street, New Orleans, La., by Laurie Foret Photography)

Stella Barcelona has always had an active imagination, a tendency to daydream, and a passion for reading romance, mysteries, and thrillers. She has found an outlet for all these aspects of herself by writing romantic thrillers.

In her day-to-day life, Stella is a lawyer and works for a court in New Orleans, Louisiana. She lives minutes from the French Quarter, with her husband and two adorable papillons who believe they are princesses.

Stella's first novel, *Deceived*, was inspired by New Orleans, its unique citizens, and the city's World War II-era history. *Deceived* introduced Black Raven Private Security Contractors. In her subsequent novels, *Shadows* and *Jigsaw*, and now *Concierge*, Black Raven took flight in thrillers that were inspired by current events. Stella is hard at work on her next Black Raven novel, *Insertion*, which will be released in 2018.

Coming in 2018

INSERTION

A Black Raven Novel

by Stella Barcelona

Made in the USA
Middletown, DE
12 October 2017